# Life's SECOND CHANCES

### The Show Me Series
BOOK 1

# Anne Stone

Anne Stone
BOOKS

# DEDICATION

This novel is dedicated to my father. He believed in me and made me promise that I would never give up on the dream of being a published author. And now, that dream is becoming a reality.

To my sister, Isabel, who has been by my side throughout this journey spending countless hours on the telephone discussing my path to self-publishing.

To my friend Chloe Barlow who introduced me to my fabulous editor.

To my editor, Melissa Schirmer, who guided me down a path of rewrites to make this book what it is today. I appreciate all of your help and support. I am proud of what you helped me accomplish.

**<u>Coming Soon by Anne Stone:</u>**
Love's Final Match – Fall, 2016
Never Lose Hope – Spring, 2016

**<u>The Show Me Series:</u>**
Life's Gateway to Happiness –
Book Two – Spring, 2016
Life's Turned Upside-Down –
Book Three – Summer, 2016

# CHAPTER ONE

"You're hired," said Mary Flynn, Principal of St. Margaret's Catholic School.

Angelina Samuels couldn't believe her ears. This was her last hope that she'd find a job before the beginning of the school year—she thought she'd end up being an aide or substitute teacher. The previous school where she'd worked since graduating from college eight years ago had closed due to decreasing enrollment. She'd wanted to teach in the Catholic schools, but it was difficult finding a job with limited positions available. She was lucky that the teacher she was replacing decided to relocate unexpectedly. With her résumé on file with the school office, she had been immediately contacted to interview for the position.

"Mary, could you show me to my classroom? I've got a lot of work ahead of me to be ready by next week. Oh, by the way, what time do the meetings start tomorrow?"

"The building opens at seven, and the opening meetings begin promptly at nine o'clock." Mary stood and came around her desk to welcome her. "Welcome to St. Margaret's, Angelina. I am excited for you to join our team. I think you'll find everyone here very friendly and welcoming. I'm sure you'll fit in without any problems." Mary smiled warmly and shook Angelina's hand. "Now, let me show you to your new home-away-from-home."

Mary led Angelina from her office. Just as they turned the corner to head down a long hallway, a body came out of nowhere, flying around the corner, running smack into Angelina. Angelina blinked once, then twice, taking in the beautiful brown-haired woman who nearly knocked her off her feet. A look of utter surprise crossed the other woman's face as Angelina stood staring at her in complete shock.

Overjoyed with excitement, Angelina screamed out Gabriella's name in delight, pulling her into a tight embrace. Both women were jumping up and down in glee. Mary looked on, not sure what was transpiring before her eyes. All she knew was that two of her teachers were more than excited to see one another.

"I take it you two know one another," Mary said, laughing.

"Yes," they said in unison, continuing their dance.

"We went to college together. I lost track of you after graduation," said Gabriella, turning back to Angelina. "What happened to you? Are you taking Lauren's place since she decided to bolt before the school year?"

"Yes, I am. Mary just hired me and she was in the process of showing me to my classroom."

"Mary, don't bother. I'll take Angelina to her classroom since it is right across the hall from mine."

Mary waved them on, and arm in arm they walked down the hallway.

"I didn't know you were interviewing for the job. I guess it came up pretty fast. When Lauren didn't show up to begin working in her classroom, Mary contacted her and discovered she was relocating and had no plans to notify her. She was a new teacher last year and had some discipline issues. I can't believe she wasn't going to let Mary know, but I guess that show's her immaturity."

"Well, I got a call from Mary this morning, and she asked me to come in this afternoon to interview. I'm stunned. I can't believe that she hired me right on the spot. I was getting a little nervous since I hadn't found a full-time job yet. I thought I was going to have to settle on being an aide or a substitute. I'd taught at St. Mark's since I graduated, but they closed at the end of the school year due to decreasing enrollment."

They stopped midway down the hallway while Angelina told her about St. Mark's closure. "I was so upset when we discovered that St. Mark's was closing. The school was over ninety years old and was so entrenched in the neighborhood. It was sad watching the enrollment decrease over the years. We saw the closure coming, but still it was difficult. Everyone wants to live in the suburbs today and people with school aged children have dwindled in the neighborhood over the years. I think I heard that the average age in the parish is something like fifty years old. I'm just really sad to see what was once a thriving school close its doors."

"Angelina, I'm just beside myself. I can't believe you are standing right here in front of me." Gabriella pulled her in for another hug. "We are so lucky to have you join the staff. You are going to absolutely love Mary. She is a one-of-a-kind principal, and she's so supportive of her teachers and staff. I'm lucky that she hired me right out of school. She's been a terrific role model to me, and I don't plan on ever leaving as long as she is here. Now, let's get you to your classroom. You're right across the hall from me. I've already finished setting up my room, so why don't I help you set up yours?"

"Would you? First of all, I need to check out the space and look at the class listing."

"You've got a lot to do to get ready for next week."

"I know I do. I'm not sure what I need, but with your help I'm sure it will take no time."

Gabriella led Angelina down the hallway to her classroom. She stopped outside the only room with a closed door. "Ready to see your new home?"

"Of course, I am! I can't wait. This day has been so surreal. Open the door already," Angelina called out. Gabriella threw open the door to Angelina's new home. She couldn't believe her eyes as she walked through the door. The room was huge! One whole wall was lined with windows that provided the best natural light she'd ever seen in any of the classrooms that she'd ever taught in at St. Mark's.

"Oh, my gosh! I love all of the light. It's fabulous."

"Yes, we're lucky. All of the classrooms have an abundance of natural light."

Angelina walked towards the back of the room and noticed the huge walk-in closet.

"Oh, my."

"What?" asked Gabriella.

"Look at all of this storage. I'm speechless, absolutely speechless."

"Now, that you've come down from this shock of a classroom, let's see what you need." They worked well into the early evening sorting through the books and materials that were in the classroom. Angelina made lists as she went of the additional materials that she would need to purchase to get her classroom together before school started the following week. She was switching grades and wouldn't be able to use anything that she had used previously. They stopped and took a break so Angelina could purchase some supplies and then returned to begin the task of preparing her classroom for the start of school.

While they were working on her bulletin boards, Angelina discovered that Gabriella lived just down the street from St. Margaret's. "I love this neighborhood. It's so family-oriented. Families are constantly milling about, taking walks, dining at the local restaurants. It can be both positive and negative living and working in the same community, but I love it and have absolutely no complaints. I love going to the grocery store and running into my students. I can't say it enough that this is a great area to live and work in."

"I'm looking forward to getting to know the neighborhood as well, along with the families. I had the same sense of neighborhood and family while working at St. Mark's. Even though I still live at home, I was able to experience those same feelings because I spent an awful lot of time in the neighborhood going to sporting events and various other parish activities. Did you move here right after school?"

"No, I lived at home for a couple of years so I could save enough money for a down payment on my house. I can't wait for you to come over and see it. It's not too large, just a starter home, but I love it just the same."

"Well, I still live at home. In time, I'd like to move out, but I'm okay living there for now. I help my mom a lot with Colleen and Wyatt. Can you believe Wyatt just turned twelve and Colleen's a junior in high school?"

"You're kidding me. I remember when she was a little thing! I can't believe Wyatt's twelve. I remember when he was born."

"Yep, I can't believe Colleen will be in college in one more year. I can still see her climbing on your bed in our old dorm room, playing hide and seek under the covers. Remember the curly mop of hair she had?"

Gabriella nodded.

"Now, it's straight as a pin," Angelina chuckled. "Oh, and can you believe she's already had universities contacting her to play field hockey for them? Time sure flies by, doesn't it?"

"It certainly does," Gabriella added in agreement. "What about Kelly and James? What are they up to?"

"Kelly is twenty-five now and is currently attending graduate school at Emory University, and James is twenty-seven. He's engaged to his high school sweetheart and has followed my dad into banking. How are your parents and brothers?"

Gabriella couldn't stop talking about her family as she helped Angelina finish hanging the remaining border on her bulletin boards. "Mom and Dad are semi-retired. As I'm sure you already know, Dad has turned over his medical practice to Alec and Joseph and works three days a week. He's kept his favorite patients, so I'm sure Colleen and Wyatt still see him. I'm not sure how much longer he'll practice since he has so many other interests. He worked so hard building that practice that I think he now believes he can successfully turn it over to my brothers.

"Alejandro just moved back to town. He lived in Madison, Wisconsin and worked for the University Hospital. He's a renowned transplant surgeon and was recruited to head up the Transplant Services here. I think deep down he decided to come home because Mom and Dad are nearing retirement, and he wanted to spend more time with them as they get older. Being the oldest, he has a sense of responsibility to take care of them." Gabriella paused, twirling her hair as she thought about her brother. "I can't believe he's been gone since he left for college almost twenty years ago. He's thirty-seven now. Although, it came out of the blue, I think he's got other stuff going on and just wants to be near family."

"What do you think is going on with him? I remember how intense he was all the time when I talked with him on the phone, and then other times he was a jokester. Do you think he is running away from someone or something?"

Gabriella just looked at Angelina—she wasn't going to comment on what Angelina was saying.

Angelina continued, "I'm just glad that he's living in town now. Maybe I'll finally have a chance to meet him in person."

"Of course, you will. I'll make sure it happens." Thinking back, Gabriella said, "That's right. I forgot you've never met face to face. He was never around us... Was he?"

"No, he wasn't."

Gabriella stepped down from the ladder after completing the finishing touches on the bulletin board. She would make sure that would happen in the near future.

The school year started without issue two weeks before the Labor Day holiday. Angelina really enjoyed all of her students, and she was excited to be working with Gabriella. They both realized how much they'd truly missed their friendship. Graduating from college and entering the workforce was a hard transition, and they both realized they'd failed one another by not keeping their friendship alive. They started spending their weekends together shopping and going to their students' soccer games. They had a ball reliving their collegiate experiences and sharing their new life challenges.

The day after Labor Day, Angelina got a call out of the blue from Maria, Gabriella's mother. Gabriella was turning thirty the following week, September 9th, and her mother wanted to throw a surprise party for her only daughter. She wanted Angelina to put together a listing of the teachers at St. Margaret's. The party was scheduled for the first weekend of October, so Gabriella would be clueless as to the surprise.

Angelina was thrilled that Maria asked for her input, and she wasn't shy about volunteering to help Maria with the details. Angelina was crafty and immediately volunteered to make all of the party favors and invitations. Angelina designed the card that would be used as the invitation. Using her various supplies, she spent the entire weekend after Labor Day cutting paper, gluing flowers and addressing the large number of invitations that Maria needed. Maria was surprised with how quickly she completed everything in such a short amount of time.

Maria had thought of absolutely everything. She'd even arranged for Alejandro to spend the afternoon with Gabriella leading up to the party: Alejandro was going to take Gabriella to a matinée showing of Miss Saigon that was playing at the Opera House. Then, he was taking her to an early dinner. Of course, the early dinner would lead to her surprise party.

Alejandro picked Gabriella up for the musical the day of the party. She wouldn't stop talking about Angelina. She was elated that Angelina was working across the hall from her. "Alejandro, you've never actually met Angelina, have you?"

"I've heard a lot about her over the years since, what was it, your freshman year?"

"Yeah, we've known one another since our first semester of freshman year. Remember, at first we lived across the hall from one another?"

"That's right. I can't believe I've never met her in all these years."

"Well, now that we're working together, we'll have to go to happy hour so you two can meet. She's met everyone in the family except you. I think after all of these years you need to put the name and face together."

"I would have to agree. I talked to her often on the phone while you roomed together, but since I never had the chance to visit you, we never met. I'd love to put the name and the face together, but I don't know about happy hour. I'm sure we can meet at some point."

Gabriella thoroughly enjoyed the musical. As they walked out of the Opera House, Gabriella looped her arm through Alejandro's. "Thank you. This was such a treat. I've wanted to see that for a long time."

"I enjoyed it, too. Now, let's go have something to eat."

"Alejandro."

"Yes?"

"Thank you."

"For what?"

"For today… For moving back home. I've missed you so much. I hardly saw you after you moved away to college. I know we've talked often but it wasn't the same… Now I feel like I have another brother again. I can see you whenever I want. I can relate to what you are doing and what you are experiencing. It's different, that's all. I love you so much."

Alejandro turned and pulled her into his arms. "I'm glad I came home, too. I missed seeing you grow up. You were only ten when I went away to school. I'd see you on holidays but that was it. I never got to experience your firsts with you. I should have been there for you, too, especially since you are the only girl in the family. We're going to remedy that now. I'm home to stay, and I expect to be as involved in your life as you want me to be. We need to plan regular outings because you mean way too much to me." Alejandro kissed her on the temple and said, "I love you, too."

Alejandro helped Gabriella into the car and pointed it towards the restaurant where the surprise party was scheduled for five o'clock. Conveniently, his phone rang as planned. He pulled off the highway to take the call. The call lasted a few minutes and they were on their way again.

"Was that the hospital?" He had talked to the person on the other end of the line cryptically so she wouldn't discover what they were discussing. He told a little white lie and said that he was speaking with his assistant who was following up on some travel arrangements.

Alejandro pulled into the parking lot of the restaurant and helped Gabriella from the car.

"I can't believe you brought me here. This is one of my favorite Italian restaurants."

"I'm glad I chose something you enjoy," he said as he opened the door to the restaurant.

As they entered the restaurant, the hostess asked if they would like to sit outdoors. They agreed since it was such a beautiful day. For a mid-autumn day, they were lucky with mild temperatures hovering in the mid-sixties. It was a welcome relief after the horribly hot and humid summer they'd had. "That's the one thing I've missed since moving back from Wisconsin. I forgot how awful the summers tend to be in St. Louis. Wisconsin is like this a good part of summer, nice and comfortable."

As the hostess led them to the patio, Alejandro winked at her. Gabriella smiled to herself thinking that only Alejandro would wink at the hostess. Unbeknownst to Gabriella, that was the hostess's cue to lead them to the backroom. She explained to Gabriella that this was an alternative route to their seating. The hostess threw open the doors and Gabriella was greeted with a loud, "Surprise!"

Gabriella was speechless as she threw her hands up to cover her mouth. She wasn't actually sure what was going on in front of her. As she walked further into the room, she noticed the streamers hanging from the ceiling and balloons scattered about the room. The partygoers all screamed, "Happy birthday!" in unison.

"What's this?" she asked Alejandro.

The room was packed with familiar faces when she noticed Angelina coming towards her from the back of the crowded room. She stopped in front of Gabriella, hugged her tightly, and said, "It's a surprise party for your birthday."

"But that was weeks ago," commented Gabriella. She turned to Alejandro and said, "You... You were you in on this, too?"

"Well..."

"Don't 'well' me—"

Alejandro grabbed her and gave her a big hug and kiss.

"Happy birthday, Sis. I'm so glad I could celebrate this milestone with you."

Gabriella greeted all of her guests. Her mother and Angelina moved into party mode, ensuring that everyone had everything they needed.

Instead of a sit down meal, Maria had arranged for a buffet to be served so that people could mingle and eat when they wanted to. The room was scattered with large, round tables covered in fall-colored tablecloths, with balloon bouquets being the focal point of each table. The yellow and orange colored balloons swayed in unison, highlighting the Mylar "Happy Birthday" balloons.

As everyone began to eat, Gabriella walked over to Angelina. She grabbed her arm and pulled her across the room where Alejandro was getting a drink. "I'd like you to finally meet someone." As Gabriella looped her arm through her brother's, she finally introduced her famous brother to her best friend. "Alejandro?"

"Yes?"

"I'd like you to finally meet my friend Angelina."

When he thought about it, he remembered seeing photos of her and Gabriella in school. He couldn't believe his eyes as he finally met her in person. Angelina was beautiful. She had honey colored eyes and long, light brown hair that had been neatly pulled back into a ponytail. Alejandro was stunned by their meeting and was pulled back into the moment

Before Gabriella could say anymore, Alejandro was reaching for Angelina's hand. "Finally, we meet."

"Yes, finally. I've heard so much about you through the years." Angelina grasped his hand and was pulled into an embrace. She was taken aback by the gesture, but realized that she felt like she'd known him forever.

Before Angelina could get accustomed to the embrace, he was being waved down from across the room. "It was nice to finally meet you. We'll talk later."

Angelina smiled as he walked away. She was excited that she finally met Alejandro, but also wished they'd had more of a chance to visit in person.

Gabriella was disturbed that he left them so quickly. She gnawed on her lip in disbelief. It had taken her over twelve years for them to meet in person. In the blink of an eye, it was over. She wanted her best friend to finally get to know him since he was such an important part of her life.

Angelina knew Gabriella was upset with her brother. "Gabriella, don't think twice about our meeting. This is your party. Have fun! Alejandro and I can talk another time. You know he's just as popular as you, the birthday girl, since he's been away for so long."

Gabriella hugged her friend. "I know. I've just waited for this moment for so long," she said as she pulled away from Angelina.

Gabriella's party went well. The dancing began after dinner, and Alejandro cut in on their father while he was dancing with Gabriella. "Were you surprised?" he asked her.

"What do you think?"

"I'm glad you were. And I'm glad I was able to participate in this celebration."

"Alejandro?"

"Yes?"

"Will you do me a favor?"

"Sure, if I can."

"Angelina has been working tirelessly during this party. Will you at least dance with her? She needs a break." Gabriella was still upset with Alejandro for walking away from his initial meeting with Angelina. She knew her uncle had summoned him, but still. This was an important moment and she wanted her brother to get to know her best friend.

"Of course I will. I am glad that you were able to reconnect with each other. I know she was an important part of your collegiate days. What happened for you to lose touch with one another?"

"I'm really not sure. I guess we became so involved in our new lives. With our first teaching jobs, we were extremely busy that first summer. Getting things together for the classroom, writing lesson plans, coming up with innovative ideas... I remember going into the classroom almost every day that summer after I got my first job. Planning, always planning. I wanted to be the best teacher that I could be, someone my students would always remember. I hope I've done that through the years. Angelina was going about it the same way. I remember we always had the same ambitions. We wanted to be the best..."

"Well, from what you've told me through the years, you've been an influence on many students. I am so proud of you."

"As I am of you. Now, go and have that dance with my best friend." Alejandro brushed a kiss across her knuckles and headed towards Angelina.

"May I have this dance?"

"Alejandro, I'd love to but I am busy at the moment. How about later?"

Alejandro reached for her hand, but she pulled it away.

He had a funny look on his face—one of surprise that she wouldn't dance with him. He knew Gabriella had been upset with him earlier when he'd been summoned by their uncle. He wanted to spend some time with Angelina, but he knew his uncle would have made a scene, so he'd left her standing with his sister.

The look Gabriella had sent his way when he walked away was the same one she used to give him when she was a little girl and he wouldn't give into her demands. She'd scrunch her face and roll her eyes at him. He knew he was in trouble with his sister, and he needed to make up to her by dancing with Angelina.

"Aww, come on."

"Give me a few minutes to finish this up, and I'll dance with you."

While Angelina was cleaning up, Alejandro got an emergency call. He had to rush to the hospital to tend to a patient who'd had a kidney transplant and was exhibiting signs of infection. Alejandro hated getting these calls. He apologized to Gabriella for having to leave early. She understood but thought he needed to have some fun in his life.

She was going to see that he did, now that he was home and living close by.

# CHAPTER TWO

The following Monday morning, Gabriella couldn't wait to see Angelina. She ran directly into Angelina's classroom, hugged, and thanked her for helping her mother organize and plan her surprise party. "I had such a wonderful time."

"I did, too. It was great seeing everyone. I was happy to finally meet Alejandro in person. Were you surprised?"

"Surprised? Yes, that's an understatement. Shocked is more like it. I wasn't sure what was happening at first, but then you came running up to me. All I can say is Alejandro did a fabulous job of keeping it from me. I thought it was his idea to take me to Miss Saigon."

"It was his idea. We weren't sure how to get you there, so he volunteered. It was really important to him that he take you to the play since you wanted to see it so badly. He wanted to make it a special memory for you since he missed so many important happenings in your life. He was like a kid in a candy store helping your mother plan this part of the surprise. He even met with the hostess at the restaurant so she knew who he was and could guide you directly to the party without question."

"Huh, so that's what that wink was about."

"What wink?"

"Never mind. Getting back to Alejandro... I thought you hadn't met before the party."

"We hadn't. Your mother arranged it all. I didn't meet him until you introduced us."

"Oh. Did you two have a good time dancing?"

"We never danced. I told him I was busy. I was getting the party favors together because one of your mom's friends was leaving, and I wanted to be sure she had one. I asked if he could wait a few minutes, and when I went looking for him, he was gone."

"Oh, I'm sorry. I thought you'd danced. He got a call from the hospital and had to go in."

"After all of these years, I was just glad to finally meet him in the flesh. I'd talked to him while we were in school, and I've met Alec and Joe many times. It's just nice after all of these years to finally meet him in person. I always enjoyed talking with him. He always knew the right thing to say to brighten my day."

Mid-October was upon them, and with it came Colleen's field hockey sectionals. Colleen, Angelina's sister, played for her high school team. She was the star of the team and a team player who always thought of her teammates first while on the field. She'd broken many of her high school's prestigious records. She was only a junior, but had already received letters from various universities that were interested in her playing field hockey for them.

The team had a game scheduled in Kansas City, which was a four hour drive from St. Louis. Colleen's parents and brother, Wyatt (who always attended her matches), were going to follow the bus to Kansas City. Wyatt loved watching his older sister play. He played ice hockey himself and was a well-respected player in his own right.

Angelina declined to take the early morning car ride to Kansas City with her parents. She was preparing for the end of the first quarter and wanted to spend the weekend working on grades. She never liked waiting until the last minute to complete the quarterly report card.

They were originally scheduled to leave directly after school ended on Friday afternoon, but at the last minute the plans were changed. The new plan was to leave at seven o'clock Saturday morning.

Angelina spent Friday evening at Gabriella's house. It was the first time Angelina had been to Gabriella's. As soon as she pulled up to the curb, she fell in love with it. The sidewalk was lined with flowers. She remembered how much Gabriella loved flowers—she had always been buying bouquets of whatever flowers she could get her hands on for their dorm room.

Gabriella had told Angelina that her home was a starter house and Angelina couldn't believe the size of it. The house fit the neighborhood. It was a typical red brick two-story with an attached garage. Angelina couldn't wait to see the inside as the outside was so Gabriella, between the size, red brick and swing that sat on the front porch.

She rang the doorbell and Gabriella answered instantaneously—she had been waiting for Angelina right by the door. She gave Angelina a quick tour of her four-bedroom home. It had a gourmet kitchen that any chef would envy, as well as a formal dining room that held a table she was sure would fit at least eight, and maybe even twelve when opened fully. She had a quaint living room that fit the house, and a huge family room that overlooked a fairly large backyard. The backyard was strewn with flowers blooming in pots and baskets of flowers hanging from a multitude of shepherd's hooks. Fall was in the air and, thankfully, St. Louis hadn't experienced a frost yet, so Angelina could fully enjoy Gabriella's brightly colored backyard and patio area.

Gabriella had ordered pizza. As they waited for the deliveryman, Angelina commented on her home. "I thought you said this was a starter home."

"It is."

"If this is what you consider a started home, I can only imagine what your next house will look like."

"It's not that big, Angelina. I've done a few updates over the years. You should have seen it when I first bought it."

"All I can say is this house is so you, inside and out—between the flowers, the red brick… and I love how you decorated it."   She barely finished her comment when the doorbell rang. They'd decided to eat in as Gabriella wanted Angelina to experience pizza from the neighborhood pizzeria. "Doesn't this remind you of our late-night pizza parties that we held in our dorm room?" asked Angelina.

"Yeah, but now we can at least enjoy our food without being interrupted by the guys from the other side of the dorm. I swear they had a homing device when a pizza crossed through the elevators doors."

"I know. They were crazy."

They finished their meal, and then Angelina helped Gabriella prepare the pictures that would hang on her bulletin board dedicated to the special events from the quarter. They learned the importance of this in one of their education classes. It helped with parent teacher conferences, as the bulletin board tied up the quarter, highlighting the field trips, parties, and whatever else occurred that was special. It was a fabulous way for parents who couldn't attend the special functions to see what occurred in their children's lives. Angelina had put the finishing touches on her display while they waited for their pizza.

During their evening, many topics were discussed. Angelina started talking about the special events they attended while in college. "Gabriella, do you remember when we had to go on that urban experience for one of our education classes, were dropped off in the middle of the city with hardly a map, and were expected to visit the city schools and find our way downtown?"

"Yeah, I do. I really enjoyed seeing all of the old, turn-of-the-century schools. The architecture was beautiful. I wish the buildings would have been maintained more." Pausing, Gabriella added, "I can understand how the buildings fell into the condition they're in. Some, in fact many, of them have since closed. Some of those neighborhoods were pretty scary."

They continued their reminiscing and hardly noticed that three hours had elapsed when the doorbell rang. "Are you expecting anyone?" asked Angelina as Gabriella stood to open the door.

"At this hour? No. I'd intended it to be just a girl's night."

Before she could get to the door, the bell rang again. "Wait a minute... Just wait a minute... Who is it, anyway?" called Gabriella. She turned to Angelina and whispered, "One should always ask before opening the door especially at this late hour."

"Me," a voice called from the other side of the door.

"Who's me?"

"You know who it is. Open the door, Gabriella."

Gabriella threw open the door and was pulled into a hug. "Alejandro, what're you doing here?"

"Saying hello to my favorite sister."

"Favorite? You mean only."

"Okay, okay. Enough of that."

Gabriella led Alejandro to the family room where they'd been working.

"What're you doing this evening?" asked Alejandro as Gabriella led him down the hallway.

"Angelina and I are working on our quarterly bulletin boards. We take pictures throughout the year and post them in our classroom at the end of the quarter. That way the students and parents can experience some of the fun activities we did throughout the quarter."

"Sounds like a good idea," he said as he moved into the room. "Hi, Angelina. How are you doing?"

"I'm fine," Angelina smiled at Alejandro. "And you?"

"I'm great!" Alejandro said with a grin. "I'm off service with the hospital for the week and can finally take it easy. Thankfully, I just have office hours. These last few weeks since Gabriella's party have been a blur—I've worked non-stop. I'm so looking forward to some down time."

"Want something to drink?" Gabriella asked as she turned towards the kitchen.

"Sure, whatever you have," he called out as she disappeared around the corner.

Alejandro stood looking at Angelina as she put the finishing touches on Gabriella bulletin board. "So, are you the creative genius behind this project? I heard you made the invitations for Gabriella's party. They were beautiful."

Angelina put down the last of the pictures. Smiling, she looked over her shoulder at him. As she flashed her smile, she chuckled and said, "No, I'm not the genius. Your sister did much of this herself… And thank you for your compliment. I had a lot of fun helping your mother."

"From what I hear, you more than helped. I know my mom really appreciated everything you did to make it a special day for my sister."

Gabriella returned with a glass of wine. They sat around the table, catching up.

"I'm sorry I didn't get a chance to have that dance with you, Angelina."

"It's not a problem. I understand. I was trying to get the party favors together for one of your mom's friends and, when I went looking for you, you were already gone. Gabriella explained that you were called into the hospital. We can have that dance anytime."

Alejandro truly loved his sister and Angelina saw it first-hand. She had no idea that he'd missed Gabriella as much as he had while he'd lived out of state. Alejandro was a kind, caring man who seemed to really enjoy his job. Even with the demands of his profession, he spoke highly of his peers and co-workers at the hospital. He was unlike any doctor that she knew. He was compassionate and didn't talk down as he spoke of his colleagues.

Angelina saw a much different side to him than she imagined when she looked back on her many conversations they'd had while she was in college. She saw the serious side to him, but also the jokester that loved to kid around. But now he was different. He seemed much more intent—serious, but he was still a loving brother.

She caught him staring at her a few times and, several times, she smiled back at him, causing him to look away.

They talked until two in the morning when Angelina finally decided to go home. She explained that the following morning she wanted to be sure and be up to wish Colleen good luck before she left for her tournament. Angelina said her good-byes while Alejandro decided to stay with Gabriella. "It's been a long time since we've done this."

"It has. So how come you came by tonight?"

"I hadn't seen you since your party and wanted to spend some time with you."

Gabriella decided to change the subject abruptly, "I've got a question for you." She'd noticed him staring at Angelina several times while they talked.

"And that is?"

"Are you seeing anyone?"

"No," he sternly replied.

"Why not?" she asked.

"I'm too busy getting acclimated to my new job."

"Come on now…"

"Not now, Gabby. I don't want to talk about it." She knew he meant business—he usually only called her Gabby when he was upset with her. She dropped her questioning for the time being. She had her hopes, but she wasn't going to share them with Alejandro.

Angelina had barely crawled into bed when her alarm blared in her ear. It was six in the morning and she felt like she'd just gone to sleep. She crawled out of bed and dressed quickly, as she wanted to see her parents off.

Angelina hugged Colleen and wished her good luck as she and her parents hurried out the door. Colleen had to be at school by seven to make the bus for their early afternoon game. "Drive safely," she told her parents as she kissed them goodbye. "Wyatt, be sure and catch the entire game on video."

"I will," he told her as he grabbed a bagel and ran out the door. "Don't forget to walk Bingo," he yelled as he closed the car door. Bingo was the family's shelter dog they'd adopted. They'd had him for the last six years. He was a mix breed that the whole family had fallen in love with when they first laid eyes on him. Within hours of him entering their house, he'd become a member of the family. He was a sweet dog who let strangers know of his presence. They didn't think he'd bite anyone, but they didn't want to test him either.

Angelina went back to bed for a few hours, then spent the day as planned. She finished grading the last of the tests that she would use for the quarter. She was pleased with her students' grades. All of them had done well. That would bode well for her, especially since this was her first quarter at St.

Margaret's. Angelina took pride in her job and loved to see her students doing well.

Angelina decided to take a break and headed to the nearest local bookstore. Her favorite mystery author had just released a new book and she wanted to start it that weekend as a reward for finishing her grades for the quarter. She also wanted to read something new, in addition to the mystery that she held in her hand. She wasn't sure what she was looking for, and was searching the endcaps for new releases when she turned and accidentally bumped into someone, causing herself to drop her book. She looked up and was surprised to see Alejandro. "What're you doing here?" she asked as she knelt down to pick up the book from the floor.

"I could ask you the same," he said as he also reached for her book. "Sorry about that. I didn't mean to scare you into dropping your book."

"You didn't scare me."

"Well, I'm glad." he said, laughing. "If you're not in a hurry to be somewhere, would you be interested in having a coffee?"

Smiling at him, she teased, "I guess if you twisted my arm I could have one."

Smiling broadly at her, he paused and said, "Okay, I'm twisting," and he reached for her arm and playfully twisted. Laughing, they headed towards the café.

The barista took their order and Alejandro graciously paid for their coffees. Angelina ordered a café mocha, while Alejandro chose a plain old cup of coffee.

"You're not too adventurous."

"What do you mean?"

"Plain coffee?"

"What can I say?" he chuckled as he led her to a table in the back of the café. They sat and talked. "Angelina, I am so glad that you and Gabriella were able to reconnect. I think she considers you a sister. She has Alec, Joe, and I, but brothers are brothers. You can't talk 'girl' talk with us."

"I consider her a sister as well. I can share things with her that I can't share with my own sister, Kelly. I guess it's because we're the same age. Gabriella's a special person. I am lucky to have her in my life."

"I know she feels that same about you." Alejandro took a sip of his coffee, "So, what're your plans for the day?"

"Well, I worked on grades earlier. I got up early since my parents, Colleen, and Wyatt were heading off to Kansas City for Colleen's field hockey game. I thought I'd take a break, and that's how I ended up here. I'm not sure how I am going to spend the rest of the weekend. I guess take it easy." Pointing to her book, she added, "And read."

"Since you have no real plans outside of reading, what about having dinner with me?"

"Alejandro, that's kind of you to ask." She was surprised with his invitation and she paused before responding, smiling broadly. She said, "Sure, I'll have dinner with you." She knew his sister would be thrilled just as she was. She had always enjoyed her phone conversations with him, but now she was able to see him a different light. When he talked, she could see the intensity on his face and witness the passion in his eyes when he discussed something close to his heart. She was excited, to say the least, to have dinner with him—she was seeing a much different side to his personality than she'd imagined coming through the phone.

They finished their drinks and he said, "Why don't I follow you home and then we can decide where to go."

"Sounds great."

"Ready?" Angelina nodded and Alejandro stood and helped her with her chair. She paid for two books: the mystery she'd originally sought out and a non-fiction book written by one of her favorite comedians. Alejandro escorted her to her car and asked that she wait while he retrieved his car.

Angelina waited in her car for Alejandro. She sat there replaying their conversation. She hadn't paid much attention to his looks at Gabriella's party and when she saw him at Gabriella's house, it was late, and she was tired after a long day of teaching. But today... today she saw him for the man he was. *Wow*, she thought. "How did I miss how attractive he is?" she said aloud to herself. He'd certainly matured into quite a man from what she remembered from his pictures. She was sure a passersby thought she was crazy talking to herself sitting alone in her car. But, she had to talk to someone, and that someone was herself.

*My gosh! He's practically beautiful,* she screamed in her head. *He has the most amazing dark eyes.* His Spanish ancestry only added to his looks with his dark skin tone. His hair was also dark and thick, cut short and made for running one's fingers through. She had to get ahold of herself. She shouldn't be thinking of Gabriella's brother in these terms. *Anyway, he wouldn't look twice at me*, she thought. *But wait a minute... he did at Gabriella's house. No, I'm sure I imagined that... And that smile. Stop, just stop it—I'm not going there. Just friends. That's right, we're just friends.*

She couldn't believe how quickly her plans had changed and, with that, she heard a short toot signifying that he was ready. She waved at him, acknowledging his presence and put her car into reverse. As she took her foot off the brake, her heart rate accelerated as she backed out of her parking space. She stopped to turn and put her car into drive. *Stop it,* she said to herself. *I'm not nervous. This is Alejandro. We're friends. There's no need to be nervous,* she thought as she drove off towards home, Alejandro following closely behind.

In her fifteen minute drive home, she convinced herself not to be nervous. This was just dinner with a friend, that's all.

She pulled into her driveway with Alejandro right behind her. Her purse toppled over when she made the sharp turn into her driveway, but she quickly grabbed the contents of her purse and motioned to Alejandro that she needed to run into the house—she didn't realize that her cell phone was lodged between the seats.

Alejandro made a quick call while he waited for her. She ran inside, quickly let Bingo out, and grabbed a jacket since it was expected to be a cool evening. She locked the house and walked over to Alejandro's car. He got out of his car and held the door open for her, even assisting her with her seat belt.

"Where would you like to go?" he asked.

"I don't care. You choose."

"Why don't we head towards Old Towne, walk around, and when we're ready we'll just pick a spot to eat."

"Sounds like a plan."

They drove for a few miles before Angelina asked Alejandro what he liked to do in his spare time. Even though she tried not to be nervous, she was. She didn't understand what was wrong with her. It's not like this was a blind date.

"I like the outdoors. I'd be outside all of the time if I could. I used to run around the lakes up in Madison, but I wasn't able to do that much before I moved home. I love going to Forest Park, but I don't get there very often due to my schedule at the hospital and the distance from my house. I wish it were right around the corner, but it isn't. I'm surrounded by farmland now: corns and cows."

"You should try and make time for yourself... I know that's hard with your schedule and all. Do you anticipate it improving?"

"I hope so. I'm still trying to get the lay of the hospital. I'm glad that I made the move, but there's always an adjustment when you change jobs."

"I know that too well. When St. Mark's closed, I was pretty lost, especially since we went right into summer. I'm just thankful that I still live at home. I was able to help my mom with my siblings.  My dad's been pretty busy at the bank, so I did the majority of the yard work. I love my family and would do absolutely anything for them."

"They're lucky to have you. Have you ever wanted to get out on your own?"

"Yes and no. I'm pretty independent, and my parents don't stop me from doing anything. I pay them rent, although I know they're putting it away for me for when I do decide to move out. My parents are great."

Alejandro parked and came around to help Angelina from the car. *He's a true gentleman,* she thought. Opening car doors, holding doors for her... She almost thought that was a lost trait of many men. Most of the men she dated let her open her own doors, never helped her from the car, and often proceeded her going through doors before her. She often wondered if all men had lost their manners. She was pleasantly surprised that Alejandro was so unlike her previous boyfriends. And she liked it—she liked having doors held open for her, liked being made to feel special.

Side by side, they walked the streets of Old Towne, looking into the windows of the closed stores. Alejandro didn't seem to mind that Angelina liked to go into the antique stores. "I have a fondness for antiques as well," he told her as they exited the final store on the block. "Hungry, yet?"

"I'm a little hungry. What time is it?"

"Just about seven."

"I guess Colleen's game should be about over. Wyatt was going to videotape it for me. Depending on my schedule, I usually try to get to as many games as I can. Today, I just didn't feel like taking the trip. I wanted to get my grades done, and I guess just vegetate a little this weekend." They stopped at a restaurant and looked at the menu displayed in the window. Neither liked what was on the menu and walked on.

"From the time I accepted my job at St. Margaret's, it's been a whirlwind with trying to get ready for the school year. I had less than a week to prepare my classroom and get ready. I was a little lost at first as I changed grades and had to start all over on my lesson plans. I pretty much like to have the whole year planned out, and I spent all of my weekends since I took the job planning that."

They walked down the sidewalk. A bunch of kids came running towards her. Alejandro put his arm around her to keep her from being knocked into. She smiled up at him and continued with the conversation.

"Gabriella helped me so much. I couldn't have done it without her. This is the first weekend that I felt I needed to take time for myself. And then I see you at the bookstore. This has been a great day. Thank you for this evening. I'm really enjoying myself."

"I'm glad. I'm having a good time getting to know you, too."

They had dinner at a pub on Main Street. It was nothing fancy, but they sat and took in the ambience. They both enjoyed a beer while they waited for their food to arrive. Angelina had ordered a plate of nachos while Alejandro ordered a BLT. "I haven't had a BLT in years," he said. "This last time was—"

He stopped midsentence and didn't finish his thought. She noticed him tense up and a look of sadness crossed his face. He looked down at his left hand like he was looking for something, paused, and then changed the subject. She felt uncomfortable for a moment, but then when he started talking again, the feeling passed.

When they had finished their dinner and were having a coffee, the weekend band started playing. The band played a mix of country, pop, and seventies/eighties music. Several couples started to dance. Alejandro glanced at Angelina, reached out his hand and said, "Shall we dance?"

Angelina nodded and stood. The band had started the opening melody to a famous ballad as they made their way across the dance floor. Alejandro escorted her to the middle of the floor where he gently pulled her into his arms. He sensed her nervousness, but didn't question it. No words were spoken. They felt each beat to the music and danced. They glided across the dance floor until the music ended. He brushed a kiss across her knuckles, thanking her for the dance. Alejandro placed his hand on her lower back, guiding her back to their table. The instant she felt his hand on her back, she jumped and her nerves returned once again. She didn't understand what was wrong with her. That small gesture shouldn't have affected her in the manner it did.

Alejandro felt her jump when he guided her back to their table. He wasn't sure what had caused her nervousness, but he decided to call it a night. "It's getting late. Shall we go?"

He paid the bill. As they exited the restaurant, he placed his arm around her shoulders and guided her from the restaurant. The nervousness he had felt earlier when they left the dance floor had disappeared. They silently walked to Alejandro's car. He was helping her into her seat when he realized that he'd turned off his cell phone while they were at dinner. As he headed around the back of the car, he turned it on and discovered that he'd missed three phone calls, all from his father.

Since it was nearing midnight, he decided not to return his father's calls. He'd never left a message, so

Alejandro didn't think it was anything too important. Alejandro drove Angelina home and walked her to the door.

"I had a really nice time this evening," she said.

"So did I. We'll have to do this again sometime soon... I know my schedule's pretty busy starting next week. Maybe we can get together and have dinner again when my schedule clears." He whipped out his cell phone. "Give me your number and I'll call you when I have some free time."

She gave him her number then he walked her to her door. Angelina unlocked the door and turned back to Alejandro. He thanked her again, turned, and left her standing in the doorway.

Angelina waved goodbye as he walked away. Reflecting on her day, she realized what a remarkable man Alejandro was. She knew she'd liked him from the phone conversations they'd had and from what Gabriella had told her over the years, but she hadn't realized what a kind person he really was. The way he spoke of his family, friends, and colleagues spoke volumes about the person he was.

It was nearing one in the morning when Alejandro pulled into his driveway. As he opened his door, his cell rang. He looked at the caller ID and saw that it was his father. "Hey, Dad. I saw that you'd called earlier but was out and thought it was too late to return your call. What's up?"

"Where are you?"

"I just got home. I'm sitting in my driveway."

"Can you do me a favor?"

"Sure. What ya need?"

"Will you go over to Gabriella's for me? Pick her up and take her over to Angelina's."

"Why? What's wrong?"

"Gabriella's been trying to get a hold of her. She wasn't answering her cell."

"Is there a problem?"

"Alejandro, Colleen was in a serious accident."

"What happened?"

"I don't know all of the details. I just know she's in the ICU at Kansas City Memorial. She was injured in her field hockey game. Her parents have tried unsuccessfully to get ahold of Angelina. They called me since I'm her physician, and I told them I'd have Gabriella go over and break the news to her."

"What can I do?"

"Just get over to Gabriella's ASAP. When you get to Angelina's, call me and hopefully I'll have some more information." Alejandro hung up the phone, closed the car door, revved up his engine, and headed straight for Gabriella's. Before he could ring the bell, the door flew open and she was running out the door.

"Hurry, we've got to get to Angelina's!"

The lights were still on at Angelina's when they pulled up. It had barely been forty-five minutes since he left her on the doorstep. They ran to the door and rang the bell. Angelina looked out the front window prior to opening the door. "Alejandro, Gabriella, why're you here? Is something wrong?'

Alejandro had dialed his father as they approached the house. The call had just connected when Angelina opened the door. "Gabriella?" she asked again as she looked at her friend.

Alejandro told his father they were at Angelina's, and he asked to speak with her. Angelina looked scared. "What's wrong? Did something happen to my parents?"

Alejandro passed the phone to her. "My father would like to speak with you."

They entered the foyer and Alejandro closed the door behind them.

"Dr. A? What's wrong?" Angelina asked.

Alejandro led her to the couch and gestured for her to sit. Gabriella and Alejandro flanked her on either side.

"Angelina, are you sitting?"

"Yes, I am. What's wrong?"

"Angelina, Colleen's been in an accident. She was seriously injured in her field hockey game and is in the ICU."

Angelina raised a shaking hand to her mouth in shock.

"What happened?" she asked, trying to hold back her emotions.

"I'm not sure. I just know she took a shot to the abdomen from a very close range and collapsed onto the field. Your parents rushed to her, but by the time they got to her, she was unconscious. They rushed her to the hospital and called me since I am her physician, but also because of your relationship with Gabriella."

Gabriella grabbed Angelina's hand, and Alejandro put his arm around her.

"I need to go there and be with my sister."

"Angelina, I'm not sure that is a good idea. Do you have a piece of paper handy?"

Alejandro heard his father's request and pulled a notepad from his pocket. He always carried a notebook with him in the event he received an emergency call. "Here," he said.

Angelina was shaking so badly that she handed the phone to Alejandro. He wrote the telephone number down for the hospital, along with the name of the doctor that was handling Colleen's case. Angelina just sat mumbling, "I should have been there…"

Alejandro disconnected the call and turned to Angelina. "What can I do?" he asked.

"I don't know," she stammered. "I need to talk to my parents. I wonder if Kelly and James know."

While Gabriella got Angelina a glass of water, Alejandro called the hospital. He was able to get through to the nurses' station and speak with the nurse in charge. "Hello, yes, my name is Dr. Alejandro Alvarez. I am a friend of Colleen Samuels's sister. She is sitting right here with me. What is her condition?"

The nurse didn't want to divulge anything in relation to her condition since she couldn't verify who they were. "Fine," he said. "Are her parents nearby so that we can talk to them?"

The nurse placed them on hold while she went to get Angelina's mother. Angelina's mother came on the phone. "Hello," she stuttered.

"Mrs. Samuels?"

"Yes."

"This is Alejandro, Dr. A's son. I am here with Angelina. I'll put her on." Alejandro handed the phone to Angelina.

"Angelina?"

"Mom… Colleen… What happened? What's wrong with her?"

"Sweetie, she somehow took a hard shot directly in the abdomen. She cried out and collapsed. By the time we reached her, she was unconscious. She has significant swelling in the abdomen and they're waiting on the CT scan. She was having difficulties breathing, so they decided to put her into ICU until they can determine what's wrong with her."

"Mom, I'll be there as soon as I can."

"Honey, no wait. Let's see what the test results reveal. I'm in contact with Alejandro's father and we'll go from there. Where is your cell phone? I tried calling several times—there was no answer."

"I don't know. I had it earlier in the day." Angelina thought for a moment and then realized that it probably had fallen out of her purse when it overturned in her car. "It must have fallen out of my purse. I think it's in my car."

"Okay. Now try not to worry. I'll call you as soon as we know something. Is Gabriella with you?"

"Yes, she is."

"Good. I don't want you alone. Is Alejandro still with you?"

"Yes."

"Let me speak with him."

She handed the phone to Alejandro.

"Hello?"

"Alejandro?"

"Yes."

"I want to thank you and Gabriella for being there with Angelina. I told Angelina that I want her to stay there until we know something. The doctors are in contact with your father. I'm not sure what's going to happen, but we may have Colleen flown back to St. Louis. We have to see how she gets through the night. I would appreciate it if you could stay with Angelina as long as you can."

"It's not a problem."

"Please watch over her. I'm sure she has some guilt since she wasn't here. I'll call with any updates."

"Thanks." Alejandro disconnected the call and turned to Angelina. "Your mom will call with any updates. Why don't you try and get some rest?"

"I can't. My sister's in the hospital in serious condition. I want to be with her."

"I realize that, but the best place for you is right here. Let's not overreact. We need to wait for a more complete diagnosis."

Angelina got up and ran to her car where she discovered her cell phone lodged between the seats. Gabriella decided to make coffee when Angelina returned from her car with her phone in hand. Alejandro sat with Angelina while she paced the room. "What could be wrong with her?"

"I can't say for sure until the test results come back. It may be nothing."

The three of them stayed-up the remainder of the night. There was little talking. Gabriella held Angelina's hand while Alejandro sat, staring off into space. He was racking his brain with her possible diagnosis.

Just before dawn, Angelina drifted off to sleep. Earlier, Gabriella had curled up into an armchair and had also fallen asleep. Alejandro had joined Angelina on the couch. She'd fallen asleep in his arms.

# CHAPTER THREE

Alejandro awoke at about seven with Angelina nestled in his arms. He softly stroked her cheek and hoped for a better day when his phone started ringing. He hated to move but knew it would be his father. Reaching for his phone, he checked the caller ID, and answered. "Hello, Dad. Any news?"

"Not yet. It's still early. How are the girls?"

"Both are asleep... Dad, what're your thoughts about Colleen's condition?"

"I don't know. I'm not there, but I am concerned with how hard she was hit. She could have a multitude of injuries depending on exactly where she took the shot."

"I know. I was going through all of the possibilities myself. I just hope it's not as bad as where my thoughts led me last night."

"I know. Alejandro, just make sure you watch Angelina. I am concerned about her. She tends to internalize everything.  I know she's probably blaming herself for not being there with her family."

"I know what you mean. Since I'm not on service, I plan on staying with her so that I can decipher the medical terminology for her."

"She's lucky to have both of you there to support her."

"Call if you hear anything, and we'll do the same." Alejandro hung up the phone.

Alejandro carefully moved Angelina from his arms and laid her on the couch while he stood and stretched out the kinks in his back. He glanced at her. Even in her sleep, she had a worried look on her face. Gabriella woke just as he was heading towards the kitchen to find some coffee. "How's Colleen?"

"Dad just called and he had no updates. He's concerned about both Colleen and Angelina. He wants us to watch her. I told him we'd both be here for her, as I was planning on staying to explain the medical jargon when we do hear something."

"You're the best," Gabriella said as she got up from the chair, walked over to her brother, and placed a kiss on his cheek. "You don't really know Angelina yet you're willing to go out of your way for her. Thank you."

"Why wouldn't I? She's like a sister to you, and I feel like I've known her for years. She's a remarkable woman," he said as he thought about their dinner conversation the previous evening.

"Yes, she is."

They headed to the kitchen to fix coffee and something light to eat. Angelina started becoming restless on the couch. He heard her and went to check on her. She was just about ready to fall off the couch when he caught her. "Angelina?" he called out.

Startled, she woke and sat up. Rubbing her eyes, she asked, "Any news?"

"My father called a few minutes ago, but he has no new news. I told him if we heard anything, we'd let him know—he is going to do the same. He'll do his best to get some answers. I'm sure he knows someone on staff at Kansas City Memorial. He'll find out what's going on."

"Thank you, Alejandro. And please, thank your father for me."

The morning went by slowly, but no news was good news. Angelina's phone rang several times, but none of the calls were from her family. She was sick with worry over Colleen's condition. She kept thinking *no news is good news* over and over again to herself. She tried to think positively, but then her mind would turn negative. The what ifs started playing in her mind...

While Angelina spent some time alone in her room, Gabriella and Alejandro sat on the patio talking. "What do you think is wrong with Colleen?"

"I'm not sure since neither Dad nor I are there. I hope we hear something soon. I don't like that it's taking so long."

Angelina sat alone in her room pondering the previous day's events. Her sister was lying in the ICU in Kansas City and she was sitting in her room. What was wrong with this picture? Her parents had told her to stay home and not travel to Kansas City and, like a good girl, she did what they said. She wanted to be near Colleen, supporting not only her, but her parents and Wyatt, too. Even though there was almost a fourteen year age difference, she had a special connection with her sister.

When Angelina first started college, Colleen was almost four. She loved playing in Angelina's dorm room when she visited. Then, after she graduated and returned home, Angelina took time helping Colleen with her homework. And when Colleen got involved with field hockey, she tried acting as a goalie for Colleen as she took shots towards a make-shift goal. They often ended her practice sessions in a fit of giggles as Angelina was definitely not a goalie or even a field hockey player. She lacked the talent all the way around.

Angelina also established a Christmas ritual with Colleen. They spent a Saturday during the holidays shopping. Angelina would treat Colleen to lunch at one of the department store restaurants, and she had paid for Colleen's gifts until she had started earning her own money to pay for them. They both spent all year waiting for their next holiday shopping spree as it was the highlight of the year for them. *What if we can't do it any longer*, she thought. And then out of nowhere this feeling she couldn't place overcame her, and she started to cry. She sat on her bed hugging herself and crying as silently as she could.

Her window was open and Alejandro heard her cries. Gabriella had just received a call from their mother and had walked to the car to give her some information, so Alejandro rushed inside to Angelina.

Softly, he knocked on her door, but there was no answer and her crying seemed to intensify. He opened the door and saw her sitting on her bed with her back to the doorway. She had no idea that he'd entered her room.

"What have I done wrong in my life? How can I correct it?" She cried to herself. She thought she felt a presence, but she must just be overreacting. Next, she felt a hand on her shoulder. Slowly, she turned and there stood Alejandro. He squatted before her, reaching for her, and she fell into his arms. He held her and let her cry. Sweeping a hand across her face, she apologized for her tears. "Sorry."

"For what?"

"For falling apart." She calmed herself as she pulled from his embrace and walked across the room. Glancing out the window, she asked if he had any updates. Alejandro shook his head no, but just then the bedside telephone started ringing. Angelina answered it with a breathy hello.

"Angelina," One word. Her name… The tone. She knew it was bad news. "Colleen is in acute liver failure," said her father.

"Wh-what does that mean?"

"The blow has caused her liver some damage and it has begun to fail."

"And?"

"Is Alejandro nearby?"

"Yes, he's standing right here."

"Please put him on the telephone."

She turned to Alejandro and handed him the phone. He said, "Yes?"

"Alejandro?"

"How's Colleen?"

Angelina's father detailed her condition.

"Yes… I understand. I'll contact my father. Yes… I will let Angelina know. What time do you expect to arrive?" Not only had her father discussed Colleen's condition with him, he'd also asked Alejandro if he would be her doctor in the event that she needed a transplant.

Angelina's father told Alejandro that they were having Colleen flown home. She would arrive sometime late afternoon, early evening. He wanted Angelina to be waiting for her at the hospital. Her parents would leave Kansas City as soon as possible, but they expected that their drive would take at least four hours since there was road construction. They would meet Angelina and Alejandro at the hospital. He and Gabriella would both wait with her. Alejandro disconnected the call while Angelina sat in silence.

"What did my father tell you about Colleen's condition?"

"Same thing that he told you. He wants me to contact my father and asked that I take you to the hospital to wait for the helicopter. Your father expects their drive to take about four hours. Angelina, I'm not going to make light of the situation. This is extremely serious."

Alejandro walked over to where she stood staring out her bedroom window. "Will she live?" Angelina asked.

"I don't know. If this becomes more critical, she may require a liver transplant."

"Transplant?"

"Yes."

"Can we find a donor? I thought people were on waiting lists for years for donors."

"Generally they are, but it's quite possible that we could find a donor quickly. It just depends. Let's cross that bridge when and if we need to."

"Are you going to be her doctor?"

"That's what your father was asking me. We'll see. Right now my father is her primary doctor, and that's one of the reasons why your parents wanted to get Colleen home. We need to let Gabriella know what's going on, and then we can leave for the hospital."

Angelina changed her clothes and gathered some things for her parents, Wyatt, and of course, Colleen. Alejandro carried the bags to the car while Angelina locked up the house. Gabriella was waiting for them in the car. She was on the phone with her father. "We're just about ready to leave. We should be there in less than a half an hour." Hanging up the phone, she relayed her conversation with her father to Alejandro. "Sounds like she'll be there in an hour or so."

"Great," said Alejandro. "Let's get moving." As Alejandro drove towards the hospital, his thoughts were on the what ifs, Angelina's were on Colleen as well as her parents, and Gabriella was worried about her friend. She wasn't talking. She was just sitting there, and that scared her more than anything. She was going to have to keep her focus on her. If she couldn't get through to her, maybe Alejandro could. He should know what to look for, as well as how to approach her and what to say.

They parked in the doctor's lot and, as they exited the car, they heard the helicopter's approach. Angelina started to shake. Gabriella reached for her hand as they hurried into the hospital. Alejandro was a few steps ahead of them.

"Gabriella, take Angelina to my office. I've already contacted my assistant who is prepared to let you in. I'll touch base as soon as I know something." Alejandro squeezed Angelina's hands and hurried down the corridor. Gabriella put her arm around Angelina and guided her to Alejandro's office. Suzie, his office assistant, was waiting for them. She led them into his office where she'd gotten a fruit and cheese platter from the cafeteria. She also had an assortment of juices and water. "I thought it might be a while, and I wasn't sure when you last ate. I'll let you know when Dr. Alvarez knows something."

Angelina sat on the couch while Suzie led Gabriella to the office kitchenette to retrieve some glasses for their drinks. "Suzie, let my brother know that he needs to come up here as soon as possible. I need to talk to him privately without Angelina knowing. I'm sure you will be discreet in advising me when he is available."

"No problem, Gabriella. I'll page him and let him know."

"Thanks."

They sat in Alejandro's office for almost two hours before Suzie let Gabriella know that Alejandro was available to speak with her. Since Gabriella was a volunteer at the hospital, Suzie asked if she could get her help with something for the Children's Hospital. She led Gabriella to an examining room where Alejandro was waiting. "Sis, what's up? Suzie told me you wanted to see me privately."

"Before we get started, any news?"

"No, they're still stabilizing her and will take her to ICU within the next half hour. Now, what did you want to see me about?"

"Angelina."

"Yes?"

"I'm worried about her. I know Dad's also worried. Can you talk to her? She hasn't said a word since we got to your office. She just sits there, staring off into space. I don't think she's eaten anything today or, if she has, it's been very little. Please, Alejandro, do something."

"Why don't you go take a break, and check with Suzie to see if they've moved Colleen? I'll talk with Angelina."

Angelina sat in Alejandro's office. So much had happened in the last twenty-four hours. She still couldn't believe that she'd run into Alejandro at the bookstore. And then, they'd gone out to dinner. She'd had a fabulous time with him, walking through Old Towne, dinner, and then when he held her in his arms and they danced. Talk about perfection. That's what she'd call their night together. It had come as a complete surprise to her, her attraction to him, if that's what she called her nervousness after their dance. And then he had asked for her phone number. She knew she shouldn't think along these terms, but she did. They'd gone on a date, if that's what you called their time together. And then, less than an hour later, all hell had broken loose. He'd returned with the news that would change all of their lives forever. Colleen was injured—no one knew her condition, and no one knew if she'd survive. The memories of the prior day overwhelmed her as she sat alone in Alejandro's office. And then, she heard a noise.

Alejandro knocked on his office door. There was no answer, so he slowly opened it and entered. He noticed she was sitting on the couch gazing down at the floor. As he gradually approached, she didn't move a muscle, even when he was directly in front of her. He reached for her shoulder, lightly placing his hand there. She appeared to be in a coma. She never moved. Finally, Alejandro gently squeezed her shoulder and said, "Angelina?"

Slowly, she raised her head and looked at his face. Tracks of dried tears trailed down her face. She looked ashen in color. She was scared to death for her sister.

"Colleen is being moved to ICU. She should be there within a half-hour… She's holding her own for now."

She nodded her head.

"Angelina, say something. What are you feeling?"

She sat there holding her hands in her lap. Not making eye contact with him, she said, "I just want her to get well. That's all."

"But what're you feeling?"

"I don't want to talk about myself. I'm only concerned about Colleen and that my parents make it home safely. Please take me to her."

Alejandro reached for her hands and pulled her from the couch. She fell against his chest. "Sorry," she said. "I lost my balance."

"Have you had anything to eat today?"

"No, nothing to speak of."

"You've got to take care of yourself. It's not going to help your parents if you end up in the hospital as well. I'll take you to see Colleen, but you will, and I mean will, only stay for five minutes. Then, I'm taking you to get something to eat."

Nodding, she followed Alejandro from his office to the ICU. He guided her through the doorway and nodded at one of the nurses who pointed to Colleen's room. Alejandro led her inside. As she crossed the threshold, she felt a cold chill overcome her. The room was so sterile—white walls, no color except for that on the various machines that were hooked-up to Colleen's body. Angelina was cold. She wrapped her arms around her middle trying to warm herself. Alejandro put his arm around her shoulders as he guided her towards Colleen's bedside. Machines surrounded Colleen, giving off incessant beeps. She watched the numbers constantly change as the machines monitored her vital signs.

Colleen laid there. She was as pale as the sheets that were pulled up to her chin. Angelina reached for her hand. "Coll, it's me Angelina."

There was no response. No squeeze of Angelina's hand. Nothing. She just laid there, pale as a ghost. If one really didn't know how sick she was, they would think she was asleep—there were no visible signs of injury on her face, hands, or arms. Angelina just watched her breathe.

Alejandro placed his arm around her shoulder, nodded, and ushered her from Colleen's room. As they exited the ICU, he told her she couldn't return for another two hours. Hopefully, by that time, her parents and Wyatt would be there.

Angelina's parents had spoken to her other siblings earlier. Kelly and James were expected at the hospital shortly. Kelly was driving in from Atlanta where she attended grad school. James was flying in from the west coast. His flight was scheduled to arrive within the hour.

Alejandro motioned for Gabriella to join them as they exited the ICU and headed towards the cafeteria. Gabriella was starving while Angelina just asked for a bottle of water—Alejandro didn't listen to her request. Instead, he ordered her a sandwich and fruit plate. Paying for their food, he led them to the doctor's lounge. Thankfully, no one was present.

Alejandro guided them to one of the round tables that filled the doctor's lounge. Gabriella was so hungry that she practically inhaled her sandwich before Angelina and Alejandro could seat themselves. Alejandro pulled out Angelina's chair and sat down beside her. He watched Angelina as she stared at her food. He nodded at Gabriella, who then excused herself indicating that she needed to use the restroom.

"Angelina, you need to eat. You almost collapsed in my office." Slowly she looked up into his caring eyes and told him that she knew it but just couldn't. Alejandro speared a strawberry from her plate and lifted it to her lips. "Eat," he said. She opened her mouth and took the strawberry from his fork. She began to chew. When she'd finished that, he chose a piece of pineapple.

Before he could spear another piece of fruit, she put her hand up to stop him. "Thank you, but I can feed myself." He smiled at her when she reached for her sandwich and took a bite. They continued sitting in silence until Gabriella returned. Then, the door opened and Alejandro's father walked in.

"Any news?" asked Angelina.

"No, but I just heard from your parents and they're approaching the hospital. I told them we'd meet them outside the ICU."

Angelina started to gather her food but Alejandro stopped her. "You need to finish before we leave here. That's an order. Dad, can you meet her parents? They probably won't be here for another half hour or so."

She looked up at him and a pained look crossed her face, her eyes becoming downcast and her lips drawn. She was doing her best to hold in her emotions.

"Please finish. You need to stay well, too."

Gabriella and her father headed off to the ICU while Angelina stayed back with Alejandro to finish eating. It took her longer than he expected for her to finish her lunch. It seemed like an hour had elapsed when only fifteen minutes had passed.

He tried to take her mind off Colleen by asking her various questions about school, but she always seemed to turn the conversation back to her sister. That's all she could focus on besides swallowing her lunch. Every bite she took seemed harder and harder to swallow as the lump in her throat grew from keeping her emotions in check.

She finally finished her meal. He was right—she did need to eat. As she stood, she felt stronger and more stable on her feet. "Okay, now I'm ready."

"Thanks for listening to me. Now, let's go." Placing his hand on her back, he guided her from the doctor's lounge back to the ICU where they met her parents coming off of the elevator.

Angelina reached for her mother and threw herself into her arms. "She looks so pale," she whispered to her mother.

"I know, dear. I know."

Reaching for her father's hand, the three of them walked down the hallway with Alejandro and Wyatt trailing behind. Alejandro's father was waiting for them outside the ICU.

"John," Angelina's father said, "How is she?"

"Right now she's holding her own, but that can change at a moment's notice. Anything can happen. To be on the safe side, I think all of you need to be tested to see if a family member is a viable donor in case Colleen requires a liver transplant."

Angelina's mother cried out and reached for her husband. "Ben, she can't die."

Ben held his wife and told her he wasn't going to let that happen. They would do everything in their power to see that she got well. Ben looked towards Alejandro and said, "Will you take care of our daughter?"

"In the event that it gets to that stage, yes I will. I agree with my father—you all need to get tested to see if any of you are viable donors. Right now, that would be in Colleen's best interest."

Jackie looked at her husband and said, "Come on, let's go." She motioned for Angelina and Wyatt to join them. Alejandro guided them to the lab where they would be tested for their viability.

# CHAPTER FOUR

Both the Samuels and Alvarez families tested to see if any of them were compatible to be a liver donor for Colleen. Angelina's parents had yet to see Colleen since they arrived, so they headed off to the ICU with Wyatt. Angelina, in the meantime, made her way to the hospital chapel. She had never been in a hospital chapel before. She was actually surprised to see the stained glass windows that lined the hallway as she approached the closed doors. The doors were heavier than she expected as she opened them and walked into the solemn room. Four sets of pews were located towards the front near an altar. Additional chairs were set-up around the perimeter of the chapel. She could hear a pin drop as she walked towards the front of the room. She was the only one present in the chapel.

She sat in the front pew and bowed her head, praying for her family but, most importantly, for her sister. She was more than scared. Colleen had been glowing with excitement just yesterday morning when she got in the car to head off to her tournament. And now, just a little over a day later, she was unconscious, lying in a hospital fighting for her life. All due to a freak accident.

Angelina had drifted off to sleep sitting in her pew when she felt someone sit beside her. Then she felt an arm drape around her shoulders and she inched her head onto their shoulder. She was in a safe place, feeling protected, and was drifting back off to sleep again when she heard the air conditioning kick on. She jumped and the arm around her shoulders tightened. She raised her head and looked up at Alejandro. "What're you doing here?"

"Thought you needed a shoulder."

Angelina became uncomfortable all of a sudden and moved out of the protection of his arm. "I see. Any news?"

"Not yet. It will take a few more hours before we hear if anyone is compatible. We're already running Colleen's information through the transplant database."

She nodded then stood up. Alejandro asked her to follow him, and he led her down a long, sterile hallway, then opened a door and entered an office.

"Where are we?"

"My offices. We just came in a different way."

Leading her down another, albeit shorter, hallway, he opened the door to his private office. He motioned for her to sit on the couch. Sitting down beside her, he reached for her hand, "Angelina, you need to rest. Please lie down while I get caught up on some paperwork. I'll wake you when I have any news."

"My parents?"

"I told them I'd take care of you. Now, get some sleep."

Angelina wanted to argue but knew better. She was scared, worried about her sister and what would happen. She also felt like she was taking advantage of

Alejandro. She knew him, but not really. As she thought about their relationship, she drifted off to sleep again. Alejandro covered her with a blanket that he kept in his office for his late night shifts when it was just easier to stay at the hospital. Instead of working, he watched her sleep. In all the years that she had been friends with Gabriella, he had no idea what a kind-hearted person she was. She was extremely caring of her family and friends. They took precedence over her wants and needs, which often caused her to withdraw into herself. He wished he'd met her when she and Gabriella were in college. Maybe his life would have been different. He couldn't think about what he'd been through in the past few years—the highs, lows, happiness, grief, and heartache. He had to focus on the here and now—Colleen and her possible need for a liver transplant.

His cell vibrated. Taking it from his pocket, he immediately recognized that it was his father. "Dad?"

"Get down here now. I think you need to get involved. It's not looking good." He didn't even respond to his father. He ended the call, jumped up from his chair and approached Angelina. Tapping her on the forearm, she awoke with a start.

"My dad just called. I am headed down to the ICU."

"Colleen?"

"Not sure what's going on. Come with me." He reached for her forearm and helped her from the couch. While Angelina had slept, Alejandro had received the news he'd hoped for. He wasn't sure what his father wanted, but he knew there was a definite solution to the situation at hand. A sense of hope was on the horizon. Guiding her from his offices, she followed him to the ICU.

When they reached the ICU, her parents and siblings were waiting for her. "Where've you been, Angelina?" asked her mother.

"I was with Alejandro. Why?"

"It's Colleen. She's taken a turn for the worse and the doctors feel she needs an immediate transplant."

"What about a donor?"

"We've found one."

"That's great. Are they far?" asked Kelly.

"No."

"Really? Who is it?" asked Angelina.

Alejandro knew who it was. He'd received an email with the confirmation prior to receiving his father's call. He began to raise his hand to her back when Alejandro's father said, "You."

Angelina was stunned. "Me?" she whispered as Alejandro placed his hand on her back. A series of emotions crossed her face; her body stiffened under the guide of his hand as she listened to Alejandro's father speak.

"Yes. You're a perfect match." John stated. Her mother crossed in front of Alejandro and grabbed ahold of Angelina.

"Yes, my dear. You'll be the one to save our Colleen."

Angelina stood there, stunned. She didn't know what to say. She had all kinds of thoughts running through her head. She couldn't believe she was the one person that could save her sister's life. She never knew that a live human could be a liver donor. She'd heard about people receiving a family member's kidney, but a liver? How could she survive without her liver?

Alejandro, guessing her concerns, explained to her that a portion of her liver would be removed and would be implanted into her sister. If all went according to plan, and Colleen's body did not reject her liver, Angelina's liver would replace Colleen's and regenerate to normal size in a matter of weeks. He explained that hers would also return to its normal size, too.

Alejandro went into detail about the surgery. It could take up to twelve hours to complete. Colleen would remain in the hospital two to three weeks. She could be discharged sooner or later depending on whether she encountered any complications.

Angelina had a dazed look on her face. Alejandro interjected, bringing her back to reality, "Angelina, we must admit you and take you for further testing. Colleen's condition is deteriorating. We must perform the transplant as soon as possible."

Dazed, she continued to stand there. She didn't know what to say or do. She reached for her mother and just hugged her. Alejandro reached for her arm and told her they needed to get moving—time definitely was not on their side.

She kissed her parents goodbye as Alejandro led her off. Gabriella followed them. She needed to support her friend and brother while Angelina's parents stayed with Colleen. Gabriella loved Angelina and her brother, and she prayed that this transplant would be successful for all involved.

Alejandro completed running the necessary tests and approved Angelina as Colleen's donor. She was still in a state of shock. She was confused with everything that was going on around her. She went through a myriad of tests herself. She didn't have a choice if she wanted to have this surgery or not. It didn't matter that she was frightened about herself. She was more worried about her sister and all the what ifs floating through her mind.

It seemed like an eternity had passed since her dinner with Alejandro. In fact, it was as though it had never happened—a figment of her imagination. And now, she was facing a major surgery herself. She realized in that moment how family's lives could be drastically changed in just the beat of a heart.

Time passed quickly but also stood still as Angelina waited to be wheeled into surgery. Prior to the surgery, Alejandro visited her. She looked so small in the bed. He could tell how scared she was, for when he entered her room, she was staring out the window. Her hands were balled into tight fists along her sides. Her jaw was tightly clenched. It had turned into an ugly weather day. Storms were predicted to move in at any time. The weather reflected her mood: dark, intense, and full of rage. She was full of anger not only because her sister was going through this ordeal, but because she hated the fact that she wasn't closer to Colleen. Yes, they had a special bond because she was still living a home, but she was much closer to Kelly since they were just a few years apart in age. She and Kelly had been practically inseparable until she went away to college. She wished that she'd made more one-on-one time for Colleen and she vowed that, if Colleen survived this crisis, she would make the time for her sister and forge that bond.

"Angelina?"

She turned and looked in Alejandro's direction. It seemed as though she didn't see him.

"Angelina?" he repeated. She looked up at him. He could tell she'd been crying. "Why are you crying?"

"Alejandro, I am so scared. I'm afraid that I won't be able to save Colleen. I know she's my sister and all, it's just—"

"Don't think like that. From all indications, everything should go well. You're a perfect match. The real concern will come after the transplant, trying to prevent Colleen from rejecting your liver. You should be fine, too… Just a few weeks of rest for you. I don't expect that you'll have any complications. Colleen's the one I'm worried about."

She nodded at him.

"Are we ready?"

"As ready as I'll ever be."

"Then let's do it." He squeezed her hand as the nurses prepared to move her to the operating room.

Alejandro performed Colleen's surgery while another surgeon extracted a portion of Angelina's liver. It was a long surgery, but both came through with flying colors. Angelina's parents went back and forth between their daughters rooms while they waited for each of them to wake from their respective surgeries. The Samuels's had just left Angelina's room when Alejandro entered. She was alone, so he decided to sit with her because he didn't want her to be alone when she woke. He reached for her hand and softly brushed his thumb along her palm. He sat there for quite some time when he dozed off.

She squeezed his hand, causing him to wake. He sat up straighter in the chair and noticed that her eyes were fluttering—she was waking up. He looked down at his watch. He'd been asleep for about an hour.

He brushed her bangs from her forehead and, as she opened her eyes, she immediately recognized him. "Alejandro?" she croaked. Her voice was raspy from the surgery.

"How are you feeling?" He could tell that she was having difficulties swallowing and offered her a sip of water. Angelina felt like she'd been hit by a Mack truck. She was exhausted and thought every bone and muscle in her body was calling out in pain. There were several intravenous lines coming from her body. She'd never had major surgery before and hadn't really known what to expect when she woke. She hadn't really thought to ask Alejandro since the surgery happened so quickly—she'd been in shock from the moment she discovered that she was going to be Colleen's donor.

"Sore," she groaned in response. "And Colleen?"

"Doing as well as can be expected. Angelina go back to sleep and I'll be here when you wake."

She nodded, turned her head away from him, and fell back to sleep.

Once he was sure she was sleeping, Alejandro went to check on Colleen. As he made his way down the hallway, he prayed that Angelina didn't wake until he returned. Even though Colleen's room was not far from Angelina's, it seemed like it was an eternity before he reached her door. He waved to her parents as he passed the waiting room. They, too, looked exhausted—no one in the Alvarez or Samuels family had slept much in the last seventy-two hours.

He checked with the nurses before entering Colleen's room. She was still unconscious from surgery, but that was to be expected. He checked her vital signs, all of the machines that were connected to her, as well as the various tubes that were attached to her body. She was still on a ventilator helping her breathe. She had a gastric tube that fed into her stomach. She had a catheter along with other various tubes in her abdomen. These drained fluid from around her liver and would remain in place for about a week. All in all, Colleen was faring well. He stopped by Colleen's parents to provide them with an update before returning to Angelina's room. He hoped that she hadn't woken while he was gone. He'd promised her that he'd be there when she woke up in the morning. He'd just reentered her room when she called for him.

"Alejandro?" she whispered. He reached for her hand and held it while she opened her eyes. He brushed his hand across her forehead, letting her know that he was there, but also checking for a fever.

"I'm here."

"Thank you. Thank you for saving Colleen."

"I didn't—you did. What matters is that she is alive and recovering. You need to rest. We'll be getting you up soon. Take it easy because you'll need to be fully rested before I will allow you to return to work."

"Yes, sir," she said. Alejandro had to leave—he was being paged over the intercom. He promised to check on her before he left the hospital for the evening.

Gabriella ran into Alejandro as he was leaving Angelina's room. "How is she?"

"Good. But Gabriella, you need to make sure she understands that she needs her rest. She'll be tired and will be susceptible to infection. I worry that when she returns to the classroom she will pick something up from one of the children."

"I'll tell her that she needs to take it easy. But I know her and she will push herself. You're going to have to play an active role in making sure she takes it easy, too. You're her doctor."

"I realize that, but I wanted to make sure you understood the importance of this. I don't expect you to do her work, but I want you to understand that she is—"

"I know, Alejandro. She's like a sister to me, and I will make sure she takes care of herself."

"Thanks."

Gabriella sat with Angelina and she spoke of Alejandro's concerns for when she returned to work. She wouldn't be able to return to work for six to eight weeks. "You're going to have to take it easy, and when you return, the beginnings of the flu season will be underway."

"I know that, Gabriella. I'll do my best to stay rested and well. I won't overdo it, I promise. I'll have you and my parents to make sure that I take care of myself."

Colleen was slowly recovering from the transplant. She had exhibited no signs of rejection. Everyone was thankful that the transplant was successful.

Gabriella visited Angelina while she was in the hospital almost daily, bringing cards and letters from her students. Angelina missed them and couldn't wait to return to the classroom. It was her avenue of joy. Her students were the family that she hadn't yet had the chance to build. Teaching provided her with an extended family. Many of Angelina's past students kept in touch with her and several that she'd worked with while she studied in college had begun to have their own families. When Angelina thought of the prospect of her own family, she often got depressed. She was thirty years old and didn't even have a prospect for a husband, let alone a chance at fulfilling the dream of starting the family she so desired. Angelina had always dreamed of having it all—a house she could call her own and a family. The size of her family didn't matter as long as she and her husband were healthy and happy with whatever came their way. One, two, three children didn't matter. She'd feel blessed no matter what.

One day when Gabriella entered Angelina's room, she surprised her with a wheelchair and another envelope stuffed with cards. "What's up with the wheelchair?"

"We're going for a ride," she said as she placed the envelope containing the cards down on the tray table and helped Angelina transfer from her bed to the wheelchair. Gabriella wheeled Angelina down the hall. Angelina had no idea what her friend was doing and then she realized they were headed to Colleen's room. Gabriella pushed through the doorway and Angelina was flabbergasted. It seemed like the entire Samuels and Alvarez families had gathered in Colleen's room.

As everyone stood around celebrating Colleen's successful transplant, her parents recalled watching the field hockey game and witnessing the series of events that led up to her injury. It had been a freak accident by nature. Somehow she'd lost her footing and was trying to recover when she was hit. "I really don't remember anything about what happened. The last thing I truly remember was leaving the house and Wyatt reminding Angelina to walk Bingo. That's it."

Her parents praised the emergency medical teams that assisted Colleen, both on and off the field. They were extremely thankful for their relationship with the Alvarez family. "John and Maria, thank you for everything," Jackie said as she hugged Maria.

"We didn't do a thing," John said as Ben shook his hand.

"You brought Alejandro to us," said Jackie.

"We had nothing to do with that," John said. "Gabriella was the one behind it—she's the one who linked our families together when the girls were in school."

"Either way, Alejandro is why we're all standing together celebrating Colleen's new lease on life," Jackie added.

Colleen reached for John's hand. "I don't care what you say, Dr. A. You made this day happen. From what I understand, you coordinated everything. Thank you!" They were lucky to be connected with them, and Alejandro's move back to St. Louis proved to be a godsend for all involved.

Angelina came home from the hospital a week after the transplant. When Angelina returned home, physically she was doing well, but emotionally she was still trying to catch up and make sense out of what happened. She had her emotionally charged moments where she found herself crying for no reason, and then she'd realize how lucky Colleen was to be alive. Life was precious. It could be taken in a moment's notice. She would never take it for granted again.

Colleen followed Angelina home a week later. Neither one experienced any complications. Time would tell if Colleen would reject the transplant, but all indications were that she would be just fine. Angelina returned to the classroom two weeks before Thanksgiving, while Colleen wouldn't return to school until after the New Year.

# CHAPTER FIVE

Angelina returned to school amongst a hail of well wishes. A special mass and assembly were held in her honor. Angelina thanked everyone for their prayers, well wishes, and cards. She graciously thanked Gabriella for her constant support. "I want everyone to know that Ms. Alvarez's family was instrumental in helping my family. Ms. Alvarez's older brother is the physician that performed the transplant on my sister. I owe so much to her and her family."

Angelina said a few more words and then hugged Gabriella. She was so thankful that Mary hired her and brought Gabriella back into her life. Both were an emotional wreck by the end of the assembly. Arm-in-arm, they walked towards Mary's office.

"Are you two going to be okay the rest of the day?" Mary asked.

"I'll be fine," said Angelina. "I just got a little emotional. Give me a minute and I'll head back—"

"No, you two take your time and go back to your classrooms when you're ready. Your aides will cover for you."

It was a pleasant day, so Angelina and Gabriella decided to take a walk outside.

"I'm blessed to have you and your family back in my life. I'm sorry that we lost track of one another after graduation. I love you, Gabriella."

"I know you do. Angelina, I regret not keeping in touch, too, but we can only move forward and acknowledge the past, knowing we'll always be in each other's lives from now on. I consider you the sister that I never had, and I love you, too."

They sat outside for the remainder of the period discussing the upcoming holidays and the year's activities leading up to their winter break. Angelina was excited to get back to her classroom. They were studying Thanksgiving and were preparing for a field trip to an Indian Reservation to participate in a mock Thanksgiving celebration. It was the first time the school had done this and everyone was looking forward to it.

Angelina had been back in school for about a week. She'd been more tired as of late, but blamed it on the fact that she was getting back into the swing of things. That morning she'd awakened with a headache, but she didn't think twice about it since she often had headaches due to her allergies. Lately, she'd also been a little on the warm side, but blamed it on the weather and the higher than normal humidity levels.

Angelina was running behind as she greeted her mother in the kitchen. She grabbed her travel mug and reached for the coffee pot when her mother started questioning her about the field trip. "I've always wanted to visit an Indian Reservation. How far did you say it was? What time are you leaving?

What time do you expect to arrive? Are you looking forward to the trip?"

Jackie didn't hesitate or even take a breath between questions. Angelina's head was pounding and she just didn't have the energy to deal with her mother. She paused before pouring her coffee and said, "Mom, last night I told you everything about the field trip. Didn't you listen to a word I said?"

Jackie was shocked by Angelina's comment. She stood and watched as Angelina quickly poured her coffee sloshing the hot liquid over the edge of the cup. Hurriedly, she reached for a cloth to clean-up her mess and slammed the lid onto the cup. She grabbed her purse and headed to the door. "I have to go I am running late." And with that, Angelina rushed through the door slamming it behind her. Angelina had been cross with her mother for no reason at all. In Jackie fashion, she'd just asked a few questions.

They boarded the bus for the field trip. Angelina seemed a little anxious, but Gabriella didn't say anything because she thought it was just the adrenaline of going on the trip. She'd actually had to pull aside several of the boys to threaten them that if they didn't behave, she'd leave them at school. Gabriella had never witnessed Angelina get upset with her students, but today she did. Gabriella couldn't figure out what they'd done. Actually, hers were behaving worse than Angelina's while they'd lined up to board the bus.

They arrived at their destination and disembarked the bus. Angelina was behind Gabriella. One of Angelina's students was a little loud and Gabriella turned around. She witnessed Angelina stumble as she reached the top of the stairs and almost fall down the stairs, but she caught herself before falling. One of Angelina's students asked if she was okay, but she blamed it on her clumsiness. Gabriella thought something was out of sorts with her and decided to keep an eye on her for the remainder of the day.

Thankfully, the school required a parent for every three students on field trips, in addition to the classroom teacher. This ratio enabled the teachers to interact more with the students and further enrich the experience for everyone.

Gabriella noticed Angelina brushing her hand across her forehead. She was pale and appeared to be warm. Several times, Gabriella saw Angelina lift the hair off of her shoulders, fanning her neck. It was a nice day and the temperatures were in the mid-sixties. Gabriella didn't think it was warm enough that Angelina needed to fan herself.

They had eaten and were watching a tribal dance when Angelina stood and headed for the back of the Exhibition Hall. Gabriella followed her with her eyes and waited for her return. She was concerned with the visible signs she'd witnessed earlier in the day. Anxiousness... Clumsiness... Overly warm. It just wasn't normal for Angelina, as she remembered her always being on the cold side. Alejandro had asked her to keep an eye on Angelina when she returned to school.

When Angelina didn't reappear, Gabriella stood and nonchalantly walked over to Mary.

"I'm going to check on Angelina. She walked out a few minutes ago and hasn't returned. I'm a little concerned."

Mary nodded. "I saw her leave, too, and was watching for her to return. Go check on her."

Gabriella headed to the ladies room where she found Angelina standing at the sink washing her hands. Her face was flushed and it looked like she'd been wiping her forehead—there was an abundance of wet paper towels sitting beside the sink. She seemed surprised when Gabriella entered. She gathered the towels and threw them into the trashcan. Gabriella didn't want her to think she was checking on her, so she went into one of the stalls. When she came out, Angelina was still standing beside the sink. She appeared to be holding onto the sink for dear life.

While washing her hands, she asked, "Are you alright?"

"Yes," Angelina adamantly replied.

She didn't believe her quick, terse reply. Gabriella didn't know what to do. She knew something wasn't right, but didn't want to press the issue and further agitate Angelina. She'd wait and see how she was when they returned to St. Margaret's; then she'd confront her. Gabriella opened the bathroom door and Angelina preceded her. Angelina barely crossed the threshold when she grabbed her side and collapsed to the ground.

"Angelina?" Gabriella cried out.

She'd fainted. Gabriella knelt down and felt Angelina's head—she was burning up with fever. Trying not to draw attention to herself, she ran for Mary. Whispering in her ear, she told her of Angelina's collapse. Mary jumped from her seat and followed Gabriella to the hallway where Angelina lay unconscious. "I'll call for an ambulance," said Gabriella. She dialed 911 and told the operator what had happened. An ambulance was being dispatched.

No sooner had she hung up with 911 then she dialed Alejandro.

Alejandro had caller ID and recognized his sister's telephone number. He'd just completed visiting with his inpatients at the hospital and was heading towards his office.

"Hey, Sis. What's up? Aren't you supposed to be on some Indian field trip?"

Gabriella could barely get the words out. "Angelina," she whispered.

He couldn't hear what she said and asked again, "What?"

Gabriella spoke louder this time. "It's Angelina. She's collapsed."

Alejandro stopped in the middle of the hallway, "Where are you?"

"We're on the field trip. Angelina's been acting a little strange today. Anxious, clumsy... So she went to the ladies room and I followed her. As she went to leave, she grabbed her side and collapsed. I've called 911 and they're on their way. Alejandro, she's got a fever."

"Damn," is all, he said. Collecting his thoughts he continued, "Inform the paramedics about the transplant. Tell them to bring her directly to this hospital. I'll be waiting for you in the ER."

"Okay," she said. "Alejandro?"

"Sis, get her here as soon as you can. I'll contact her parents and let them know she's on her way."

"Alejandro, what could it be?"

"I don't know. We'll have to see when she gets here. Try not to worry. I'll take care of her."

"I know you will."

Alejandro took a deep breath when he hung up the phone. He moved his hand through his hair in disgust. He'd warned her about returning to work too soon and for her to call him in the event she felt like she was coming down with something. "Damn," he uttered as he flew down the stairs, running towards the ER. He was going to secure an examining room and then call her parents.

The paramedics arrived at the Exhibition Hall within four minutes of Gabriella's call. They tried to be discreet—Mary gathered the parent chaperones from Angelina's class and informed them what was happening. They were shocked, but knew to remain calm for the sake of the students. The paramedics had moved Angelina out of the doorway and into an adjoining conference room. They didn't want to frighten the children. While the paramedics were examining her, Gabriella gathered her chaperones and informed them of the situation. She'd be escorting Angelina to the hospital.

Gabriella told the paramedics exactly what Alejandro had instructed her. Her fever was 103.5. They further questioned Gabriella as they wheeled Angelina out of the building. "Her doctor will be waiting for her in the ER."

"How were you able to arrange that?" the driver asked.

"He's my brother. He performed the liver transplant."

The paramedics had heard of Alejandro through the grapevine. "Didn't he just move to St. Louis?"

"Yes, he did, and I'm so thankful for that."

Gabriella rode in the ambulance, holding Angelina's hand the entire way. She was worried about her friend. She was warm and so pale. Alejandro had been worried about her returning to school and he was right. Gabriella talked softly to Angelina as the ambulance sped down the highway to the hospital. She prayed that her brother would find the answers quickly to what was ailing her.

The ambulance pulled up at the ER. Before it came to a complete stop, Alejandro was prying open the doors. He helped Gabriella from the ambulance. "Alejandro, she's so warm and pale."

Nodding at her, acknowledging her concerns, he assisted the paramedics in removing the stretcher from the ambulance. He noted Angelina's paleness and asked about her vital signs. The paramedics filled him in as they wheeled her to the examining room that he'd set aside. Gabriella made her way to the waiting room and watched as Angelina's parents ran in from the parking lot. Gabriella threw herself into Angelina's mother's arms. "She collapsed on the field trip."

"I know that, Dear. Alejandro called us. What happened? She didn't quite seem herself this morning, but I thought she was just a little fatigued from returning to school. She jumped at me about something trivial. I ignored it, but now I guess I shouldn't have."

Gabriella recounted what had transpired throughout the day. "I should have said something to her sooner, but I decided to wait until we returned to school. I should have spoken up. It's my fault."

"It's no one's fault," said Alejandro. No one had noticed him enter the waiting room.

They looked to him for answers.

"I don't know anything yet. We're running tests. It's going to be awhile before I know anything. She just woke up and is a little out of it. She's aware that she's in the hospital."

"Can I see her?" her mother asked.

"Go on in. I'm making arrangements to transfer her directly to a room. She's going to be here until we diagnose her condition. And she knows that!"

Alejandro seemed a little upset. When Angelina had awakened in the ER, he'd asked her when she started feeling poorly. At first she didn't answer him. He pushed further, "Angelina, answer me. When did you start feeling bad?"

She couldn't look at him. She hadn't been feeling well for days. She attributed it to her return to work and the fatigue from getting back into her daily routine. Finally, she told him. "I haven't felt well for a few days now."

"Why didn't you call me?"

She couldn't answer him. She looked him in the eyes and shrugged her shoulders. A lone tear trailed down her cheek. Dejectedly she said, "I don't know." She turned her head from him and closed her eyes.

Alejandro stared at her for a few moments. Not wanting to comment further, he left the room.

After speaking with her parents, Alejandro returned to Angelina's room. She was facing the wall and he walked over to her and laid his hand on hers. He could tell she was fighting back tears. Slowly she turned her head towards him and whispered, "I'm sorry."

He didn't know what to say in return. Instead, he brushed her hair from her eyes, grasped her hand and said, "I'll take care of you. Don't worry. You're going to be fine. Just relax and let me do my job."

She nodded in reply and squeezed his hand. With that, two nurses entered the room notifying him that they were going to transfer her to a room. He squeezed her hand and walked from the room. He was livid with her but couldn't show it. She knew she'd been sick and didn't do a thing about it. He hoped that she hadn't waited too long to seek medical attention. He wanted to diagnose her condition as soon as possible. He didn't want to see her or her family suffer any more. They'd been through so much in the last two months.

Alejandro joined Angelina in her room after her parents left for the evening. She was sitting alone in the darkened room with only the bathroom light illuminating her features. He thought she was asleep until he saw her brush her hand across her face. He knew she'd been crying. He quietly entered her room and walked to her bedside. She'd felt his presence. She glanced up at him with tears in her eyes and began to cry.

Alejandro reached for her and drew her into his arms. He let her cry. "Just let it out." She didn't know why she was crying. Her emotions took over and the tears started falling out of nowhere and she couldn't control them.

She held onto him.

When she'd finally let out her final sob, he pulled her away from him and looked into her eyes.

"I messed up," she said. "I should have come to see you. I feel so stupid… I—"

"It's not your fault. I probably wouldn't have come to see me either. Stop feeling guilty, and let's figure out what's wrong. Your test results should be in shortly. Just lie back and try and get some sleep."

"Thanks." She laid back and closed her eyes, falling asleep almost instantly. Alejandro sat beside her for quite some time before he too decided he also needed some sleep. Tomorrow was only a few short hours away and he would see to it that they knew what was causing her fever. He had his guesses, but wanted to wait for the test results.

Alejandro spent the night on the couch in his office. He didn't want to leave the hospital. He'd instructed the staff to call him as soon as the lab results came in—he wanted to react as quickly as possible.

Early in the morning, his phone rang. The results were in. Alejandro ran to retrieve them. As he reviewed them, he decided to run a few more tests. He went to Angelina's room to see how she was doing. Upon entering, he saw that she was awake. She was staring straight ahead. "Angelina," he said.

Glancing in his direction, she blinked her eyes a few times before realizing who it was. "Alejandro?"

"Yes," he said as he walked towards her. "How are you feeling?"

"The same. I might not be as warm, but I still don't feel like myself."

"I got your results, but I want to run a few more tests before I'm sure what's wrong."

"You're the doctor. You know what's best."

He moved the chair from the corner of the room to her bedside. He sat there for a moment before he said,

"Why didn't you let Gabriella know you weren't feeling well today?"

"You mean yesterday?"

"Semantics… Why?" he demanded.

"I don't know. I guess I thought I was fine. But then…" She looked at him and then looked away, "I… I guess I was scared."

"Scared?"

"Yes. Colleen's been doing so well and… I guess I didn't want to jinx her with me getting sick. I know that's stupid reasoning but… I don't know. I'm sorry."

"Sorries don't count. You're only hurting yourself, not me. Angelina, you have to be honest with me, your parents, and especially yourself. I know you're independent, but it's okay to rely on others. It's okay to say you don't feel well. It's okay—"

"Enough" she barked. "I get the picture. You've done a great job of painting it." She turned her head away from him. She was embarrassed by her behavior. She was definitely stupid for not listening to her body and not informing him of her illness. Now, the only person that could help her was upset with her, but she really didn't care what he thought of her for not letting others know of her condition. She just wanted to feel better soon. She wanted to get on with her life and back to her students. They meant more to her than what Alejandro thought of her.

"Alejandro, please go. I'd like to try and get some rest." She rolled onto her side, away from him. That was his cue to leave. He knew she was mad at him. What else was he to do? In time, she'd realize how serious this was. She'd get over it.

# CHAPTER SIX

Alejandro diagnosed Angelina's illness: It was Peritonitis caused by the surgery. It wasn't uncommon—somehow bacteria had entered the body during surgery. He was bothered by the diagnosis but knew she'd recover.

He entered her room. She was still lying on her side. "You awake?"

Slowly rolling over, she looked at him with the same expression he'd seen on her face when Colleen had first been admitted to the hospital—downcast eyes, drawn face. He believed this expression helped her hold her emotions at bay. She blamed her illness on herself. This was not something she could have prevented on her own—its origins began during her surgery.

"It's Peritonitis, an inflammation of the lining of the abdominal cavity, the peritoneum. It's a thin membrane the covers the abdominal organs and the inside walls of the abdomen. I'm going to treat you with antibiotics. You'll have to stay in the hospital for a few days."

There was no reaction from Angelina. She just laid there. He approached her and she rolled back to her side.

"Do what you have to do."

"Angelina?"

"Please go. I just want to be alone."

Alejandro left her room and headed to the nurses station where he entered the necessary information into her chart for the course of antibiotics. He was worried about her. It was still early, so he called Gabriella before she left for school. "Are you coming by the hospital today?"

"Yes. We're getting out early, so I thought I'd come by after school. Why?'

"I don't know... Just talk to her. She seems withdrawn. Let me know what you think."

"I will. Alejandro, she's been through an awful lot these last few weeks. Give her some time. I know she's scared. I know she knows she made a mistake not contacting you. Just give her some time. This just happened yesterday."

"I'm just worried about her."

Gabriella visited Angelina that afternoon. She brought her a huge envelope filled with handmade cards from her students. Gabriella noticed that Angelina seemed quiet, but she didn't comment on it. She'd give her some time to see if she'd snap out of whatever was bothering her.

Gabriella sat with her for several hours. They discussed the field trip and decided they wanted to do it again the following year. "It was a great teaching experience. I think it was neat that we got to meet

Native Americans and see them perform their ceremonial dances."

"I enjoyed it too, Gabriella." Angelina was sitting up in bed. She still had a slight fever, but seemed to be feeling better. "What're your plans for Thanksgiving?"

"Going to my parents. And, of course, I plan on coming to see you."

"I sure messed up this holiday. Our family has so much to be thankful for. Colleen's well and..."

"Angelina, what's wrong?"

"I just messed up, plain and simple. I screwed up our family plans by being here in the hospital. I just—"

"Stop right there. Is that what's bothering you?"

Angelina nodded. "That and..."

"Angelina, you didn't know. I probably would've ignored the signs, too. I would have thought it was due to returning to school and dealing with that. Stop beating yourself up."

"But—"

"Not buts. Just stop it and move on. Your job is to get better. Do you hear me?"

"Yes."

Gabriella stayed until Angelina's parents arrived. Her parents were ecstatic that Alejandro had discovered what ailed her. Peritonitis was serious, but treatable. They visited for a while until Angelina showed signs of tiring. They told her they'd return the following day and have a quiet Thanksgiving celebration with her.

"Please don't plan on having dinner here. Eat at home. I'll be fine. Just come for a visit."

"Angelina," her father started, but a nurse walked in to take her vital signs.

"Go home, and I'll see you both tomorrow. I'll be fine. I'm in good hands."

"Are you sure?"

"Of course I am. Please enjoy the day. I'll be fine. Do I have to keep repeating myself?"

"No."

Her parents both kissed her and told her they'd be back early the following day. They could watch the Macy's parade together. She nodded in agreement as her parents walked from the room.

Angelina thought about all that she could have done, should have done, to prevent her illness. She was sitting alone, wondering what could have been, when she started to feel faint. She thought that her temperature was rising, but she was more than likely imagining it since she was upsetting herself by contemplating the what ifs.

It was nearing midnight when Alejandro visited Angelina for his final round of the day. He'd been called into an emergency surgery and was behind in his schedule. Upon entering her room, he noticed that she was asleep and thrashing about in bed. He reached her side and noticed that her face was flushed. He felt her forehead. She was burning up with fever. He hurried from the room looking for Angelina's nurse. "Monica," he called. "When was the last time that Angelina Samuels's temperature was taken?"

"About an hour ago. Why?"

"What was it?"

"I think it was ninety-nine degrees. Let me check." Monica checked Angelina's chart. She was right—her temperature had been ninety-nine degrees when she'd last taken her vital signs.

Alejandro knew her fever had risen. "Let's take it again. I think it's risen."

Sure enough, Alejandro was correct. Her temperature had spiked to almost 104. Alejandro checked her medications and ordered some more tests. Something just wasn't right.

Alejandro finished rounding with Angelina. He'd spent the previous night sleeping in his office and he imagined he'd do the same thing tonight. He needed to discover why her antibiotics weren't working.

For some reason, he was starting to feel close to her. He was feeling things he shouldn't be feeling as a doctor with his patient. He didn't know why she was constantly on his mind. He imagined it was because of her friendship with Gabriella. *That's what it is* he thought.

Instead of going back to his office, he pulled up a chair beside her bed. Stretching his long legs out in front of him, he watched her sleep. She had such sadness about her. She looked fragile. He sat there thinking about the changes that he'd gone through recently. Moving to St. Louis was the best decision that he'd made in a long time. He was with his family and that was the best thing for him. Hopefully, he'd be able to overcome what had happened two years ago. His family had come to Madison to help him deal with the events of the tragedy, had helped him try and get on with his life, but they had to return home to St. Louis. Once he was alone, he realized he couldn't face going home on a daily basis. He'd spent

most of his nights curled up on his office couch.
When he had gotten ill, he realized he needed more
rest. He couldn't go on sleeping in his office. He had
no life other than work. He needed his family. And
that's when he decided to look for a new job, if not in
St. Louis, at least maybe a little closer. Once he'd
made up his mind, there was no looking back. Before
he could even contact someone about his decision to
relocate, he was being contacted to head up the
Transplant Unit of the hospital in St. Louis. He'd
thought then that things were going to work out for
him...

Now, he was in St. Louis where he wanted to be.
He was forging new bonds with his family. He'd
finally gotten to meet Angelina. Although he wished
they'd gotten to know one another under better
circumstances, he was still happy they were able to
become friends.

While he sat with Angelina, he received the results
from the rushed lab work, but he still needed to run
more tests. Morning light was fast approaching. Then,
he'd run a few more extensive tests hoping to find
answers.

The nurse returned to Angelina's room at around
three in the morning. He'd drifted off to sleep
somewhere between two and three. The nurse tapped
him on the shoulder with the latest temperature
reading.  Her temperature had gone down, but it
wasn't where Alejandro wanted it to be. He scowled.

Angelina was still sleeping fitfully. He thought of
waking her, but decided not to. At least she was
getting some sleep—more than him, anyway.

Alejandro headed off to the doctor's lounge for a
quick shower and then to his office. It was

Thanksgiving. He should have something to be thankful for today, but he knew that today would end up being a day full of sadness—he was pretty sure what Angelina's test results would reveal. He called his parents. He knew his mother would be up at the crack of dawn preparing for the holiday. "Mom, is Dad up yet?"

"He certainly is. Would you like to speak with him?"

"Why else do you think I'm calling?"

"Alejandro, don't get testy with me."

"Sorry, Mom. I just need to speak with him, okay?"

"Sure, son. I won't take your tone of voice too seriously. Just remember that this time."

"Sorry, Mom." He heard the phone being passed, "Dad?"

"Alejandro?" his father said into the phone. "What is it? Why are you calling so early? It's Thanksgiving."

"It's Angelina."

"What's wrong? Is she no better?"

"No, she's not. Actually, her temperature's gone back up."

"What do you think is causing it?"

"Peritonitis. But there's something else going on, too. I'm going to run a few more tests today. I'm not sure I'll be there for dinner."

"Do what you have to, but I know your mother will be disappointed."

"I know. I'll do my best."

"I know, son. Do you want me to come by and see her, too?"

"Not necessary. You're not her physician any longer."

"I realize that."

"It's up to you, but it's not necessary."

"Let me talk it over with your mom, and I'll try and stop by early this morning before your mother starts going crazy with her preparations."

"Thanks, Dad."

John hung up the phone and filled Maria in on Alejandro's conversation concerning Angelina. "You're going to the hospital, aren't you?"

"I was hoping you'd say that."

"Well, of course. Angelina is like family."


John appeared at the hospital mid-morning. "How's she doing?"

"I sent her down for some more tests and am waiting for the results to come back."

"What are you thinking?"

"I think she just needs to be on a stronger antibiotic, but we'll see. This infection is a lot worse than I first thought. I just wish she'd come in sooner instead of waiting until she'd collapsed."

"I understand your concern, but there's nothing you can do about that now. She's here and that's what matters."

"It's just…"

"There's more isn't there? What aren't you saying?"

"Dad, I can't be sure. I want to see what this latest round of test results show. Then, I'll know for sure."

Alejandro waited for what seemed like an eternity for the test results, but in all actuality it was only three hours. Angelina's parents came by with Colleen and they watched the parade with their daughter. James, Wyatt and Kelly would check in on Angelina after dinner so her visitors would be spread out, allowing Angelina to nap when needed.

Angelina's spirits seemed better when her family was around. Colleen started to tire, so they decided to depart.

"Are you sure you're okay with us leaving?"

"Absolutely. You take Colleen home so she can rest. I'll have my own Thanksgiving here. Don't worry. I'll call if I need anything."

"Darling..."

"Mom, just go. I'm fine. Please."

Her family left mid-afternoon. Alejandro had sequestered himself to his office. He went through all of Angelina's test results. Rubbing his hand across his forehead, he reread the test results. *How can this be* he asked himself. "This can't be happening to her," he muttered. How would he tell her? How? When should he do it? Today being Thanksgiving, he didn't want her to start associating this news with this festive day. But he couldn't keep the news from her any longer—he needed to tell her.

Alejandro grabbed her file and walked to her room. "What should I say? How should I tell her?" He spoke aloud to himself, hoping that someone would answer him. But of course, the voice he was looking for was silent. No one answered his plea. He took a detour to the hospital chapel and said a brief prayer. He asked the powers that be to give him the strength he needed to share this news with her. He needed guidance to help him tell her the news that would devastate her and shatter her dreams... Dreams that would never come true.

# CHAPTER SEVEN

Angelina was sitting alone in her room when she'd felt a sudden sadness overcome her. It occurred shortly after her family left, but she didn't think it stemmed from their departure. It was something else. She sat in bed studying the cards she'd received from her students. *Her children*, she thought. She loved to experience their firsts. First time being able to read, first time learning a math fact… So many firsts occur in school. She just loved it. She couldn't wait to experience that with her own children. Someday that would happen.

Angelina hadn't dated much while she was in school. She studied hard, making excellent grades. After graduation, she'd focused her efforts on being the best teacher possible. She wanted each child's experience to be unforgettable so they'd remember her as the teacher that taught them something special. She wanted to be that influence with her own children and wanted to be that mom that everyone looked up to.

Angelina was fingering one of the cards when Alejandro entered her room. She thought that by reading them, she'd lose that overwhelming feeling of sadness. She was thinking about Lauren, whom she tutored after school. She'd gladly do anything to see her succeed.

"Angelina," Alejandro spoke "What are you doing?"

"Looking at some of the cards Gabriella brought by. You should see how creative some of these kids are." She looked up at him and he seemed troubled. "What's up?"

"We need to talk."

She began to get worried.

Alejandro sat down in the chair beside her bed. He clasped his hands together and hung them between his legs. He stared at his hands. He didn't know what to say or how to begin. He knew this conversation would change her life forever. He didn't want to be the bearer of bad news. It would crush her, and he knew she would never forgive him. This was Thanksgiving, but today she would have absolutely nothing to be thankful for.

He looked into her eyes and said, "Angelina, I got the rest of your test results back." Clearing his throat, he looked away from her, then back again. Taking a deep breath, he looked away from her a second time.

By the way Alejandro was behaving, she knew something was terribly wrong. "Alejandro, just spit it out. Tell me what's wrong."

He looked at her with a pained expression and she watched the color drain from his face. "I don't know how to tell you this." Pausing, he continued, "Angelina, the infection is a lot worse than I thought."

"And?"

"Well, it's settled in your pelvic area."

"What does that mean?"

"You have severe scarring that's affected your fallopian tubes." Alejandro let out the breath that he'd been holding. He looked down and then back up into her eyes.

A myriad of expressions ranging from surprise to dread crossed her face. Angelina gasped in understanding, her hand immediately dropping to her stomach.

Alejandro saw the gesture as she tightly closed her eyes to keep the tears at bay. He confirmed her worst nightmare. "I'm afraid you won't be able to have children," he said as she stared at him in horror.

Angelina was in shock. She didn't know what to say or how to react. Gasping, she turned away from him. He reached for her hand, but she pulled back, clutching the sheet against her. When she looked back towards him, her eyes were welling with tears. Slowly, a tear escaped her eyes and trickled down her cheek.

"Angelina, I'm sorry." Alejandro could feel her pain emanating from her stiffened body.

She brushed the tear away. "How? Why? It's my fault. I should have gotten here sooner."

"That may not have prevented this. I can't say for sure. I just know the Peritonitis is the leading cause. The infection travelled to your pelvis and caused severe scarring of your fallopian tubes."

"You know today is Thanksgiving. There are so many things that we should be thankful for. I am thankful for Colleen's health... I am thankful for my job and reconnecting with Gabriella and your family, but today will always live in my heart and be on my mind. I will always connect this moment to what should have been a day of thanks, but instead it turned into my worst nightmare. I will never be able to say I am thankful for my own family because it will never happen. Right now, I don't know that there's anything left to say. Just please leave me alone. And please, don't tell anyone else about this— this is between me and my doctor."

Alejandro wasn't surprised by her reaction, so he did as she wished. Slowly, he stood and left her room. This diagnosis had also brought a reality to him. As a doctor, he'd become immune to so many things. He placed all emotions aside when dealing with a diagnosis such as this. But for some reason, this situation had removed that barrier. He was feeling her sadness, too.

He called Gabriella and told her not to visit Angelina. "Why?" she asked.

"Just because I think she needs some time to herself. Her parents visited earlier and she just wants to be alone. She's suffering the after-effects from her fever and infection. She needs time to rest and recuperate."

Gabriella started to question him, but he told her to leave it alone and do as he asked.

Gabriella did the direct opposite of what her brother requested and decided to phone Angelina herself. She wasn't going to listen to her brother— she'd determine if what he said was true. "Hey, Angelina, how are you? I thought—"

Angelina cut her off and told her she just wanted to be left alone. "No, I'm fine. You enjoy the day. My family has already been by, and I'm fine. Really, have a happy Thanksgiving."

"Angelina?"

"Really, Gabriella. I'm fine. I'm just a little tired and would like to take a nap. I'll see you maybe tomorrow." With that, Angelina hung up the phone.

Gabriella had heard the sadness and even tears in her voice, but didn't want to press her. She knew she wasn't feeling well and guessed that was why she seemed so emotional.

Alejandro joined his family for Thanksgiving dinner. Everyone was in attendance. Gabriella had arrived late morning to help her mother with the preparations while Joe and Alec didn't show up until dinner was ready to be served. Both of them had rotated in and out at the hospital, checking in on their pediatric patients that were hospitalized. It wasn't unusual for them to have several children in the hospital during the holidays.

His father questioned Alejandro about Angelina's test results, but Alejandro didn't disclose them. His father knew that he'd diagnosed something in addition to the Peritonitis, but didn't want to press him.

Alejandro's mother outdid herself with the sumptuous feast. He realized as he sat at the table how much he was thankful for. He'd missed too many of these meals and he was just happy to be home with his family. Family was important to him and he knew they'd help him from slipping back into the memories that had almost consumed him.

Alejandro somehow got through the meal with his family, his thoughts never leaving Angelina. His mother knew something was amiss, but didn't press him. She'd learned through his tragedy not to bother him about certain things. When he wanted to share his thoughts and feelings with her, he would. Apparently now was not the time.

Alejandro soon decided he'd had enough of his family and needed to leave. He approached his mother and thanked her for a fabulous meal.

"Alejandro, please stay."

"I've gotta go," he said. Kissing her goodbye, he shook hands with his father and brothers, then hugged Gabriella goodbye. She knew something was wrong with him when he hugged her, so she decided to follow him from the house.

"What's up?" she asked.

"Nothing. Why?"

"You've been kind of withdrawn all evening. I'd like to help."

"There's nothing you can do, Gabby. Just leave me alone and I'll handle it myself." Alejandro had been awfully quiet during the meal. They'd all expressed what they'd been thankful for, but Alejandro just sat there staring at his plate. All he could think about was Angelina and her earlier comments. He, in some regard, felt the same way. That was one of the reasons why he'd left Wisconsin. He'd never have his family either. When it was his turn to express what he was thankful for, he spoke of his decision to return to St. Louis.

Gabriella didn't want him to leave under these circumstances. "Alejandro, please?"

"Gabby, stop! I'll be alright. I just want to go home."

She nodded. She knew he was beyond listening to her. Giving him one last hug, she watched him get into his car and drive away. He drove in the opposite direction of his home, though. She wondered where he was going, but decided not to worry. He was a grown man with issues that only he could resolve. She'd be there for him when he was ready to talk. They'd all be there for him.

Alejandro left his parents' not knowing exactly where he was going. He drove around until he found himself pulling into his parking place at the hospital. *Why am I here,* he wondered. Deep down, he knew why he was there. Slowly, he emerged from his car. He didn't bother with his lab coat—he was there as a visitor, not a physician. As he entered the hospital, he nodded to several nurses who greeted him with a "Happy Thanksgiving, Doctor." As he saw it, today was not a happy day. It was not a day of thanksgiving. It was a day filled with sadness and broken dreams. A young woman's fantasies had been shattered in one brief conversation. He wanted to make things right. But how could he?

He sought the chapel again for some insight. He always believed that prayers helped—that's how he had gotten through his tragedy. He prayed often. At times, he found solace; other times, he succumbed to his grief. He had a difficult time dealing with his past. He carried it with him every day. He only hoped that he could give comfort to Angelina during the trying days ahead.

He glanced at his watch and realized he'd been sitting in the chapel for close to an hour. It was nearing nine o'clock and he didn't know what to do. Should he check on her, or just leave the hospital? After all, he'd driven all this way in a complete fog of memories. He needed to try and deal with his feelings and also help her get through this. He'd be there for her. He wanted to be the shoulder that she could cry on. He needed to do this because he'd had no one there for him when he was going through his own personal crisis.

Alejandro exited the elevator and headed for her room. Just as he prepared to enter, Monica, Angelina's nurse, motioned for him to join her at the nurses' station.

"Doctor, I just wanted you to know that she hasn't eaten all day. Her temperature is normal, but I'm worried about her. She seems to have withdrawn even more since this morning. I was going to put a call through to you, but thought it could wait until tomorrow."

"I'll check on her." He knew what was bothering her. How was he going to deal with this? His thoughts and feelings kept rushing through his head, one disappearing just as quickly as the next one surfaced. He couldn't begin to put a sentence together. He knew he needed to do something to help her, but what?

Taking a deep breath, and asking for assistance from above, he entered her room. She sat in bed with her hands folded loosely around her as if she were protecting her unborn child. But he knew differently. She wasn't protecting anything except her feelings. She didn't hear or notice him enter—she was in a totally different world. Quietly, he walked to her bedside. He whispered her name, but she didn't respond. Speaking a little louder, she finally heard his voice.

"Go. Please go," she whispered.

"No. I want to stay. I want to help you. I need to help you…"

"Please, Alejandro. I just want to be alone."

"I know you do, but I think you need someone right now… Someone to help you deal with this. You're grieving, and I want to be here for you. Please. I need to do this."

"Why?"

"Because I do. I can't explain it to you right now, but someday I will." Alejandro sat down on the bed and reached for her hands. Holding them loosely, he looked into her eyes. "Let me be here for you…"

Looking into his eyes, she nodded and closed hers eyes to prevent the tears from falling. They sat alone in silence. When she finally drifted off to sleep, he exchanged the bedside for a chair and held her hand into the early hours of the morning. He'd see her through this. For some unexplained reason, he couldn't remove himself from this situation. He'd gotten too close to this patient. He now understood why doctors never treated family members, and Angelina was no ifs, ands, or buts. He couldn't put aside the fear that he caused her illness due to his own lack of follow-up. He knew she'd returned to the classroom and he should have insisted on watching her more closely.

Peritonitis was always a possibility with surgery. Never in a million years would he have thought that she'd contract an infection. Never. And, then, that infection becoming the cause of the scarring to her fallopian tubes and her infertility. Maybe if he'd seen her more often he'd have picked up on something. But "maybe" was also a big word and more than likely he wouldn't have seen the signs until they'd manifested themselves as they did. He was going to remedy that now. He'd follow her as closely as she allowed.

Shortly after three in the morning, he awoke. Angelina was squeezing his hand. "Alejandro, please go home. I'll be fine. You've spent the last two nights away from your bed. Please go home."

Alejandro nodded. Rising from the chair, he gave her a kiss on the cheek and told her to get some sleep. He'd return early to check on her.

She knew he wasn't going home. He would just exchange the chair for the couch in his office.

Rolling onto her side, she tried to sleep. All she could think about was the family she always wanted. She was going to have to get past those dreams. Her students would have to be her family. She'd nurture them and see them grow, hopefully influencing some as they traveled down the path of life.

Angelina fell asleep at dawn. She knew she'd somehow find the strength to persevere. It may take her time, but she'd overcome this. At least she and Alejandro were the only ones that knew about her condition. That would make things easier—she never wanted to tell her parents about this latest health development. If her mother knew, she'd make her see an endless stream of doctors to arrive at the same conclusion. All she wanted was to heal and move on with her life. To alleviate any questions, she made a commitment to herself: she'd never fall in love and marry. She just wouldn't. That way, she wouldn't have to deal with the issue of grandchildren. Her mother dreamed of Angelina providing her with the first grandchild. Often times, she referred to

Angelina's "ticking clock." Angelina had enough of her mother's desires. From the time she'd been a little girl, Angelina dreamed of marrying and having children. The infection was causing her to reevaluate her life. And now, she believed having kids and being married was not part of her calling. Everyone else in her family could marry and provide them. She just wouldn't be one of them.

She decided that when she got up, she'd pretend there was nothing wrong, that the news of yesterday was long forgotten, never to raise its ugly head again. She didn't want her parents to worry any more than they currently were. Today was another day and the beginning of a new time in her life. She could act when she wanted, and now she was going to be that actress. Her role would evolve over time, but she knew she could do it. She'd just have to fool Alejandro, that's all. Only time would tell if she succeeded. Soon, she wouldn't have to deal with him at all. Once she was released from the hospital, their dealings would be over. She would only have to hear of him through Gabriella. She could deal with that. She knew she could.

Angelina was released from the hospital the following week. She was told to take it easy for an additional week. She wanted to return to school before the winter break began—she needed to do it. Not only for herself, but for her students as well.

Angelina returned to school feeling much better. Her students were surprised to see her and couldn't believe their eyes when they entered the classroom. Angelina was sitting at her desk when the school bell rang for the morning. She'd only decided to return to school late in the evening the prior Friday, so no one, including the teachers, knew of her return except Mary and Gabriella.

Angelina snuck into her classroom under the radar, so when her students discovered her, cheers rang out. The other teachers whose classrooms were nearby ran from their rooms to see what the commotion was all about. Everyone was thrilled with her return, including herself. It was time to move on and start the next phase of her life.

Angelina believed in her students writing a daily journal. She hadn't read them for some time and decided she needed to review them prior to the break. Angelina stayed late every evening since her return. She knew if Alejandro was aware of this, he'd have a coronary, but technically she wasn't his patient any longer and was no longer his concern. She needed to catch up and determine what her substitutes had done with each of her pre-planned lessons. Angelina had her lesson plans sketched out for the entire year. She'd worked hard at completing this after Mary hired her. Since she was now teaching fifth grade instead of second grade, it took her weeks to feel like she was where she needed to be organizationally in school.

She remembered the night she ran into Alejandro at the bookstore and the ensuing events that led to where she was today. Mary had visited Angelina while she was recovering and told her how lucky both she and St. Margaret's were when she discovered her résumé at the school office. Never in all the years that she'd been a principal had she seen a teacher so prepared when she'd needed to find a substitute on a moment's notice, not only once, but twice. She said

Angelina was a wonderful teacher and a role model for all.

The evening before classes were ready to dismiss for winter break, Angelina was sitting in her classroom. She'd completed all of her holiday shopping and wanted to finish reading the last of the journals. If she completed this task, then she'd have the entire break to herself. She could rest and just hang out at home with her family and not feel guilty for not working.

It was almost six o'clock. She'd gone out and gotten herself a bite to eat and was just starting on the last journal, Lauren's. Once she finished, she could go home and finish getting her presents together for her students. She always purchased a book and a new set of pencils for each student, as many of her students had either lost their pencils or sharpened them to bits by winter break. She always had their name inscribed on the pencils, too. That way, everyone knew who they belonged to.

The last assignment she'd given them for their journal was to write about someone that played an important role in their life. She assigned this specifically since, after the first of the year, the school was sponsoring their first Career Day and she wanted her students to be prepared and start thinking about it in advance. It would be a fun learning experience for all. Angelina was impressed with the journals that she'd read so far, as many of her students were influenced by their parents or grandparents.

She took a sip of water and began reading Lauren's journal. Her writing had greatly improved since the beginning of the school year. Often times,

Lauren stayed in at recess because she wanted to complete a thought. Angelina couldn't believe the depth that went into each entry.

Lauren titled her journal entry, *"The Most Important Person in My Life."* As Angelina read Lauren's journal, she was amazed with what she was reading:

*The most important person in my life is Ms. Samuels. I'm sure you may ask why? But why not? She treats us like her own children. Nothing is too important for her. She stays late on a whim to help anyone who needs the extra help. I don't want you to think that my parents aren't important to me. They are. They love and support me. They give me anything that I need. They feed and clothe our family and provide us with all the love in the world.*

*Ms. Samuels has taught me that nothing is too small to care for. I know that I have issues in school and I am working really hard to get good grades. Last year, I could've cared less about school. But this year is a different story and Ms. Samuels is the difference in my life. I know now that I am not stupid. I just have to work a little harder than everyone else. She has taught me that I can do anything I want. I just have to set a goal and I can achieve it. She has an "I can do" attitude, and that's what's made the difference for me.*

*Ms. Samuels will someday make the perfect mother. She'll be a role model for her own children. Someone they can look-up to. I know I look up to her.*

*She has changed my life, and I hope that I can continue to make her proud of me.*

*Thank you, Ms. Samuels. You've changed my life. I hope someday to be a teacher just like you. Loving and caring and always willing to help the underdog like myself. You're the best teacher in the whole wide world. I am so lucky to have had you in my life.*

When Angelina had finished Lauren's journal, she was a wreck. Tears cascaded down her face. She didn't realize what an influence she truly was in her students' lives. She knew she helped some become the achievers they were always meant to be by giving them that little extra push to reach their potential, but Lauren was special, and she was lucky to have her as a student at this time in her life. Angelina reread the entry and cried even harder. She wanted to be the perfect mother, but knew that dream would never come to fruition. Yes, her students were her children and they'd be that way the rest of her life.

Alejandro was running late for his meeting with Mary. She wanted to see if he would be a speaker at Career Day. Unfortunately, he'd been tied up in surgery and was late for their scheduled appointment. He'd relayed a message to her about his delay and she informed him that she'd wait for him. It was late when their meeting concluded. When he started to leave St. Margaret's, he noticed Angelina's car in the parking lot. He asked Mary for directions to her classroom and, as he strolled down the long corridor, he thought he heard someone crying. He dismissed that thought from his mind. Why would someone be crying? Everyone should be gone except for Angelina. Her car was the only car in the parking lot, as Mary was expecting a ride from her husband.

He stopped in the hallway. Again, he heard the sobbing. Angelina's classroom was at the end of the hall. Her door was partially open. Was she the one that was crying, or was he just imagining it? He picked up his stride and found himself outside her classroom. Glancing in the room, he saw her seated at her desk. Indeed she was crying. Her back was to the doorway, but he saw her wiping tears from her eyes.

Opening the door, he walked into her room. She didn't hear him. Soft music was playing in the background. "Have Yourself a Merry Little Christmas," was the current song of choice. He stood there watching her. She was totally oblivious to his presence. As he reached to place a hand on her shoulder, he said, "Angelina?"

She didn't seem surprised at his presence. She didn't respond to his touch or voice.

"Are you alright?"

She turned and began to cry even harder. She threw herself into his arms.

"It's okay, sweetheart. Just let it out."

She held onto him like there was no tomorrow. She cried and cried, and as her sobs grew louder, he stroked her back and her hair. "It's going to be alright.    Whatever's troubling you, we can get through it together."

"No we can't," she said through her tears. "Nothing can fix this. Nothing."

Alejandro wasn't sure what she was talking about. She was sitting in her classroom crying. Why? He had to know what had upset her so. "Did something happen to you? Are you in pain?"

"No," she cried.

"Then, what is it?"

She pointed to Lauren's journal and continued sobbing. *What's that,* he thought. It's just a notebook. Why would that cause her the tears? She placed her head on his shoulder and continued holding onto him.

Alejandro held her for a time before she was able to speak. Wiping her face and pulling herself from his embrace, she handed him the journal. He read Lauren's entry and understood. Reaching for her, he grabbed her into another tight embrace. He brushed a kiss across her forehead. "We will get through this. Together," he stressed. "I am going to see to it that you get the help you need."

"I'm fine," she said. "I just had this moment where—"

"Enough, Angelina. You're not okay. You need to talk this through. Share your feelings with someone."

"I don't want to see a counselor. I can get through this on my own."

"No, you can't. You need to talk to someone. Please, let me help you."

"I don't want anyone to know about this. You're the only person that knows."

"Well, I'm no counselor, but let me be the one you talk to. I want to do this for you."

She nodded and was drawn again into his arms. "I trust you, Alejandro. Please help me."

"I will. I'll help you through this," he said.

"Please help me get over this sadness. It's just consuming me. I feel like I'm grieving for a lost child, but we both know that isn't the case."

He tightened his hold on her. He knew, in his own way, what she was experiencing. He hoped that time would heal her wounds.

They sat in her classroom for a few minutes longer when she said, "By the way, what are you doing here?"

He explained to Angelina that Mary had contacted him about appearing at Career Day. She wanted him to partake in the presentations. Neither Gabriella nor Angelina knew that Mary had asked him to participate. She was saddened by the fact that he was going to speak.

"Why the sad face?" he asked.

"Well, she wouldn't be asking you to speak if Colleen hadn't needed the transplant, or I wouldn't have gotten sick."

"Why do you say that?"

"How else did she learn about you being a miracle worker?"

"Well, I don't consider myself a miracle worker. I just do my job."

Angelina was done for the night. She gathered her things while Alejandro watched her.

He walked her from the building and asked if she'd like to go get a drink.

"I have so much to do."

"Like what? Tomorrow's the last day for a few weeks. Whatever could you have to do?"

"I guess nothing really. I was just going to pack up my stuff for tomorrow. Wyatt can probably help me tomorrow morning, though. He's already out of school for winter break."

"Sounds like a plan to me. Why don't I follow you home? You can drop off your car and I'll drive."

"Okay."

Alejandro followed Angelina home. He met her at her car where she was struggling with her backpack. "Here, let me help you."

She handed over her backpack and he grabbed the remainder of her things. Her parents were surprised to see him when they walked through the door.

"Alejandro, what a surprise. What are you doing here?"

"It's good to see you both. Happy Holidays," he said as he turned towards her father and shook his hand. Angelina's mother wondered why the two of them were together. Alejandro explained, "I was meeting with Mary regarding St. Margaret's upcoming Career Day and saw Angelina's car. We decided to celebrate the holidays with a quick drink. So, since I was following her home, I thought I'd check on Colleen, too. Is she here?'

"I'm sorry, she isn't. She's out with some friends finishing some last minute shopping."

"Well, let her know that I stopped by."

"It's great seeing you. Angelina, do you need help with anything?" asked her mother.

"I'm glad you asked. Since I'm going out with Alejandro, I was hoping Wyatt could help me pack my car for tomorrow."

"No problem, Angelina," Wyatt called from the other room. "Show me what you want done and I'll do it while you're out."

"Thanks, Wyatt. You're a sweetheart."

Angelina showed Wyatt the packages that needed to be loaded into her car. She kissed her mother goodbye, and Alejandro placed his hand on her back as he escorted her out the door. Her mother had a smile on her face. *Maybe, just maybe*, she thought to herself. "I hope she can find happiness," she accidentally said aloud.

"What did you say?" asked Wyatt.

"Nothing, son. Nothing at all."

# CHAPTER EIGHT

Alejandro opened the car door for her. She was starting to have second thoughts on going out with him. *What am I doing,* she asked herself. *Why am I going out with him?* She'd been at an all-time low when he found her crying in her classroom. She guessed that she'd just given in to his kindness. He knew her secret, and he also knew that she needed to talk with someone. That someone was him.

"Thank you," she said.

"For what?" he asked.

"For being my friend."

"Think nothing of it. I consider you a friend as well. Now, let's have that drink, relax, and enjoy ourselves. Heaven knows we both need to do it more often."

She nodded.

Alejandro stopped at a local bar/restaurant. He was hungry, and they headed for the restaurant side of the building. The waitress took their drink order. They both ordered a glass of white wine. They looked over the menu while they awaited their drinks. "What looks good to you?" he asked.

In all actuality, she wasn't hungry. She'd indicated her hunger to appease him, for if she declined his offer, he would worry about her not taking care of herself. What he didn't know was that she'd grabbed a bite to eat before he'd found her crying hysterically in her classroom. She'd get something light to eat and blame it on the fact that she normally didn't eat this late. She knew that with his schedule, he ate at all hours of the day. Eating after nine o'clock wouldn't bother him in the least.

Angelina ordered a salad while Alejandro ordered a dish of pasta. "Is that enough for you?"

"I'm not used to eating this late. This will tide me over. I'm fine."

"I just want to make sure that you're taking care of yourself. Any problems of late?"

"No. I feel great," she quickly responded.

"Good," he said. Their meal arrived in record time since the kitchen was about to close—they were practically alone in the restaurant. He felt as though they could talk under these circumstances as no one should interrupt them. They finished their meal and he asked Angelina if she was in the mood for coffee, which she gladly agreed to. The waitress brought their coffee and indicated that they could stay as long as needed. She was going to clean up around them, but if they needed additional coffee, they just needed to ask. Alejandro paid the bill and then turned back to Angelina. Her hand was positioned next to her coffee cup. He didn't know what came over him but he reached for her hand. She was reluctant at first, but allowed him to hold it.

"Let's talk."

"About what?" she asked. She knew where the conversation was headed, but she would try and take it in another direction.

"As if you didn't already know," he stated.

Looking away from him, she took a deep breath and swallowed, "Do we have to do this now?"

"Why not? Is there ever going to be a better time?"

Looking him straight in the eyes, she said, "I guess not."

"Angelina, you need to talk to someone. You don't want to see a counselor. You don't want anyone else to know what's going on. I think I'm it. I am the only person you can share this with. I promise our conversations will go no further than us. Angelina, you're too important to me. I don't want to see you suffer. Even though I contributed to your suffering, I want to see you happy."

"Contributed? What do you mean by that?"

"Well, the surgery caused this problem, and then I didn't follow up with you as closely as I should have when you returned to school."

"Let's not go there. I don't want you to have any guilt. If anyone should be blamed, it's me. I should have sought your help sooner, but I didn't. I can't change that. I can only try and move forward with my life. It won't be as I imagined. My parents won't understand my decisions or reasoning, but it's up to me to explain it to them."

"What're you talking about?"

"That I will never marry or provide them with grandchildren. That's my decision."

"Angelina, you shouldn't think along those lines. You can still marry and have a family, it just may not be your own biological children."

"Alejandro, I don't want to go there now. It's been a long day and I just want to forget about it. Please, do that for me."

He looked away from her and dropped her hand to the table. "It's getting late. How about I take you home?"

"Okay." She got up from the table and he escorted her to the car. Prior to closing the door, he got down on one knee, looked her in the eyes, and said, "We will have this conversation, Angelina. And it will be soon."

She didn't have a chance to reply. He stood and slammed the car shut with a loud thud.

Neither spoke on their drive home. He pulled into her parents' driveway and turned off the motor. "Angelina, I'd like you to go out with me tomorrow. The hospital is having a dinner in honor of the holidays. I don't want to go by myself. Will you be my date?"

She didn't know what to do. He'd been so good to her that she felt she owed it to him to attend. She thought for a moment. She liked Alejandro and decided she wanted to spend the evening with him. She turned towards him and said, "Yes, I'll go with you."

"Great. Be ready by six. Cocktails start at six thirty."

"That's fine. I'll be ready." Thanking him for the evening, she got out of the car and headed to the door. Waving goodbye, she entered the house. "What have I just done?" she asked herself out loud.

"Angelina, is that you?" her mother called.

"Yes, it's me."

"Who are you talking to?"

"No one."

"But I heard you talking."

"Mom, Alejandro asked me to join him for a holiday dinner tomorrow night. I accepted."

"Darling, that's fabulous. He's such a kind and caring man… A brilliant surgeon."

"Mom, stop. I just accepted because he helped me out tonight. That's all. Don't get your hopes up because nothing is going to happen between us. Please just leave it alone."

Angelina's mother wanted to believe otherwise. She agreed to leave Angelina alone about this, but a mother could hope and even dream, couldn't she?

Angelina's last day of school flew by. Before she knew it, she was wishing everyone a Merry Christmas and Happy New Year. She requested that they all have a wonderful holiday and joked that they shouldn't ask for too much from Santa. Each of her students thanked her for their gifts as they left the classroom.

Angelina hadn't had a chance to talk to Gabriella. All day long she wanted to be honest and up front with her friend about attending the hospital's holiday dinner with her brother. Angelina walked across the hallway after her last student left. Gabriella was packing up her things and tidying up her classroom for the extended break.

"Hey there. What's new?" Angelina called out to Gabriella.

Gabriella turned around and said, "Not much. What about you?"

This was the perfect opportunity to tell Gabriella about her planned evening with Alejandro. "Well, I've got something to tell you."

"And it's…?"

"I kind of have a date with your brother this evening, if that's what you want to call it."

"You what?" Gabriella was too excited for words. She couldn't contain herself. Smiling broadly, she started jumping up and down. Turning around in circles with a look of glee on her face, she stopped abruptly. She grabbed ahold of Angelina, pulling her in close; she started throwing rapid fire questions at her.

"He asked you out on a date? When? Where? Oh my gosh!" Gabriella said as she spun around in delight.

"Well, it's not really a date. He just asked me to attend a holiday dinner that the hospital is hosting."

"Well, to me that's a date."

"In my eyes, it isn't. It's just easier to use the word date instead of—" *In fact, what would you call these "so-called dates"* she wondered.

Angelina felt like she was on some type of game show and Gabriella was looking for just the right answer. Little did Gabriella know, they'd sort of been having these so-called dates off and on for the past few months.

Angelina proceeded to tell Gabriella about the previous night. "He caught me at a low point when he surprised me in my classroom. I'd read Lauren's journal and I got a little upset about what she wrote. Anyway, he was here talking to Mary about Career Day."

"I didn't know about that."

"Well, don't let him know I told you. I think he wants to surprise you. Anyway, we went out for a drink and something to eat. When we were leaving, he asked me to be his date tonight for the hospital holiday party. He didn't want to go by himself."

"That's wonderful," Gabriella responded. "It's about time he started dating again."

"Gabriella, we aren't 'dating.' This is a one-time thing."

"I don't care what you call it. He's going out with someone. He doesn't want to be alone. That's just…"

"I'm not following you."

"Don't mind me. I'm just happy for my brother."

"Whatever you say, but I don't get what you mean by your comment about him dating again."

"Forget it. Just be sure and have a good time. You owe it to yourself and to him as well. You've both been through a lot lately."

She hadn't finished dressing when the doorbell rang. Colleen answered the door. She had no idea about their date.

"Dr. A.? What are you doing here?"

"I've come for your sister. I'm taking her to dinner."

"Oh. I didn't know that."

Alejandro seemed surprised that Colleen wasn't aware of their date, but then again, she hadn't been home when they'd left the prior evening. He'd also dropped Angelina off rather late for a school night, and he was sure that Angelina had left before Colleen got up.

"How are you feeling, Colleen?"

"Great thanks to you." She let Alejandro in and led him to the living room where her mother was reading. "Mom, Dr. A is here for Angelina. Did you know they were going out?"

Her mother popped up off the sofa and said. "Indeed, I did. I'm so pleased with this development."

"Mrs. Samuels. Don't get me wrong, but Angelina's just doing me a favor."

"I know. But can't a mother dream?"

"Well, yes she can, but…"

Colleen called for Angelina. "Your date's here," she yelled.

Angelina appeared at the top of the stairs. As she descended the stairs, she absolutely took his breath away. She was dressed in a gorgeous red sequined dress that fitted her slender body like a glove. It had a scooped neckline with capped sleeves that fell just above her knees. Her hair was pulled up into what Alejandro would call a messy bun with tendrils of her light brown hair hanging loosely around her face. This truly wasn't a date he thought, but it sure felt like one. She looked absolutely stunning, more beautiful than he ever could have imagined. He couldn't take his eyes off of her.

Angelina had no intentions for this to go any further than dinner. And in all actuality, he didn't either. He just needed her assistance for this one function, and that would be the end of it. He'd made a pact with himself. He was never going to give his heart to someone again because, when it ended, it would be like he was living his nightmare all over again. He never wanted to experience those feelings again.

Alejandro greeted her at the bottom of the stairs. He couldn't believe his eyes. She was… He checked himself. *I can't go there.*

"Angelina, you look beautiful," her mother chimed in.

"Yes, you do," added Alejandro. He reached for her hand and helped her down the last step.

Silence ensued as they looked at one another. A strange sensation passed through her hand as she looked-up at him. A wave of nervousness temporarily overcame her until Colleen interjected, "Have a wonderful time," breaking the spell they were both under. Colleen then reached up and kissed Angelina's cheek. She whispered in her ear, "You do look beautiful." Smiling at the couple, Colleen turned towards the door and opened it for them.

Alejandro released her hand, and then placed his against the small of her back as he guided her out the door. She could hear her mother saying, "Enjoy yourselves."

Angelina giggled as she walked down the sidewalk.

"What's so funny?" he asked.

"Nothing. I was just thinking about something my mother said. That's all." She was remembering their earlier conversation when her mother learned about their date and how she went on and on about Alejandro.

Alejandro left it at that as he opened her car door. Being the gentleman that he was, he aided her again with her seatbelt.

"What are you doing?"

"Helping with your seatbelt."

"You don't have to do that."

"Yes, I do. Your mother would expect it."

"Stop that," she said. "Don't even go there. This is an evening about friendship and nothing else."

"Back at you," he said. "Friendship." He closed the door and walked around the car. As he opened his door, he noticed the drapes moving in the front window. He was sure it was her mother checking them out. She had hopes and dreams for her daughter, but he knew otherwise. Those dreams, as Angelina told him, would never come true. He wanted Angelina to get on with her life. He wanted to help her see that she could have it all. He could counsel her to believe that even though he knew he would not play a part in her dreams. He kept reminding himself that he just needed a partner for the evening. If they had a good time, maybe she would agree to be his date for other hospital functions. He knew he was never going to have another long-term relationship. He'd had it once, and never wanted to go there again.

They arrived at the hotel where the event was being held. A valet stood at Alejandro's door as he placed the car in park. He handed Alejandro a claim check as he exited the car. The doorman opened Angelina's door and Alejandro was right there as she exited the car. He presented her his arm, which she immediately reached for. They walked into the hotel looking more like a couple than either of them desired to be.

He escorted her to the ballroom after he checked their table seating. Angelina was nervous. She'd never been to an event where so many professionals surrounded her. She didn't realize it, but she squeezed Alejandro's arm a little tighter. He looked down at her and smiled. "Come on," he said. "Our table awaits us." He guided her to their table and pulled out her chair. Alejandro asked her what she'd like to drink and went to the bar to retrieve their drinks.

She waited there for Alejandro to return, looking around at the ballroom filled with holiday decorations. She'd been to many holiday parties in this same ballroom, but never did she remember how beautifully decorated it had been. Tonight, clear balls were hanging from the ceiling filled with holiday lights, giving the appearance of ornaments. Holiday lights were woven into the garland that was strung around the doorways. The room was a sea of various gold and silver decorations. If she had one word to describe the room, it would be "magical." She felt like she was living in a fairy tale with all of the twinkling lights that surrounded the room.

She couldn't believe the chain of events that led to this evening. She was sitting in the grandest of ballrooms celebrating the holidays with Alejandro. She was having difficulty putting words behind her thoughts. She didn't know what she'd done to deserve Alejandro's attention.

She was deep in thought when Alejandro returned to the table.

"White wine for my lady," he said as he handed her the drink.

Smiling up at him, she thanked him. They were presently alone at their table. Taking a sip of his wine, he started their conversation by asking about her day.

"It was good. I'm going to miss seeing my students."

"What are your plans for your break?"

"Nothing really. Gabriella and I are going out one day, but other than that I have no plans. I guess I'll help my mom around the house. As you could tell by the decorations, Christmas is a big event for her."

"Yes, it's quite festive."

"Well, Christmas Day is huge at our house. I don't know why she continues with all of this, but I guess she does it for Wyatt and Colleen, but it's not like they still believe in Santa Claus."

"Traditions must mean a lot to her."

"Yes, they do."

As the night progressed, they enjoyed a wonderful meal and conversations with his peers and their spouses. Alejandro introduced her to the table as a friend of his sister's—they didn't need to know that she'd been his patient. The head of the hospital's wife, Trudy James, was sitting beside Angelina. Angelina explained her longtime family connection with Alejandro's family to Trudy.

"Actually, Alejandro's father was my Pediatrician. I knew he had a daughter my age, but we didn't actually meet until college and we became fast friends. And then I didn't actually meet Alejandro until he moved to St. Louis earlier this year. I'd heard all about him and his accomplishments through Gabriella. He does such marvelous work."

"Yes, he does. We were lucky to get our hands him. He's so well respected throughout the country."

Alejandro turned to Angelina and joined in on her conversation. The last of the dinner dishes had been cleared and the band began playing. Placing his hand on hers, he asked her to dance. Smiling up at him, she agreed. Alejandro grabbed her hand, and led her to the dance floor. Pulling her into his arms, he asked if she was having a good time.

"Yes, actually, I am. Everyone at the table is really nice. Not stuffy like I expected."

"Stuffy?" he scoffed.

"Well you know."

"Know what?"

"Know how doctors can be. They all have such egos."

Alejandro smiled at her and she continued, "Of course, I don't consider you amongst their company."

Laughing, he said, "I'm glad."

She was surprised that Alejandro was such a good dancer. He spun her around the dance floor. Even with the hall as crowded as it was, he was still able to keep up the flow of the dance without running into anyone. She was impressed to say the least. They danced until the band took a break, and he led them back to their table. She appeared to be getting tired. Knowing that she'd had a long day, he asked her if she wanted to leave.

"Not unless you do."

"Are you sure? You're looking tired."

"I'm fine, really," she said. "Let's just get something straight. Tonight, you're not my doctor. Got it?"

He nodded. "I just thought you'd had a long day, that's all."

Smiling, she said, "Come on. Let's dance some more." She reached for his hand and pulled him up from the chair. Begrudgingly, he headed back to the dance floor with her. They danced until the band called it an evening at eleven o'clock.

Alejandro reached for her hand and, as a couple, he led her from the ballroom. She'd had a wonderful time. While they waited for the valet to bring his car around, she began to shiver.

"Cold?" he asked.

"Not really."

"Let me warm you up," he said as he placed his arm around her and drew her close. "Better?" he asked.

"Yes. Thank you," she said as she drew closer to him, feeling the warmth emanating from his body.

The valet delivered Alejandro's car and opened the door for Angelina. She hated to leave the warmth of his arm around her. Alejandro once again assisted her with her seatbelt. Smiling at her, he closed the door. They drove home in silence as each pondered the events of the evening. When he pulled into the driveway, she turned to him. "Thank you. I had a marvelous time."

"No, thank you. I'm glad you decided to go. Otherwise, I would have begged off and stayed home this evening. It was good for me to socialize with my colleagues outside the hospital."

Alejandro exited the car and came around to open Angelina's door. She'd already started to exit the car when he reached for her hand. "Let me help you."

"Thanks again," she said as they walked to the door.

"Maybe we can do this again sometime." He said as she made her way up the front steps.

Turning back to him she said, "That would be fun." Not sure what else she should say or do, she told him to have a great holiday.

"Aren't you coming over to my parents for their Christmas open house?"

"Gabriella did mention it. Let me see what's going on here and I'll try and make it."

Both of them were a little uncomfortable. Neither knew how to end this evening, so he reached for her hand, shook it, and said, "Sounds good." Dropping her hand, he started to turn away but added, "Take care."

With that, he turned and waved goodbye, disappearing into the confines of his car. She watched him as he started the engine and slowly backed out of the driveway. She stood on the doorstep and watched as his taillights disappeared around the corner. Sighing, she opened the door and entered the foyer. She closed the door on what had turned into a fabulous evening.

# CHAPTER NINE

Gabriella couldn't wait to discover how their date went. She phoned Angelina early the next day to see if she'd like to meet for lunch and finish some last minute shopping.

Angelina missed her call since she'd been busy running errands for her mother and had forgotten her cell phone. As soon as she got home, she checked her messages and saw Gabriella's number pop up. She knew what she wanted and really didn't want to discuss her evening with Gabriella. She waited to return her call until the next day and, like a good game of phone tag, had to leave Gabriella a message.

Two days later, they touched base and Gabriella couldn't contain herself. "So tell me, how was it?"

"Gabriella, I'm in the middle of something right now and can't talk. Would you be able to meet tomorrow for lunch?"

"If I have to wait that long," she whined.

"Sorry, but I'm really busy helping my mom with something. That's all I can offer."

Gabriella agreed, so they met for lunch the next day and did some last minute shopping.

"I can't believe today is Christmas Eve," said Gabriella. They'd both finished picking up some last minute gifts and were hoping to enjoy a relaxing lunch.

"I know what you mean. This year has been a whirlwind with everything that's happened." said Angelina as they sat down at their table for lunch.

Gabriella had decided to not overwhelm Angelina with her questions about her dinner with Alejandro's peers. "How are you feeling these days?"

"Pretty good, although I still get a little tired in the afternoon. Otherwise, I'm fine."

"Have you spoken to Alejandro about this?"

"No. I didn't think it was necessary."

"Well, you know he'd probably want you to call him. He worries about you."

"I'm fine. Okay?" Angelina wondered if Gabriella was snooping for Alejandro's benefit. Then, she thought again and realized that Gabriella was just a concerned friend.

Gabriella nodded, but made a mental note of her tiredness. "So, since we're on the subject of my brother, how did your date go?"

"Gabriella, it really wasn't a date."

"You said it was a... No, I think you said... It doesn't really matter what you said exactly, how was your evening?"

"I had a nice time."

"And?"

"And, what?"

"What about Alejandro?"

"I think he enjoyed himself, too. Look, Gabriella, Alejandro just needed someone to accompany him for the evening and he asked me. There's nothing to it.

Please get any thoughts of us dating out of your head—it's not going to happen."

"But?"

"No buts, Gabriella. We went as friends and that's it." Angelina looked down at her watch and noticed the late hour. Her family was putting the last minute touches on their Christmas Eve celebration. "Look at the time—I better get moving so I can finish helping my mom with dinner."

As they were waiting for the waitress to return with their credit card receipts, Gabriella asked her if she was going to attend her parents' open house the following day.

"I don't know. You know how crazy it gets at my house. We'll have to see."

"I understand," said Gabriella, but she wondered if that was truly the case.

They hugged at their cars and wished each other's families a Merry Christmas. "Now, don't forget about tomorrow."

"I know, Gabriella. I said I'll try to come and I mean it." Angelina waved goodbye as she drove off. Gabriella was worried about her friend and would mention her concern to Alejandro when she saw him later that evening.

It just so happened that both of their families attended midnight mass. Usually Gabriella's family attended mass on Christmas morning but, since they were having an open house, they decided to go earlier. Midnight mass was a tradition for the Samuels's family, as both Colleen and Wyatt sang in the children's choir.

Angelina's parents, along with Wyatt and Colleen, left early for church. Kelly and James were right behind them in a separate car. Angelina decided to drive herself. She was slow in getting ready since she'd taken a nap after returning from lunch, and she lost track of time when she discovered that it was almost midnight. She knew mass would be crowded and thought she'd have a hard time finding a parking place. She lucked out in finding one, and as she got out of her car a familiar car pulled up beside hers. She couldn't believe her eyes. It was Alejandro.

"What are you doing here?" she asked.

"Same as you. Since my parents are having an open house this year, they decided to attend midnight mass. Where's the rest of your family?"

"They're inside. I was running a little late." As they entered the church, they discovered how crowded it actually was. There were no seats available near either of their families, so they decided to sit together. An usher led them to a pew that barely had enough room for the two of them. Alejandro motioned for her to enter the pew. As they kneeled, his arm brushed against hers. She looked up at him and smiled. They were packed into their pew like sardines. Several times, she knocked into him as she tried to get situated. She looked at him and mouthed an apology. He just smiled back.

Mass was beautiful, and Alejandro gave her a hug at the sign of peace. She was taken aback by it and smiled at him. When mass was over, they joined their families who were huddled outside. Jackie invited everyone back to their house for an impromptu celebration.

Angelina and Alejandro walked to their cars. "Are you okay with me coming over?"

"Why wouldn't I be?" said Angelina.

Alejandro followed her home and helped her from the car. He followed her inside where the rest of the clan had already gathered. Her mother was in her element: entertaining. In no time, she prepared a meal that others would have taken hours putting together. Angelina looked in awe as she watched her mother pull an endless amount of dishes from the refrigerator. Angelina quickly stepped in to assist her mother set up the buffet while her father prepared drinks for everyone. She had no idea that her mother had anticipated having the Alvarezes over after mass. By the way her mother talked, it had already been set up days in advance with Maria and John. Everyone had a fabulous time enjoying the food and conversation.

Colleen approached Alejandro who was standing with Joe and Alec. She hugged him and thanked him for everything that he'd done for her. Then, she turned to his brothers and said, "I guess I'll see you both in a few weeks."

"Well, I don't know about that," said Joe. "Isn't your appointment with our father?"

"It is," said Colleen. "But anytime I'm in there I seem to see both of you, too. Even if it's just in passing."

"That's true. It seems like I see Wyatt an awful lot, too," said Alec. Since they worked together, they always made it a habit of trying to stay abreast of all the patients that passed through the office. Their father believed it was important that they were all aware of the special cases that flowed through the practice.

Jackie cornered Alejandro when he was on his way to grab a cookie. "Did you have a nice time with

Angelina at the hospital dinner? How was the food? What did the ballroom look like?" Alejandro wasn't sure what hit him. She tried asking him one question after another about his evening with Angelina. Before he could react to her questioning, Gabriella interrupted her asking her if she could have a recipe for the delicious cookie that she held in her hand.

The Alvarezes left at around three in the morning. Alejandro turned to Angelina as he was putting his coat on. Smiling, he asked if she planned on attending his parents' open house.

"It all depends."

"On what? Surely you can find time to come over for a little while."

"It's just that…"

"What, Angelina? Are you not feeling well?"

"I'm fine. I've just been a little tired of late."

"Are you taking your meds?"

"Yes."

"Why don't you get some rest and see how you're feeling later on. I'd be more than happy to come by on my way to my parents' to check on you."

"That's not necessary. I'm fine. You have a blessed Christmas and I'll see you later."

"Fine, but I certainly hope to see you tomorrow."

"I'll try to come. I promise."

Alejandro didn't believe Angelina. He was concerned about her tiredness. But the more he thought about it, the more he realized that she'd been working pretty hard lately trying to get back into the swing of things. The winter break would do her good. She'd be able to catch up on her rest and, hopefully, start the year off on solid ground.

Alejandro's parents' open house was scheduled for two o'clock. On his way over, he ran by Angelina's. Jackie answered the door. "Alejandro? What a pleasant surprise."

"I was in the neighborhood and thought I'd stop by and thank you for last night. Or should I say this morning? I can't believe you were able to put that together at a moment's notice."

"I'm used to it. It was nothing really. I had already pre-planned it with your parents. I'm just so glad you were able to come by, too. This year was a hard one for our family, and yours helped us get through it. I just wanted to do something, in thanksgiving, for all their support and friendship through the years."

Alejandro smiled. "It's not a problem. That's what we're here for. By the way, is Angelina around?"

"She is. I think she may be lying down. Do you want me to get her?"

"Well…"

At that moment, the telephone rang. Jackie pointed in the direction of Angelina's bedroom. He wasn't sure if he should seek her out, but decided there was no reason not to. He remembered where her bedroom was, as he'd found her there in tears the morning after Colleen's accident.

Softly knocking on her door, he listened for a response. He thought he'd heard a faint "yes" and opened the door. Angelina was lying on her bed with Christmas carols playing in the background. He approached her and realized that she was asleep.

He started to leave when she called out. Alejandro turned and walked back to her. "What are you doing here?"

"Checking on you. I was concerned earlier and thought I'd stop by on my way to my parents."

"Isn't this out of the way?"

"No."

"I guess you're wondering why I'm resting? I wanted to come over to your parents' and thought I should take a nap first."

"And?"

"I feel great. Now, if you'd leave me alone, I'll get dressed and come over shortly."

"I've got a better idea. I'll wait and take you on over. I've got to go by the hospital later and, since your house is on the way, I'll bring you back home."

"Are you sure?"

"Yep. I'll go keep your mom company while you dress. I'm sure she'll enjoy that," he said, laughing as he strolled from her bedroom.

Angelina quickly dressed in a pair of khakis and a holiday sweater. She met Alejandro in the kitchen where her mother was entertaining him with one of her stories about Angelina growing up. "Ready?" he asked, almost thankful that she appeared when she did. All he knew was that Jackie could sure tell a long-winded story.

Nodding, she put on her coat and kissed her mother goodbye.

"Have fun," her mother happily said. She crossed her fingers as the couple left the house. Hopefully her prayers would be answered. She'd prayed especially hard at mass when she'd seen them together at the back of church. She hoped that they were developing a close friendship or, better yet, a relationship. Jackie had learned over the years not to interfere in her children's lives, although at times she forgot her own mantra. She didn't want to ruin a good thing for her daughter.

It seemed like second nature when Alejandro opened the car door for Angelina and clicked her seatbelt in place. He was such the gentleman. They drove to his parents' while Christmas carols played on the radio.

"I thought you were off this week. Gabriella told me you were going to help her do something around her house." Angelina asked.

"I am, but I just wanted to check up on a patient whose family is out of state. I didn't want her to spend Christmas all alone. I thought I'd take her a plate from my mom's."

"You're so sweet. That's such a nice gesture. Can I come along, too?'

"If you want," he said, smiling at her kind offering.

They arrived at Alejandro's parents'. When his father opened the door, he was surprised to see Angelina on his arm. "Angelina, my dear, it's so good to see you." His father looked questioningly at Alejandro.

"I stopped by Angelina's on the way over. Gabriella had invited her, and I thought since I had to run by the hospital after I was done here, I'd do the gentlemanly thing and bring her with me since her house is on the way to the hospital."

His father thought he was making excuses for his decision to pick Angelina up, but let it slide. Alejandro was an adult and could do whatever he wanted with his personal life.

Gabriella was excited to see Angelina. "I wasn't sure you'd come."

"I wouldn't miss it for the world." Glancing at Alejandro across the room, she finished her thought, "I took a nap to make sure I'd enjoy the rest of the day." She said this loudly enough for him to hear.

Maria had invited their neighbors along with some of the office staff from the practice. She'd also invited the Samuels, but Jackie declined because she thought it had been too much for Colleen. Maria decided to have an open house this year because she wanted to do something different for the holidays, especially since Alejandro was home for the first time in many years.

Alejandro made sure Angelina had everything she needed. He acted as though she were his date, constantly checking on her, topping off her drink, and making sure that she tried one of his mother's specialties. As he walked out the door, Maria handed Alejandro the plate she'd made for his patient. "I even have a little something for her. I hope she isn't too lonely."

"That's why I'm going by. Being in a hospital is hard enough, but when you're alone during the holidays it makes it even harder."

"Alejandro, you're too caring of a doctor. Do you realize that?" his mother asked.

"I do the best I can. I want all of my patients to feel special. Each and every one of them is important to me." He glanced over at Angelina and smiled.

They left for the hospital. Angelina guarded the plate of food while he drove. "So, we're all special to you?"

"Huh?"

"You said all of your patients are special."

"Indeed they are."

They chatted as they drove. He was still going on about her mother's generosity that morning. He never thought he'd end up at the Samuels's for an early morning meal. When they entered the hospital, he placed his hand on her back and guided her through the halls to his patient's room. This small gesture was becoming a force of habit for him.

He knocked on the door before entering Jessica's room. She was sitting in a chair reading. Glancing up, she smiled and excitedly said, "You came."

"Of course, I did. A promise is a promise." He handed her the plate his mother prepared, along with the small gift that his mother sent along.

"I hope I'm not too late and that you haven't already eaten."

"No. I held off ordering my meal. I thought I'd eat a little later."

"Jessica. This is my friend Angelina."

"You're friend? Sure, Doc."

"She is. Actually, she's my sister's best friend. They went to college together and now teach at the same school."

"Whatever you say," she said as she glanced back and forth between the two of them. She thought they were standing awfully close to one another to just be "friends."

They spent about an hour with Jessica. She was thrilled he'd taken time out of his holiday to bring her dinner and a gift. It made her feel special. "Jessica," he said. "I'm off the rest of the week and Dr. Miles will be covering for me."

"I know. I already met him. He's nice, too."

"Well, I hope so. I only want people working for me who have good bedside manners. That's important to me," he said as he stood to leave.

"It was nice meeting you, Angelina."

"Same here, Jessica," she added as she grabbed her purse and stood. The strap from her purse slipped from her shoulder and, noticing it, Alejandro instantly reached for it and settled it back on her shoulder.

As they walked to the door, Jessica thanked Alejandro again for coming by. She winked at him and told him to take care of Angelina. She was a special person, too.

Alejandro took Angelina by his office so he could gather a few files to take home with him. "You know, Alejandro, you are a special doctor."

"Well, thank you. I try."

"No, you are. You sure brightened Jessica's day."

"Well, what can I say?"

"Alejandro, you're a one-of-a-kind doctor. Your patients are not just patients to you. You treat them like family... And that's the difference. We need more physicians like you and your dad. It would definitely make a difference in the medical community."

"I hope to bring physicians with my same philosophy here, too. It's important to treat your patients with respect and dignity. They're people, too."

Alejandro grabbed his files and they left the hospital. It was getting late, so he took her directly home. Angelina asked if he wanted to come in, but he declined saying that he better run by his parents' again. He wanted to help them clean up after their open house. Since this was his first Christmas home in a long time, he wanted to spend a little more time with them.

Alejandro pulled into Angelina's driveway and thanked her for joining him. "It meant a lot to Jessica for us to come by."

"It certainly did. Thank you for letting me go with you. It made me feel like I did some good today."

"You do good every day. Teaching is a specialty that not enough people appreciate."

"I guess you're right."

"No. I know I am. You're shaping the children of tomorrow. You are instilling beliefs in them. You're guiding them on their path to the future."

"Enough already, I'll let you go. Please wish your parents a Merry Christmas and Happy New Year. Tell Gabriella I'll call in the next day or so. You take care and I'll see you soon. Again, thanks for today. It was special."

Alejandro helped her from the car. As she exited, she got her feet tangled up in the strap of her purse. Thankfully, Alejandro was paying attention. He grabbed her as she fell into his arms. "Damned purse," she murmured. "I'm sorry, Alejandro. I stepped on the strap of my purse and tried to keep walking while I was still holding it. Thanks for saving me."

Alejandro looked down into her eyes and smiled. "I'm glad I was here to catch you. You need to be a little more careful and stay out of the way of your purse," he laughed. "Now, get inside and I'll see you soon." He gave her a hug and wished her a Merry Christmas. Little did Angelina know, her mother witnessed her fall into his arms. From her angle, it looked as though Alejandro had pulled her directly into his arms. Jackie was ecstatic with what she'd just seen. Maybe her prayers would be answered. Only time would tell.

Angelina opened the front door and hurried inside. Her mother happily greeted her. "Did you have a nice time?"

"It was great. I had a wonderful time at his parents'. I had a really nice talk with both Alec and Joe. After, Alejandro took me by the hospital and I met one of his patients. We took her some dinner and a Christmas gift. She was so thankful and appreciative of his time. You know, Mom, he is a special doctor. There aren't many physicians that would take their patients a home-cooked meal, and on a holiday nonetheless."

Jackie smiled at her daughter and said, "Indeed, he is a special man." Smiling she looked away and whispered under her breath, "Special indeed for my daughter."

Angelina took it easy the next several days. Out of the blue, one afternoon, her phone rang. She wasn't expecting a call. In fact, the caller was lucky her phone was even on. Glancing at the caller ID, she didn't recognize the number. "Hello?" she said.

"Angelina, it's Jessica, Dr. Alvarez's patient. How are you?"

"Just fine and you?" Angelina had given Jessica her phone number on Christmas in the event she got lonely and wanted some company.

"Great. I'm feeling a lot better. I was wondering if you had any free time. I'm a little lonely and looking for some girl talk. Are you interested?"

"Sure. I'm not doing anything. When would you like me to drop by?"

"Whenever you have a chance."

"Let me finish up a few things around here, and I'll come by in a little while."

"Thanks. I look forward to seeing you."

Angelina changed her clothes. She'd enjoyed meeting Jessica at Christmas and thought it wouldn't hurt her to spend some time with her. In all actuality, she'd forgotten that she gave Jessica her number.

Angelina arrived at the hospital mid-afternoon. She brought Jessica some Christmas cookies that she'd made with her mother and sisters.

"Thanks for the cookies. You didn't have to bring me anything. I just asked you over because I was bored and was looking for someone to talk to other than doctors and nurses."

"No problem. I wasn't doing anything today. I'm happy that I was free so I could come by."

They talked for hours and were fast friends. They had so much in common. Jessica was from a relatively large family, except they lived a good distance from the hospital and could only visit on weekends. She was also studying to become a teacher. Jessica had been in and out of the hospital after having a kidney transplant six months earlier.

When Angelina was just about ready to leave, someone knocked on the door and in walked Alejandro. He was surprised to see her. "Angelina, what're you doing here?"

"Visiting Jessica. Hey, I thought you were off this week."

"I am, but I stopped by my office and thought I'd check on Jessica."

"That's so nice of you. Thanks for stopping by," Jessica said. Alejandro asked Angelina to wait outside the room while he examined her. He then motioned for her to return when he was done. When a nurse came in to check Jessica's vital signs, Angelina decided to leave. Alejandro was right behind her.

"Wait," he called. She stopped and turned around. "Where're you going? Anywhere special?" he asked.

"No, not really. Why?"

"Want to have dinner?"

She didn't know what to say. He'd been so good to her that, after thinking about it for a moment, she agreed. "Sure," she said.

"Do you mind coming by my house? I'll make us something there."

"Just give me the directions."

Alejandro did so and she phoned her mother while she waited for him to grab the files that he needed from his office. She told her mom that something came up, and she wouldn't be home for dinner. Surprisingly, her mother didn't question her further.

Angelina met Alejandro outside his office and they headed towards the parking garage. Alejandro walked towards the prime parking that the doctors used, while Angelina headed towards the elevator that would take her to the third floor where her car was parked.

It turned out that he lived a short distance from her parents, but Alejandro's house was in a more rural area. While her parents lived in a subdivision, Alejandro's house was surrounded mainly by farms. He'd just arrived and was exiting the car when she pulled into the driveway. He waited for her at the front door while she grabbed her coat from the back seat of her car and he showed her inside. Alejandro's house was quite large for a bachelor. She was surprised by the size.

"Glass of wine?" he asked as he closed the door behind them.

"Sounds great."

He led the way to his bar that was located in the family room and poured her a glass of wine; then he reached behind himself for a door that he opened and flipped a switch, filling the room with a soft jazzy tune.

In no time at all, he'd whipped up a terrific dinner. He sautéed some shrimp and added it to a fabulous sauce that he'd pre-made and threw it over some angel hair pasta. He also served a green salad and crusty dinner rolls.

"Where did you learn to cook like this?"

"Lots of practice. I used to watch my mom in the kitchen when I was growing up."

Dinner passed in a blur for Angelina. She enjoyed every bite. She gathered the plates and carried them to the sink where he stood rinsing off the dishes. "Wish I could cook like this."

"Maybe I can teach you." He turned and placed the dishes in the dishwasher. Refilling their glasses, he led her into the living room where he'd already lit a fire in the fireplace. "Sorry, but I can't offer dessert other than Christmas cookies, which I'm sure you're tired of."

"Yes. I never thought I'd say this, but I've had my fill of Christmas cookies for another year. Thanks, though."

He showed her to the couch.

"This is really nice, Alejandro. Thanks for asking me to join you."

"I'm glad I ran into you. Thanks for visiting with Jessica—her family can't make it here very often."

"She explained that they lived out of town and could only see her on weekends. Do you think she'll be in much longer?"

"No. I'll let you know when she's ready to be discharged. That way you can say goodbye."

"Thanks. I hope to stay in touch with her when she returns home. I'm glad that she called earlier. I really enjoyed our talk."

They sat in the living room drinking their wine and listening to the soft music playing in the background. He turned towards her and removed her glass from her hands. Placing it on the end table, he reached for her hands. "I know now probably isn't the time to talk about this, but there never will be a good time."

She looked at him, wondering where the conversation was headed.

"Angelina, have you thought anymore about talking to a counselor?"

She was shocked that he would bring that up now. In her eyes, he'd just ruined their perfect evening. "Alejandro, let's not go there now. Please... I'm having a really nice time this evening and don't want to think about that right now." She withdrew her hands from his.

"Angelina. You're going to have to deal with it sometime. Let's talk about it now. Please."

She looked him in the eyes, then looked away. Taking a deep breath, she glanced back at him and nodded.

He reached for her hands again and held them ever so tightly in his. He wanted her to feel his strength, his desire to help her. He'd do anything for her since he was the only one that she trusted with her secret.

"Angelina, have you thought about this lately?"

"Thought about it?" she said. She didn't know if she should share with him everything that she'd been going through. Nightly, she had nightmares. Nightmares that started with her happy, holding a newborn, and then always ended in the hospital room learning the news of her condition. That was one of the reasons why she'd been so tired. She was afraid to sleep for fear of waking in tears with her heart pounding.

Looking away from him, she didn't know where to begin.

He pulled on her hands and shifted his body so that he was now facing her. "Tell me what you're going through. It's only going to keep tearing you up."

Taking another deep breath, she faced him. Tears were gathering in the corners of her eyes. She was trying to control them from slipping down her face. She didn't want to cry in front of him—he'd seen enough tears from her. Gathering her thoughts, she said, "I think about this daily." She stopped talking and looked at their clasped hands. "I can't sleep at night. I have nightmares. I wake up in tears, always with a pounding headache." Closing her eyes tightly to fend off the tears, she wrinkled her forehead. Drawing her hands to her eyes, she rubbed them with such intensity that her actions caused Alejandro to pull down her hands and draw her towards him, into his arms. She needed to be held closely to wave off her fears. After settling into his arms, she laid her head on his chest and continued her story. "That's why I've been so tired. I'm afraid to sleep."

"Angelina, why haven't you called me?" he questioned as he smoothed his hand through her hair.

"I don't know. I guess I didn't want to bother you."

He set her away from him, startling her in the process. "It's not your issue to deal with alone. I'm here. I've always been here for you. I promised you that I'd be here for you when you elected not to talk with a counselor or your family, and I am."

"I know what you said."

"Didn't you believe me?

"I don't know. You're so busy. And—"

"I meant what I said. I'm definitely not too busy for you."

"I know you say that but—"

"Angelina, look at me." When she refused to look at him, he removed one of his hands from hers and placed a finger under her chin. Lifting her chin upward, he forced her to look him directly in the eyes. "I would never say something that I didn't mean. I don't take this issue lightly. I want to see you deal with this situation, not sweep it under the carpet, or you'll carry it with you for a long time."

Sighing, she looked away. "I don't know what to do, Alejandro. I've wanted a family since I've been a little girl. Gabriella and I dreamed of this together…"

"You can still have a family, just maybe not how you intended."

"I can't go into a relationship with this monkey on my back."

"Why not?"

"I just can't..." Angelina sighed. "Question for you."

"Okay."

"If you were in a relationship, and wanted to have a family, wouldn't you want the children to be yours and not someone else's?"

"To be truthful, I will never have a family myself. But if I were to get married and have one, it wouldn't matter to me. As long as I was with the woman I loved, it wouldn't matter."

"Why won't you have a family?"

"That's not important. This is about you and your inability to have children, not me."

"But, Alejandro—"

"I said no." He stood and abruptly walked away from her. Placing his hands in his pockets, he turned towards her. He needed to get the focus of their conversation back on her. "I'm sure that when you disclose your medical condition to your boyfriend, he'll understand. If he doesn't, then you weren't meant to be together. You can't help the fact that you got sick. He should understand, and if he can't, then he's not good enough for you."

She stood and reached for him. "Alejandro, I don't think I'll find anyone as understanding as you. You understand the issue. Most men won't. They'll want their own biological family, and I can't provide that."

"Stop," he said. "Just stop. Why do you believe that? There are good men out there, you just have to find one."

Shaking her head, she walked away from him. He went to her and placed his hands on her shoulders. Turning her towards him, he pulled her into an embrace and just held her. She buried her face into his chest and finally released her tears. He held her while she cried and then led her back to the couch. They sat in silence with the music playing softly in the background.

Before Alejandro realized it, she was asleep in his arms. He fell asleep a bit later, but was awakened by her sobs. It was nearing eleven according to the clock on the wall, and she'd been asleep for a couple of hours. He softly nudged her, trying to awaken her from her dreams until he was successful. Wiping the tears from her face, he asked if she was alright. Nodding, she pulled herself from his arms and stood. "I think it's time I go home." Without a thought, she gathered her purse and headed towards the door. He stood and reached for her. She avoided his arms and opened the door. "Thanks for dinner. You're a wonderful cook." Crossing the threshold she added, "Have a Happy New Year."

He stood in wonder—he was perplexed by her behavior.

She ran down the sidewalk to her car. Tears were streaming down her face.

Alejandro just stood in the open doorway. He wasn't sure what had just happened, what had caused her to run. One minute, she was sleeping in his arms, and the next she was running away from him. If he desired to have a relationship again, he knew he would choose Angelina. He shook his head in disbelief... She was a remarkable woman. She could be his and he could watch over her always—she was a special person in his life and his family's life as well. But then again, he also believed that it would never happen.

Angelina drove home in tears. *What just happened to me?* she thought. She had awakened, wrapped in Alejandro's arms, and it felt so right. This couldn't be happening. He didn't want a family and she couldn't have one. What was she going to do?

She sat in her driveway for a few minutes while she composed herself. Just as she exited the car, her phone rang. She didn't bother to check the caller ID and just answered it.

"Are you alright?" the caller asked.

"I'm fine, Alejandro. I just got home. Thanks again for this evening."

"Angelina?"

"As I said earlier, I don't want to go there. I've had enough. I don't want to discuss this anymore tonight." She terminated the call, entered the house, and went straight to her bedroom, ignoring her mother's call. She had to think, and she could only do that alone, without interruption. Her cell rang again and she ignored it. Before she turned it off, she checked the caller ID. It was Alejandro. Sighing, she placed her phone in her purse. Tomorrow was another day. In fact, tomorrow was New Year's Eve. She'd end the day with the hopes of making the New Year a better year than the one that was on the way out.

# CHAPTER TEN

New Year's Eve dawned with an approaching snowstorm. As long as Angelina could remember, St. Louis always had a winter storm that affected the holiday parties, and this year would close with what the weather forecasters were calling a snow-pocalypse.

Angelina's family decided to celebrate the close of the year by renting a downtown hotel suite. Angelina, at the last minute, decided to stay home. She wasn't in the partying mood. Her parents were disappointed, but seemed to understand.

Earlier in the day, Gabriella called to talk. Angelina told Gabriella of her family's plans and her decision to stay home by herself. Gabriella listened to her friend and wished her a Happy New Year. Upon disconnecting the call, Gabriella phoned her brother who was home. She informed him that Angelina was going to be alone and that she would have joined her, but she had a date.

"Alejandro, I'm worried about Angelina. She just didn't seem herself. There was such sadness in her voice. I can't put my finger on it but—"

Alejandro interrupted his sister. "Aren't you always worried about her?"

"No… I mean yes. Hell, I don't know. All I know is that I just got off the phone with her, and she's going to be by herself this evening, of all evenings, New Year's. Can you believe that? Her parents are celebrating downtown. They're going to have a blast. It's just that I am concerned because she just didn't sound herself. That's all."

"Well, what do you want me to do?"

"I don't know. I just thought you should know."

"Thanks for the call. And Gabriella?"

"Yes?"

"Happy New Year."

He disconnected the call and went about his day.. He knew Gabriella expected him to do something since she was alone, but he was alone, too. *What did it matter?* he thought.

It had started snowing right after he got off the phone with Gabriella. Before he knew it, almost a foot of snow had fallen. At around six o'clock his power flickered off and on, and then went out and came back on. According to the news sources, more than half of the city was without power. He was thankful that his power decided to stay on, at least for the time being. The winds were howling and the visibility was next to nil. They were experiencing blizzard-like conditions, and it reminded him of the countless snowstorms he'd encountered while living in Wisconsin.

The forecasters predicted that overnight the storm was expected to dump an additional six or more inches of heavy snow on the St. Louis area. For some reason, his mind drifted to Angelina at home in this horrific snowstorm, most likely without power. He told himself he was crazy for worrying about her, but he strapped on his snow skis and headed over to Angelina's. Often Alejandro would strap on his skis during a snowstorm when he lived in Wisconsin and tonight was no different. He loved to watch the snow fall as he skied. He discovered he was a little out of practice as he glided down the country roads that led to her house. It took him longer than he expected, but when he approached her street he discovered that she was indeed without electricity.

He dropped his backpack onto the front steps while he removed his skis. Brushing the snow from his hat and coat, he knocked on the door.

At first Angelina thought she was hearing things, but the pounding on the front door continued. She was scared, wondering who would be knocking on her door during this intense storm. She looked out the side window and discovered a rather tall man standing at her door. His back was to the door and she was leery to open it. She wondered if someone had gotten stuck in the street, but she hadn't seen any traffic for what seemed like hours. When she didn't answer right away, he turned back towards the house and that's when she saw it was Alejandro.

She quickly opened the door. "Alejandro, what're you doing here?"

"Gabriella told me you were going to be alone, and I was concerned that you were alone without power."

"Come in, but I'm fine," she said as she reached for a coat hanger from the coat closet. "You didn't have to come all the way over here." She snuck her head back out the door, not understanding how he made his way to the house. "How did you get here? I don't see your car."

"I skied over."

"Oh, really? You skied all the way over here? That's something you don't see in St. Louis."

"I know, but I always did it while living in Wisconsin."

"Let me get your coat. Are you cold?" she asked as she grabbed his coat and hung it up in the closet.

"No. I'm fine. I actually worked up a sweat skiing over here. What about you?"

He knew she was freezing. She had on two pairs of socks, a turtle neck, a sweatshirt, and was preparing to put her winter coat on.

"I'm a little cold," she said.

"A little? Look at all the clothes you have on. I'll light the fireplace."

"Thanks," she said. "I don't know why I didn't think of starting a fire a long time ago." She sat on the couch and covered herself with a blanket while Alejandro started the fire. He joined her when the fire was blazing. Before she knew it, she was starting to get warm.

They sat in silence watching the fire catch and die down before he asked her if she was alright. He'd passed on Gabriella's concern about not joining her family downtown. "How come?"

"Huh?" she said.

"How come you didn't want to join your family?"

"I wasn't in the mood."

"Because of our discussion last night?"

"Yes… No… I don't know."

"Angelina, let me in. I want to help you. I didn't want to upset you. I only want to be the ears that you need to work through this."

She burrowed further under the covers. She was freezing. Alejandro moved towards her and pulled her into his arms. "You'll be warmer." She nuzzled into his side and wrapped her arms around his waist. "Thanks."

They sat huddled on the couch, lost in their own thoughts. Out of nowhere she said, "Alejandro, what's happening here?"

"What do you mean?"

"It seems like we're together all the time. You want to help me. I know you do. It's just that I don't know... I want to... I just can't."

"Can't what?"

"I'm so confused," she said as she started playing with the zipper pull on his jacket. Wrinkling her nose she added, "Alejandro, I feel like we're dating. We share so much with each other. Lately, we're together all of the time. I just—"

Alejandro placed his hand on her jaw and turned her head towards him, stopping her mid-sentence so she'd look him straight in the eyes. "How would you feel about that?"

"What?'

"Dating."

"You want to date me?"

"Well, yes, actually I do. You're so special, Angelina." Stopping, he swallowed loudly, briefly closing his eyes and continued, "I'm going to be upfront with you. If we were to date, you have to understand that it will go nowhere. It will just be for us to have someone to hang out with. I'll never get involved in a full-fledged relationship. You have to understand that."

"Why not?"

"Just because. That's why. I have my reasons," he said seriously.

Shaking her head, she said, "You want me to share my issues with you. Why can't you share yours with me?"

"I just can't right now." Stopping momentarily, he took a deep breath, expelled it and said, "Maybe someday I'll tell you, but right now it's still too fresh for me, and I just can't."

"How about just being good friends. Right now that's all I need."

"Good idea."

They sat wrapped in one another's arms as they tried to stay warm. As midnight approached, he said, "Angelina, if you found the right man, do you think you'd get married and have that family?"

"I've thought a lot about what you said last night. If I could find someone as understanding as you, I'd say yes. But in all honesty, I don't think I'll ever find him."

He twirled her hair in his fingers. "You're sure about that?" His eyes twinkled. Sitting there, she'd made him think about having his own family again. He had a lot to deal with, but maybe... Maybe he could make her dreams come true. He wasn't sure where those thoughts came from since two hours ago he was adamant about not having a family of his own. But first he knew he had to deal with his own issues. Only time would tell. "Do you have any champagne? We can have our own celebration."

"My parents refrigerated a bottle earlier today. Can you open it?' Unfolding from the warmth and comfort of his arms, she led him towards the kitchen and retrieved the chilled bottle.

Alejandro opened it with ease while she got the champagne flutes. "Let's toast. To the New Year. Let it be filled with good health, happiness, and love."

She nodded and took a sip from her glass. "Yes, I agree. To good health, happiness, love, and most of all honesty." She looked him directly in the eyes and said, "If we're planning on 'hanging out together' as you call it, we have to be honest with one another. Agreed?"

He looked away for a moment and then looked back, shaking his head, "Agreed, but it will take time... Time for me to be able to share what happened in my past. Please be patient with me and I'll eventually tell you." He took a gulp from his glass.

"That's all I can ask for." Smiling at him, she took another drink from her glass. Then they heard a myriad of booms in the distance. Her neighbors were shooting off fireworks early on this cold, wintery night. She assumed they were ushering out the end of this hellish year with the hopes of a promising start to the New Year.

Alejandro checked his watch just as it was approaching twelve. He started a count down, "Five... Four... Three... Two... One... Happy New Year!" He reached for Angelina, pulled her into his arms, and planted a kiss on her lips. Both were surprised by his actions. She was taken aback but returned his kiss.

Hand in hand they headed for the couch where he wrapped themselves in the blanket. Holding her in his arms, he said, "This feels right, doesn't it?"

She agreed as she snuggled closer, "Yes, for some reason, it does." Never in her wildest dreams did she anticipate the start to the New Year would play out as it just did. Kissing Alejandro was definitely the start to the New Year that she needed.

They sat watching the fire die down in the fireplace. "Penny for your thoughts," he said.

"I was just thinking," she said as she snuggled closer.

"About what?"

"I don't know... I guess that I am lucky to have you in my life. I'm fortunate to have Gabriella as my friend. If it weren't for her, we'd never have met."

"Let's not get nostalgic here."

"It's true. Alejandro, I don't know where our friendship will lead, but I want you to know that you're important to me, and that I never want to hurt you."

"And I hope I'll never hurt you. We've got to take this one day at a time, but I believe that no matter what happens, we'll always be friends."

They continued watching the fire. Before she knew it, Alejandro was asleep. She looked up at his face. It was the first time that she'd truly seen him relaxed. *What happened to you,* she wondered. *I'm not going to dream too big. You're a wonderful man, but I'm not going to let myself get hurt. I'll be objective and take this one day at a time. Friends, that's what we'll be. Friends.* She snuggled deeper in his arms and drifted off to sleep.

She heard a noise and woke up. She was still wrapped in Alejandro's arms.

"You okay?"

"Yeah, just heard a loud noise. That's all."

"It's the snow plow trying to make it down the street. It stopped snowing, but it started again."

"I thought you were asleep."

"I was, but I woke up a while ago. Come on, let's get some sleep. I think it'll be quite some time before it stops snowing. Look at it outside."

She glanced out the window and it was snowing with an intensity that looked like it had no plans on ending anytime soon.

He tightened his embrace as she laid her head on his shoulder. "Thank you for being here with me. You've made this evening unforgettable."

"Go to sleep."

"You, too."


Alejandro's phone interrupted their slumber. Sleepily, he answered. It was his mother and she was concerned about him. She'd tried calling his house numerous times and couldn't reach him, finally deciding to try his cell in hope that he'd answer. He told her he was with Angelina. He explained that Gabriella had told him about her being alone in the storm.

"That's gallant of you. The roads are impassable. I don't think Angelina's family will make it home today. I'm sure they'll check in with her, but you need to stay with her and make sure she's okay."

"Mom, she's fine. She's resourceful. But to put you at ease, I'll stay until the electricity comes back on." They talked a few more minutes and then he hung up.

"It was my mom telling me how bad the roads are… I'll stay until the electricity comes back on."

"You don't have to do that. I'll be fine."

"I want to."

She thanked him, and asked if he was hungry. It was almost eight in the morning. He nodded that he was.

"We have some leftover sweet rolls from yesterday. I think we might have some bagels and cream cheese, too. I'm sure the cream cheese is fine, being that it's freezing in here. I'm sorry, but coffee is definitely not on the menu."

"It's not," he chuckled as they made their way to the kitchen.

They ate breakfast and returned to the living room where he stoked the fire, bringing it back to life. It was her turn for her phone to ring. It was her mother. "Honey, I'm so worried about you being alone. Are you staying warm?"

"I'm fine, Mom. I'm not alone. Alejandro came over last night to check on me. Gabriella told him that I was staying in and would be alone. He was concerned about me since the electricity is out all across the county."

"Wonderful," she exclaimed. Jackie was beside herself. She knew her daughter's New Year was starting off on the right foot.

"Mother," scolded Angelina.

"Oh, Angelina, can't I dream?" Angelina sat there shaking her head in disbelief. She couldn't get over her mother. In her own way, she always seemed to be interfering in her children's lives, even if she really did nothing but express her thoughts.

She told Alejandro that her family didn't expect to return home until the following day. The roads were treacherous, and the authorities were telling everyone to stay off of them except for emergencies.

"Well then. What are we going to do?" she asked.

"What do you want to do?"

"Let's talk some more. Get to know one another better... Tell me why you chose to become a transplant surgeon."

He stood up from the couch and started pacing the living room. He walked to the fireplace and placed his hands on the mantle. Bowing his head, he took a deep breath and turned towards her. "My best friend in high school became ill. They weren't sure what was wrong with him. After running a multitude of tests, they discovered he was in kidney failure. He was immediately placed on the transplant list, but didn't live long enough for a donor to be found. I knew then that I wanted to be a surgeon. In his memory, I decided to be a transplant surgeon. I wanted to make a difference. I'm sorry that Jacob didn't live to have a transplant, but hopefully through the awareness programs that I have developed, I've made a difference in someone's life."

Angelina walked over to him, placing her hand across his heart and said, "You've made a difference. A huge difference. Look what you did for my family. I'll always be grateful for all you did for Colleen. You're a special person, and I'm lucky to have you in my life." She gave him a hug and kissed his cheek.

She stepped aside and reached for his hand. Grasping it, she pulled him back towards the couch. "I'm getting a little chilly. Let's cuddle."

Alejandro smiled and followed her to the couch where they huddled under the blanket. They rehashed the holidays, discussing her mother's get together and his parents' open house. By noon, the electricity had been restored. Alejandro ensured that she had everything she needed, then indicated he needed to go home. She thanked him just as their lawn service appeared to clear the driveway and sidewalk of the massive amounts of snow. He donned his skis and she gave him a goodbye hug. "Be careful going home," she said as he started down the sidewalk. Waving his hand goodbye, she saw him turn the corner towards his home.

*What an eventful start to the New Year*, she thought to herself. *I think this year shows promise, and I'll go along with anything that he agrees to. Maybe half-dreams can come true.* She closed the door behind her and headed to the kitchen.

# CHAPTER ELEVEN

Angelina spent the remainder of her break taking it easy. Her parents returned home the next day after spending another night away from home due to the storm. She helped her mother take down the holiday decorations. She forgot what a chore it was taking down and putting away the multitude of decorations that seemed to multiply on an annual basis. She couldn't believe that the holidays were over. She and Alejandro had spent an enormous amount of time together during the holidays. She wasn't sure where they were headed but she enjoyed dreaming about the possibilities. She hadn't seen him since New Year's. He was on service at the hospital and wouldn't be available. Depending on how many patients he was treating, he generally spent most of his time at the hospital, often sleeping on the couch in his office.

She spoke with Gabriella. Neither mentioned the time she'd spent with Alejandro during the holidays. She knew that his mother knew that he'd spent time with her during New Year's, but she wondered if he'd shared the news with Gabriella. Eventually, they'd all have to know about their "dating."

The evening before she was scheduled to return to school, she was in her bedroom preparing for the next day. She wanted to get to school early, as the new year held such promise. She was just finishing getting her bag together when her phone rang. Forgetting to check the caller ID, she answered, "Hello?"

"Hello, there. What are you doing?"

"Getting ready for bed."

"Ahh," the caller said. "Then I guess I'll let you go."

"Don't you dare," she replied. "I haven't talked to you in days."

"Sorry about that. I had a couple of really rough ones. I didn't know whether I was coming or going."

"I'm sorry to hear that. I hope you were able to get some rest."

"I'm fine. Don't worry about me. I'm worried about you. Are you ready to return to school?"

"Why wouldn't I be?"

"Well?"

"Stop it. I'm fine. I got ample rest during my break. I think I learned my lesson…"

"I guess I'm just being overprotective. I know you're okay."

"Thanks for the vote of confidence. Now, what about you? Are you off service yet?"

"Actually, that's why I'm calling. Want to go out tomorrow night? Celebrate the New Year and your first day back at school."

"Sure. Alejandro?"

"Yeah."

"I haven't told anyone about us."

"Us?"

"Well. You know what I mean. I haven't even told Gabriella."

"Thank you. Angelina, I have to do this my own way."

"I understand. We'll take it slowly and see what happens."

"Don't expect too much out of me—I don't really have much to give. We're just friends, right?"

"Whatever you say."

They continued to chat, and Alejandro could tell she was getting tired. "I'll see you tomorrow. Do you mind if we meet somewhere?"

"No. I think that's a good idea. I don't want my mother hounding me with speculation." They agreed on a restaurant and ended their conversation.

Angelina had a horrible start to her first day. She'd awakened with a pounding headache. She dressed and went down for breakfast—she had to be ready for school, regardless of any headache.

Her mother could tell she wasn't feeling well. "You okay?"

"Yeah, I've just got a killer of a headache." She was running behind, so she quickly grabbed her breakfast and hurried out the door. Just as she was ready to close the door, she told her mother she wouldn't be home for dinner as she had a meeting.

"What about your headache?"

"I'll deal with it. See you tonight."

Her mother wished her a good day, but wondered what she was up to.

Angelina's class was out of control. They were forced to have indoor recess due to the abundance of snow and wind chill temperatures. Her head continued to throb and the noise levels were making it worse by the minute. Somehow she got through her day and had never been happier when the bell rang.

Gabriella came by on her way out. She could tell Angelina still wasn't feeling well. "You still have that headache?"

"What do you think? I couldn't wait for this day to end."

"It's always hard getting back after a long break… Come on, let's pack you up and go home."

"I have somewhere to go tonight."

"Call if off."

"No. I'll be fine."

"Okay… See you tomorrow. I hope you feel better."

"Thanks."

Angelina organized her classroom and graded a few papers from the day. She wished that her headache would go away. Nothing seemed to help. She was just going to have to grin and bear it. She hadn't seen Alejandro in a week and was looking forward to their dinner. She didn't want to miss their evening. She missed him.

Alejandro was waiting for Angelina in the bar area of the restaurant. He saw her park her car, then noticed her hand pressed to her forehead. She was holding her eyes. She sat in her car for a good minute before opening the door. He watched her walk towards the restaurant. He didn't want to overwhelm her with his concern, so he decided not to say anything.

When she entered the bar, he walked towards her. He placed his hand on her shoulder and gave her a quick peck on the cheek. He looked into her eyes and could tell she wasn't feeling right. He wasn't going to push her. "Rough day?"

"You could say that. The kids were out of control. Indoor recess, mind you, so they couldn't get rid of their excess energy. Plus, I woke up with a killer of a headache."

"Still have it?"

"You could say so… But I'm fine. A good night's sleep will remedy it."

"You know what, instead of dinner here, let's go to my place and we'll order in and relax. Maybe that will ease your headache."

She smiled at him, nodded, and then followed him to his house. He'd placed a delivery order on the way from the neighborhood deli so they wouldn't have to wait for their meal. The driver met them as they pulled into his driveway. She was thankful that they'd gone to his house—it would be much quieter. She could take her shoes off, let her hair down, and relax.

Alejandro dimmed the lights in the dining room, and they ate their meal. He'd ordered the house special that included a salad, deli sandwich, and even dessert—chocolate chip cookies. He cleaned up, and they moved to the family room where he put on some soft music. He sat beside her on the sofa and pulled her into his arms. "Close your eyes," he said as he started to massage her temples. Before she knew it, her headache had lessened, and then it was gone.

"Boy, you sure have magic fingers. I feel better already."

They sat on the couch listening to the music. He'd told her about his week at the hospital. "Another chaotic one for the books," he said.

She listened intently and then turned to him, "I missed you."

Surprisingly, he nodded in agreement as he played with her hair. "I missed you, too. There were times when I was in my office late at night and wanted to call you."

"Why didn't you?"

"Did you want a phone call at three in the morning?"

Turning in his arms, she looked him directly in the eyes. "From you, I'd say yes."

"Well, thanks. Maybe next time I'll pick up the phone and make that call."

She smiled at him.

"Angelina, I haven't said a thing about us to my family."

"Nor I. We're just friends hanging out having a good time. Right?"

"Right... At least for now. As I said, I don't know if—"

"I know. Let's just take it one day at a time. I'm definitely not looking for anything long-term. I just want someone to go out and have some fun with. You're it right now."

"Thanks for understanding."

What Alejandro didn't know was that she didn't understand. She wanted to know what his issues were. She imagined, in time, he'd tell her. She'd be patient.

It was nearing ten o'clock and Angelina needed to get home. "Thanks for the evening. I had a great time, especially after I got rid of my headache. I'll call you again if I need your magic fingers."

"Anytime," he said. He walked her to her car. He gave her a hug and quick peck on the cheek. "I'll call you tomorrow."

"I'll look forward to it."


Her phone rang at five thirty the next morning. She'd already showered and dressed for the day. Alejandro couldn't get her off his mind. He was up the entire night trying to get through his dictations when he phoned her.

"Good morning," he said. "I hope this is a better start to your day than yesterday."

"Good morning to you, too. And yes, the day is beginning so much brighter than yesterday." She meant this only because of his call.

"Just thought I'd check to see if your headache returned."

"Nope. It's been gone since that fabulous massage. Did I mention you have the best fingers?"

"Only about a half-dozen times. Seriously, though. How are you?"

"Fabulous. What better way to start my day off than by taking a call from you. How come you're calling so early?"

"Couldn't sleep."

"Alejandro, really now."

"How about I couldn't get you off my mind. I tried to complete my dictations and all I could think of was you. I—"

"Alejandro…"

"Are you busy tonight?"

"I have a meeting at the end of the day to discuss Career Day."

"Oh, thank you for reminding me. I'm supposed to attend that as well."

"You are?"

"Mary asked me. How about we decide after the meeting if we want to do something?"

"That's fine. I'll see you later."

"Angelina."

"Yeah?"

"Have a good day. And if that headache returns, just think of my fingers massaging your temples." She ended the call with a huge smile on her face. The day couldn't pass fast enough for her.

Angelina couldn't wait until four o'clock when their meeting was scheduled. She went to make a call during her afternoon break and noticed she had a voicemail message. It was from Alejandro.

"Angelina, it's me. I'm going to have to beg out of our date this evening. Something's come up that I have to deal with. I'm sure I won't be done before four. I'll call Mary and let her know. I'm sorry. I was really looking forward to seeing you. I'll call you later, I promise."

Angelina was saddened by his message. She was so looking forward to seeing him. She should have never listened to his voicemail because now the rest of her day was ruined. Thankfully, Mary began the meeting on time. All of the teachers and many of the speakers were present. The meeting was about half over when they heard a noise in the hallway. The door opened and in walked Alejandro. He'd somehow made it to the meeting. As he entered, he found

Angelina with his eyes. A huge smile crossed his face. Gabriella wasn't able to ignore it, especially when he chose the vacant seat across from Angelina. She also had a humongous smile on her face—the likes of which Gabriella hadn't seen in a very long time. Gabriella wasn't going to let that non-verbal communication go. She couldn't wait for Mary to end the meeting so she could confront them to see what was going on.

Throughout the remainder of the meeting, Alejandro couldn't keep his eyes off of Angelina. All that Gabriella could think about was that something was going on between them.

The meeting ended and Mary approached Alejandro. "I didn't think you could make it."

"I was able to complete the procedure that I needed to. I knew how much this meeting meant to you, so I knew you wouldn't mind if I was late."

"Not at all. Thanks for coming. I know how busy you are."

Alejandro felt Gabriella approach. "Hey, Gabby. How are you?"

"Fine." Looking over her shoulder, he could see Angelina mingling with several of the speakers.

Gabriella could tell that Alejandro wasn't paying attention to her. Turning, she saw who he was looking at. Angelina. "Be straight with me. What's going on here?"

"What do you mean?"

"Out with it Alejandro." Turning, she pointed at Angelina. "What's going on here?"

"I have no idea what you're talking about."

"Fine. Don't tell me, but I'll find out."

Shrugging his shoulders, he asked her what she was doing that evening. "Nothing. Why?"

"Want to get a bite to eat?" With that Angelina walked over. She smiled sheepishly at him. Returning the smile, he said, "Hi, Angelina." He didn't want Gabriella to catch on to them. "I just asked Gabby to join me for dinner. Are you game?"

She wasn't sure what he wanted her to say. While she was pondering his invitation, Gabriella said, "Come on. Join us. It sounds like my brother's treating."

"Well then I guess I can't pass up the invitation."

They went to a neighborhood restaurant known for its salads and buffalo wing sauce. The sauce was used on anything from chicken strips on a salad to chicken sandwiches, and most of all its famous buffalo wings.

When Gabriella excused herself to use the restroom, Alejandro said, "She's onto us."

"What do you mean?"

"She thinks something's up between us."

"Well, isn't there?"

"Yes. No... You know. Anyway, I don't want her freaking out and pushing us into something we're not ready for. Act like you have no idea what she's talking about. I want us to progress on our own terms and not our family's."

"Most definitely. She won't get anything out of me. Thanks for warning me."

When Gabriella returned, she looked at them. She thought they looked a little sheepish, but didn't question them. She'd find out what was going on.

They finished dinner and were talking when Alejandro's cell rang. He needed to return to the hospital. He paid the bill and left. Gabriella and

Angelina decided to walk back to school. Gabriella brought up Alejandro's name several times, but Angelina quickly changed the subject each time. She wasn't ready to discuss her brother.

Once they arrived at school, Gabriella immediately left to go home while Angelina returned to her classroom to retrieve some papers that required grading. She was halfway to her classroom when her phone rang. It was Alejandro. "Where are you?"

"Leaving the hospital. What about you?"

"On my way to my classroom. Gabriella already left, but I needed to grab some papers that need grading tonight. Why?"

"Want to come by my house for a while?"

"I'd love to, but it's getting late and I need to grade these papers. I promised my student's that I'd have the results tomorrow. They're anxious."

"How about I help you grade them, that way you'll be able to get through it twice as fast."

"You really want to help me?"

"Sure. I really want to see you."

"You're sure?"

"Yep, I'm more than sure. See you in fifteen minutes."

"Sounds like a plan."

Angelina arrived at his house exactly fifteen minutes later. He was waiting for her with a glass of wine in hand.

"Wow," was all she said as she took the offered glass. She walked in with her backpack filled with the tests that needed grading. He'd already setup shop in the family room. Between the two of them, they graded the math tests in record time. Letting out a deep breath, she thanked him for his help. "I can't believe we graded these tests in a half hour. I know it would have taken me at least an hour or more. Are you for hire?"

Laughing, he put down his stack of papers and pulled her into his arms. "I'm for hire anytime as long as my payment is this." He looked into her eyes, smiled, and kissed her.

She put her arms around his neck and pulled him closer. "I think I could get used to this."

They spent the rest of the night sitting in one another arms, necking like high schoolers. "We've got to stop this. I feel like I'm back in high school. except this time I'm comfortably sitting on a couch and back then I was stuffed like a sardine in the backseat of a compact car," she said.

When it was nearing ten, Angelina told him that she needed to get going. "I had a fantastic evening."

"As did I. I'm on-call tomorrow, and I need to stay pretty close to the hospital. Would you like to come by and have dinner?"

"Wow!" she said. "You want me to come to the hospital? Wouldn't we stand out as a couple?"

"Nah… Most people would think you were there for a check-up or maybe even visiting a patient. If you come around six, most everyone will be gone. I'll call you at the end of the day and let you know if that's a problem. I never know one minute to the next how my day is going to play out." He walked her to her car and again pulled her into his arms for one last kiss.

*What am I getting myself into,* he asked himself. *I think she's getting under my skin. Eventually, I'm going to have to tell her about my past.*

# CHAPTER TWELVE

The next day Angelina wore a new dress. She greeted her mother in the kitchen. Her mother immediately complimented her on her dress. It was navy blue with long sleeves that were piped in white on the cuffs. It hung just below her knees, and was cinched at the waist with a navy colored belt. It wasn't anything special but perfect to teach in.

"I love that dress. Is it new? The color looks lovely on you. Are you going somewhere today?"

Her mother could ask more questions in a matter of seconds and Angelina elected to dismiss them all except for one. "No, I'm not going anywhere. I have a meeting this evening. Why?"

"You just look really pretty today, that's all."

"Thanks, Mom. I appreciate it. By the way, I'm not sure when I'll be home."

"You're having a lot of meetings lately."

"We're preparing for Career Day and I think the planning's a little bit more intense than Mary thought." Angelina thought the excuse sounded plausible. Hopefully, her mother would buy into it. "See you sometime this evening." Angelina walked out the door hoping her mother didn't see through her lie.

During Angelina's afternoon break, she checked her phone to see if Alejandro had left any messages. There were none, so she thought their date was still on. She'd just walked Lauren out after their tutoring session when her phone rang. Breathlessly, she answered it.

"What's wrong and why are you out of breath?"

"I'm fine. I just ran in the door to catch my phone before it went to voicemail. Are we still on?"

"Yep. Come by my office at six."

"See you then."

"Angelina?"

"Yes?"

"I'm looking forward to seeing you. Drive safely."

Angelina smiled as she hung up. He was looking forward to seeing her... Before leaving for the hospital, she applied a fresh round of make-up. She, too, couldn't wait to see him.

"Mrs. Samuels, it's Gabriella. How are you?"

"Wonderful. And you?"

"Great. Is Angelina home? I tried her cell and got her voicemail. I need to ask her a question."

"Gabriella, she's at school. She told me she had a meeting to attend regarding Career Day."

Gabriella didn't know what to say. There was no meeting that she was aware of. She decided to play stupid. "Oh, that's right. She's on a special committee. I forgot all about it."

"I'm sure her phone is off because of that. Why don't you try her later?"

"I will. Thank you." Gabriella wasn't sure what was going on with Angelina. Now she was lying to her mother. Something was up, and she was going to get to the bottom of it. She hoped her friend wasn't in trouble.

Angelina pulled into the hospital garage right at six. She checked her lipstick one last time and entered the hospital. Almost immediately she heard her name being called. She turned and ran directly into Alejandro's father. "Ah, Dr. A. It's good to see you."

"How are you feeling, dear?"

"I'm feeling really well. Thank you for asking."

"What are you doing here?"

She knew she was going to get caught, so she quickly came up with an excuse. "Uh, I'm here to see a friend."

"I'm sorry to hear that. I hope she gets better."

"Well, thank you. I think she's actually going to be released tomorrow."

"That's good. I'd better let you go. In fact, I'm late for dinner myself. Take care and I'll see you soon."

Angelina blew out a breath as Alejandro's father headed for his car. *That was a close call*, she thought. Just to be safe, she took the first available elevator up just in case Alejandro's father returned. When she finally made her way to Alejandro's offices, she was a nervous wreck. Her hands were shaking and she was slightly pale. She knocked on the back door and Alejandro answered it.

"What's wrong? You look like you've seen—"

"Your father."

"What did you say?"

"I just ran into him. I had to think quickly, so I told him a lie—I said I was visiting a friend."

"Come here," he said as he pulled her into his arms. His offices were empty except for the two of them. "You're shaking…"

"I know, I am. I was so surprised to hear someone call out my name. And to top it off, that someone was your father."

He guided her down the hallway to his private office where their dinner awaited them. He sat beside her on the couch.

"I thought I was going to get caught. I told him I was checking on a friend."

"Did he believe you?"

"I think so. I took the first available elevator to a patient's floor just to be on the safe side."

"Angelina, my dad didn't think twice about it. Let's forget about it and eat." Alejandro had ordered take-out from the on-site Italian restaurant. They started off with a green salad. He also ordered a pasta dish, eggplant parmesan, and chicken marsala. They shared all of the dishes and, as they ate, they talked. She recounted her day and how happy her students were that she'd found the time to grade their tests. "I still can't believe you helped me grade them."

"Why?"

"Well, isn't that beneath you?"

"Why would you say that? Any time that I can spend with you is well worth it. As I said last night, I'll help you anytime."

"I think I'll call you when I have to calculate grades at the end of the semester."

"I'll be ready."

Just as Alejandro was ready to serve the tiramisu, they were interrupted when he was paged over the hospital intercom. "I better go. Do you want to wait around?"

"No, I should go home. I don't want to raise any red flags with my family."

"Here, take the dessert with you. I'll call you tomorrow."

"Thanks again for a lovely evening." Pointing at the tiramisu, she said, "Thanks for this, too. It's my favorite dessert."

"I'm just sorry our evening had to end so early. Come here." With that, he drew her into his arms, kissed her, and wished her a good evening. He walked with her to the end of the hallway and headed off to deal with his patient.

Angelina's mother was waiting for her when she got home. Since she'd lied to her mother about her whereabouts, she hid her dessert in her backpack. She couldn't wait to dig into the creamy layers of lady fingers.

"Angelina. Where were you?"

"I was at a meeting. Don't you believe me?"

"No, actually I don't. Gabriella called looking for you. She couldn't reach you on your cell."

"Oh," she said. "Well, I was at a meeting. I'm sorry she didn't remember that." Angelina's face flushed.

Her mother noticed, but decided against continuing her line of questioning. Whatever Angelina was up to, she was sure she had good reason for keeping it to herself. Eventually she'd discover what was going on with her daughter.

Angelina rushed to her room and called Alejandro. He answered on the second ring. "You okay?"

"Yeah. We've got problems."

"What's wrong?"

"My mother. She knows I lied to her about my meeting."

"Why do you say that? Did she catch you with your dessert?"

"No, she didn't."   She informed him of their conversation. "I'm worried what Gabriella's going to say."

"Don't. I'll deny anything if she brings you into the equation, and you can do the same. What's the problem?"

"I hate lying."

"If anyone finds out, we'll blame it on me."

"Alejandro."

"Just stop worrying. I'll handle it."

"But?"

"No buts. Now, do you miss me?"

"What do you think?"   She talked softly because she didn't want her family overhearing their conversation. "I can't wait to see you again. Are you on call the rest of the week?"

"Unfortunately, yes. But I'm off the entire weekend. Why don't you come over Saturday morning and we'll talk without interruption? How does that sound? And, maybe by then, we'll know where we stand with our families."

"Give me a call and let me know when you want me to come over. Again, thanks for a great dinner. I really enjoyed it. Goodnight."

"'Night. And Angelina? Sweet dreams."

"Thanks." Angelina disconnected the call with the biggest smile on her face. Maybe they were going somewhere. Hopefully their planned talk would settle the true status of their relationship. She went to bed dreaming of what might be.

The next morning, Gabriella was waiting for Angelina at the door to her classroom. Angelina saw her and wasn't looking forward to their discussion— she'd have to lie again. "I called your house last night and spoke to your mom."

"I know, she told me."

"Where were you?"

"Shopping."

"Shopping? She told me you were at a meeting."

"You know, I think she got mixed up. I told her I was going shopping for some materials for my classroom. I'm sure she misunderstood me."

"Your mom misunderstood you? Come on, Angelina, where were you?"

"Like I said, shopping."

"Fine, whatever." Gabriella gave up and walked away.

She knew Gabriella didn't believe her. She just hoped that she didn't put two and two together. She didn't believe their stories would hold up with Gabriella. She was intuitive, especially when her brother was involved. She was sure Gabriella had already figured out that something was up between them. She'd have to get in touch with Alejandro before Gabriella called him.

Angelina's day was an up-hill battle from the moment she entered her classroom. Between dealing with Gabriella, and then having to deal with a student cheating on a test, she thought she was going to lose it. During her morning break, she called Alejandro at his office, but he was with a patient and couldn't take her call. She didn't want to leave her name with his secretary, so she called his cell and left a message. "She's onto us," she said and then hung up. At lunch, she checked her phone and he hadn't returned her call. While she was heading off to pick her students up from music class, the school secretary stopped her in the hallway. She was carrying a huge bouquet of flowers. "These are for you."

"Me?" she asked.

"Yep. They were just delivered. I wonder who they're from."

Angelina felt giddy with excitement. "Is there a card?"

The secretary found one and pulled it out.

Angelina opened it. Two words were printed on it: "I know." She knew who they were from. She'd call him as soon as school let out for the day. Angelina asked the secretary to take the flowers to her classroom while she picked up her students from music class. Angelina was thankful for the day-ending bell. Her students rushed from the classroom, which was great because she couldn't wait to speak with Alejandro to thank him for the flowers. Angelina was packing up her backpack when Gabriella stopped by her classroom as she was leaving for the day.

"Where in the world did you get those flowers? They're gorgeous!"

"A friend."

"Who? Let's see the card." Angelina tried to keep the card from her, but Gabriella snatched it.

"There's no name. Just, 'I know.'"

Angelina was getting very frustrated with Gabriella's interference.

"Well, I know who they're from and that's what counts." Angelina snapped at Gabriella. She turned away from her and walked to the back of her classroom.

"Angelina, what's going on here?"

"Nothing. Why?"

"Why are you mad at me?"

"Can't I get flowers from a friend?"

"Yes, but—"

"That's enough Gabriella. Just leave it alone, okay?"

"Okay… I'll stop bothering you." Gabriella was perplexed by Angelina's attitude towards her. "See you tomorrow." Gabriella said as she marched from her room.

Angelina also said goodbye, but she was sure that Gabriella didn't hear her. Gabriella could be Gabriella and when something got under her skin, she didn't give up until she got her answers. Except this time Angelina wasn't going to give in—Gabriella would just have to live with it.

When Gabriella left Angelina's classroom, she was concentrating on her own thoughts. She uttered under her breath, "I'll stop bothering you, but I won't give up on getting my answers from my brother." Gabriella knew that she could be over the top at times, but that was just her personality. She wasn't angry with Angelina. She just wanted to know what she was hiding. She assumed she was possibly involved with someone, but Angelina hadn't shared anything of that nature with her. She hoped it was her brother, but didn't know for sure.

Angelina left the flowers in her classroom to avoid the questions that she knew she'd get from her mother. She called Alejandro from her car—this time, he answered.

"Did you get my surprise?"

"Yes, they're gorgeous. Thank you so much. It was a nice surprise… Alejandro, I think we really have a problem. I know Gabriella thinks something is going on between us."

"I'll deal with her. Don't worry."

"But I do."

Ignoring her comment, he asked, "So, how was your day?"

"Other than dealing with Gabriella and a student cheating, it was great. Your flowers really helped turn it around. They're absolutely beautiful."

"I'm glad you liked them and were surprised. I wanted to do something special for you because I know this sneaking around is really hard on you. We'll talk this weekend about what our next steps are. What're you doing this evening?"

"What I do almost every night—grading papers."

"I'd love to help, but I'm a little busy here. If I get a chance, I'll give you a call later on."

"Call me after ten o'clock. I should be in my bedroom and my parents won't hear me."

"I'll do my best. If I get busy, I'll talk to you sometime tomorrow."

Smiling into the phone she said, "Thanks again for the flowers. They made my day."

Angelina spent the evening grading papers and helping her brother with his homework. She looked at the clock, and it was nearing ten. She didn't want to miss Alejandro in case he called, but Wyatt was having a hard time with his math, and Angelina wanted to make sure he understood the concept before he went to bed.

She was so relieved when Wyatt finally understood it and started putting his things away. Turning to her parents, she wished them a goodnight. She rushed to her room and waited for his call. It never came. She decided to grade the remainder of her papers because she didn't want to go to sleep. Just as she was beginning to doze off, she heard a muffled ring. She'd placed her phone under her pillow so it wouldn't wake her family in the event that it rang. Grabbing it, she said, "Hi." It was almost midnight.

"Sorry I'm calling so late. I had an emergency. I hoped that you were still awake. Did you get all of your paperwork completed?"

"Just finished. Wyatt was having some problems with his homework, so I helped him."

"What a sister."

"Yeah, right."

"Any issues this evening with your family?"

"None especially since I left my flowers at school. Maybe it's blown over."

"Time will tell."

They talked a few more minutes and Alejandro got another page. He didn't mention Gabriella, so she assumed she hadn't caught up with her brother.

"Gotta go. Sorry about that."

"That's fine. Get some rest."

"I will. You, too."

They ended their conversation shortly after midnight. She had a hard time getting to sleep, finally drifting off around dawn. She got about an hour's sleep when she heard her mother pounding on her door.

"Angelina, are you okay?"

When she didn't answer, her mother entered her room. Angelina was brushing the sleep from her eyes.

"Guess I overslept." Looking at the clock, she couldn't believe the time. She jumped up from bed and hurried to the bathroom. She took a shower and dressed in record time. She was forced to skip breakfast and made it to school just in time for the first bell. What had happened to her? *Alejandro*, she thought. She just couldn't get him out of her mind.

She checked her phone during her mid-morning break. Alejandro had left her a message. He hoped that she'd been able to get some sleep. He told her he'd had a horrendous evening. The page that he took turned into a lengthy surgery. He was tired, but would call her later in the day when his schedule permitted.

She somehow got through her day and was exhausted when the last bell rang. On the way home, she decided to forgo grading papers that evening and elected to stay in her room. She sat on her bed, trying to relax. Soft music played in the background and her mind kept drifting off. She was dreaming—dreaming of a possible future with Alejandro. She knew she shouldn't go there because he'd adamantly told her that he wouldn't enter into a full blown relationship, but time would tell, she thought. She wouldn't push him. They were fine being friends… But she could hope.

He didn't call that evening, and she slept much better. She got up at her usual time and had just finished dressing when her phone rang. It was Alejandro. "Sorry I called so early, but I wanted to apologize for not calling last night."

"That's okay. I know you're busy."

"Another busy night, but I was able to get someone to cover for me tonight. How about coming over for dinner?"

"I'd better skip dinner. I'll come over after. I don't want my mother to get any more curious."

"That's fine. I'll see you when I see you. Have a great day."

"I will. You, too." Smiling, she hung up the phone, gathered her backpack, and headed off to the kitchen.

"Angelina, was that your phone that rang earlier?"

"Ahh, no."

"Are you sure? I thought I heard you talking to someone."

"No, that was a gimmick on the radio. That's all."

Hurriedly, she ate her breakfast. She needed to get out of the house before her mother questioned her further.

Her day went well. Gabriella left her alone, and there were no cheating scandals for the day. She couldn't wait until she saw Alejandro. She ate dinner and helped Wyatt again with his math homework. Her mother noticed that she kept looking at the clock. Right after seven, Angelina decided she needed something for a project she was doing in her classroom the following day.

"Angelina, that's not like you to forget to stop on the way home," commented Wyatt.

"Well, I did." Now Wyatt was questioning her behavior. Pretty soon her entire family would know she was up to something.

Grabbing her purse, she headed out the door. Alejandro lived only a few minutes from her house, and she was there almost before she could take another breath. She was going to be caught, and soon.

Alejandro was waiting at the door when she pulled into his driveway. He was anxious to see her. He opened the door and pulled her into his arms.

"Come here," he said. "I've dreamed about this all day." He began kissing her, then pulled away. "What's wrong?"

"We've got to talk."

"About what?"

"Us. We've got to decide what we're going to do. I am going to get caught in all of these lies."

"Angelina, take a breath and calm down."

"Wyatt's onto me now. I can't stay long—I told him I was running off to the store to get something for my classroom."

"Can you stay an hour?"

Nodding, she agreed to that. He poured her a glass of wine. He hoped that she'd take time to relax. Handing her the wine, they sat down on the couch.

"This is good. I'm feeling better."

"Good." He pulled her into his arms and held her. He began to play with her hair. She loved it when he did that. "Angelina, I know we need to talk. I'd hoped we could tonight, but I can tell we definitely don't have the time. I promise we will this weekend."

She nodded and sat wrapped in his arms. She'd drifted off to sleep when he nudged her awake. "Angelina, it's almost ten. I guess you'd better go."

Cringing, she said, "Ten o'clock? Oh my gosh. What am I going to do?"

"First of all, you're going to take a deep breath. Then you're going to kiss me. After that, I guess I'll have to let you go home."

They briefly kissed and he walked her to her car. "Drive safely."

"I will. Now I've got to make up another story to explain why I wasn't home earlier," she said, anxiously.

"I'm sure you'll come up with a believable one. I'll try and call you tomorrow, but I'm not sure how busy my schedule will be. We'll definitely talk before Saturday." He kissed her goodbye and watched her as her car lights disappeared around the corner. Where was he going with this? He didn't know. It felt good, but he didn't want to betray… He couldn't think about his issues. He needed to go inside and review the file of a patient he was seeing the following day.

Angelina pulled into her driveway and saw the curtains in the front window move. She was sure it was her mother watching for her. She was thirty years old—she should be able to come and go as she pleased. If not, maybe she should think about moving out. Her life would be her own.

"Angelina, where have you been? I was getting worried."

"Shopping for my classroom."

"At this late hour?"

"I lost track of time. I stopped by the bookstore on the way home and got a coffee. I got involved reading a magazine."

"You're sure about that?"

"Mom, I am thirty years old. If I can't come and go as I please, maybe I need to look for a place of my own." Angelina stormed down the hallway towards her bedroom.

Jackie couldn't believe her ears. Where did that tirade come from? Angelina never spoke to her in that manner. She wondered what had gotten into her daughter. She'd noticed the change in her around the end of last year. She'd hoped to get answers soon.

# CHAPTER THIRTEEN

Angelina and Alejandro spoke on Friday to set up a time to meet the following day. She was nervous. If he wouldn't address his issues and allow them to share with their family what was going on, then she'd just have to break it off—she couldn't continue lying to her family.

Her parents were attending a hockey tournament with Wyatt, so she didn't have to worry about them. She dressed and drove over to Alejandro's home. She couldn't eat because she feared the outcome of the day.

The phone rang and Alejandro answered it immediately, thinking it was Angelina. Instead, it was Gabriella.

"Alejandro, what's new?"

"Not much. I've been busy at the hospital. Why? What about you?"

"Oh, not much. Whatcha doing today?"

"Ahh… I'm going out… And—"

His doorbell rang. Phone in hand as he answered the door, he placed his finger to his lips, but was too slow; Angelina had already said hello.

"What was that? Who's there?" asked Gabriella.

"Ahh, no one. You just heard the television."

"Alejandro, you don't watch TV. Who's there?"

"What do you want, Gabby? I told you I'm busy today."

"Well, I want to come over. I need to talk to you."

"Gabby. I told you, I'm busy."

"You mean you don't have five minutes for your sister?"

He looked at Angelina who still stood on the front porch. He stepped aside so she could enter. Pacing, he said, "Fine. Why don't you come over this evening for dinner? I'll cook."

"Why not sooner?"

"Gabby, you're pushing too hard. If you can't make it for dinner, then I guess we'll have to do it another time."

"That's fine. I'll see you at five." Gabriella wasn't too happy with her brother. She wanted answers and she wanted them now.

Alejandro hung up the phone and looked at Angelina. She looked distressed. He just knew they were in trouble. Both of them were digging a grave. They had to decide what to do today, before Gabby came over and before Angelina had to deal with her mother again.

"Boy am I glad to see you," he said as he pulled her into a tight embrace.

She immediately pulled away. "We have to talk, and now!"

Alejandro didn't like her tone. *What's wrong now,* he thought.

"Come on in and sit down. Something to drink?"

Looking up at him, she asked for a stiff drink.

"How about orange juice instead?" he said as he turned towards the kitchen.

"I guess I'll have to settle for that."

Alejandro returned and handed her the glass of juice. She immediately set it aside. Sitting next to her, he reached for her hands. Grasping them tightly, he looked into her eyes, "What's wrong?"

"Alejandro," she said. "We have to decide where this 'whatever we have' is going. I can't continue to lie to my parents, to Gabriella…"

"I know." He pulled her into his arms. "I'm just not—"

"Not what?" she snapped at him, withdrawing from his arms and standing. "Alejandro, we have to figure this out."

"I know."

"Is that all you have to say is 'I know?'"

"Angelina, it's complicated."

"How?"

"It just is."

"Tell me what the issue is."

"I can't. I can't deal with this right now."

"Well, either you deal with it or I'm out of here. I can't continue down this path. I'm on pins and needles all of the time. My mother knows something's up. My relationship with Gabriella is strained…"

"I realize that. It's just I can't share this with you or anyone right now. I have to deal with it myself."

Turning the tables on him, she said, "Maybe you should talk to someone about whatever's going on with you."

"Don't have time…"

"You know what, Alejandro. All you seem to have is excuses. Until you figure this out, we're over  You need to deal with whatever's going on with you. If you won't find someone to help you, then you'll have to deal with it by yourself. I guess I'll be seeing you around."

"Angelina, don't do this. Please… Stay. Let's talk. We can work this out."

Angelina didn't look back while he pleaded with her. She grabbed her purse and, with head held high, she waltzed through the front door and out of his life. Tears were streaming down her face as she left. She thought they could make this work. She thought she could help him get through whatever was troubling him.

Angelina got in her car and drove away from Alejandro. Her cell rang several times, but she ignored it. She decided to run by school and work in her classroom—she always found solace there. She was there for only a few minutes when she started crying. Maybe she would feel better if she went home instead. There she could try and figure out what had just happened.

Alejandro's day was ruined. He'd planned on having a nice chat with Angelina, then that all fell apart. He spent the remainder of the day thinking about her. He knew he had to deal with his past, but he just couldn't right now. He kept pushing the memories aside, hoping time would heal his wounds.

Gabriella appeared promptly at five. He'd completely forgotten about their dinner. He'd been dealing with his thoughts and feelings since Angelina had walked out. He knew he'd looked a sight when he answered the door. "Gabriella?"

"What's up with you? You look like you've been through the ringer today."

"It's been a crazy day. How about a rain check?"

"How about you tell me what's going on with you and Angelina."

"What're you talking about? There's nothing going on with us."

"Come on, Alejandro. Are you two dating?"

Emphatically he said, "No." Now if she were asking him earlier in the day, he'd had to have lied. Now, his answer was the truth.

"Come on. You are."

"No, we're not. Now did you get out of me what you wanted?"

"Not really. I think you're dating, but I'll believe you for the time being. What about our dinner? Aren't you cooking?"

"Let's go out. I don't feel like cooking."

They went out for dinner. He enjoyed spending time with his sister, even though she could care too much about his personal life sometimes. They talked about the upcoming Career Day and what he was planning to present. They discussed the program he was trying to implement at the hospital. They finished eating and had been at the restaurant for quite some time when they started getting dirty looks from their waitress, so they decided to leave and call it a night. Alejandro gave his sister a hug, a quick peck on the cheek, and said goodbye. Alejandro drove by Angelina's house on the way home, wishing he'd get a call from her but knew he wouldn't.

The following Wednesday, Mary held her last planning meeting for Career Day.

Alejandro entered the teacher's lounge prior to the meeting. He immediately saw Gabriella. "Where's Angelina?"

"She went home with a migraine."

"Really?"

"Yes, she didn't look too good either. She said she's been getting them lately, but today she just couldn't push through it."

He wondered if he was the reason for her headache, but didn't get into it with his sister.

Their meeting lasted longer than expected, and Alejandro got a call right at the end of it. He had to go back to the hospital.

Career Day was scheduled for the end of the month and Alejandro didn't know if he could wait that long to see Angelina. January always seemed like such a long month and two weeks was a long time to wait… He was going crazy not talking to her. He wondered how she was doing with their separation.

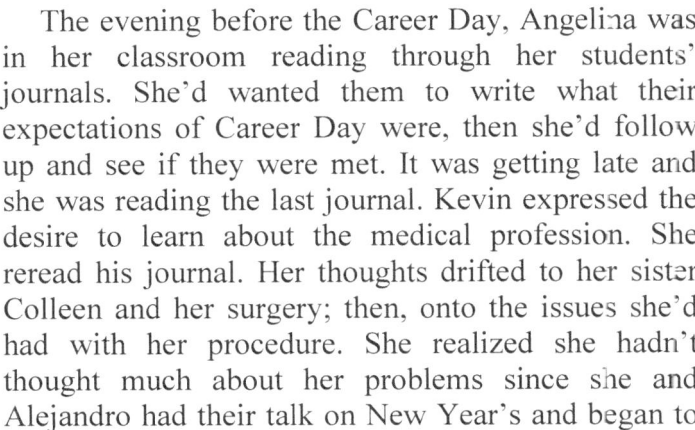

The evening before the Career Day, Angelina was in her classroom reading through her students' journals. She'd wanted them to write what their expectations of Career Day were, then she'd follow up and see if they were met. It was getting late and she was reading the last journal. Kevin expressed the desire to learn about the medical profession. She reread his journal. Her thoughts drifted to her sister Colleen and her surgery; then, onto the issues she'd had with her procedure. She realized she hadn't thought much about her problems since she and Alejandro had their talk on New Year's and began to tear up. She wiped the tears from her face, but they continued to fall.

She heard a noise and looked up. Alejandro was standing in her doorway. Just her luck, he'd caught her crying again. He walked into her room and looked her squarely in the eyes. He opened his mouth to speak, but stopped. When he neared her side, he brushed his thumb across her cheek, catching one of the tears. Smiling, he said, "Last time I came in here you were crying."

"Yeah, just thinking about some stuff. That's all."

"I've been thinking about you a lot lately. I miss you."

"I miss you, too. But you know why this won't work. Until you can deal with—"

"I know. I'm just sorry that it's come to this. Can you just tell me what upset you?"

"I asked the class to think about what they wanted to get out of tomorrow. Kevin indicated that he wanted to hear about the medical profession."

"That caused you to cry?"

"Yeah. I was thinking about Colleen and my infection, and I just teared up. I'm fine now."

"Sure?"

"Yeah. I've got to get going. I have a lot to do before tomorrow. My mom is expecting me for dinner and I need to pick Wyatt up from school."

"I won't keep you. I'll see you tomorrow."

Angelina packed her bag and locked her classroom. Alejandro waited and walked her to her car. "Angelina?"

"I'll see you tomorrow," she said. He stepped back from her car as she got in and drove off. He'd really messed things up. He needed to fix them. He needed to open up and share things with her. Maybe he'd be able to do that soon.

The next day, Angelina was anxious. She didn't want to face Alejandro or Gabriella during Career Day. She was afraid Gabriella would bring up her brother, and she just didn't want to talk about him.

She made it through the day without any incidents. Alejandro was just as gracious as ever. Angelina attended his second-to-last presentation before the day was over. She sat in the back of the classroom while Alejandro spoke about his profession and described what he did as a transplant surgeon, how he changed people's lives when they thought nothing could be done to save them. He discussed what it meant to be an organ donor.

Everyone was glued to their chairs while Alejandro spoke. He spoke eloquently about why he did what he did. He brought the presentation down to the level of the students so they could fully understand what he did—he saved lives. He got some excellent questions and received the loudest round of applause that Angelina had heard the entire day.

Angelina was proud of him. She left the room as the children stood to move onto their last speaker. Alejandro hadn't realized she was in the room—he had been so engrossed in his presentation. By the time he looked towards the back of the room, she was gone and the last group of children was entering the room.

Mary gathered all of the speakers in the gym at the end of the day to thank them and to present everyone with a plaque. Alejandro and Angelina shared a glance across the room. She smiled at him then looked away. Gabriella caught the exchange and knew she had been right—something was going on between them.

Gabriella decided not to question them. She'd wait and see if anything more happened. Angelina seemed reserved as of late, and Gabriella didn't want to push her. They shared everything when they were in college and, when they first rediscovered each other at the beginning of the year, she seemed like her old self. But since she'd had her medical issues, Gabriella had seen a change in her friend. She didn't know if she should worry or not. Maybe she was imagining it and maybe not. If it continued, she'd contact Angelina's mother to see what she thought. Something was wrong and, by God, she'd discover what was troubling her.

Spring came early with horrendous rains. They'd had a terrific amount of snow pack and the rain was causing it to melt too fast. The ground was still partially frozen and the weathermen were forecasting flash flooding throughout the entire area.

Alejandro hated this weather. It brought back too many memories, memories he tried to forget... memories he knew he'd have to deal with if he ever wanted a relationship with Angelina.

Alejandro was off service for the week and had stayed close to home—he didn't want to be out in the storms, and he had enough to do around the house anyway. He'd never completely unpacked from his move and decided he'd try and finish. All of the boxes were stacked in closets or were stored in the basement out of sight.

It was early evening and a huge storm was passing overhead. Warnings continued to scroll across the television. He was watching the news (which he rarely did) when his phone rang. Checking the caller ID, he saw it was his sister.

"Alejandro, I'm worried."

"What about?"

"Angelina. She was running home to change her clothes and then she was coming over to work on grades—"

Interrupting her, he said, "It's that time again?" Alejandro's mind drifted away. He recalled a conversation he'd had with Angelina earlier in the year. She was going to call him to help with grades. Well, he knew that would never happen.

"Alejandro, she should have been here a long time ago."

"What do you want me to do?"

"I don't know. Her cell phone just goes to voicemail. I tried her house, but there was no answer. I'm really worried about her."

"Do you want me to go see if she's home?"

"Would you? With the rain and potential flooding…"

"I'll call you when I know something."

Alejandro put on his raincoat, grabbed his phone, and headed out. He was sure she was on her way over to Gabby's, but thought it didn't hurt to check. As he pulled out of his garage, the rain fell hard on his windshield. When he got to the end of his driveway, he noticed how much water was actually standing in the street. He wasn't going to panic. He turned out of his driveway and headed towards Angelina's. He had to drive much slower than normal due to the ponding on the road, but made it to her house without incident. There were no cars in the driveway. He called Gabby again. She said that Angelina still wasn't there and hadn't returned any of her messages.

Alejandro didn't know what to do, so he drove towards Gabby's. As he approached the intersection near her house, he looked ahead and saw Angelina sitting in her car. Luckily, he was at the top of a hill while her car had stalled at the bottom and her emergency flashers were on. The water was rising quickly and panic was starting to set in. Grabbing his umbrella, he left his car in the middle of the street and headed towards her car. The current was getting swift and he was having a difficult time getting to her—the water almost upended him, but his adrenaline kept him going. When he reached her car, she looked panicked.

"Alejandro, please help me," she said through the window.

He pulled open her door and she threw herself into his arms. As quickly as possible, he made her grab her backpack and purse.

"Hurry up," he yelled to her. "We need to move to higher ground." She grabbed onto his sleeve as he led her back to his car. He opened his car door and practically threw her in. He got in the driver's side and, before he knew it, she'd thrown herself into his arms again.

"Oh my God," she said. "Those waters came out of nowhere. My car stalled. My cell wasn't working. I knew I needed to get out of there, but I was so frightened." Angelina gasped for breath.

"It's okay," he said as he stroked her back. "You're okay. Hey, I need to call Gabby and let her know you're fine. Then we'll call a tow truck and have your car towed. She was worried and sent me out to look for you."

"Thanks," she said as he made his calls. She watched his face and hands while he was on the phone. He seemed composed, but his hands were shaking. When he got off the phone and told her he was taking her to his house, she sighed in relief. They waited for the tow truck and then headed for his house. Her family was out for the night and she didn't want to go home alone.

They pulled into his garage and he turned off the motor. She watched him. He didn't move, but continued to grip the steering wheel. She asked him if he was okay, but he just sat there with his shaking hands glued to the wheel. She touched his forearm. With a look of panic in his eyes, he turned his head towards her. "Alejandro," she said. "Are you alright?"

He slowly nodded. Releasing his hands from the steering wheel, he looked her straight in the eyes and said, "It's time."

She looked perplexed.

"It's time that I share my past with you."

He exited the car and reached for her hand as he opened her door. He pulled her from the car and placed his hand on her cheek. "It's time I told you about Tammy and Michael." She had no idea what he was talking about, but she didn't want to interrupt him. She smiled at him and squeezed his hand. She had the feeling that he needed her strength. Hand in hand they walked inside, removing their coats as they entered through the mud room. He reached for her coat and hung it up in the closet next to his. He led her directly to the couch in the family room. She sat while he turned to watch the rain fall in sheets against the window. Closing his eyes, he took another deep breath and turned to Angelina. "I need to tell you about my wife and son."

Her eyes widened in shock, but she didn't say anything. *Wife and son?* she thought. Gabriella had never told her that he'd been married and had a child. Angelina was shocked to say the least, but she would give him the benefit of the doubt and hear what he had to say.

He started pacing back and forth and his hands were clenched at his side. He seemed as though he was reliving an event. Abruptly, he stopped. Turning to her, he said, "They died on a night like tonight. This is what I've needed to deal with. I guess I'm being forced to face it tonight. Tonight I was able to rescue you, but on that night I wasn't able to save my family." He walked over to the sofa and sat down. He leaned forward and folded his hands between his legs. Sighing, he sat back on the sofa. Staring straight ahead, he began to tell her his story.

"I met Tammy at UW Hospital. She was a nurse in Pediatrics. I'd performed a heart transplant on an infant and she was my patient's nurse. We made friends quickly and then began to date. We had so much in common. I'd never been in love before, but I fell head over heels in love with her almost right away. We were married within a year and Michael came along just after our first anniversary. We were ecstatic. He was the sweetest little boy. He looked exactly like his mother."

Pausing, he continued. "Tammy and I had been married four years. We'd been trying to have another baby. It was late spring and we were inundated with heavy rains. It had rained nonstop for three days. The rivers were all overflowing their banks. The farm fields were flooded. Tammy hadn't been feeling well, so she decided to go to the doctor. I'd been on service and couldn't go with her. Actually, I was in surgery at the time of her appointment. As I said, it was raining heavily. She was on her way back from the doctor when her car was swept away in a flash flood. The car overturned and she and Michael drowned." Closing his eyes, he finished his story. "She'd just found out that she was expecting our second child."

Angelina reached for his hands. "Alejandro…"

"I went through some pretty dark days. My family came up to support me, but I just couldn't handle it. Gabby stayed with me for a while. She helped me pack their things and donate them to charity. She'd wanted me to talk about it, but I couldn't. I couldn't face the fact that I'd lost everything that meant anything to me. I'd loved her with all of my heart and she was gone. I'd never see her smiling face again… I'd never see Michael grow up… I couldn't face the fact that I wasn't there for her. I'd promised to protect her always and I wasn't able to do that. She died on my watch. I should have been there to save her. I shouldn't have let her drive that day. I shouldn't have—" He stood abruptly and walked to the window. He just stared out at the rain.

She didn't know what to do or say. She was in shock. She stood and walked towards him, placing a hand on his shoulder. He turned and she pulled him into her arms.

"I didn't protect my family… It was my fault…"

"It was no one's fault, Alejandro. It was their time to go. You need to look at it as though there was another plan for them. You need to stop blaming yourself."

He burrowed his head into her shoulder. "Angelina, when Gabby called and asked me to go looking for you, I almost said no. These storms have had me on edge remembering all that happened. Then, I thought about how I wasn't there for Tammy, but maybe I could be there for you. When I saw your car stalled at the bottom of the hill, my heart went into my throat. I thought, 'not again.'"

He raised his head and looked into her eyes. "I couldn't get to you fast enough. I knew that I was going to do all that I could to save you. I couldn't believe the current when I reached your car. I knew that in a matter of minutes your car was going to be swept away. I knew I needed to get to my angel... to save and protect you."

"What did you call me?"

"My angel. Even though you might not realize it, you've led me down a path to face my past. You've pointed me in the right direction. I had to deal with my feelings. Before I moved here, I'd swept them under the rug. Tammy and Michael didn't exist in my heart any longer. I just couldn't face the fact that I'd never see them again. I knew I needed to relocate. I knew I needed to face their death. I was afraid that if I accepted their deaths, though, that I would move on and forget them. And that's something I never want to do."

"Come on, let's sit down," she said. They both moved back to the couch.

"This move was the best thing for me. After their deaths, I made a promise to myself that I would never marry and have children again. But after I met you, I was starting to doubt my pledge to myself. You were starting to make me feel again—have feelings that I never thought would be possible after losing Tammy. I knew I had to deal with them before I could commit to you, but I couldn't deal with my memories. We've been apart for almost two months because I couldn't face my fears. I was afraid to make a commitment. A commitment that could… I wanted to be your boyfriend without my baggage."

"Alejandro, they were your family. They were a part of you. You should never forget them."

"I know. It's just that I didn't feel that I could move on until I dealt with their deaths. Tonight, you've been here for me. You've helped me deal with my past."

"I'm glad I could be here for you."

"Angelina," he said as he placed his hand on her cheek. "I know I have a long way to go, but with you by my side I know I can face my past—overcome it and move ahead. I can't promise you anything, but will you stay by my side and help me through this?"

"Of course I will. Did you even have to ask?"

He pulled her towards him. Their lips met briefly in a soft kiss. Pulling away, he said, "Thank you." He pulled her into his arms and held her there for hours. They just sat there. No words were needed. He was dealing with his past and she was there supporting him. He'd get through this, she knew it in her heart. They'd survive and move on to a future of their own.

# CHAPTER FOURTEEN

Angelina sat in his arms until the rain subsided. It was almost nine o'clock when she called her parents to let them know what had happened. They were at a school function when Angelina called them. "Alejandro came by and pulled me from my car. What? Oh, yeah. Gabriella had sent him out to look for me… I was on my way over to her house and she got worried when I didn't show up and she couldn't reach me. I lost cell service during the storm… I'm at his house right now. I didn't want to go home by myself." She reached for his hand and smiled at him. "What? Yes, my car was towed to the house. Alejandro is going to take me home soon. Yes, I'll be fine. See you later."

Alejandro squeezed her hand and smiled at her. "My parents won't be home until later. They're playing it safe with the rain."

"When do you want to go home?"

"I don't care. I am content right where I am." She looked away from him and didn't know if she should confront him with her questions.

He sensed that something was on her mind, "What's wrong?"

"Ah, nothing…"

"Come on, Angelina. I know you pretty well and I know when something's bothering you."

"It's just…"

"Just what?"

"Where does this leave us?"

"I'm not sure. I know that I still have an awful lot to work through and I know you're a special person in my life. I'd like a relationship with you, but I'm not sure that I'm ready for that. And I don't think it's fair to you if I can't give you one hundred percent."

"Alejandro, I understand and I'd like to help you. I don't expect for you to be able to commit yourself to anyone until you resolve your feelings about your family. Let's just see where this goes. I'm also nowhere near ready to commit to a relationship. The only thing I ask is that we be up front with our families. I can't lie to my parents and Gabriella any longer."

"I understand. Why don't we approach it like this: we experienced this life altering situation with the flash flooding, we've decided we mean a lot to one another, and we're exploring a possible relationship. Angelina, we have pasts that we have to deal with before we can move forward. We both know that."

"Pasts? I don't have a past relationship that I need to deal with."

"Maybe not, but you do have to deal with your infertility problem."  He saw her swallowing her fears. "I don't think you've really addressed that. But I know I can help you, and you can help me deal with Tammy and Michael."

Nodding her head she said, "Okay. But Gabriella…"

"I'll deal with her. I'll just tell her what I told you. She can believe what she wants to believe. We'll act like nothing was going on between us before tonight. Agreed?"

"Sure."

Alejandro drove her home and waited until her parents arrived. The flash flooding had dissipated and the rain had almost stopped. They were sitting closely on the couch when her parents walked through the door. Her mother rushed to her and pulled her into her arms. "Angelina, I'm so glad that you're alright. Alejandro, thank you for saving our daughter."

"Think nothing of it. I'm just thankful Gabriella was concerned enough to contact me. I'm glad I got there before something really happened to Angelina." As Alejandro spoke, she turned back to him with a broad smile on her face. They talked for a period of time before Alejandro indicated that he needed to leave. Angelina walked him to the door. Hugging him, she asked if he'd call her later. Reaching for her hand, he told her he'd call, but he needed to run by Gabriella's first.

"Are you sure?"

"Yeah, it's something I have to do."

"Okay," she said as she pulled him closer. "I'm looking forward to your call."

Alejandro hugged her and headed for his car. She walked out onto the front porch and waved goodbye. She hoped that he would be okay talking to Gabriella. She decided that maybe she should go with him. She rushed to his car before he pulled from the driveway. "Alejandro?"

He heard her voice before he saw her standing next to his car. He slowed the car and put it in park. "My

God, Angelina. You scared me to death. What's wrong?" he asked as he jumped out of the car.

"Nothing." She was regretting running to his car.

"Angelina?"

"Can I go with you?" She looked into his eyes with a pleading look on her face and reached for his hand. "Please?"

Alejandro thought for a moment. "Are you sure? Gabby can be quite a handful…"

Softly, she spoke, "I don't want you going through this by yourself. I'd like to be there with you. I care about you too much and just…"

He didn't even ponder his next comment. "Go tell your parents that you're running out with me for a bit." Smiling at her, he released her hand and pushed her towards the door. She looked back at him then threw herself into his arms. "Go on, go. I want to get going."

Angelina turned towards the door, paused, and smiled at him. Then, she rushed through the door to tell her parents that she was leaving.

Alejandro was waiting for her and opened her door as she neared. She slid into the seat and slapped his hand away as he tried to put her seatbelt on. "Mother's looking and I don't want her to get any ideas that we may be dating before we're ready to tell her. She'll start asking questions and won't stop. You know how she can be."

Alejandro laughed at her statement remembering all of the questions she asked him at Christmas. "Fine," he said as he closed the door and noticed the drapes moving back in place. He slid into his seat and, shaking his head, said, "Your mother… She's quite the matchmaker."

"She thinks she is. I don't want her getting involved with us too soon. Don't get me wrong, I love her to death, but she can be quite overbearing at times. I don't want to have to worry about her right now. I just want to see where this may lead. I want to do this with just us walking down this path and her not pushing us."

He reached for her hand and squeezed it tightly. "I know what you mean. But with Gabby, we're going to have to be up front with her or she'll continue to meddle. I'll be straight with her and tell her that we need to figure this out ourselves." He released her hand as they drove over to Gabriella's.

They pulled up in front of Gabriella's house. The lights were still on. Alejandro turned off the ignition and turned towards Angelina. "Let's do this. Let me do the talking and everything will be fine. Gabby is just going to have to understand that we're going to take this slowly and we don't want her interfering. You mean a lot to me, Angelina. Come on, let's get this over with."

She met him in front of the car and they walked hand-in-hand to Gabriella's door. Alejandro rang the bell. They saw Gabriella look out the window before she opened the door. "So, to what do I owe this visit?"

Alejandro motioned for Angelina to precede him into her house. "Just thought we'd come over for a bit."

"Would you care for anything to drink?"

Alejandro indicated he'd take a beer if she had one. Angelina also requested one. Alejandro seated himself on the sofa right next to Angelina and patted her knee. When Gabriella appeared in the doorway, he winked at her and smiled. "It's okay," he whispered as Gabriella approached with their drinks.

She handed them their drinks and said, "You two look pretty chummy."

Alejandro looked at Angelina; then glanced up at Gabriella. "Well, we've been through something tonight."

"I know. Angelina, it sounded so scary."

"It was."

She said nothing more as Gabriella looked to Alejandro. He took a swig of his beer and looked down at the floor. He leaned over his knees, rubbing his hands back and forth in front of him. He took a deep breath and looked up at his sister. "It brought back an awful lot of bad memories, too."

Gabriella looked at her brother. She couldn't believe what she was hearing. He was thinking about that God-awful night. Alejandro looked over at Angelina and then said, "Gabby, tonight I told Angelina about Tammy and Michael."

She looked at him in shock. "You did?"

"Yes, I did," He reached for Angelina's hand. He needed her strength. "I thought it was time." Swallowing with difficulty, he continued, "Gabby, I need to start dealing with my past. If I am going to begin to have a future, free of misgivings, I have to face it."

Angelina squeezed his hand for she wanted him to know that she was with him through his pain.

"Saving Angelina made me finally start to confront that night. I have to face my fears head on. I have to deal with the fact that there was nothing I could've done to prevent Tammy's accident."

He looked at his hand entwined with Angelina's and smiled at her. "Gabby, I don't want to offend you with my next comment, but I have to say this. Angelina and I have become quite close as of late."

Gabriella started to comment, but he put up his hand to stop her. "Please, listen and let me finish before you say something."

She nodded.

"As I said, Angelina and I have become close lately. I can't dive into a relationship until I deal with Tammy and Michael's deaths, though. This evening, Angelina and I talked about them. She's helping me cope with their deaths. We've decided that we have a special bond, one that we'd like to explore without any family interference."

Gabriella's eyes widened, but kept her mouth shut.

"I realize you have our best interests at heart; however, if we're to have a chance at a relationship, we need to figure it out on our own. No meddling from you and no meddling from her parents. I can't say where this is going, but we want to take it slowly. I have issues to deal with, as does Angelina. Together, we're going to deal with them. Do you get my drift?"

Gabriella smiled and said, "Yeah. I know I was interfering by harassing you, Angelina. I'm sorry. I promise I won't ask any questions. I'll wait for you both to let me know where this is going. But first, I want to say that I am happy for you two. I know that you'll both get through this together, and I look forward to seeing you in a relationship. I know I'll get overexcited at times, but I've known for a long time that you both should be together. I hope and pray that you get through this time together as a couple. You're meant to be together." She stood and gave both of them a hug. "I love you both."

They continued talking, but when Angelina stifled a yawn, Alejandro patted her knee and indicated that he should take her home. Gabriella thanked them both for coming by and told Angelina she'd see her at school the next day. Angelina proceeded out the door. Gabriella stopped Alejandro with a hand on his arm. She gave her brother a big hug. "I'm so happy you've finally decided to share your feelings with someone." She patted him on the cheek. "Don't be a stranger," she called as he walked down the sidewalk.

"I'll try not to. Talk to you soon." With that, he helped Angelina into the car and drove off down the street.

Gabriella was so excited that her brother was finally opening up to someone about the family he'd so tragically lost. She just hoped that he continued to share his feelings with Angelina. They'd make a great couple. Hopefully they would be able to make it through the difficult and trying days ahead.

# CHAPTER FIFTEEN

They both made it through the next several weeks with no interference from either of their families. Angelina went to school and continued to tutor Lauren. Alejandro experienced a few difficult cases. He had to deal with a small child going through a transplant. Unfortunately, the child lost its life. It dealt Alejandro a serious blow. They'd been scheduled to attend a function the evening of the child's death.

Alejandro called and left a message for Angelina. "It's me. I hate leaving this message but I thought it best since we had plans for this evening." Dejectedly, he continued, "I need to cancel. Something's come up and I'm going to have to take a rain check."

When she listened to the message, she knew something was wrong. She was scheduled to begin spring break, and she was looking forward to spending time together. She dialed his cell so she could leave him a personal message. Surprisingly, he answered.

"Hey, there. Did you get my message?"

"Yeah. I thought this was a special dinner with your colleagues?"

"It is. I just have to cancel."

"You sure it's just that?"

A moment passed before he answered, "Yes. I just need to handle something that can't wait. I'll talk to you later."

Something just wasn't right. She decided she'd pretend her night was still happening. Her parents knew she was going out for dinner, so she dressed and left her house, deciding she'd head over to his place.

She wasn't sure whether he'd be home but decided to try. She pulled up in front of his home and noticed most of the lights were on. Generally, that meant that he was home. She rang the doorbell and waited. There was no answer. She rang it again and when no one came to the door, she decided to leave. Just as her feet hit the driveway, he opened the door. "Angelina," he sighed.

She turned around. He looked awful. She couldn't figure out what was wrong. She turned and headed back towards the door. He ushered her in and walked silently into the family room. He'd been drinking—there was a half-bottle of wine sitting on the coffee table.

"You okay?"

"Honestly?"

She nodded.

"No," he said. He sat down on the couch and put his hands over his eyes. "Sorry about tonight. I just couldn't go out and face my colleagues. It was supposed to be a happy occasion, and I'm definitely in no mood to celebrate."

Instead of sitting beside him on the couch, she sat in the chair across from him. "Alejandro. What's wrong? What happened? You were looking forward to tonight to celebrate the grant that the department received."

He didn't respond but just sat there. She wasn't exactly sure what to do. She could tell he was hurting. Was it her? A patient? She had no idea what was troubling him.

He reached for his wine. "Would you like a glass?"

She nodded. He stood and went over to the bar and retrieved a glass. He poured her wine, handed it to her, and returned to his seat on the sofa. He didn't utter a word while he performed this task. She took a sip of her wine and looked at him. He had deep, dark circles under his eyes. He looked like he hadn't slept in days. She sat there for a few moments, then stood and went to the couch. She squatted down so that she was eye level with him. She reached up a hand and stroked his cheek. He raised his head and looked into her eyes. He didn't say a word. She wasn't sure what he needed, but she drew him into a close hug. She wanted him to know that she cared and was there to support him in any way possible. She held him for some time before he gestured for her to sit beside him. He reached for her and drew her close. She laid her head on his shoulder. No words were spoken. They held one another until they were interrupted by the ringing of his cell phone. He withdrew it from his shirt pocket and glanced at the caller ID. It was Gabriella. He elected to ignore the call, then turned off his phone.

Almost an hour had elapsed since she'd arrived, and he said his first words since pouring her a glass of wine. As he stroked her hair he said, "I did all that I could and he still died."

Angelina wasn't sure what he was talking about, so she waited for him to continue. He took a deep breath and explained. "Dakota was a five-year-old boy. He would've been the same age as Michael. He was born with a congenital heart defect. He needed a heart transplant. A heart finally became available, but he was just too weak. He made it through surgery, but died in recovery."

She snuggled closer while he told his story.

"Normally, these situations don't affect me. I guess I've built this tough outer shell, but this was just too close to home. Michael didn't die because of a medical condition, but they were the same age... Had their whole lives ahead of them... I guess since I'm trying to deal with Tammy and Michael's deaths, my feelings are just too close to the surface. This has zapped all of my energy. I'm so tired. I don't know what to do."

"I think you should stretch out on the couch. Put your head in my lap and try and go to sleep."

"That sounds great, but I've got a better idea. Will you join me in my bedroom? Just lie with me for a while so I can take a short nap. That would mean so much to me."

She agreed. He reached for her hand and drew her up from the couch and led her to his bedroom. They removed their shoes and lay atop the covers. He pulled a throw from the foot of the bed to cover them. She laid her head on his chest and they both drifted off to sleep. Angelina awoke with a start at around two in the morning. She glanced at the clock and gasped. She couldn't believe she'd slept that long.

Alejandro felt her anxiousness and woke as well. "It's after two, Alejandro. I've got to go. Not that my parents keep track of me, but I do know that my mother worries until we come home."

"Where did you tell her you were going?"

"Out to dinner."

"Oh, I'm afraid what she'll think." He leaned over and kissed her, then sat up. "Come on. Let's go. I'll follow you home. If needed, I'll talk to your mom."

"That's not necessary. I'll handle her."

"Don't argue with me. At least let me follow you home and let my chivalrous side shine."

She got up, put her shoes back on, and straightened her clothes. He reached for her hand and led her towards the garage. He got into his car and waited for her to back out of his driveway. He followed her car closely as she drove home. He pulled up at the curb while she pulled into the driveway. He exited his car and met her at hers. He opened the door as she grabbed her purse, reached for her hand, and drew her into an embrace. "Thank you," he said. "I don't know what I would have done without you tonight."

"I didn't do anything. I just sat there and listened."

"That's what I needed. I needed to talk. I didn't need someone to sit and analyze me. What you did was special, and I'll never forget it." Alejandro was facing the front of the house and saw the drapes move as he held her. "I think we have an audience."

She withdrew from his embrace and turned towards the house. The draperies were still moving. "Doesn't surprise me in the least. Come on. I guess we'd better get this over with."

"What do you want to tell her?"

"I don't know. I guess I'll just wing it and see where she takes the conversation." Arm-in-arm, they walked to the front door. Angelina's mother didn't even let her open the door—as she reached to put her key in the lock, the door flew open.

"My God, Angelina. Where have you been? I've been so worried. I thought you were just going out to dinner. It's almost three in the morning."

"Mom."

"Don't 'mom' me. I want an explanation."

"Mom, I'm thirty years old. I don't need you waiting up for me." She was about to continue when Alejandro placed his hand on her arm.

"Mrs. Samuels, I am sorry that Angelina didn't get home earlier. She was at my house."

"Doing what?" She was upset. She thought her daughter had been in an accident. "I tried to reach your cell phone. No answer. Just what the hell were you doing?" Her mother was losing all control.

"Mom. Stop it. As I told you, if you keep interfering in my life, I'm going to move out."

"Angelina, enough," said Alejandro. "Mrs. Samuels, Angelina was helping me deal with a problem. I'm sorry that I didn't think for her to contact you but we fell asleep."

"Fell asleep?"

"Mom, it was innocent. But I don't need to explain that to you. Alejandro and I are friends. I was a friend helping another friend. Now, if you'll leave us alone, I would like to say goodbye to him."

Her mother stomped off.

"Sorry about that. I'll talk to her about us tomorrow. She's just overprotective. But just so you know it, I've threatened to move out several times over the last couple of months. It's nothing new to her."

"Has it been since we've been seeing one another?"

"Yes, but how many people my age still live at home?"

"It's what you're most comfortable with. I don't want to cause problems with your family. Maybe we just need to let her know that we're dating."

"We are?" she asked with a huge smile on her face.

"I believe we are. You've helped me out so much lately. I'm finally dealing with my issues after two years, and it's all because of you. I think I can move forward now and actually give this thing a shot—take a chance on a relationship with you."

"Oh, Alejandro." She threw herself into his arms and kissed him. She was so happy. He'd finally made a break through. Now she had to make sure that they continued moving forward. She knew that they could make this work if they did it together without any expectations.

Angelina was beside herself. Alejandro wanted to take a shot at a relationship with her. After wishing him goodnight and a safe drive home, she headed off to her bedroom. She was too excited to fall asleep. She laid in bed until almost dawn when she finally drifted off to sleep. Her cell phone awakened her around seven thirty. It was Alejandro.

"Get any sleep?"

"No, not really. You?"

"What do you think? I want to come by this morning and talk to your family."

"No, I'll deal with it myself."

"Angelina, please. I need to do this. I need to do it for myself. It'll help me heal. Please allow this."

"If you say so… First, let me make sure my parents are here. I'll call you right back."  Angelina got dressed and went to the kitchen. Her mother was sitting at the table downing a cup of coffee.

"Mom, are you and Dad going to be around for a while?"

"Why?"

"Are you?"

"We were planning on it."

"Don't go anywhere. Alejandro wants to come over and talk to you."

Her mother agreed and took another sip of her coffee. Angelina returned to her bedroom and called him.

"I'll be over in an hour."  He took in her silence and continued, "It's going to be alright. I'll do all of the talking. You have nothing to worry about… Just so you know I've contacted my family. After we confront yours, we're headed over to my parents to share our news."

She could hear the smile on his face as he ended the call.

Exactly one hour later, the doorbell rang. Angelina's father greeted him. "Come on in, Alejandro. We're in the family room."  Angelina's father led the way.

Alejandro suddenly became extremely nervous. His palms, which never sweat in the most stressful of situations, were slick. Angelina was standing near the couch while her mother was seated in a chair. Her father sat down in the accompanying chair next to her mother.

"Alejandro, please have a seat," her father indicated. He was trying to be amicable.

The only open seat was on the couch. Angelina sat and he joined her. They were seated inches apart. Alejandro glanced at her and smiled. He began to address her parents as Mr. and Mrs. Samuels when her father stopped him.

"Please call us Ben and Jackie."

Alejandro nodded, "Ben and Jackie, thank you for seeing me on such short notice."

"Think nothing of it," her father said. "Would you care for something to drink?"

Angelina thought her father was being too nice.

"I'm fine. Thank you, Ben." Alejandro wasn't sure what he should do. Should he reach for Angelina's hand? He didn't know what he had gotten himself into. He'd planned his speech on the way over, but he just couldn't find the words. Angelina reached over and grabbed his hand. She knew he was nervous. She smiled at him. Her smile and slight squeeze of his hand gave him the encouragement to continue. Swallowing, he started. "I want to explain to you about last night, but first I have to share something with you. Something from my past."

Jackie looked over at her husband. She wondered where this was going.

"The first time I met Angelina in person was after I moved to St. Louis shortly before Colleen became ill. I knew I didn't want a relationship in my life. I'd had one and..." he stopped for a moment.

"Had one?" her mother questioned.

"Mom, please. Let him finish."

"Let me step back for a second. When I lived in Wisconsin, I met and married a very special woman." He paused again. Alejandro was having a difficult time getting through this. Jackie knew by the sound of his voice and the look on his face that something was troubling him. Angelina squeezed his hand and he continued.

"I was married for a year, when we had our son, Michael. We wanted another child and kept trying… We'd been having one major thunderstorm after another. Tammy, my wife, had a doctor's appointment. She and Michael were on their way home when they encountered a flash flood. Their car was swept away. They were both killed. Tammy had just found out she was pregnant with our second child."

"Oh, my!" cried Jackie.

Alejandro put his hand up to stop her and continued, "I went through hell after the accident. I couldn't get past it. That's the main reason why I returned to St. Louis. I needed my family around me. I'd made up my mind that I'd never enter into a relationship again because I just couldn't put my emotions out there—I couldn't face losing my family again. I started to form a bond with Angelina, but I knew I couldn't have a relationship. Several things occurred and when Angelina had her flash flood experience, it really dealt me a blow. It took me back to Tammy and Michael's accident. That evening is when I shared my story with Angelina. Angelina knew where I stood, but she had also been convincing me that I could do anything I wanted, I just needed to deal with my past. I've been working on it."

He looked over at Angelina and smiled. This time it was his turn to squeeze her hand. She returned his smile. "Yes, Jackie, you've been right all along. Angelina and I have been seeing one another, but we didn't want anyone to know. I didn't want questions. Last night we were scheduled to attend a celebratory dinner with my colleagues. I called her and cancelled. I'd had a rough couple of days at the hospital... Actually I lost a little boy. He was five. The same age Michael would be. It hit me really hard, and I knew I couldn't attend the event."

"Alejandro, I'm so sorry."

"Thank you. Angelina had a feeling something was wrong. She came over to my house last night and she helped me through a very difficult time. As a result of that, I decided I had to give our relationship a chance. Angelina means way too much to me. Will this go anywhere? I don't know, but I know we have to give us a try. Yes, we both have issues to deal with. And maybe, just maybe, we both can help one another. I'm not going to promise you anything, but what I will promise you is that I will never hurt your daughter. She is a remarkable lady, and I'm lucky to have her in my life." He turned to Angelina and winked at her. "Will you please give me the privilege of dating your daughter?"

Jackie spoke, "Alejandro, wow, I can't believe you just asked us for permission to date our daughter. That's so noble of you. I've never heard of anything such as this. I promise I'll stop my meddling. I'd be more than happy for you to date Angelina."

Alejandro hadn't asked for Angelina's hand in marriage. He'd just asked, or rather told, her parents that he wanted to date their daughter. *Who did that in this day and age?* he thought.

Jackie stood and motioned for Alejandro to stand. She embraced him. "I'm sorry for what you've gone through. I promise to not interfere in your relationship."

Angelina couldn't believe her eyes. She thought they could get through anything after dealing with her mother.

Jackie motioned for everyone to join her in the kitchen where she served a light breakfast. While Jackie was preparing their food, Alejandro looked over at Angelina with such emotion in his eyes. He reached for her hand again. Raising it to his lips, he brushed a soft kiss across her knuckles. He mouthed, "Thank you." She smiled back at him.

After breakfast, Alejandro told her parents that they were headed over to share their news with his family. He'd wanted both families to know of their relationship so there would be no further questions that they had to approve or deny. As they went to leave, Ben shook Alejandro's hand and thanked him for sharing his past with them. He also indicated how happy he was that Angelina had such a wonderful man in her life. "Just remember," he said shaking his finger at him, "don't hurt her."

"I won't. I think we're both going into this with our eyes wide open. We know we have issues that we can't ignore, and that's what our obstacle will be."

Ben wasn't sure what Alejandro meant by "dealing with our issues"—he wasn't aware that his daughter had any problems. Maybe Alejandro just vocalized it in that manner.

Jackie hugged them both goodbye and asked Alejandro to join them for dinner in the upcoming week. He agreed since he was off and wouldn't be interrupted by the hospital.

"That wasn't so bad, was it?" Angelina asked when they were in his car.

Alejandro turned to her as he started the car. "It was at first. I couldn't verbalize what I wanted to say. All my practiced words left me, but with you by my side I was able to get control and speak from the heart. Now we just have to deal with my family. I called Gabriella to make sure she'd be there. I only want to do this one more time."

She nodded. Alejandro backed out of the driveway and pointed his car in the direction of his parents' home.

Alejandro's family greeted them with open arms. When Angelina started to refer to his father as Dr. A., he immediately corrected her. "Don't you think it's about time you called us John and Maria?"

Angelina was shocked by their acceptance, and before Alejandro's confession of their relationship. She nodded and smiled.

They knew something had to be up since everyone in the family was standing around with a look of approval on their faces. His mother couldn't contain herself as she pulled Angelina into an embrace. "Yes, dear. Please call me Maria."

Angelina hugged his mother back and agreed to use their first names. *That was easy,* she thought. Did they know something?

Maria led them into the formal living room. They sat and started with small talk. "Oh, school's fine. I really like St. Margaret's. I was lucky to find the school and even luckier to reconnect with Gabriella."

On cue, Gabriella entered the room. "So, what's up? Why did you call us all here, Alejandro?"

He reached for Angelina's hand. He looked into her eyes, then looked at his mother. "I wanted to let everyone know that Angelina and I are dating."

"Wonderful!" exclaimed his mother.

"I knew you'd get there. How long has this officially been going on?" shouted Gabriella. "I told you I'd stop my meddling. And it worked. You're finally together."

Alejandro briefed his family on what had transpired with him and Angelina over the last several months. Gabriella couldn't contain herself any longer—when Alejandro finished his story, she ran over and hugged them both. Words could not express Gabriella's happiness. From the moment she introduced her brother to her best friend, she'd hoped this day would come. Now she could only hope and pray that they both could get through whatever issues remained. She wanted Angelina to be the sister she never had.

Both Alejandro and Angelina were glad that they'd finally told everyone about their relationship. Now, they could stop worrying about hiding their relationship and move forward to see where things took them.

# CHAPTER SIXTEEN

All that remained of the school year was the final mass and annual school picnic. An hour remained before mass, so she decided to reminisce with her class. She wanted each child to have a chance to share something about the school year that had affected them.

Angelina truly loved her students. She had a special bond with this class and was going to miss them dearly. As they went around the circle, the students thanked her for being such a great teacher. They talked about their field trips and, when one student brought up the trip prior to Thanksgiving, Angelina started to get a little emotional. She held it in check, but could feel the tears. Lauren asked her if she were okay. She nodded and said that something had flown in her eye. Reaching for a tissue, she dabbed her eyes and gathered her composure. She still hadn't really dealt with her infertility.

Another student brought up Career Day. He'd learned a lot and wanted to explore being an architect while another student said that he was thinking about going into the medical field. "Ms. Samuels? You know Dr. Alvarez really made me see what I could do to change someone's life. I'm thinking about being a doctor just like him."

Angelina smiled and told Bret that she would pass it along to him. "Yes, Dr. Alvarez is a wonderful doctor." She again started to think about her infertility and wondered where these thoughts were coming from. She knew that she was going to have to deal with them sooner rather than later. Just as she finished her thought, the bell rang signaling that it was time for mass.

They walked to church and headed down the aisle when a flash caught her eye. She looked over and was surprised to see Alejandro seated in a pew. His watch face had caught the sun's light. He bowed his head and she acknowledged him with the briefest of smiles. She thought he had been working at the hospital, but then noticed some of the other participants from Career Day seated throughout the church.

Seeing Alejandro brought a fresh wave of tears to her eyes. She blinked them back, but he saw them glistening in her eyes. He was so attuned to her feelings that he wanted to be near her, so he decided to move from the pew he was in to the one directly behind her. She felt him as he genuflected into the pew. As he kneeled upon entering the pew, he placed his hand on her shoulder and squeezed it gently. He bent forward and whispered into her ear, "You okay?"

She shook her head and he added, "What's wrong?"

She whispered, "I'll be fine. Just let me sit here."

He finished his prayer and sat back in the pew. He could see her wiping her eyes, but let her be. He'd see her when school ended.

During the homily, the priest reviewed all of the special events that occurred throughout the school year and then called each person up that helped make the school year special. He specifically recognized those involved in Career Day. He thanked them for helping the students become aware of the many different avenues they could pursue. He also addressed Alejandro's involvement with Colleen's transplant. Alejandro thought the priest went a bit overboard, but he stood proudly and listened to his accolades.

As Alejandro stood in front of everyone, he kept his eyes trained on Angelina. Her head was bent low and he could see that her eyes were closed. When he returned to his seat, he briefly placed his hand on her shoulder. She kept her head bowed. He couldn't figure out what was wrong.

At the sign of peace, she turned to him. He hugged her and whispered, "Hang in there. We'll talk shortly."

She nodded and turned back to the front of church. When the final song was sung, she walked her students back to the classroom for the final bell of the year. She stood at the door as each student left, receiving many hugs and well wishes for the summer.

Lauren was the last student left in her room. She hugged Angelina and thanked her for her help and support throughout the year. She told Angelina she'd see her that evening. As she started to leave she said, "You're the best. You helped me so much this year. You taught me to have confidence in myself. One day you're going to teach everything you taught me to your own children. I hope that I can share with them how you changed my life. Thanks again, Ms. Samuels."

Angelina barely held it together as Lauren bounded out of the room. Angelina headed back to her desk and put her face in her hands, tears pouring from her eyes. Then, she felt strong arms encircling her shoulders. Alejandro had walked into her room while her head was down. He comforted her the only way he could, by holding her. She started to cry openly. Thankfully, he'd closed her door when he'd entered her room.

As her tears slowed, he moved around her chair and knelt in front of her. "Sweetheart, what's wrong?"

She started to wipe her eyes. Alejandro reached into his pocket for his handkerchief and wiped at the tears that were cascading down her cheeks. Then, he handed her his handkerchief.

"I guess a lot of emotions today. We were reminiscing about the year and the Thanksgiving field trip was discussed. It brought up a lot of unhappy memories."

"Angelina, we need to deal with this."

She nodded.

"I want to help you."

"I know you do. Let's discuss this later."

He smiled at her and reached for her hand. "Follow me home so I can change, and then we'll come back for the picnic."

Angelina grabbed her purse and threw it over her arm. Alejandro drew her into an embrace, then they walked arm-in-arm out of her classroom.

Mary greeted them as they were leaving the building. "Are you feeling alright, Angelina?"

Alejandro spoke for her. "She's fine." He squeezed her shoulder and said, "Will we see you this evening?"

"Alejandro, you're coming to the picnic?"

"Wouldn't miss spending the night with my girl."

Mary's eyebrows rose in a question.

"Oh, I guess you weren't aware, but Angelina and I are dating. All she's been talking about for weeks is playing those carnival games together."

Mary smiled and said, "Congratulations. I'm happy for you." She had had a feeling something had been going on between them for a while.

Alejandro didn't want to stall any longer— Angelina needed to get out of the building and deal with her latest bout of emotions. He said their goodbyes as he led her to her car. He followed her home and, just as they pulled into her driveway, his cell phone rang. He took the call outside while she changed her clothes, then they headed over to his house.

While he changed, she grabbed them something cool to drink. He joined her on the deck and sat beside her on a chaise lounge. She handed him his drink.

"Alejandro, I know I need to deal with this, but..."

He reached for her hand.

"Every time I think about last fall... Colleen... Everything, I get so emotional. I haven't been able to sleep..."

"When did this start?"

"I...I haven't been able to sleep for months. I guess I've just been hiding it from everyone. I think it's catching up with me. Alejandro, I need your help. Please help me." She started to cry again. He joined her on the chaise and gathered her into his arms. "I'm here Angelina. Don't worry. I'm here, and I'll help you." He held her until she stopped crying.

She looked up at him and brushed her hand across his jaw. "You're my knight in shining armor. You always seem to be there when I need you the most... I love you." She couldn't believe she'd finally said those three words. She loved him. "I'm sorry. I shouldn't have said that."

"Why? That's how you feel, isn't it?"

"Yes. It certainly is."

"Angelina, I care for you so much, but I can't say those words just yet. Maybe someday I'll be able to, but not right now."

"I understand." Angelina knew he'd been through an awful tragedy, but she'd put her feelings out there and she hoped he'd feel the same way about her one day.

He jumped up from the lounge chair, grabbed her hand, and said, "Let's go. I can't wait 'till I see what I win at the duck pond."

She laughed, hugged him, and thanked him for everything. "You know no one at school, besides Gabriella and now Mary, knows that we're dating."

"Well, I guess we're going to surprise quite a few people this evening, aren't we?" He placed his arm across her shoulders and led her out the back door.

They parked near the rectory. Just as he was helping her from the car, Father Xavier approached them. "Dr. Alvarez, Angelina. How are you?"

"Just great, Father," responded Alejandro. Fr. Xavier seemed surprised to see them together. Alejandro decided to face this head on. "Father, Angelina and I are dating."

"You are? I wasn't aware of that." Fr. Xavier was surprised, but seemed pleased with the news. He chatted with them for a few more minutes, then headed to the cafeteria for dinner.

"Angelina, let's go check out that duck pond," Alejandro said. As they neared the games, they ran into Gabriella. He hugged his sister, and she in turn hugged Angelina.

"You okay? You seemed a little upset in church this afternoon. I couldn't get over to you before mass began, and then I saw Alejandro sitting behind you."

"I'm fine." She reached for his hand. "I'm so lucky to have your brother in my life." She reached over and placed a peck on his cheek.

"We're both lucky to have him."

"Enough. You're both going to inflate my ego." They laughed and enjoyed their evening.

To anyone who saw them walking around the picnic, they definitely appeared to be a couple in love. Angelina, looking up at him and smiling, while he was often seen laughing at any small comment she'd make.

They ran into Lauren and her family. Lauren hugged Angelina and smiled up at Alejandro. Her parents engaged them in conversation. Lauren's mother thanked Angelina numerous times for helping Lauren after school. As they were ending their conversation, Lauren turned to Alejandro and asked him, "Are you two dating?"

Alejandro was surprised with her question, but nodded and said, "We are."

"Good. I'm happy for Ms. Samuels. I told her today that she's the best. She helped me so much this year. She taught me how to succeed and have confidence in myself. I told her that someday she was going to teach everything she taught me to her own children. I hope that someday I can share with them how much she changed my life."

The light bulb went on for him. He knew why Angelina had been upset when he'd joined her in her classroom. Her tears always seemed to go back to the fact that she couldn't have children.

Lauren's family said their goodbyes and wished her a good summer. He wasn't going to confront her with this latest revelation until later.

Angelina encountered several more of her students throughout the night. At one point, he looked at her and thought she looked absolutely exhausted. He was afraid to comment on it, so instead he told her how tired he was.

He grabbed her hand and said, "I'm totally exhausted. Do you mind if we head on home? I had to fill in for a colleague today and the patient was more difficult than anticipated."

She agreed. "Yeah, let's go. Now that you say it, I'm pretty tired myself."

He wasn't actually tired, but wanted to get her home so she could get some sleep.

They pulled up at Angelina's house and her parents were standing in the front yard looking at the flowers her mother had planted earlier in the day. Her father approached the car and opened Angelina's door. Alejandro came around as her father helped her exit the car.

"How was the picnic?" her mother asked.

Alejandro smiled at them, "It was a lot of fun. I met several of Angelina's students—"

Her father interrupted them, staring at Angelina, "Sweetheart, you look exhausted. Are you feeling alright?"

"Yes, I'm fine. It's been a long week. Packing up my classroom for the summer and all…"

"Well, I'll let you and Alejandro say goodnight then. Alejandro, it was good seeing you."

"Nice seeing both of you, too."

Angelina's parents went inside. Alejandro put his hand on her shoulder and looked her directly in the eyes. "We need to spend some time together. Alone… Without interruptions."

She nodded in agreement. She knew what he was talking about.

"I'm off this weekend. Why don't I come over tomorrow and pick you up? Pack an overnight bag. We'll go for a drive and see where we end up. We need time together so we can address our issues. You okay with that?"

"Yeah, but why do I need to pack a bag?"

"Just in case it's too late to bring you home. I promise nothing will happen unless you want it to."

She nodded her head.

"Angelina, please get a good night's sleep. You need it."

"I know. It's just that I have dreams…"

"I know. We'll deal with that this weekend. Now go to bed and I'll come by tomorrow around nine and we'll start to confront your demons."

# CHAPTER SEVENTEEN

Promptly at nine, the doorbell rang and Colleen answered the door. She was surprised to see Alejandro. "Hey Doc, whatchya doing here this early?"

"Your sister and I have a date."

"Oh… So, are you and my sister getting serious?"

Alejandro was startled by her question. He knew Angelina loved him and, in all actuality, he loved her, too. "What do you call serious?"

"Colleen, it's none of your business," Angelina called from upstairs.

"Angelina!" Colleen huffed.

"Don't 'Angelina' me. I'm going to go say goodbye to Mom and Dad. Behave yourself, Colleen."

"Sorry, Doc. I'm just worried about my sister, that's all. She's seemed pretty sad lately. I hope you can cheer her up. If you and my sister are getting serious, I'm all for it. You're good for her."

"Thanks. I'll try and put a smile back on her face. Sound good to you?"

"Yep, sure does. Just take care of her." Colleen gave Alejandro a quick hug before Angelina entered the room.

Angelina said her goodbyes as Alejandro reached for her bag and they walked out of the house.

"Where are we going?" she asked as they headed towards his car.

"Why don't we just drive and see where we end up?"

"Let's go to the Botanical Gardens. We can stroll through the gardens and find a quiet place to talk."

"Good idea. It's not too warm, and we can get lost there for as long as we want."

They arrived at the gardens shortly and walked the perimeter. They passed the Rose Garden and strolled through the Chinese and Japanese Gardens before they found a secluded path near the Herb Gardens that led to a brook with a small waterfall. At the end of the pathway was a wrought-iron bench, and they sat down. Several birds were bathing in a small pool while a rabbit nibbled on a sprig of grass. It was the perfect setting to begin their conversation.

Alejandro drew her close. She laid her head on his shoulder.

"This is nice," she said.

"Sure is." Pausing, he continued, "Talk to me, Angelina. Tell me what's going on."

"It's just…"

"What?"

"I don't know where to begin. What to say. I don't know if I can put it into words."

"Try. Otherwise, this pain is going to consume you. It's the elephant on your shoulder, weighing you down, causing your sleepless nights. We won't be able to move forward until you do."

She sat there quietly, then placed her hand on his thigh. He pulled her in closer. "I thought I'd dealt with this a while ago, but, out of nowhere, it reared its ugly head again." She took a deep breath. "The last time we talked, I thought I'd come to grips with my infertility. Then, as the school year came to an end, I started to reflect on the year. My mind kept drifting back to Colleen's accident… the surgeries… my infection… At times, I feel like I just can't take it any longer. I've been thinking that teaching might not be the right profession for me."

Alejandro was shocked by her confession. "Where's this coming from? From what I can see, you're an excellent teacher. Your students love you. Look at all the good things they said about you last night. How could you think about giving up a career that means so much to you? Look how you affected Lauren's life."

"I know. It's just that…"

"Just what?"

"Whenever I look at my students, I think of what might have been."

He reached for her jaw and turned her face towards him. "What do you mean by that? Angelina, you're a natural. You care so much for each of your students. You're such a role model to them—"

"I know, but I'm to the point that I want to be that role model for…" She couldn't keep up this conversation. She jumped to her feet and began to pace in front of him. Alejandro stood, reached for her hand, and led her back to the bench. She sat down and he squatted in front of her, grabbing her hands.

"Go on."

She started to tear up. As a lone tear cascaded down her cheek, she said, "I want my own child. A child borne from me, and… and… I can't have that." She broke into uncontrollable sobs.

He pulled her into his arms and let her cry. "Angelina, you can still have children, just not borne from you. There are other options that you can explore when the time is right. You can still be that mother you want to be."

"But what about my husband? How will he feel that I can't have his child? Alejandro, I am so torn with this…"

"I realize that, but Angelina I don't care whether you can physically have my child or not, just raising a child together would be magical. Seeing you as my child's mother… I can't put into words how overjoyed I'd be. Angelina, you're a special woman. I'm so lucky to have you in my life." He pulled away from her slightly and came to a decision.

"Angelina, look at me."

She raised her tear strewn face.

"Sweetheart, we can make it through this together. Promise me that you'll always love me, because I love you more than life itself."

There, he uttered the three magical words that he swore he would never say again. There, squatted before Angelina, he came to an understanding of what was right before his eyes. Angelina was his angel that was sent by Tammy. Tammy wouldn't want him to spend the remainder of his life without someone to love or share his heart with. He was a remarkable man and needed her in his life.

Angelina was speechless and couldn't believe what she was hearing. Alejandro said he loved her. She had to make sure that she heard him correctly. "Could you repeat that? Did you say what I thought I heard you say…?"

"Yes, Angelina. I love you with all of my heart. I think I've loved you since the night of Colleen's accident. I want to be honest with you. Deep down, I feel responsible for your infertility. I should have been more in tune with what was going on with you. I should have insisted that Gabriella keep me aware of how you were doing. But I can't look back now. What is, is—we can only move forward and try and deal with the cards that have been dealt. I love you and will stand by your side through whatever we may encounter. Angelina, you mean the world to me. I don't want to see you unhappy. We can adopt. We'll do whatever we can to have our own child, one that we can raise together. A child that you can teach how to read and write. You are a fabulous role model, and I want you to be that role model to our children."

"Alejandro, I'm confused. I don't understand why you keep referring to having our child… Raising our child. What are you saying?"

He guessed that now was the best time to ask her a very important question. Since he was already on bended knee, he reached for her hand and intertwined it with his. He placed his other hand softly on her cheek. "Oh, Angelina… how I love you. You mean the world to me. I never thought I'd be saying 'I love you' to another woman. You helped me deal with my fears… my past… Sweetheart, I love you. I love you for who you are. I love you for the teacher you are. You've taught me so much. I think you'd be crazy to give up on the world that means so much to you. We can deal with whatever faces us together. I'll always be there to support you, support your dreams, support your everything."

Looking directly into her eyes, he said, "Angelina, will you be the mother of my children? Because I know we'll have children together. I don't care that they won't be borne by you. All I care is that we'll raise them in a family filled with love."

She wasn't exactly sure she if he was saying what she thought he was saying. Then, she heard the magical words, "Angelina, will you marry me?"

Angelina was in total shock. The whole direction of their conversation had done a one-eighty. She opened her mouth to speak, but no words would come. She swallowed deeply and tried to find her voice. "Alejandro, are you sure? Because there's no going back."

He nodded.

She saw a tear escape his eye and fall down his cheek. When she saw that tear, she knew he truly loved her and that he wanted to spend the rest of his life with her. She reached up and brushed the tear aside. "Yes," she whispered. "Yes, I will marry you."

He pulled her into a tight embrace and held her. Moving back slightly, he looked directly into her eyes. "You're my life. Your pain is my pain. Your happiness is my happiness. Your dreams are mine. Together we will make it through whatever obstacles are presented to us because I know our love can survive anything." He leaned in and kissed her. She embraced him… Oh how she loved him.

He pulled away. "I'm sorry I don't have a ring for you. I hadn't planned on asking you to marry me today. I wanted to do it romantically, with candlelight, wine, soft music…"

"This was the perfect setting. It was so unexpected. It took me by complete surprise."

They would deal with her infertility together and, if needed, she would seek counseling. Today, she was going to bask in the glow of his pronouncement of love for her.

They decided to hold off on sharing their engagement. They wanted to enjoy being in love before sharing it with the world.

That evening, they enjoyed a quiet dinner at his house. "When do you want to get married?" Alejandro asked.

Angelina laughed, "Alejandro, I don't know. I'm still in complete shock that we're even *getting* married. All I know is that I want to enjoy our engagement and take our time. I don't need to rush into marriage. Even though I know I can't wait to become your wife, I still need time to fully deal with my infertility before we marry. I don't want to carry that baggage into our marriage. I hope you understand."

"I do. I'll do whatever you want. I don't care when we marry, just that we do. I love you so much."

"And I you."

They finished their dinner. It was getting late. He would have loved for her to spend the night in his arms, but thought better of it. He drove her home and walked her to the door. She asked him in, but he declined.

"See you tomorrow?" he asked.

"Of course. We can discuss our plans as to when we tell our families. You know I'm going to have to stay away from your sister. She'll see right through me."

"I know. She's going to be ecstatic to have you for a sister. I think she's been praying for that from the moment she officially introduced us."

"I would agree with that."

He kissed her and left her standing at the front door. She was glad that her family had already gone to bed and her mother hadn't waited up for her. She would be overflowing with joy when she learned of their engagement. She'd been dreaming of this day forever, even if there was one part of her dream that would never come true... Being her child's biological grandmother. She'd have to break the news to her family at some point. She knew she'd have to face the facts squarely and be up front with them before the wedding. She didn't want to set expectations that would never happen. She was infertile and would never have her own children, but she was forever lucky to have Alejandro in her life. He was understanding and knew the medical reasons behind her inability to have his children.

Angelina went to bed but couldn't sleep. She tossed and turned for well over an hour when she decided to give Alejandro a call. He answered immediately.

"Can't sleep?" he asked.

"How did you know it was me? The phone didn't even ring"

"Because I was getting ready to call you. I can't sleep either."

"Alejandro, I just want to say that I love you so much. I'm so lucky to have you in my life…"

"Angelina, I feel the same way."

"We have so much to think about. My mind keeps spinning…"

"I know, so does mine."

"How about I come over early and we'll start trying to answer some of those questions together?"

"Sounds like a plan. I better let you get some beauty sleep. Not that you need beauty sleep at all, since you're already so beautiful to me. I love you unconditionally."

Angelina chuckled, "I know you do, and I love you, too."

They said their goodnights. Angelina was the happiest she'd been in so long. She just hoped that she could make Alejandro happy, knowing that she couldn't bear his children.

# CHAPTER EIGHTEEN

Angelina awoke with an intense headache. She jumped into a hot shower to try to relieve it, then dressed and joined her family in the kitchen. Rubbing her hand across her forehead, she tried to drink a cup of coffee.

"Angelina, you okay?" asked Wyatt.

Wearily, she looked up at him. "Yeah, I just have a monstrosity of a headache. That's all."

"What time did you get home?"

"It wasn't too late."

"What did you and Alejandro do yesterday?"

Angelina's thoughts drifted back to the perfect day that it had been. She replayed everything... Walking through the gardens, their conversation, and, to top it off, him asking her to be his wife. What a day!

"Angelina?" Colleen placed her hand on her sister's arm.

She drifted back to the present. "What did you say?"

Wyatt repeated his question.

"Oh, we walked around the Botanical Gardens. The roses were in full bloom. It was beautiful."

"Maybe you have such a headache from being outdoors… Could be allergies."

"That's true." Angelina knew better than that, though. It wasn't from being outdoors—her headache stemmed from lack of sleep. She was lucky if she'd gotten two hours of sleep last night. She was just too excited. Her life was going to change shortly. She was the luckiest woman in the world, in love with a wonderful man. Angelina tried to finish her coffee, but couldn't choke it down. She threw the contents down the drain, washed her cup, and placed it into the dishwasher. She reached for her purse and withdrew her keys.

"Where're you off too?"

"Alejandro is off today. I told him I'd come over this morning."

"Weren't you just with him?" her brother asked.

"What's it to you?" She waved goodbye and headed out the door.

Her parents sat at the table, shaking their heads. They both knew something was up with their daughter, especially when she didn't finish her coffee.

Angelina pulled up at Alejandro's. Before exiting the car, she rested her forehead on the steering wheel. She hadn't had a headache this bad in a long time. She knew she needed to put a smile on her face when he answered the door. If only she could. Slowly, she exited the car and walked up the sidewalk. She didn't even get a chance to ring the doorbell when the door opened in front of her.

"What's wrong?" he asked.

"Nothing, why?"

"Don't lie to me, Angelina. I saw you sitting in the car with your head resting on the steering wheel."

"Oh," she said.

He grabbed her hands and pulled her into the foyer. Quietly, he closed the door and pulled her into his arms. He kissed her forehead, then led her towards his bedroom. She didn't resist. He brought her to his bedside, then squatted down to remove her shoes. All the while, nothing was said between them. She laid down and he joined her. Pulling her into his arms, she placed her head on his chest. He stroked her hair, then massaged her temples. No words were needed.

After they laid there for a while, he spoke, "Better?"

She nodded into his chest.

"What's wrong?"

"Killer of a headache."

"Did you take anything?"

"No. I thought it would go away, but it's only gotten worse."

Alejandro got up and went to the bathroom where he retrieved a pain killer for her. He handed her the pills and a glass of water. She downed it, then he rejoined her in bed.

"Thanks," she said.

He nodded. "Go to sleep. We'll talk when you wake." He held her until she fell asleep. He considered himself the luckiest man alive. He was holding his future wife in his arms—a moment he thought he'd never experience again. As he looked at her, he realized that he would never tire of watching her sleep. She was so beautiful. She was his and he'd never let her go. Whatever their issues were, they would face them together along with the help of their families. He would see to that.

He decided to let her sleep, so he rose and went to his study. He'd read some medical journals until she woke, and then they'd talk. He sat at his desk with his back to the doorway, staring out the bay window that overlooked the backyard. With his forefinger on his temple, he watched a bird taking a bath, a squirrel scampering up the oak tree while a rabbit was gnawing away at the grass... Deep in thought.

She watched him from the doorway, wondering what he was thinking. She'd slept for several hours before waking alone in his bed. She laid there smelling his cologne on the sheets. As she rolled over, she saw his pillow. She pulled it into her arms and squeezed it. Soon she would be sharing his bed with him. She'd be lying in his arms and awakening to his warm touch. Oh, what a dream... a dream that she couldn't wait to come true.

She approached him. He remained in his own world. She wrapped her arms around his neck and brushed a kiss on his cheek.

"Feel better?" he asked.

"Much. Thanks for that. I just needed a little sleep."

"I take it you had a sleepless night?"

"What do you think? Of course, I did. I couldn't get yesterday out of my mind. It was... It was magical. I can't believe you asked me to marry you. I'm still in shock. I don't think I've ever been this happy in my entire life."

He spun around and pulled her onto his lap. "Ready to have that chat?"

She snuggled deeper into his arms. Nuzzling his cheek, she nodded. "Now?"

"What else do you have—"

Before he could finish his thought, the phone rang. It was his mother. She wanted to know what he was doing.

"Angelina's here and we're just talking. Why?"

"Why don't the two of you come over for a late lunch? The whole family will be here."

He relayed his mother's request, and Angelina nodded her head in approval.

"How about we come over in the next hour or so?"

"Sounds great, I can't wait to see you both."

Alejandro hung up the phone. "Sorry about that."

"Why are you sorry? I enjoy being around your family. This way I can get to know them better."

"I know, but we planned on discussing our future and all…"

"We can do that another time. It's not every day that your mother invites you over to have lunch with the family."

They arrived at his parents' house an hour later. As they exited the car, they could see the family gathered around the pool in the backyard. Alejandro ushered her through the gate, announcing their presence as it closed behind them.

"Are we missing anything?" Alejandro asked.

Maria pulled Angelina into a welcoming hug while his father shook Alejandro's hand. "It's so good to see you, dear. I'm happy you could join us."

"Thanks for inviting us." Alejandro pulled out a chair for Angelina. She seated herself next to his brother, Alec. It was a little warm, but not too bad for a summer day. Alejandro's father was grilling by the pool. Angelina wanted to help Maria and Gabriella prepare the remainder of the meal, but they wouldn't allow it. They wanted her to sit and get to know his brothers.

They'd been sitting for a while when Alejandro came up behind her, leaned down, and whispered in her ear, "How are you feeling?"

"Fine."

"No more headache?"

"It's better, but not totally gone."

Alejandro went inside and came back with another round of pain killers and a glass of water. "Here, take these."

For the second time that day, she complied and took his medication. She nodded her thanks.

Maria appeared with a plate of fruit. "You're not feeling well?"

"Just a headache. I'm fine otherwise."

"Maybe you should go inside and get out of the heat."

"I'll be okay."

Gabriella joined her friend at the table. She kept staring at Angelina. She could tell that something was different about her, but couldn't determine what it was.

They enjoyed their lunch, but when afternoon storms threatened, they went inside. Alejandro joined Angelina on the couch, placing his arm around her shoulders.

"What's new?" inquired Gabriella.

"Not much. Just trying to relax. It was such an exhausting year for me that I need to take a little time and chill out. Soon, I'll start planning for next year." Planning, she thought. Not only planning for the school year, but her upcoming wedding. Boy, she and Alejandro really needed to talk. She didn't know how long she could keep their engagement from his sister. She was her best friend and Angelina wanted to share her exciting news. Maybe they could discuss their plans on the way home. Alejandro was on service the entire next week and she would hardly see him.

They said their goodbyes to his family. Alejandro opened the passenger door and Angelina eased into her seat. Just before he closed the car door, he reached in and gave her a soft kiss on the lips. "I've wanted to do that since we got here. You look so beautiful."

He closed the door and walked around the car. As he did this, he noticed Gabriella peeking out the front window. They needed to talk today about their future before Gabriella confronted him.

"That was fun," she said as he started the engine. She reached for his hand. "Alejandro, we need to talk about when we're going to tell our families."

"I know. Gabriella kept looking at me like she'd already figured something out. I caught her looking out the window as I helped you into the car."

"She's pretty perceptive."

As he pulled the car into his garage, he asked her to join him on the patio. He retrieved cool drinks from the kitchen while she settled at the patio table. When he joined her, he dropped a kiss onto her head and sat down.

"While I was inside, I checked my calendar. Do you think you can wait until the Fourth of July?"

"For what?"

"Our announcement."

"That's only two weeks away. Why?"

"I thought I'd have a barbeque to celebrate the holiday. We'll invite both of our families. This'll be ideal since I haven't had a party since I moved back. What do you think?"

"That's a great idea."

"I'll call your mom and invite your family. Okay with you?"

"Yeah. We'll have to go shopping."

"I need everything," said Alejandro. "Do you want to go shopping next week after I get off? Let's plan on Friday evening, dinner and shopping."

"Sounds like a winner to me."

# CHAPTER NINETEEN

Alejandro called Angelina's house the following morning. "Jackie, hi. It's Alejandro. How are you this fine Monday morning?"

"I'm good. How about yourself?"

"Hanging in there. I'm on service the entire week, so it'll be a long one. Hey, the reason I'm calling is I wanted to ask you something. What's your family doing for the Fourth of July? I was thinking of having a barbeque and wanted to invite you all over. My family is planning on being there, too. This will be the first party I've thrown since moving back." Alejandro felt like he was rambling a bit, so he stopped to give Jackie a chance to respond.

"We have no plans that I am aware of." She didn't have to think about her answer at all. "Yes, we'd love to come over and share the holiday with you and your family. Is there something that we can bring?"

"No, I've got it all taken care of. Just bring yourselves."

"Thanks. I'm looking forward to it. I'll make sure we're all there."

"Well, if I don't see you before, I'll see you on the Fourth. I'll make sure Angelina provides you with the details. Say hello to Ben for me."

"Okay, Alejandro. Thanks for the invitation."

Alejandro hung up and quickly dialed Angelina. "Well, I did it."

"Did what?"

"I invited your family for the Fourth. Your mom said that everyone would be there. I told her you'd fill her in on the details."

"Are we still going this weekend to get the tableware?

"Yep. I'll try and give you a call this evening, but you know how my schedule is when I'm on service. I feel like I'm going to have a hectic week."

"I'm sorry to hear that. If you have some time, I can run by the hospital and meet you for lunch or even dinner."

"I'll call and let you know what works best for me. I love you."

"Love you, too."

Angelina didn't hear from him until late Thursday. She was sitting in her bedroom, making lists of things they needed to handle for the weekend, and they still needed to discuss their future plans in more detail. Angelina was getting ready to turn off the lights for the night when her phone rang. It was Alejandro.

"How's it going?"

"I'm wiped out. It's been a long week, just like I thought it would be. I was covering for another doctor and he ended up having some critical patients that I had to handle. Then, I had my own patients to deal with… But enough about me. What have you been up to?"

"I'm sitting here making lists."

"For what?"

"What do you think?"

"I don't know."

"Try your barbeque with our families and our wedding plans."

"Oh, yeah. We still need to discuss that."

"We do. Are we still on for tomorrow night?"

"Yep. How about seven? I'll swing by and pick you up on my way home. Then, we can grab something quick to eat and go shop."

"Sounds good. Gosh, it feels like forever since I last saw you, kissed you…"

"Angelina, I feel the same way. I've missed you so much. I've found myself day dreaming about you… Us. Normally I am so transfixed while I'm at the hospital, but lately all I find myself thinking about is you at the most inopportune times."

Angelina laughed quietly, "I went shopping with your sister today and couldn't stop thinking about you, either. Gabriella kept asking what was wrong because I kept zoning out. I told her nothing was wrong, but knowing her she knows something's up. She's too perceptive."

"Yeah, I know. We only have until next week, and then our secret will be out and we can openly discuss our plans."

"I can't wait to see you."

"Nor I you. Hey, I've gotta go—I'm being paged."

"See you tomorrow."

"Yeah. I'll try and give you a call in the morning. Love ya."

Alejandro didn't arrive at her house the following evening until well after nine. He'd called and told her he'd had an emergency and didn't know when he'd see her. He told her to go ahead and have dinner, and he'd try and stop by if it wasn't too late. She was disappointed since she hadn't seen him since the previous Sunday. He apologized, but told her he couldn't help it. She understood, but was still saddened by the fact that she wouldn't see him as expected.

She'd pretty much given up on seeing him for the night when the doorbell rang. She looked at the clock and it was nine thirty. She was alone except for Colleen and Wyatt—her parents were attending a dinner reception. Her siblings were watching a movie while she'd been sitting in the living room, wondering if he would appear.

She answered the door and looked up at him. He looked drained. He had dark circles under his eyes, and he looked like a walking zombie.

"Alejandro, you look absolutely exhausted."

"I'm beat."

"Why didn't you go straight home?"

"Because you sounded disappointed on the phone. I felt bad about the whole evening, and I wanted to make things right."

He reached for her hand and pulled her out onto the front porch. She closed the door behind her.

"Come here," he said as he pulled her into his arms. "God, how I've missed you," he said. He held her for a moment, then placed his hands on either side of her face and kissed her. It felt like heaven being in his arms again.

She realized that he probably hadn't eaten yet, so she broke off the kiss and asked him if he wanted something to eat. At first, he said no, but she persuaded him to stay and have at least a bite of something. She led him back into the house as Colleen called out to her, "Angelina is everything alright?"

"Yes," she called.

She led Alejandro into the media room. "Sit down and I'll bring you something to eat."

"What happened to you?" Wyatt asked, giving Alejandro a once-over. "You look like you've been through the ringer."

"It's been a long week."

"Hey, I hear we're coming over to your house on the Fourth."

"Yep. I think it'll be a good time." As he finished his statement, Angelina appeared with a sandwich and fruit salad. "Thanks."

Alejandro ate his dinner and stretched his legs out in front of him. He became engrossed in the movie they'd been watching. Angelina just watched him. All she could think about was how lucky she was to have him in her life.

When the movie ended, he stood to leave.

"Hey, we're going to watch another. Are you in?" asked Wyatt.

"Well..."

"Come on and stay. We like having you around," added Colleen.

"I'll take that as a compliment. Thanks, Colleen."

Alejandro tried, but just couldn't make it through the second movie—he drifted off halfway through. When Angelina realized he'd fallen asleep, she covered him with a blanket and let him sleep. It was nearing midnight when she finally tried to wake him. Angelina placed her hand on his arm and shook it. He was out to the world. She knew he needed his sleep, but she didn't want him oversleeping in case he needed to go back to the hospital the next morning. She shook his arm harder and he woke with a start. He was out of it at first, then realized where he was.

"Oh Angelina, I'm sorry I fell asleep," he said brushing sleep from his eyes. "I wasn't much company."

"You needed your rest. Come on, let's get you home."

Alejandro stood and reached for her hand. "Walk me out?"

She nodded and squeezed his hand. As they walked out the door, they met her parents as they were coming in.

"Hi. How are you?" asked Alejandro.

"We're pretty good. Looks like you've had a rough day, though."

"More like a week's worth."

"Well, we'll let you go. See you on the Fourth."

Alejandro said his goodbye and Angelina walked with him to his car. "Call me when you get home."

"Sure." He pulled her into his arms and held her again before kissing her goodnight. "I'll call you in a few."

Alejandro was good to his word—he called her within ten minutes of leaving her house. He told her he had to go in the following day, but asked if she would meet him at his house at noon. He was sure he'd be there by then. "I love you Angelina. Sorry about tonight."

"No need to apologize. You just get some rest and I'll see you tomorrow. Love you," she said. That was the last thing he remembered, for he barely made it to his bed. He didn't know when the last time was that he'd been that exhausted.

He got a good night's sleep and actually made it home from the hospital well in advance of the noon-time he'd given Angelina. He spent some time working around the house when he heard the doorbell. It was Angelina, all bright-eyed with a huge smile on her face.

"Come here," he said and pulled her into his arms.

She sighed and said "This feels so good." She began to kiss him. He pulled away and grabbed her hand.

"Come on, let's go. We have a lot to do today and I want to be able to spend some quality time with you. Did you bring a change of clothes? I thought we'd go somewhere nice for dinner. I feel like I've been neglecting you lately."

"You haven't. You've just been busy at the hospital. I fully understand what's ahead after we marry. You're unplanned schedules, late night hours, and all. Don't worry about it."

"I do. I want to spend as much time as I can with you."

"Let's not worry about this now. Come on. Let's get what we need for next week."

They ate a quick lunch at a local pub and ventured to the store where they purchased various paper products, snacks, and drinks. He'd buy the meat and other perishable foods the following week. They went back to his house and put everything away. He led her to the patio where they shared a bottle of wine and enjoyed the late afternoon cloudless day. They discussed the party and the time everyone should arrive. She told him she'd come over as early as possible to help decorate and prepare the food.

"I'm just happy to be off that day. Actually, I'm off the remainder of the week."

"Really?"

"Uh huh. We'll have to do a day trip or something. Get away, just the two of us."

"Sounds like fun."

They spent the remainder of the afternoon enjoying one another's company. Then, they changed and went to dinner. He'd been planning the evening all week long. He was dressed in a suit and she in a beautiful emerald green dress with spaghetti straps. It was cut low in the front and back. He'd never seen her look so beautiful.

They arrived at the five-star restaurant and were greeted by the valet. As Angelina exited the car, Alejandro pulled her arm through the crook of his and escorted her into the restaurant. He'd called ahead and requested a private dining room. The hostess greeted him.

"Yes, Dr. Alvarez," she said. "Follow me."

Angelina was surprised that they didn't have to wait—with it being a Saturday evening, the restaurant was packed. The hostess led them through the center of the dining room towards the back which was lined with private dining rooms, each containing separate balconies that overlooked the vineyard below.

Angelina was amazed with the room. "What have you done here?"

"Ah, nothing special. I wanted to spend a quiet evening with you, and what better way than to have our own private dining room."

"You didn't have to do this. I would have been satisfied with sitting—"

"Shh," he said. "Let's enjoy our evening. I haven't been able to spend much time with you at all this week. I want this to be special. Okay?"

She nodded.

A waiter joined them with a bottle of wine. "Sir, would you care to sample?"

Alejandro approved the wine and the waiter poured her a glass, then topped off his and left them alone to enjoy their drink. Alejandro ordered dinner for her as well. He seemed to know everything she liked.

As they sat enjoying the ambience of the room, they discussed the Fourth of July party and how their family would react to their news.

"I think Gabriella will be too excited for words," Alejandro said. "And for her, that's something to see since she's always got something to say."

Angelina laughed.

He asked her about the start to the school year since it would be upon Angelina before too long. "I'm pretty much ready, I just have to deal with the student-specific stuff. I'll finish that when I get my class list. At least this year I won't have to redo everything. My lesson plans are pretty well mapped out for the year. I've also developed all of my supplemental materials. I feel good and can't wait to get back to school."

At that moment, their waiter came to serve them their first course. They both started with a nice garden salad topped with shrimp. For Angelina's main course, he ordered her a chicken breast covered with a creamy sauce that included roasted red peppers and artichokes. He ordered a blackened tuna steak for himself. Both meals were accompanied by roasted red potatoes and mixed vegetables. The waiter continually topped off their wine glasses throughout the meal.

"This meal is spectacular."

"It is," he agreed.

They finished their meal and then their waiter returned with dessert. Alejandro knew how much she loved crème brûlée and surprised her with it. The waiter turned and reached for a bottle of champagne that had seemingly appeared from nowhere.

"I'll take care of that," Alejandro said, thanking him.

The waiter left the room. Angelina felt like something was going on—butterflies started to creep into her stomach.

Alejandro reached for her left hand. Squeezing it lightly he spoke, "Angelina, you're so important and mean so much to me. You've helped me get through a really difficult time, something I could never have begun to deal with on my own. I love you so much."

"I feel the—"

"Shh, let me finish."

She nodded, her eyes never leaving his face.

"Angelina, I know we still have a lot to sort through between the two of us, but I want you to know that I will always, and I do mean always, be there for you. Those days that you're sad, I want you to share them with me. Whenever you decide to share your infertility with your family, I want to be there with you. To support you."

He stood and walked over to where she was sitting. He got down on bended knee and said, "I wanted to do this right. When I asked you to marry me at the Botanical Gardens, I surprised not only you, but myself as well. It was the right time and the right place, but all along I wanted you to experience a magical evening."

He withdrew a jeweler's box from the inside of his jacket and said, "Angelina, my love, will you do me the honor and be my wife?" When he completed the question, he opened the ring box. There sitting on black velvet was the most beautiful diamond ring Angelina had ever seen in her entire life. She was speechless.

"Well?" he asked.

Tears started to glide down her face. "Oh my," she said.

He silently wiped her tears.

"I'm stunned. Of course I'll marry you. This ring is stunning. I'm…"

He withdrew the two carat marquise-shaped diamond ring from the box and placed it on her finger. He raised her hand to his lips and kissed her finger.

"Alejandro, when did you have time to buy this?"

"I've had it for quite a while. One day I was walking by the jewelry store and decided to take a peek inside. As soon as I walked up to the counter, I saw your ring. I didn't think twice. I just purchased it. I wasn't sure when, or even if, I would ever ask you to marry me. Then, I wasn't sure if you'd even say yes, but I thought I had to have this ring just in case.

It spoke to me, and I knew exactly how it would look on your finger. It looks exactly how I imagined…" He pulled her into his arms and kissed her. "Now, how about that champagne?"

They enjoyed the remainder of their dinner. Indeed, it had been a magical evening for both of them. "I want to give you my ring back."

"Why?"

"Because I don't want my family to see it before the party."

"Good idea. I'll place it back on your finger soon, I promise."

They ended their evening and he drove her home—she'd returned her car to her parents earlier in the day. They said their goodbyes, and he told her he'd give her a call the following day. It was only three days until the Fourth and he couldn't wait to share their secret. He wasn't sure how their families would react, but he knew he should ask her father for her hand in marriage first. But when? He'd figure it out.

# CHAPTER TWENTY

The evening before their big day, Alejandro went to purchase the remainder of the food for the party. He'd worked late and found himself at the grocery store near midnight. Angelina had requested a specific dressing for her salad, and he had no idea where to find it in the store. He felt bad, but had to call her. Sleepily, she answered her phone.

"Did I wake you?"

"Alejandro, what's wrong? Are you okay? Where are you?" she asked. He could hear her sit up in bed.

"Settle down, sweetheart. I'm fine. I am standing in the middle of the grocery store right now, and I have no idea where to find your salad dressing."

"You're where?"

"At the grocery store."

"Why'd you go now? We could've gone tomorrow."

"I wanted to sleep in a bit. I need to be on my game…"

"Now, Alejandro. I don't think it will be that bad."

"I'm only kidding. Seriously, I'm beat and just want to try and get a good night's sleep. I wanted to make sure I got everything so we won't be hurried before everyone arrives. That's all."

She told him where the dressing was located and that she'd see him around nine. "Will that be too early?"

"Nah. I should be good to go by then. I'll let you get back to sleep. Angelina?"

"Yeah?"

"Tomorrow's going to be our big day. There's no going back."

"No... No going back."

"I love you," he said as he ended the call and completed his shopping. When he got home, he placed everything in the refrigerator and headed off to bed.

Surprisingly, he slept well. He woke around seven, showered, and dressed for the day. He wanted to get Angelina's dad aside without her knowledge before their announcement.

Angelina appeared promptly at nine. He opened the door and she almost knocked him off his feet as she carried in bags full of additional groceries.

"My goodness, you practically upended me. What do you have in there?"

She ignored him and headed to the kitchen. He followed and watched as she unloaded the bags. She was on a mission and continued to ignore him.

"You alright?" he asked as he placed an arm around her waist, kissing the side of her neck.

"Yeah. Why do you ask?"

"Well, you haven't said a word since you came flying in the door."

"Sorry about that, I've got a lot on my mind."

"You do?"

"Well, this is the first time we've entertained. I want it to be perfect."

"Anything else bothering you?"

"Like you don't know."

He pulled her into his arms and hugged her. He moved his hand to the side of her face and caressed it. She looked up into his eyes and smiled. "This is going to be a perfect day. I just know it. My mother's going to be so excited."

He smiled back at her, then reached down and gave her the good morning kiss he'd been dying to give her since she first arrived.

"Come on. We've got to decorate. Then I've got to start on the salads and—"

"Can you just chill out for a minute?" Alejandro said with a laugh. "We have plenty of time to get everything done. When is your family coming?"

"I told my mom to be here around two. Is that okay?"

"Yep, sure is. I told my family the same thing. When do you want to tell them about us?"

"You surprise me."

He nodded and gave her a quick peck on the cheek and headed outside.

They completed decorating and took a breather around noon. She fixed them a quick bite to eat and they sat on the patio eating when they started discussing their wedding.

"Alejandro, when do you want to get married?"

"Well, I know we have to wait a minimum of six months because of the pre-marital planning classes with the church."

"Yeah, I know. I'm not looking forward to those."

"Me neither, but we have to."

She stared at him, then spoke. "Let's see. This is July. The earliest we could probably get married would be January. I hate to think about getting married in the middle of winter. You know I've always wanted to get married in either April or October. I don't know, what do you think about the end of April?"

"Angelina, we don't have to make a decision today. At least we've started to think about it. You also have to factor in school. You'll have to talk to Mary about when, or if, you can get time off during the school year."

"And your schedule?"

"That's not a problem. As soon as we decide on a date, I'm putting it on the calendar. I plan on taking at least two weeks off."

"That's sounds wonderful."

They had just finished icing down the drinks when the doorbell rang. Angelina didn't even look out the window, she looked at her watch. It was one forty-five. "Wanna bet?"

"Nah."

"It's my mom."

"You think?" he said with a smirk on his face.

"Oh yeah."

She opened the door and there stood her mother, all decked out in red, white, and blue. Behind her stood her father. Wyatt and Colleen were strolling up the sidewalk, arguing about something.

"Mom, Dad, come on in." She held the door for them. "Come on, you two. What are you arguing about now?"

Colleen shrugged her shoulders and Wyatt just looked at her. "Nothing, really. Why?"

Angelina made a face at them, "Just wondering. Where are James and Kelly?"

"They're driving separately. They got stopped at a red light." Turning back to the driveway Jackie added, "Here they come. They just pulled up at the curb."

Angelina waited for James and Kelly. They rushed through the door saying their helloes as they headed off in the direction of the kitchen. Angelina was just about to close the door when Gabriella pulled into the driveway. She jumped out of her car with a platter of fruit and breezed through the door, giving her friend a peck on the cheek.

"Hey, there. Long time, no see."

"It's only been a few days."

"Just giving you trouble, that's all. Where's my brother?"

"Outside."

"Let me say hi to him and then I'll help you out. Oh by the way, Joe and Alec are running late. They were at some charity run earlier and just finished up."

All of the women gathered in the kitchen while Angelina's father joined Alejandro on the patio. Wyatt located the television and was watching the baseball game.

Alejandro set his plan in motion. Ben was helping him finish up a few things in the backyard. They were rearranging the patio furniture when Alejandro stopped and said, "Ben, can I talk to you for a minute?"

"Sure. What's up?"

Alejandro pulled two drinks from the cooler and walked to the back of his property with her father. He acted as though he were showing Ben something along the fence line.

Angelina saw him raising his arm and pointing at the ground. She turned back to her guests and thought nothing of the conversation.

Alejandro turned to her father and started his planned conversation. "Ben, I'd like to talk to you for a few minutes about Angelina."

"Is something wrong with her?"

"Oh no, nothing along those lines. I wanted to talk to you about... Well..." He looked away and then back at Ben. "Ben, your daughter means the world to me. We've gotten very close over the last several months."

"Angelina's special. You know she decided not to move out of the house because she enjoys helping with Colleen and Wyatt. I just wish she would stop feeling like she needs to help us. I wish she'd move out on her own. I think she needs that to grow as a person."

"Ah, Ben, that's what I want to talk to you about."

Ben just looked at Alejandro. "So you agree?"

"Well, in a manner of speaking. I know this may sound like—" He stopped for a minute, then continued, "Ben, I've asked Angelina to marry me. Before we said anything to our families, I wanted your approval. We decided we wanted to tell everyone today, but before we did, I wanted to talk to you first. As I said, your daughter means the world to me. Never in my wildest dreams did I think that I'd marry again, but I can't think of living my life without Angelina in it. I'd like to ask you... May I have her hand in marriage?"

"Well, of course you can. I can't think of anyone else that I'd want her to marry. You're perfect together. Her mother is going to be thrilled."

"I know she is. Can we keep this conversation between ourselves? I want to see the expression on Jackie's face when we tell everyone. I think it will be priceless."

Ben shook Alejandro's hand and told him he couldn't wait for the day that he could refer to him as his son-in-law. Alejandro felt relieved that the conversation was over. He didn't expect Ben to not accept him into his family, but wasn't completely sure.

By the time Alejandro and Ben finished their conversation, they were joined by his father. John helped start up the barbeque. He and Ben stood around while Alejandro gathered the meats that had been prepared earlier in the day for grilling. Conversation flowed and everyone enjoyed their meal. Ben even asked if he could hire Alejandro for grilling. Alejandro just laughed.

Jackie started to clear off the table. "I'll be right back with dessert."

Gabriella and Angelina gathered the remaining dishes while Jackie carried the dessert to the table. Alejandro stood as Angelina rejoined everyone. He reached for her hand. Everyone was talking about the fireworks scheduled for later in the evening.

"You know, I think we'll be able to see them from the backyard. At least that's what my neighbors have told me."

"I can't wait," said Maria.

Angelina looked up at Alejandro and smiled. She whispered, "Everyone is getting along so well."

He smiled and nodded. He placed his arm around her shoulders and led her towards the edge of the patio. She knew what was ahead and started to get butterflies. She couldn't wait for him to spill the beans. She especially wanted to see the expression on her mother's face when Alejandro shared their news. She looked at their families. Within the next few minutes, all of their lives were going to change. Soon, they'd be joined forever by marriage.

Alejandro tightened his hold on her. He took a deep breath and exhaled. Everyone was so involved with their conversation that they didn't notice his nervousness. He felt around inside his pocket for the jewelry box that he'd put there before dinner.

"May I have everyone's attention?" Alejandro called.

Everyone looked up in their direction.

"First of all, I would like to thank everyone for coming. This is a special occasion, as it's the first time I've entertained in my new home. Now, the real reason for this party…" He looked down at Angelina and smiled. "I'm sure everyone knows how close Angelina and I have become over the last several months."

Angelina looked out at her family. Her mother was anxiously listening to Alejandro. Alejandro reached for her hand while he reached into his pocket with the other. "Today, I spoke with Ben…"

Surprised, Angelina turned and looked up at him.

"I asked Ben for Angelina's hand in marriage."

Angelina looked directly at her mother. A smile broke out across her mother's lips and she shrieked.

Gabriella started to cry as he withdrew the jewelry box from his pocket and removed her ring. "Ben said yes and so has Angelina." With that, he placed her ring on her finger. Everyone jumped up in jubilation. Instantaneously, she was pulled into hugs by her mother, Maria, and Gabriella.

"I'm finally going to have you as my sister! When's the lucky day?"

She looked over at Alejandro. "We haven't set a date yet. We're working on it."

He winked at her while he dealt with his mother and father.

Kelly, Colleen, James, and Wyatt stood in the wings while Angelina dealt with her mother, Maria, and Gabriella's excitement.

Colleen was the first to approach her. She threw herself into Angelina's arms. "I knew it! I just knew the two of you would get married."

"You did?"

"Uh, huh," she added as Kelly approached her sister.

"I'm excited for you, sis. He's a great guy from what I've seen." Kelly kissed her sister on the cheek.

James and Wyatt added their congratulations, then all four Samuels siblings turned towards their soon-to-be brother-in-law. James extended his hand to Alejandro. "Congratulations, and welcome to the family," he said.

"Thanks," Alejandro said as he was then drawn into a hug with Colleen.

"This is the best Fourth of July, yet," Colleen said as she hugged him and pulled away. "Congratulations! I'm so excited for Angelina and, of course, you as well."

Alejandro laughed at Colleen's statement. Kelly and Wyatt both took their turns welcoming him to the family.

Joe and Alec were the last to approach the couple. They had arrived shortly before Alejandro's announcement. They both hugged her and told her they were happy that Alejandro was finally going to make an honest woman out of her. Angelina glared at both of his brothers.

Alejandro pulled her into his arms. "They're kidding you know."

She looked up at him, smiled, and broke out into a fit of laughter. "Of course, I do," she said

Alejandro felt like he was a true member of the Samuels family, and he knew Angelina felt the same way about his family.

The remainder of the evening passed in a blur. Shortly after the fireworks, Jackie and Ben left while John and Maria elected to stay for a bit longer. Gabriella couldn't get over Angelina's ring—she hadn't seen anything so beautiful. "Did you pick it out or did my brother?"

"He surprised me. Actually, he told me that one day he just went into the jewelry store, saw it, and bought it without thinking twice. He didn't even know if he was going to ask me to marry him, but just in case he did, he wanted me to have this ring specifically. I was shocked when I first saw it."

"I haven't seen you look this happy in a long time."

"I know. It's been hard keeping our engagement from everyone."

"When did you get engaged?"

"Officially, the day after school let out."

"Wow. How were you able to keep it a secret?"

"It wasn't easy, but Alejandro wanted to announce it today. He wanted the entire family here. I can't believe he asked my dad. That's just so…"

"Romantic?"

"Yeah, and boy can your brother be romantic when he wants to be." Angelina recounted to Gabriella the day he'd asked her to marry him at the Botanical Gardens, then when he surprised her with the romantic dinner and her ring. "Your brother means everything to me. He's helped me, too. He continues to help me daily deal with some issues that I have surrounding the transplant."

Gabriella looked perplexed.

"I'm fine, really. It's just some emotional stuff, don't worry."

"I won't. I'm just glad that the two of you got together."


By midnight, Angelina and Alejandro had completed clean-up. It was a comfortable July evening as they sat together on a chaise lounge. He held her tightly in his arms, nuzzling her neck and giving her a quick kiss.

"What a day," she said.

"It was terrific. Did you see the look on your mother's face when I told everyone about us? I wish I'd had a camera. I'll never forget it."

"It was great. She's thrilled. She told me she knew we'd get married from the get-go. She absolutely loves you."

"Well, I'm thrilled that she does. I won't have to butter her up."

Jabbing him in the ribs, she said, "Ahh, come on now."

"Kidding, only kidding. I love your family."

She turned in his arms and looked him in the eyes. "I've got a question for you."

"Yeah?"

"Just when did you talk to my dad? He never said a thing to me or my mother."

"This afternoon."

"When?"

"I led him into the backyard. This was important to me—I wanted his approval. I know it sounds kind of old fashioned, but it's something I needed to do. Especially with everything your family's been through lately… Colleen's illness, your infection… I just wanted to make sure he was okay with us before I announced it to the world."

"Alejandro, thank you for doing that. I had no idea you felt that way. Do you still feel guilty about what happened to me? Please be honest."

"Yes… no. At times I feel responsible for your infection. What if I'd done something differently? What if I'd kept a closer eye on you? Maybe we'd have a chance at having our own children…"

"Stop it. There's nothing you could've done. It happened. We'll get through it together. No one is to blame. Get it out of your head."

"Okay."

They sat in each other's arms and fell asleep in the moonlight. They were at peace. He'd shared his intentions with their families and he was content. He was with the woman he loved more than life itself.

Neither of them woke until the early morning hours when dawn was creeping into the eastern sky.

He laid there looking at his angel. And that she was. He was lucky to have her in his life. Yes, he had guilt. In all honesty, he felt responsible for her infection. He'd have to live with that for the remainder of his life. And now that they were getting married... When they wanted children, he'd have to face it again. He knew he'd be able to get past it, but would she? That was the million dollar question that they'd both have to face. Right now he was just happy to have her in his arms.

He knew they'd have to face tons of wedding questions over the next few days. He just hoped she'd be able to get through it without her mother bringing up grandchildren. The thought of that sent a knife through his heart. He didn't want her to have to deal with that right now. She was just starting to face her future without her own children.

# CHAPTER TWENTY-ONE

Angelina checked the school calendar and determined that Spring Break was in mid-March. She didn't want to get married then, so after much deliberation, she decided on April. After talking with Alejandro and Mary, she decided to take the last two weeks of April off. They decided to marry on April 16th, which was a Saturday. The first thing Alejandro did was mark out his calendar, as nothing was going to stop him from marrying Angelina.

Angelina, being the event planner, got through a good portion of her to-do list before school began. She'd picked out her wedding dress, as well as the bridesmaids' dress. She didn't want too large of a wedding party—Gabriella would be her maid of honor and her sisters would be bridesmaids. They chose Alejandro's cousins to be the flower girl and ring bearer, and his brothers would be his groomsmen. He'd chosen his father as his best man. The reception would be held at the country club, and they would marry at the church she'd grown up attending.

Everything was coming together. Angelina didn't have to worry about school as she'd completed her planning well ahead of time. She felt stress-free as she began her second year at St. Margaret's.

Angelina's fellow teachers first learned of her engagement when Mary stood up at the opening faculty meeting and said she had an important announcement to make. Angelina hadn't been wearing her engagement ring because she'd jammed her finger playing tennis the night before and couldn't get her ring on.

"I want to share some exciting news."

Neither Angelina nor Gabriella knew what she was going to say. This was the first time they'd been with any of their colleagues since summer began. None of them even knew she'd been dating Alejandro except for Mary.

"Many of you know the story of Angelina's sister, Colleen. You also know that Gabriella and Angelina went to college together." There were only two new teachers in the school, so everyone else knew their background. "But what you don't know is Angelina and Gabriella's brother became engaged over the summer. They plan to marry the middle of April."

Cheers rang out. Angelina sat with a huge smile on her face. Gabriella reached over and squeezed her hand.

"She and Alejandro have been dating for quite some time. Since they'd been through such an ordeal with her sister's liver transplant and then her illness, they wanted to keep it low key. I wanted to start the year off with this fantastic news. Last fall was full of sadness for their families, but now this year they have a lot to celebrate. I wanted to share with Angelina our best wishes. And on that note…"

The secretary wheeled out a cake. Angelina was shocked. She couldn't believe that Mary had gone to all of this trouble for her. "Let's celebrate the start to a new and successful year along with Angelina's engagement."

Angelina was surrounded by her fellow teachers. She was overwhelmed by their happiness for her and Alejandro. It took her a minute to catch her breath. When they asked where her ring was, she reached inside her shirt and pulled out her engagement ring. When she'd hurt her finger, she'd placed it on a chain around her neck so it would be with her until her finger improved.

"Oh my, look at that," said one of the teachers. "That is the most beautiful ring I've ever seen…"

She shared how he'd proposed the day after school ended for the summer break. Another teacher shouted, "Gabriella, what do you think?"

"Well, they kept it a secret from us for almost a month. Alejandro had a Fourth of July party and that's when they told us. I'm just so excited to have her as my sister. It's something I've wanted for a long time."

Mary started to cut the cake when Alejandro walked in the room. "Ahh… and here's the lucky groom-to-be."

Everyone turned at once. Alejandro stood at the back of the room in total shock. Mary had called him earlier in the day and asked that he come by school. She'd wanted to discuss a matter with him and wouldn't take no for an answer. Thankfully, he had a light day and was able to work the late afternoon meeting into his day.

"What do we have here?"

"A celebration to honor you and Angelina."

"Huh?"

"On your engagement, silly."

"Oh," he said as he neared Angelina and placed a kiss on her cheek. "This is quite a surprise. You didn't have to do this for us."

"I wanted to kick the year off on a good note and thought, what better way than to announce your engagement and have a little celebration?"

"Well, thank you," he said.

The teachers stood around for a few minutes discussing their wedding plans. After helping clean up, Alejandro walked Angelina to her classroom. "That was a nice surprise."

"It certainly was. I had no idea she was going to do that. I was going to announce our engagement in a few weeks."

He reached for her hand and looked at her swollen finger. "How's the finger?" he asked as he inspected it.

She shrugged her shoulders.

"Looks a little better, but it's still swollen."

"Yeah."

"I wish you could wear your ring."

"I am." He didn't know that she wore it around her neck. She pulled the necklace out and showed him. "It's next to my heart where I can feel your presence."

She turned and hugged him tightly. "Do you have to go back to the hospital?"

"Nah, I'm done for the day."

"Come on, let's go celebrate."

"What are we celebrating?"

"The start of a new school year, us, and anything else we can think of."

He placed his arm around her neck and pulled her close as she reached for her purse. They walked from her classroom and right into Mary.

"I was just coming to see you."

"You were?"

"Yes, what are you doing right now?"

"We're headed out to have a drink. Want to join us?"

"Sure. How about I meet you at the pub around the corner?"

"Great idea."

Mary skirted down the hallway ahead of them as Alejandro turned to Angelina. Smiling, he said, "Sorry about that."

"Not a problem. I like her. She's a great boss and really seems to like me for some reason. Maybe that's because of my handsome fiancé."

Mary joined them for a quick drink. "I just want to tell you how happy I am for the two of you. You're an absolutely perfect couple."

They smiled at one another.

"So what are your plans? I'm sure you're going to have plenty of children."

They looked at each other. He smiled at Angelina and placed his arm across her shoulders. "In time," he replied. "We have so much to do over the next few months." Changing the subject, he asked if she was planning another Career Day. Internally, he breathed a sigh of relief. He wanted today to be a happy one for them and didn't want to have to face the reality of her situation.

For the most part, Mary's question concerning children didn't seem to faze Angelina in the least. He hoped that she was beginning to face her situation without as much sadness. He wanted her to get past it.

Thanksgiving was upon them and Angelina's class was scheduled to return to the Indian Reservation for the mock Thanksgiving celebration. The evening prior to the field trip, she went over to Alejandro's. She knew he was home working on a presentation that he was scheduled to give the following week at an out-of-state conference. She was anxious. She needed him to calm her nerves, to make her see that everything was alright. They'd been over and over her situation. She'd listen to him, see the light of day, and forget about it. Then, she'd have periods of sadness and fall right back into its trap. She needed him tonight more than ever.

On the way to his house, she saw a young family taking a walk. The father was pulling two children in a red flyer wagon while the mother carried a smaller child papoose like. Seeing that particular scene threw her over the edge. She felt like a knife had coursed right through her heart. It took her breath away. She needed Alejandro.

She pulled into his driveway and swiped at the remaining tears on her face. She had to get control of herself. She didn't want to upset him. He needed to complete his presentation, but she also needed him, too. She sat in her car for a few more minutes composing herself, then walked to his front door and rang the bell.

It took him a few moments for him to answer. He was surprised to see her and looked at her questioningly. "Sweetheart, what's wrong?"

She rushed into his arms and broke into tears.

"Honey, come here. Are you okay?" He led her towards the kitchen. He couldn't comprehend what was wrong with her. He'd talked to her earlier in the day and she seemed fine. She was completing preparations for the field trip and… *That's it*, he thought—the field trip. He sat her at the kitchen table and retrieved a cold glass of water for her. Sitting down, he reached for her hand. Clasping it, he said, "It's the field trip, isn't it?"

She couldn't look at him. She just nodded her head.

Too many memories, he thought. "I understand."

She looked up at him. "I was on my way over here and I was doing okay until I saw… I saw the cutest family on a walk. Mother, father, and three smaller children. The father was pulling the older two in a wagon and the mother carried the youngest. My heart ached after witnessing that…"

"Angelina, we can have that. It just might not be our 'own.' If it makes you feel better, we can start exploring adoption right away. Right after we get married. If that will help you get through this, I am all for it."

"It's just… I need to get over it on my own, but I can't seem to quite clear the final hurdle. I think I'm there and then something throws me back two paces. Alejandro, I think I need to tell my mom. Maybe that's why I can't cross the finish line. My secret keeps holding me back from getting on with my life. What do you think?"

"That's a possibility. Maybe you'd feel free if you told her."

"I think so. It's just that I have to find the right time. With the holidays and everything…"

"As long as you've decided to tell her, you'll find the right time. In your heart, you'll know when it's best."

She smiled at him.

"Do you want me there with you? You know I want to support you. I want her to know that you haven't been alone on this journey. We're in this together and I want her to know that we'll have children. Someway, somehow."

"Alejandro, you're my lifeline. Without you, I'd have no direction. I'd be going from one day to the next without purpose. You give me that purpose. I don't know what I'd do without you."

He held her for a time and then said, "Better?"

She nodded. "You always make me feel better. That's why I sought you out tonight. I just hope I didn't ruin your creative genius for the evening."

"Why would you say that?"

"You were working on your presentation, weren't you?"

"I'm pretty much done with it, just finishing my graphics."

"That's good. I didn't want to burden you again with my life."

"Your life is my life. Nothing is too big or too small for me. That's what I'm here for, and pretty soon I'll be your husband. I want to share everything with you. The good and the bad, the ups and the downs… Everything. Don't you ever think that you're bothering me. I love you way too much to put anything between us. I want you to feel comfortable that you can share anything with me. Got it?"

"Got it."

"Maybe you shouldn't go on the field trip?"

"No. I have to face my demons. I feel a lot better just seeing you and talking to you. I'll be fine."

"You know I'm just a phone call away. I should be at home most of tomorrow working on my presentation. Call me if you need me. Please, no heroics."

She nodded in agreement. It was getting late and she needed to get home. She had to rise earlier than normal the next day. She wanted to make sure that her emotions were in check before she boarded the school bus for the Reservation.

She slept fairly well after having her meltdown the evening before. She was almost to school when her phone rang. "Hi," she said.

"Better?"

"Yes. Much."

"I just wanted to call and check on you. You're sure you can make it through the day?"

"I'll do my best, and if I have any problems I'll call you. I promise. You always help me to see the light at the end of the tunnel. I'll be fine."

"You know how much I love you."

"I know. I've gotta go. I'm just pulling into school. I love you."

Alejandro got off the phone and immediately called his sister. He wanted to make sure she understood Angelina's shakiness for the day.

"I know. I've been worried about her all week. I know she has a lot of memories from that day. Collapsing and all…"

He started to say more, but realized that his sister had no idea what came out of that horrific time. "Just keep an eye on her for me."

"Sure. I'll call you if I need to."

"Thanks, Gabby. You're the best sister anyone could have."    He hung up. He'd worry about Angelina the entire day.

Angelina boarded the bus with Gabriella right behind her. Gabriella placed a hand on her shoulder as they climbed the stairs. "You okay?"

"Yeah."

They sat together on the bus. It was a relatively long ride to the Reservation. Abruptly, Angelina spoke. "I had a little meltdown on your brother's shoulder last night."

"You did? What happened?"    Gabriella didn't want her to know that she'd talked to Alejandro earlier that morning.

Angelina proceeded to tell her the story, of course leaving out the parts surrounding having children. "Just a lot of memories came crashing back at me. I felt sorry for him because I interrupted his work."

"I'm sure he didn't care. He'd do anything for you. You know that, don't you?"

"Yeah. He's the best thing that's ever happened in my life. I don't know what I'd do without him."    She smiled at her future sister-in-law. "You know I love you, too."

"I know you do, and I can't wait until I can call you my sister."

The remainder of the day went off without a hitch. Angelina was involved in all aspects of the field trip. She participated in the scavenger hunt that led the students all around the Reservation looking for various artifacts that they'd studied in class. She pointed out the numerous headdresses and the intricate beadwork that several of the craftsmen were working on. She was also able to enjoy the tribal dance that she missed the previous year. She didn't let the memories consume her.

Gabriella knew Angelina experienced flashbacks to when she collapsed, but she made it through the day without incident. Angelina thoroughly enjoyed her day and she couldn't wait to return the following year.

Alejandro spent his day with his phone by his side. He worried that Angelina would need him. By the time the clock reached two, he realized she'd probably made it through the day. He felt that if she shared her medical condition with her family, she'd be able to deal with her situation much better. She'd have him, along with their families, to lean on when she was having a difficult time.

Alejandro had worked off-and-on on his presentation for most of the day when he decided to take a drive. Before he knew it, he'd pulled into St. Margaret's parking lot. He wasn't sure if they'd returned from the field trip, so he decided to remain in his car until the final bell.

He'd been there only a few minutes when the bus pulled into the parking lot. He saw her sitting next to the window towards the back of the bus. He thought she looked okay.

Just as the students were ready to disembark, she saw him. A huge smile broke out across her face. She turned to the person sitting next to her then waved.

He stood beside his car while he waited for her to exit the bus. He decided he'd walk her in, visit with Mary until the day ended, and then talk with her. He had an idea that he wanted to share with her. He walked over to the bus and waited for her to disembark—she was one of the last to exit. He reached for her hand and helped her down the last step.

"This is sure a surprise," she said and smiled up at him. She leaned up and gave him a peck on the cheek.

Alejandro placed his hand along her back and walked with her towards the building. "I'm going to have a word with Mary. I'll see you after the bell."

She looked over her shoulder and smiled back at him. She mouthed a "thank you," then turned as one of her students began talking to her.

Alejandro surprised Mary.

"To what do I owe the honor of this visit, Doctor?"

"Just thought I'd stop by and say hi, that's all."

"Really now?"

"Actually, I had an ulterior motive... Are you ready for the holidays?"

Mary commented on her family's traditions for Thanksgiving.

"I can't believe its next week. Time sure flies by."

"It certainly does. Before you know it, the wedding will be here."

Alejandro nodded, "I know. I can't believe it."

"So, what are your plans? Is Angelina going to keep teaching?"

"As far as I know, she's planning to. The children mean too much to her to stop doing what she loves. From what I've seen, she's a fabulous teacher."

"Yes, she is. I would hate to lose her. She inspires us all." With that, the bell rang. Alejandro wished her a good holiday and headed towards Angelina's classroom. He waited until all of the students left and then entered.

"Hey, there," he said. She was at the back of the room rummaging through her closet.

"Hi," she said and continued her efforts.

"Need help?"

"Nope. Just found what I was looking for."

He sat at her desk and watched the enthusiasm on her face when she pulled a huge display from the closet. She was preparing to change out her bulletin board for the month of December.

"What's up?" she asked.

"I was worried about you all day. Since I was home, I decided to come by and make sure you were okay. And I have a proposition for you."

"I'm fine. Better than I thought I'd be." She approached him, "So, what's this proposition about?" He stood while she put her bulletin board materials aside and gathered her purse. "Why don't you tell me at home? I think I've had enough today and just want to go home."

"That's fine. Come on, I'll follow you."

"I want to go to your house."

"I'll follow you home so you can drop off your car, then we can pick up something for dinner."

She nodded at him as she locked her classroom. Mary waved goodbye as they left the building. He followed her home and they went inside to have a brief conversation with her mother. Then, they headed to the grocery store.

As they drove back to his house, he could tell the day was beginning to take its toll on her—she was developing dark shadows under her eyes. He reached for her hand and clasped it. No words were necessary.

By the time they reached his house, it was nearing six. They elected to eat first. Alejandro fixed dinner while she watched. He knew she'd had a rough couple of days and wanted her to relax. "Sit there. This is my treat. I'm fixing dinner. No arguing."

"Well, when you put it that way." She drank a glass of wine while he prepared their meal. Swirling the wine in her glass, she said, "The kids really enjoyed the trip. I can't believe how well they listened. We had absolutely no discipline problems."

"That's good. I know how hard it is to sometimes control them outside of the classroom." He served their salads while the main course finished cooking. He reached for his glass of wine and told her how he'd finished his presentation. "I wish I wasn't going to have to be out of town next week."

"You'll be back for Thanksgiving won't you?"

"Yeah. I just wanted to be here for you. If I would have realized that Thanksgiving was the same week as this conference, I would've turned down the speaking engagement."

"Alejandro, I'll be fine."

"I know. I just wanted to be here, that's all."

They ate their dinner and cleaned up the kitchen. He poured them each another glass of wine and led her to the couch in the family room. They sat down and he pulled her into his arms while she placed her head on his shoulder.

"This feels so good," he said.

"It does… Now, what did you want to talk to me about?"

"Yesterday, you said you wanted to tell your mother about your infertility."

She nodded her head while he stroked her forearm.

"I want to run this idea past you."

"Okay."

"I was thinking that probably both of our families need to know."

She nodded again.

"What do you think about having our parents to dinner next week? I think they both should hear the news at the same time."

"It's going to be hard any way we tell them. I think it's a good idea since I'll only have to deal with this once. Our parents can then pass it along to everyone else."

"We can cross that bridge when we get there. We might want to tell them ourselves later on. But, I thought by doing it this way, we'd do it together. I want them to know that I've been through this with you from the beginning—that I'm fully aware of your condition and I support you. "

"When do you want to have them to dinner?"

"It's up to you."

"Let's do it the day before Thanksgiving. Depending on how that goes, maybe we can tell the remainder of the family on Thanksgiving."

"Are you sure about that?"

"Yes. I have a lot to be thankful for. I know this isn't the best news in the world but I've kept it from them for a year now. I'll be fine as long I have you by my side."

He hugged her close and brushed a kiss on the top of her head. "Always," he said.

# CHAPTER TWENTY-TWO

Alejandro called Angelina's parents the next morning and invited them for dinner the following Wednesday. Then, he called his mother. "Mom, what're you doing for dinner next Wednesday?"

"Preparing for Thanksgiving. Why?"

"I'd like you and Dad to join Angelina's parents for dinner at my house."

"Alejandro, what are you thinking? You know how busy that day is for me."

"Mom, I need you to be here."

Sighing deeply, she said, "Okay, Alejandro, we'll be there. Whatever the reason, it must be important to you…"

Alejandro gave her a time and explained that he would be out of town the first part of the week. "I'll see you Wednesday?"

"I just hope I get everything accomplished before we come over."

"Get Gabriella to help you. You know she will."

"I know. I just thought I'd just give you a little trouble, that's all."

"Just think of this as a relaxing evening before a big day. You need it, Mom."

Alejandro made it through his presentation and took an early flight home. He wanted everything to be perfect for their dinner. He wasn't sure how Jackie would take the news. He knew there'd be questions as to why she didn't tell them before now. He knew it was Angelina's decision, but he feared Jackie would lash out at him. He'd been the one to diagnose her condition and had known about it all along. He feared she would accuse him of feeling sorry for her daughter and not really loving her. He wondered if he felt guiltier than he previously thought. He had to get these thoughts out of his head because before he knew it they'd be sharing this with both of their families. He didn't worry about his parents, but dealing with her parents just troubled him.

Everyone arrived on time and the pre-dinner conversation focused on the wedding and upcoming holidays. Parties were being planned, and even Alejandro offered to throw a pre-holiday party.

Jackie kept reiterating how happy he made her daughter. "I haven't seen Angelina this happy in years. You're good for her Alejandro."

Alejandro served Caesar salad, roasted chicken, parsley new potatoes, and roasted asparagus for dinner. Both Jackie and Maria complimented him on a fabulous meal.

When dinner was over, they moved into the living room for after dinner-drinks. Alejandro shifted his gaze to Angelina. He walked over and placed his arm around her. He led her to one of the couches and sat beside her. She reached for his hand. Clasping it for strength, she turned to her parents. "Mom, Dad,

Maria, and John, I need to tell you something." She looked up at Alejandro and took a deep breath.

"My dear, what is it?" asked Maria.

"I have to share something with you that I've known about for some time now."

"Angelina?" her father asked.

"Dad, please. Let me continue. This is hard for me." Alejandro squeezed her hand. "Remember last year when Colleen had her transplant?"

"Yes, how could we forget," her mother said.

"Well, after that I got that infection… Well, I was a lot sicker than you knew."

"Angelina. Are you sick again?" her father asked.

"No, I'm not. But I have to tell you something. Something that I've kept from you for the last year… Something that has begun to eat me up inside. I realized with Alejandro and I getting married that I have to share this with you. If I don't, I won't be able to go on as the wedding gets closer."

"Sweetheart, what is it?" Jackie was becoming unglued while she sat on the couch.

Angelina looked down at her hand intertwined with Alejandro's. "First of all, I want you to know that Alejandro and I truly love one another. I've loved him since the moment I first laid eyes on him. What I'm about to share with you, I could never have begun to go through without him by my side. He's been my rock and I just want you to know that." She smiled up at him. "Any decisions made, were made by me and I don't want you to think Alejandro played a part in any of it."

Everyone was sitting on the edge of their seats, holding their breath.

"At the time of my infection, Alejandro was my doctor. We hadn't begun to date. I had feelings for him but I didn't really know what they were. I guess after my diagnosis it all started to come together. He was my... Well I've already told you how important he is to me."

John reached for his wife's hand. He had a feeling he knew where this conversation was headed. He glanced at his son and gave him a look that was returned. Jackie continued to stare at the couple. She had no idea what her daughter was about to say, and she definitely wasn't prepared.

"Last Thanksgiving, I was pretty sick. I'd sent you and Dad home to spend the rest of the day with the family. Colleen was... Oh never mind... Alejandro had spent the entire time at the hospital from the moment the ambulance brought me in. He was unbelievable. He never left my side. He knew I had the infection, but he also knew that there was something else wrong with me."

Alejandro unclasped his hand from hers and drew her close. She looked up at him. He nodded at her to continue.

"After you left me that day, Alejandro came in and shared the news with me."

John again caught his son's eye. He gave him "the look" and nodded. Yes, his beliefs were true. He just waited to hear it confirmed from her lips.

"The infection was a lot worse than he'd first thought. It had spread."

"Spread where?" her mother asked.

"To my..." she swallowed. "To my fallopian tubes. As a result of the infection, I can't have children."

Jackie gasped and started crying. Maria looked at her husband with tears in her eyes. Ben just stared at his daughter… And Alejandro.

Alejandro held onto the love of his life. He brushed a kiss to her temple and whispered to her that he loved her.

They sat there for a few moments before his father spoke. "Are you sure?"

Alejandro nodded. "Yes, there's nothing that can be done."

"Why? Why did you keep it from us?" her mother cried.

"Because it was about me. Because… I guess I couldn't deal with it. And if I couldn't deal with it, how could I expect you to?"

"But, Angelina. We're family. Who else knows about this?"

"No one. Only Alejandro."

Jackie glared at him.

"Jackie, I couldn't tell you. I was her doctor and she wanted no one to know."

"Why tell us now?" her father asked.

"It was getting more difficult for me. I thought that I'd dealt with it, but I realized last week that I hadn't. I needed to tell you so I could move on with my life… Our life. I have a lot to be thankful for. I have a wonderful fiancé and a great family.  I just needed to get it out."  She clasped her hands and continued. "I want to share this with the rest of the family tomorrow. This is hard enough for us, and I want you to promise not to say anything to them. For my own sanity, I have to be the one that tells them. I know it will be difficult—"

"Dear, don't worry about that," Maria said as she stood and approached her. "Can I give you a hug?"

Angelina stood and was enveloped in a warm embrace. His father followed. "Angelina, I'm sorry to hear this. But I know you and Alejandro will work through it."

She smiled up at her future father-in-law and said, "Yes, we will."

Alejandro returned to her side and forced her to glance at her parents. They were in shock. Alejandro walked over to them and said, "I want you to know that I did everything that I could. The infection moved so quickly..."

"But that wasn't enough. You're—"

"Mom, he's not responsible. He did everything he could to make me well." She reached for his hand. "Mom, Alejandro has enough guilt himself. He wished he could've done more, but it just wasn't meant to be. I had an infection and that's it. I'm well now. I just have to deal with the fact that I can't have my own children. You'll have grandchildren, they'll just be adopted."

Jackie looked at them. "I know you did everything that you could, Alejandro. I'm just sad for Angelina. She's wanted to be a mother her whole life."

"And she still can. The only difference is that they won't be our own biological children. I want you to know that we'll have children. We'll still love them as though we created them ourselves. Children are important to both of us and we'll never give up that dream. It may challenge us, but I want you to know that we'll see our dream fulfilled."

Angelina's parents were the first to leave. Jackie hugged her daughter and told her she'd see her at home. She'd promised not to mention it to her siblings. It was her news and she needed to share it. John and Maria stayed longer. John cornered Alejandro in his office while Maria helped Angelina clean up. "Son, I'm sorry to hear this news. Have you looked at—"

"Dad, there's nothing that can be done. She has extensive scarring. I was too late. Just too damn late…"

"Son, don't blame yourself. You did everything that you could."

"I know. I'm just sad. That's the only word I can use. She's wanted children her entire life."

"I know, Alejandro. You'll have them. Someday. Now, I'm concerned about your guilt."

"Dad, yes I have guilt. Guilt that I didn't realize until just recently, but we'll get through this together. I'm just concerned about Angelina. I hope that by sharing this she got some closure. I don't expect her to ever get over it. I just want the pain to lessen to where she can deal with the sadness a little more."

"I understand."

"Thanks, Dad. I knew you would."

"Angelina, honey. Thank you for sharing this with us."

"It was important for me to share it with both of our parents at the same time, just as it was with Alejandro to share our engagement. You'll be my mother-in-law soon. I couldn't leave you out of this conversation. You're too important to me. I know my mother's not too happy with me for keeping this from her, but I wasn't ready to deal with it." Pausing, she continued, "I'm ready to deal with it now. Maria, thanks for understanding. I can't wait to call you my mother as well."

"Oh, dear, thank you. I'd always wished for another daughter, and now I will have one." She hugged Angelina and that's how Alejandro and John found them moments later.

"What're you two doing?" asked John.

"Oh, just having a 'mother-daughter' talk, that's all."

John walked over to them and reached out for Angelina. He gave her a hug and kiss. "I can't wait to have you for a daughter, too. You're a special woman, Angelina. We both love you very much."

Angelina looked towards Alejandro. "I love you both as well. I can't wait to be a part of your family."

Alejandro smiled. He'd truly found a remarkable woman in Angelina. They had one more hurdle to face and then they'd be on the home stretch.

Angelina and Alejandro decided to attend the Thanksgiving Day parade that was held downtown and asked Wyatt, Colleen, and Gabriella to go with them. James was planning to participate in a touch football game with his college friends, and Kelly was driving in from Atlanta and wouldn't be expected until early afternoon. Gabriella declined since she needed to help her mother. Wyatt thought it was too cold outside, but Colleen elected to go. She'd never been to the parade and made a big deal about seeing Santa. Angelina laughed at her and Alejandro went along with the fun.

Alejandro drove and all Colleen could talk about were the upcoming holidays. Since she hadn't been able to enjoy the holiday shopping the year before, she was anxious to begin. In previous years, she and Angelina had shopped together. The first Saturday of December, Angelina would treat her to lunch and they'd shop. Last year, neither was able to partake in their ritual, but this year both of them were well.

"Hey, Doc?"

"What?"

"Angelina and I take one day during the holiday season and shop together. What do you think about joining us? Start to make it a tradition that we can share?"

"That sounds like a fabulous idea. You need to let me know when you've planned for your day of shopping so I can clear my schedule."

Angelina looked back at her sister, smiled, and winked at her. Angelina mouthed a "thank you," for including him in their special day—it meant a lot to her. Alejandro would fit into their family without any problems, just as long as her mother didn't try to continue to blame him for her infection. She acted as though she didn't, but after last night's quick exit, she wasn't too sure.

The three of them enjoyed the parade. Colleen loved Santa Claus's parade down Main Street. "I think we should go see Santa when we all go shopping."

"Come on now, Colleen. Are you kidding?"

"Would I kid about something like that?" she said with a huge smile on her face. "We need to have our picture taken with the big man."

"Whatever you say, Colleen," Alejandro said, laughing.

The parade was over by noon when they piled back into Alejandro's car for the return to her parents' house and Thanksgiving lunch. Maria had invited Angelina's family to dinner where they'd share their news with the remainder of the family. Lunch went well, then Angelina went over to Alejandro's parents' to help with the last minute preparations. His parents greeted her with hugs and she smiled at them. They asked how she was doing.

"I'm having a good day. We had a great time at the parade."

"That's good, dear," replied Maria.

"I made Alejandro bring me by early so I can help you. After all, we did interrupt your preparations with our dinner last night."

"Dear, think nothing of it. I intentionally gave Alejandro grief. I knew I'd have all the help I needed between John and Gabriella. Alec and Joe... Well, they'll just show up to eat. Now, why don't you rest? I'm sure you're worn out."

"I'm fine. I'd rather not think about it. The hardest part was telling our parents. That part's over. Don't think that it's not going to be difficult telling our siblings because it is... It's going to be especially hard telling Gabriella." Smiling at Maria, she continued, "I'll be fine—"

Alejandro interrupted her. "You'll be fine? What's going on?" he said, concerned.

"Nothing, dear. I was just having a conversation with your mother, that's all. Everything's good."

He gave her a funny look and walked out of the room.

"Angelina, he worries about you. You realize that."

"Yes, I know he does. He has his own guilt for not diagnosing my illness sooner. Deep down, he blames himself. I wish he wouldn't, but I think that's just the doctor in him. He wants to cure everyone, but that's just not possible. I definitely don't blame him. I love him and know that he would never do anything to hurt me."

Gabriella entered the room just as Angelina finished talking. "Hey, there. How's my sister-in-law to-be doing today?"

"Great. We just came back from the parade. Colleen, Alejandro, and I watched Santa Claus arrive."

"Sounds like fun," she said sarcastically.

"Oh, come on now. You don't still believe in Santa?" Angelina laughed as she helped peel the potatoes for dinner.

Angelina's family arrived at five thirty. They were early, but Jackie stressed that Maria could use the extra help. The men gathered to watch football while the women finished the last of the preparations. Dinner went smoothly as Maria served all of the Thanksgiving mainstays: roasted turkey, stuffing, mashed potatoes, sweet potato casserole, green beans, rolls, cranberries, and pumpkin and pecan pies for dessert. They all gave thanks for health, happiness, and the upcoming nuptials. They reminisced about past Thanksgivings, and it was decided that the families would take turns hosting Thanksgiving Day dinner.

The dishes were washed and everyone was sitting at the table chatting. Alejandro reached for

Angelina's hand under the table. He squeezed it and smiled at her. She knew it was time to share their news with the remainder of the family.

"May I have everyone's attention?"

Everyone stopped talking and glanced in her direction. Looking down at her hand entwined with Alejandro's, she took a deep, deep breath. "There's something I need to share with everyone. What I have to tell you, I've already shared with our parents. Now it's time to complete the circle." She closed her eyes and paused. "This isn't easy. I've needed to be honest with everyone for a very long time, and the time is now." Alejandro looked at her. She felt his strength being channeled to her and had a new-found confidence.

"I know everyone remembers last year when Colleen and I went through the transplant surgeries."

They all nodded.

"I know everyone remembers when I developed my infection last Thanksgiving."

Again, they nodded their heads.

"Well, I was pretty sick, and I've been dealing with this secret since then. But I'm able to share it with you today because I have Alejandro here to support me. He's my rock and without him I'd never been able to get to this point... Last Thanksgiving, Alejandro diagnosed my condition." She paused as they listened intently. "As a result of my infection, I have severe scarring and can't conceive."

No one said a word, staring at her wide-eyed.

"I can't have children."

Gabriella was stunned. Colleen stood and walked over to her sister. Standing behind her, she hugged her from behind. "I'm so sorry, Sis."

Kelly reached across the table for her sister's hand. She didn't know what to say—she had tears in her eyes. She squeezed her hand and tried to smile at her.

And Gabriella, she didn't know what to do. She turned towards her brother. Alejandro stood and walked towards her. She met him half-way and pulled him into a tight hug.

She couldn't speak. She just held onto her brother.

"Gabriella, it's okay. We're going to be okay."

"You must be devastated."

"I'm fine. We've known for a year now. It's been the hardest on Angelina."

"But I know how much you want children."

"We'll have them. We'll just have to adopt, that's all."

She withdrew from his arms and walked towards Angelina who drew her into an embrace.

"I wanted to tell you so badly. I just couldn't."

"Why now?"

"The field trip to the Indian Reservation made me finally confront my demons. That was a difficult day for me—I almost didn't go. I realized that I would face this depression every year if I kept this secret to myself. I had to confront it. Alejandro's been wonderful. On several occasions, when he came to St. Margaret's during the Career Day planning, he caught me being an emotional mess. Each time he was supportive and understanding. He's a special man with a kind heart. He hated seeing me go through this. He's suffered almost as much as I have. He blames himself. He thinks he should have seen something... Or been more aware of my condition to prevent it. Even though he's a miracle worker in a sense, he's not a magician. He's—"

Gabriella interrupted her. "Angelina, is there something that I can do?"

"Just be there for me when I have a bad day, which I'm sure will happen."

Alejandro stood by Angelina and placed his hand at the small of her back.

"It's hard, at times, working with my students. There're days when I've just wanted to cry the entire day—"

"Shh, Angelina," he said. "Why don't we go into the family room and—"

"No, I'm alright, Alejandro. I want to talk to Gabriella."

He nodded and left them alone.

Alejandro's brothers confronted him in the study. Joe and Alec were concerned about them as a couple, but also for him. He'd been through so much with Tammy and Michael's deaths. "Alejandro, you okay?"

"Alec, I'm okay now that we've told everyone."

"Did you look at everything?" asked Joe.

"Of course. The scarring is too severe for her to conceive. I was just too late. Too late…"

"Stop beating yourself up."

"It's just—"

"Alejandro, be thankful that's all that happened to her. Be thankful that she's alive to share your life."

"I know, Alec. It's just so hard seeing her have to face this. All she's ever wanted was a family."

"And she can still have that with you."

"I know."

Both Alejandro and Angelina fielded questions the remainder of the evening. They were both exhausted when Alejandro said, "You ready?"

"Don't we have to stay?"

"Mom will understand. Let's just go be alone together. It's been a rough twenty-four hours and I just want to hold you."

She agreed.

"Mom, Dad, I think we're going to go."

"Of course, go ahead. It's been a difficult couple of days for the two of you. We understand. Angelina, please come by soon." Angelina hugged Maria and thanked her.

"How about we go to lunch next week? We're off school one day. I'll call you to set up the time."

"That sounds wonderful." Maria hugged Angelina one last time and watched as they left the house. John knew how rattled she'd become since hearing the news the previous evening. He hugged his wife as they watched their son pull away from the house. "He's had a rough time of it these last few years."

"He certainly has. But he's strong, and with Angelina by his side they'll get through this together."

# CHAPTER TWENTY-THREE

As Christmas approached, Colleen contacted Alejandro to see if he was still available to go shopping. She caught him just as he was headed off to see a patient. "Hey, Alejandro, it's me Colleen."

"Well, hello there. How're you feeling these days?"

"Great. The reason why I'm calling is to see if you're still available to go shopping this weekend?"

"It's on the calendar. What time should I pick you up?"

"We like to get there when the stores open, but if that doesn't work for you…"

"Nope, it works for me. The earlier the better. That way we can get in a whole day's worth of shopping, right?"

"We're not that bad. Generally, we shop a bit, have lunch and then shop some more. Usually we're exhausted by early afternoon with the crowds and all."

"I promise I'll be prepared and have my walking shoes on," he said, laughing. "On a serious note, I can't wait to spend some time with you and your sister. And after we get married, I want to be a part of your lives just as much as Angelina is. Even though I can be busy at times, it means a lot to me to have you in my life."

"Thanks. It means a lot to me, too. I know you were my doctor—I mean *are* my doctor, and I don't want that to change with you marrying Angelina. Alejandro, you make her happy. I'll be glad to call you my brother, too."

"Okay. Well, I'm on my way back to the hospital. I'll see you early Saturday."

"See you then." Colleen disconnected the call and smiled. She cared a lot about Alejandro. She couldn't believe that he'd made time to go shopping with them. That said a lot about him and she was very impressed.

Saturday morning arrived and Colleen was anxious to finally go shopping. She wondered how he'd react to this yearly event. Only time would tell.

Alejandro phoned Angelina just after five thirty in the morning. Sleepily, she answered. Never did she think he'd be calling her at that time of the morning. "Hello?" she said tiredly.

"Good morning, sweetheart. Did I wake you?"

Practically jumping out of bed, she said, "Wake me? What time is it? Did I oversleep?"

"Its five thirty, and no you didn't oversleep. I'm just up extra early. I'm on my way back from the hospital. I wanted to check on a patient before we went out."

"Everything okay?"

"Yeah, I just wanted to look at some lab results. You know how I am."

"I know. What else is on your mind?"

"I thought I'd come by earlier than we'd planned, if that's okay with you. Thought I'd surprise Colleen and take you both out for breakfast. You know, so we could become fortified for our exhaustive day. I would assume that you start out like gang busters. Can't have you both tiring out on me too quickly."

"Oh, Colleen would love that. What time do you want to pick us up?"

"Seven?"

"That's early."

"Well, don't the malls open extra early now with the holidays? Thought we could grab breakfast and be there by eight-thirty or so. After all, we have a lot of shopping and this maybe the only time I have. I'm pretty busy the next couple of weeks."

"Let's see, it's almost six. I'll go wake Colleen. She'll be thrilled. As it is, she can't believe you're taking the time to join us."

"I wouldn't miss it. So, I'll see you in about an hour."

Alejandro knocked on the door promptly at seven. He didn't want to ring the bell for fear he'd wake the remainder of the house. Colleen answered the door with a broad smile on her face. She was just too excited for words. She threw herself into his arms, thanking him for taking them to breakfast. "I can't believe you want to do this. You're the best!"

"Stop inflating my ego. I want to do this. As I've told you before, you all mean the world to me and I want you to feel a part of my family, too."

"I do, and I know Wyatt does as well. Your family's great. Your dad's always been terrific with us. I'm just getting to know your mom, but I like her.

Alejandro, we're just lucky that Angelina is marrying you."

Angelina walked down the staircase with a huge smile on her face. "You're here already?"

"Yep, I was actually sitting in the driveway. Didn't want to go home and come back. Thought I'd complete a few dictations while I waited. I didn't want to wake everyone up."

"That would've been okay. You really didn't have to sit in your car. I was up and Colleen flew out of bed when she heard you were coming to take us to breakfast."

He put his arm around her shoulder and guided her towards the kitchen where her parents were enjoying their morning coffee.

"Are you prepared for your day? These two can really 'shop 'til you drop.'" Angelina's father said as he drank his coffee.

"I've heard about some of their past shopping expeditions. Worst case, if they out-shop me, I'll just sit down with the packages and wait for them."

He walked behind Angelina and Colleen as they window shopped. They'd been shopping for almost two hours and had little to show in purchases. He couldn't hear what was said, but he noticed that whenever Colleen pointed to something in a window display Angelina always had a smile on her face. She seemed really happy lately.

From what Angelina had told him, they'd grown closer since Colleen's transplant. Angelina tried to spend more time with her—they went shopping weekly and made it a point to have a spa day once a month.

Angelina stood outside a store while Colleen went in to make a purchase. She watched her sister interact with the clerk. She was thankful that Colleen had recovered without any complications from her surgery. There was always the concern that she could reject Angelina's liver, but so far she didn't show any signs that this would happen. She knew Alejandro always had an eye on Colleen. She knew that he'd be there for the family in the event that happened.

Alejandro came up behind Angelina and put his arm around her waist. "She's definitely in her element," he said. "Isn't she?"

"That she is. She loves to shop. And, on that note dear sir, I think we need to do some shopping ourselves." They waited for Colleen and then Angelina and Alejandro decided to do their own separate shopping. Colleen and she paired-up leaving Alejandro to shop alone. This allowed Alejandro the time he needed to pick-up a few gifts for Angelina and her family. He wanted them to be a surprise. They met for lunch and then shopped the remainder of the day together.

By four o'clock, Alejandro was exhausted as he dragged the packages along—he'd become the package carrier after lunch. He was amazed by the stamina that both of them had for fighting the crowds and bargain hunters.

While Angelina was shopping in the last store for the day, Colleen sat next to Alejandro. She reached over and placed a kiss on his cheek. "Thanks for the best day ever. I had a fabulous time."

"As did I. You and your sister are quite the shoppers. I didn't believe your father this morning, but you certainly can... what is it they say?"

"Shop 'til we drop?"

"Yeah."

"So have you bought Angelina's gift yet?"

"Would I tell you?"

"Yes…"

He smiled at her and told her he was having her gift made. Other than that, he wasn't telling her. Angelina joined them and asked if they were ready. Alejandro nodded "You two have about killed me. I'm beat."

"You do look a little worse for wear."

"This was truly a demanding day—almost as bad as one of my longest surgeries. I'm so glad that I wore comfortable shoes. I don't know how either of you could shop in those heels."

"We're used to it," chimed in Colleen.

"Come on now. It wasn't that bad," added Angelina.

He pulled her into his arms. Placing a kiss on her forehead he said, "I'm just kidding. I had a blast!"

The weeks leading up to Christmas passed quickly, and before they knew it Christmas Eve was upon them.

Both families attended midnight mass together on Christmas Eve. A light breakfast was scheduled to be held at the Samuels's after mass (although it wasn't nearly as impromptu as the previous year), while the Alvarez's were hosting dinner the next day.

Angelina rose early on Christmas morning after going to bed at nearly four in the morning after enjoying her mother's party. She arrived at Alejandro's just before noon. He'd given her a house key, so she let herself in.

Angelina recalled the day that he'd given her the key to his house. She was supposed to meet him at his home after work one evening and he was late. It was a cool fall evening when he finally showed up. Angelina was tired after dealing with inside recess at school for the umpteenth time in the last two weeks and she just wanted to get warm by the fire and relax. She snapped at Alejandro when he arrived, letting him know that she didn't appreciate him letting her sit in the driveway on a cold fall day.

Alejandro had taken her mood in stride since he knew she'd had a rough couple of weeks at school. He'd been thinking about giving her a key to his house for a while, so he decided to make a big deal out of it.

That weekend Alejandro made her a steak dinner with all of the trimmings: salad with baked potatoes, green beans almandine, and a chocolate cake for dessert.

She had run off to the bathroom when he went to serve the cake. When she returned, a box wrapped in brightly colored paper sat next to her cake. A huge bow sat on top of the box.

She looked at him. "What's this," she asked.

He shrugged his shoulders. "You'll have to open it to see,' he said as he watched her shake the box.

"There's nothing in here," she said.

"I'll guess you'll have to just open it and see."

She pulled the bow from the box and plopped it on his head.

"Whaddya do that for?"

"So you can celebrate, too."

"I'm celebrating just watching you open it."

She ripped the tape off the box and pulled aside the paper. A small white box the size of a jewelry box sat before her. She hadn't a clue what was inside since she already had her engagement ring. They weren't celebrating anything special that she was aware of.

She eased the lid off the box and looked inside. She flipped the box upside down and another box similar to a jeweler's ring box fell into her hand. She turned it over and stared questioningly at it.

"Open it," Alejandro urged her, nodding at the box.

She flipped open the lid and that's when she saw the key. "What's this for? I don't need a new car."

"Silly, it's a key to my house." He smiled at her. "After what you put me through the other night when I was late... I don't want to have to go through that again."

"I wasn't that bad."

"Yes you were and, even if that hadn't have happened, it was long overdue. You're going to be my wife soon, and you should be able to come and go as you please. My house will soon be your home, too."

She smiled at him. His gesture meant the world to her.

"Thank you. I promise not to abuse it until after we're married." She reached over and kissed him. She then grabbed a fork and shoved a mound of cake into her mouth.

She found Alejandro sitting in front of the Christmas tree, staring into his clasped hands.

"Something wrong?" she asked.

"No, I was just sitting here thinking about us, about next year at this time. We'll be married and starting our own traditions."

"We most certainly will." She walked over and sat beside him with her packages. Reaching over, she gave him a quick kiss and said, "Come on. Let's open our gifts."

"Are you like the kid in the candy store?"

"Of course! Especially today."

They took their time as they exchanged gifts. Angelina gave Alejandro several dress shirts and complementary ties, along with an Irish knit sweater. She also bought him a new tie-tack with the engraving "With love, A."

He loved his gifts. He gave her a new coffee mug that he'd purchased from the Botanical Gardens. It had pictures of the various gardens they'd toured the day he asked her to marry him. The Herb Gardens were proudly showcased on it with the intricate labyrinth that surrounded it. He wanted her to put it on her desk at school, so she could store her pens neatly. And, whenever she looked at it, she could relive their special day when he asked her to marry him.

"I love this, and every day I'll think of the magical day and your proposal. That day is never far from my thoughts." She gave him a quick kiss and moved on to her next gift. It was a beautiful silk scarf that she could wear in her hair or around her neck. He also gave her a bottle of her favorite perfume. The last gift he'd hid under the sofa cushion. While she was cleaning up the wrapping paper, he reached for it.

"One last gift for my lady," he said and handed her a beautifully wrapped package.

"Alejandro, you've already given me so much."

"Stop talking and just open it."

She nodded and carefully began to open the gift, not wanting to tear the paper.

"Just open it already!"

"Well, I don't want to tear the paper. I love it and want to save it as a reminder of our first real Christmas as a couple. Now, just let me be…"

He watched her with a broad smile on his face. She removed the paper and slowly opened the box. Inside sat a velvet jeweler's box. He couldn't wait to see her face when she opened the box. She glanced up at him and said, "What's this?"

"Open it."

She lifted the lid and was taken aback. Inside laid the most gorgeous pair of emerald and diamond earrings that she'd ever seen in her entire life. A huge emerald was the focal point of each earring, and they were surrounded by diamonds; then, there was a drop that contained a smaller version of the main earring. She'd never seen anything like them. As she stared in awe, the diamonds winked back at her. She was speechless.

"Do you like them?"

She looked up at him with tears in her eyes. "They're beautiful. I'm speechless…"

She reached over and kissed him. She placed both hands on either side of his face and said, "I can't believe you did this for me. I can't wait to put them on." In her rush to get to Alejandro's for their gift opening, she'd forgotten to put on earrings. She removed the earrings from the box while Alejandro watched her put them in. She jumped off the couch and ran to a nearby mirror. "They're absolutely beautiful."

Alejandro approached her from behind and placed his hands around her waist. "No, you're the one that's beautiful. I'm so lucky to have you in my life. I love you."

"I love you, too." They stood in front of the mirror, relishing the moment. He turned her in his arms and said, "I wish we were getting married right this very moment. I can't wait to call you my wife."

She smiled at him.

"You're the light of my life. Our wedding day can't come soon enough."

They shared a beautiful moment in one another's arms when Angelina noticed the time. She couldn't believe how quickly the afternoon had flown by. Hurriedly, they cleaned up their mess and headed over to his mother's house for dinner.

She and Alejandro had shopped together for his family's gifts. One evening they had a marathon wrapping session while enjoying takeout pizza. She didn't realize how much they'd purchased on their shopping excursion with Colleen until she had to wrap all of the gifts. Angelina had met him at home after work. She'd used her key for the first time. It was an exciting moment for her, but it also felt strange entering his house alone without him by her side.

She expected Alejandro home within the hour, so she ordered pizza and pulled out all of the presents from the hall closet where he'd stored them.

She wanted to be organized when he got home, but what he found brought tears to his eyes. He hadn't laughed so hard in a long, long time. Presents were scattered about the room. Piles that had been neatly stacked were laying on their sides. Wrapping paper lay in various states: Some packages half wrapped, other's had paper cut and lying beside them, yet others rolls of paper were unfurled from their roll lying beside the package to wrap. Additional rolls of paper stood on their end against the wall. And the ribbon…

He looked at her as she tried to apply tape to a package and broke out in a fit of laughter. "What the hell happened here? It looks like the wrapping fairies lost their way."

He grabbed her hand and pulled her towards the couch where it, too, was covered with tissue paper, tags, and other supplies. "I see you need my help with this simple task."

"Simple? You call this simple? Look at all of these gifts. I think they've multiplied three-fold since we went shopping."

He continued laughing. "Well, I have to be honest—I did add a few. But why are so many packages in different stages of being wrapped?"

She glanced at him. He knew she'd have a good reason—at least what she thought was a good reason.

"Well," she said as she looked at him and then about the room at the packages. "Ah, to tell you the truth, I don't know why. I thought I'd finished wrapping that one," she said as she pointed to the package half-wrapped, "but then I found the perfect paper for another gift…" She looked back at him and watched his face. He was giggling and was ready to break into another fit of hysterics.

"I don't know. I guess I lost my focus," she said as she also started laughing.

Before they could begin to get organized, the doorbell rang announcing their dinner. They enjoyed their pizza. Then, Alejandro retackled her organizing and, before they knew it, all of the presents were wrapped. "See, I knew it wouldn't take us too long... That is, after we started over."

"I was just trying to match the paper to the person to the gift. I guess I got a little carried away. I wanted everything perfect, especially since it's our first Christmas together as an engaged couple."

"Honey, next time just grab a roll of paper and wrap. You don't have to put hours of thought into it."

They laughed and took in the mess that was once the family room.

"Next time, I promise I'll do better," she said as she rolled up some of the remnants of paper. They'd packed the gifts into bags and stored them in the hall closet.

They grabbed the bags then and headed for the garage where they piled them in the car. She thought they were going to be late, but they were actually the first guests to arrive.

As soon as she walked into his parents' home, Maria noticed her earrings. "Angelina, let me see." She pulled her into the last remaining rays of sunlight and gazed at her earrings. "Alejandro, they're gorgeous."

"Maria, I was shocked when I opened them. I've never seen anything so beautiful."

"Alejandro designed them himself."

"You did?" Angelina said, turning to Alejandro.

"I did. I wanted to do something special for you. I knew you'd look fabulous in emeralds and diamonds, and I wasn't wrong."

Angelina helped Maria with the finishing touches in the kitchen while Alejandro spent time with his father. The remainder of the family arrived and they shared a fabulous dinner, after which they opened their gifts. Everyone loved the earrings that Alejandro had given her. The holidays were a happy occasion for both families. Before they knew it, the wedding would be upon them, and the families would be forever joined.

# CHAPTER TWENTY-FOUR

In the blink of an eye, winter was over and the final preparations for the wedding had kicked into high gear. Career Day had come and gone, but Alejandro wasn't able to participate due to his schedule, so his brother Joe stepped in for him. The April wedding was less than a month away and the teachers at St. Margaret's threw Angelina a surprise bridal shower during their faculty meeting. Gabriella had been tasked with delaying her to the meeting, so she asked Angelina for help with a bulletin board. Angelina was standing on a chair, stapling a new spring border to the bulletin board, when she realized they were late for the meeting. "Gabriella you know how I hate to be late."

"I know, so do I." Angelina climbed down from the stepladder and handed Gabriella the remaining bulletin board supplies.

"Come on, we've got to get going. Mary's not going to be happy that we're late.

I'll help you after the meeting," Angelina said as they hurried from the room.

Gabriella let her precede her into the meeting room. Everyone shouted "Surprise!"

Angelina was taken aback. All of the teachers and staff had gathered to throw her a wedding shower. She turned to Gabriella and said, "You were in on this, weren't you?"

"What do you think?"

The room was decorated with balloons and streamers. A huge congratulations sign was stretched across the wall opposite the entrance. A table strewn with gifts sat off to the side, while cake and punch sat below the sign.

She immediately pulled Gabriella into an embrace, thanking her for helping her fellow teachers keep this a surprise from her. She'd known about the other bridal showers that were held in her honor, but this one totally took her off guard.

They hadn't registered for wedding gifts, as Alejandro had a house that was completely furnished. Gifts didn't mean anything to them. She just wanted to marry the man of her dreams and, in two short weeks, her dream would come true.

The entire staff was invited to the shower, including the janitors and rectory staff. Everyone on staff loved Angelina and wanted to help her celebrate such a wonderful occasion. They were overjoyed with her upcoming marriage. Angelina had never talked much about her relationship with Alejandro—she kept it close to her and really only let certain people in. She guessed it had to do with what both of them had been through to get to this day. Everyone knew Alejandro and loved him dearly, but no one knew that he'd been married before, had a family, and lost them in a horrific accident. No one needed to know that, and no one needed to know about her condition.

Questions were being thrown at her from all directions. Where was she going to live? Where were they going on a honeymoon? And of course, the question of children came up. Gabriella caught her eye. She wondered how she would handle it.

"Alejandro and I want to have a family. I'd like as many children as we can have. Alejandro is open to whatever I want…"

*Good answer*, thought Gabriella.

Angelina got through the questions and seemed no worse for wear. She told them they were going to live in Alejandro's home. She had no idea where they were going on a honeymoon, as Alejandro refused to tell her the exact location, only that it was somewhere warm.

Gabriella helped her load the abundance of gifts into her car. She turned to her and said, "I'm proud of you."

"Why's that?"

"Because you answered the questions concerning children so matter of fact."

"It's true. We'll have what we have. If it's one, two, or more children, it'll be what it is. I can't control it and neither can your brother. I'm fine now. I've pretty much dealt with my problems, and when I'm sad I turn to your brother."

The next two weeks passed in a blur. Angelina spent that time running around getting last minute gifts for her bridesmaids. She'd already ordered them engraved wine glasses, but she then found little photo albums that she wanted to make them with photos from the rehearsal dinner and wedding day.

She also put together the wedding favors that would be at each place setting. She bought small organdy bags that she filled with miniature mints, and she secured each with a wedding bell that she made out of beads. Each guest would also receive a small gift bag that contained a small bottle of wine. The label was a copy of their wedding invitation.

On her last day at school, Angelina's class threw her a party. Her classroom mothers put the party together and surprised her by also inviting Alejandro. Mary had called her to the office while her aide led the class to the gymnasium for PE class. When she returned, the doors were closed to the gym. She opened them and another, "Surprise!" rang out. Angelina looked around and couldn't believe her eyes. She'd been totally surprised twice in just a matter of days. Her class had decorated the gym with balloons and streamers and the room mothers were serving refreshments. She was even more shocked when Alejandro walked out of the coach's office. He walked over and gave her a hug and kiss on the cheek.

"What're you doing here?"

"I got a call from Mary. She told me your students were throwing you a shower and wanted me to attend. I guess they wanted to check me out to make sure I was acceptable for their favorite teacher," he said jokingly.

"Oh, come on now," she playfully slapped his forearm.

"Kidding, only kidding. They just wanted me to be a part of it."

They shared in the refreshments and were encouraged to open their gifts together. Alejandro gestured for her to open them. He just wanted to watch his beautiful fiancée enjoy this time with her students. He was overjoyed watching her open the gifts, oohing and ahhing over everything she opened.

They received many handmade gifts which made them even more special. Pot holders that were crafted using a loom were made by several students. She received a mosaic hot plate that she could tell was handmade as it was signed by her student and dated with her wedding date. They received handmade embroidered guest towels and towels embroidered with the letter A. Lastly, they received a quilt whereby each student drew a picture and signed their name on the fabric. These were all sewn together and then quilted. She'd never be able to forget the kindness of the class, especially when she looked at the quilt.

She was happy, truly happy. Alejandro hoped he'd be able to keep the smile that she'd been wearing permanently etched on her loving face.

Angelina looked over at Alejandro and smiled at him. She wanted him to help her open their gifts, but he declined, "I'm enjoying watching you."

"Well then, you can at least wear this," She started to slap him with the sticky bows that were attached to some of the gifts. Her students and parents burst into laughter when they saw the playful manner between the loving couple.

"Thanks everyone," said Alejandro. "I especially want to thank you for inviting me. I had a great time, especially now that I look like a flower bouquet."

The kids all broke out in laughter. Angelina reached over and brushed a kiss on his cheek which everyone loved.

"No, seriously. Thank you for including me in this day. It means a lot to me and Ms. Samuels that you went to all of this trouble for us. We will always remember this, and I know Ms. Samuels, as well as I, hold a special place in our hearts for each of you. I wasn't invited to any of Ms. Samuels's previous bridal showers, so I now have a better understanding what goes on at these events," he said, laughing "All kidding aside, I want each of you to know that it means a lot that you wanted to include me in today's event."

Alejandro helped clean up while Angelina returned to her classroom for the last class of the day. He joined again her as she released the kids. She received hugs and best wishes on her wedding. Alejandro had already carried their gifts to his car, so they headed to the teacher's lounge for her final goodbyes. Mary hugged her and informed her she'd see them at the wedding. Gabriella stopped by and wondered why her brother was there. "I attended the shower held by her class," Alejandro said.

"I didn't know that you were going to be here for that."

"I called him," Mary replied. "Several of Angelina's students thought it would be neat for Alejandro to be here."

"I'm surprised you could get off."

"It was touch and go today, but nothing was going to keep me from being here."

They finished their goodbyes and, hand-in-hand, he walked her to her car.

Angelina followed Alejandro to his house. She wanted to organize the gifts she'd received. She'd put them all away and write her thank you notes after they returned from their honeymoon.

After they carried the gifts in, Angelina turned to Alejandro and put her arms around his neck. "I can't believe we'll be married by this time on Saturday."

"I know. I can't either. We just have to get through the rehearsal and dinner tomorrow."

"I want to remember everything... I don't want it to fly by. It's the only time I plan to get married and I want to enjoy every minute of it!"

"I promise you, honey, we'll enjoy it."

The rehearsal at the church went well, as did the dinner hosted by Alejandro's parents at their country club. His father gave a toast that brought tears to her eyes. "First of all, I'd like to thank everyone for being here to participate in my son and soon-to-be daughter-in-law's special day. I'd like to say a few words about Angelina. I've known her since she was a baby. Being her pediatrician, I watched her grow into a beautiful woman. Never in my wildest dreams did I believe she'd become a part of my family. I watched her friendship with Gabriella grow, and she always referred to Angelina as the sister she never had. Then Alejandro moved back to St. Louis and helped Angelina's family when Colleen became ill. That was a life changing moment in both of our family's lives. Angelina's subsequent illness brought her and my son together in a way only they can describe. He cared for her, but she also helped him through an extremely trying time in his life.

"Angelina, I want to thank you for bringing our Alejandro back to us. You've helped one another through some difficult times. I don't think either of you could have gotten through these times without the other. We love you and welcome you into our family as our daughter—to Angelina."

Everyone raised their glasses in honor of the bride. She glanced at Alejandro with tears in her eyes. He leaned over and kissed her on the cheek, whispering how much he loved her. She smiled at him as his parents approached, giving them both hugs and kisses.

Maria told Angelina that she was thrilled to be able to refer to her as her daughter now. "You're the best thing in the world for my son. You make him happy. Thank you for putting the smile back on his face."

The rehearsal dinner ended and Alejandro drove her back to her parents' house. "I guess the next time I see you will be tomorrow when you walk down the aisle."

She nodded.

"Angelina, I love you with all of my heart, my soul... I want you to feel like you can tell me anything, good or bad. As our marriage grows, we need to continue to communicate. I know I'll be busy at times, but we can't forget that. Communication is the key to a happy, healthy marriage."

"I know, sweetheart. I'll always tell you when I'm happy or sad. And right now, I couldn't be happier. I never thought in my wildest dreams that I'd marry you, Alejandro. It's a dream come true, and I won't do anything to jeopardize it. You're my world and nothing is going to stand in the way of our happiness." She reached over, grabbed his face between her hands, and gave him one last kiss before she would see him as she walked down the aisle. "I love you, for always and forever."

"You're my life, Angelina. I'll do everything and anything to make you happy. Always remember that."

Colleen woke Angelina from the best night's sleep that she'd had in a long time. She was content and happy with where her life was headed. Colleen prepared her sister breakfast in bed. After eating, all of the girls pampered themselves at the spa, then headed over to their favorite beauty salon where they had their hair and make-up completed by their favorite beautician. The men, on the other hand, had scheduled an early game of golf prior to their late afternoon wedding. Jackie couldn't believe how relaxed everyone was. She figured it was a good sign.

The photographer Angelina hired not only followed the women around for most of the day, but also the men. Photos were taken of the men goofing around on the golf course, while the women were photographed with green masks on their faces and with their hair in curlers.

Angelina wanted to showcase the fun along with the serious side of the wedding. She couldn't wait to see Wyatt hamming it up in front of the camera while riding around in a golf cart. And she couldn't wait to see what photos came out of their day at the spa—her mother's face covered in a mask. *Priceless,* is all she could think when the photographer was clicking away. Angelina didn't even know if her mother realized she'd had her photograph taken.

They all laughed endlessly until it was time for hair and make-up, and that's when the importance of the day struck Angelina. She was marrying

Alejandro, the man of her dreams. The entire time leading up to this day, Angelina took everything in stride—nothing bothered her. Her true nervousness had gone away once she'd told their family about her infertility.

But now, the nerves rushed at her from all sides. She worried that her dress wouldn't fit even though she knew it did. She worried about the flowers, her hair, her make-up, the reception... until she took one look in the mirror. She closed her eyes and took a deep breath. She pictured Alejandro standing at the end of the aisle, waiting for her as he did the night before at the rehearsal. His hand reached out to her. The smile on his face and the love that shown for her in his eyes... That memory from only the day before brought her out of her stupor. Her nerves dissipated and a feeling of calm overcame her.

The women all drove to the church where the wedding party planned on dressing. When Angelina appeared from the dressing room, everyone stood in awe. Jackie had never seen her daughter look more beautiful. It brought tears to her eyes.

Angelina's hair had been styled in an up-do with soft curls that framed her face. Her dress was a spectacular off-the-shoulder, beaded with Austrian crystals that carried all the way down her eight-foot train. Her veil was exquisite and contained the same intricate beading in her headpiece. She wore a single-strand pearl necklace that contained a diamond drop in the center, along with a pair of matching earrings that complemented her dress. The jewelry was a wedding gift from her parents.

Maria walked over to her and grasped her hands. "My dear, you're absolutely beautiful. My son is so lucky." Tears glistened in her eyes.

Gabriella could hardly contain herself. She turned away and walked from the room. Angelina noticed her disappearance and wondered why she'd left. Colleen gleefully spoke of how gorgeous her sister looked. "I've never seen you look so…"

"Marvelous," chimed in Kelly. "Angelina, you're stunning. Alejandro won't be able to take his eyes off of you when you walk down the aisle. You're going to take his breath away." She smiled at Angelina as she herself became emotional.

Gabriella paced the hallway outside the dressing area. Alejandro strolled down the corridor towards the patio area where the photographer was waiting, taking candid shots of the wedding party. Alejandro saw a tear on his sister's face and approached her. He wiped it from her face and asked why she was crying.

"She's beautiful, Alejandro. She's going to take your breath away…" And with that the photographer captured a moment between brother and sister that was priceless.

"I'm sure she is. I can't wait to see my bride."

Every other pew was decorated with a floral spray that matched that of the bridesmaids. Peonies were Angelina's favorite flower and it was showcased in the sprays, along with roses and baby's breath. The sweet smell filled the church.

Candles adorned the altar, along with several large displays of peonies, roses, and a multitude of other spring flowers. No expense was saved when it came to the flowers.

The organist began playing as both of their mothers were escorted down the aisle. Surprisingly, Jackie was dry-eyed. Maria had a handkerchief clutched in her hand which she used to dab her eyes when she saw her son standing so stoically at the front of the church. Maria had a flash back to another day such as this—the day Alejandro and Tammy were married. She looked at her son. He was happy then and he was happy now. He'd overcome the tragedy of losing his wife. And today… today was about the future, not the past. They'd always have their memories, but today was about making new memories, not dreaming of a past that could never be recovered.

Alejandro stood beside his father. The processional music began as the bridesmaids, escorted by his brothers, walked slowly down the aisle. The bridesmaids were all dressed in peach-colored, tea-length dresses that complemented the grandeur of Angelina's dress. The groomsmen were dressed in tuxes with coordinating peach-colored bow ties.

There was a brief pause in the music, and then he saw her standing at the end of the aisle. Alejandro was breathless. His sister was right—she took his breath away.

Angelina had the most beautiful smile on her face as her father walked her down the aisle. Alejandro had never seen her look so beautiful or so happy. Her father raised her veil and kissed her cheek as he handed her over to Alejandro. Alejandro reached for her hand and winked at her, mouthing, "I love you."

She smiled and nodded in return. She squeezed his hand as they turned towards the priest. She caught

Alejandro's eye several times during the ceremony with a chaste smile and a wink only he could see. He was almost her husband. As she looked around the church, she took in the beauty of the flowers. She could smell the peonies that stood beside the altar. Her bridesmaids looked beautiful and the groomsmen were just as handsome. It was her day—no, their day. She was doing her best, taking in every glance, every smile, and every tear. This was the day she'd dreamed of her entire life. She almost let it slip away when she'd been overcome with her reaction to the effects of the peritonitis. She had been reacting to the situation. In all honesty, she had known she'd marry. It just took Alejandro's belief in her, and his desire to love her that pulled her through those days.

They made it through the majority of the ceremony without any tears. As they began to exchange their traditional wedding vows, the tears started to flow. Thankfully, she'd stuffed a handkerchief into the kneeler and was able to extract it without difficulty. She squeezed his hand especially hard when she reached the "in sickness and in health" portion of her vows. Tears were cascading down her cheeks. He knew she was reflecting on what they'd already been through together. As he said his vows, he choked up a bit, somehow getting through his without tears.

They both gave their mothers red roses during the ceremony. Jackie pulled Alejandro into an embrace and thanked him for making her daughter so happy. Maria dabbed at her eyes when the couple approached. Alejandro hugged her when he handed her the rose. She turned to Angelina and pulled her into an embrace, whispering that she loved her.

They shared their kiss as a married couple after they were pronounced husband and wife. As the organist played the recessional, they walked hand-in-hand down the aisle, taking their time as they soaked in the moment. They partook in the family photography session, both at the church and nearby park, before heading off to the reception. At the park, as they exited the limousine, a couple greeted them as they walked their dog. They were in awe at what an attractive couple they were and wished them a lifetime of happiness. Angelina glowed, as she'd never been happier.

The wedding party gathered outside the reception doors. As they were announced, the doors opened and loud applause rang out. The receiving line was held at the reception so everyone could enjoy the cocktail hour. The couple was flanked on either side by their parents. At one point, Angelina couldn't see the end of the line and then Mary came into view. She hugged and kissed Angelina, telling her she was the most beautiful bride she'd ever seen.

"I couldn't agree more," said Alejandro as he pulled her towards him.

The reception hall was decked out with the same floral arrangements that were in the church. Large vases of flowers stood on either side of the wedding party's table. Floating candles lit the tables. The napkins were tied with peach-colored ribbon that matched the color of the day. A string quartet played in the background while waiters passed around hors d'oeuvres for the guests who had already greeted the couple. Between family, friends and business acquaintances no one was left off the list of invited guests. The room was packed to its limit—six hundred guests were expected.

Everyone enjoyed their meal as toasts were given throughout for the happy couple. Both of Alejandro's brothers spoke, but Alec's toast really hit home.

"To my brother and his ever beautiful wife," Alec said as he raised his glass. "Alejandro, you've chosen the perfect woman. You complement one another, and I haven't seen you happier. Both of you have experienced your own challenges on your way to this day. We recognize them and know that any challenges you face in the future you will face together as one. I'm proud to call you, Angelina, my sister. I know I speak for my entire family... We welcome you with open arms. To the happy couple." After completing his toast, Alec approached them. He pulled Angelina into a hug, telling her how happy he was for them and then rapped his brother on the back, again offering his congratulations.

The reception flew by as they spent time dancing and circulating among their friends. When it was time for their first dance, Alejandro pulled her into his arms, brushing her forehead with a soft kiss. "Are you having fun?"

"I am," she said as she looked up into his eyes. "I'm taking each moment and burning it into my memory. I love you, and I've so enjoyed our day."

They danced to a classic wedding song. Then, she danced with her father and he danced with his mother. Next, he danced with Jackie.

"I'll do everything in my power to keep her as happy as she is today. I want to see that smile plastered on her face always. I love Angelina, Jackie."

"I know you do." Jackie said as Alejandro spun her around on the dance floor.

When it came time to toss the wedding bouquet, all of the single women gathered: Gabriella, Kelly, Colleen, and all of the single teachers from St. Margaret's. Cheers rang out as Angelina prepared to toss her bouquet and turned her back to the ladies.

"One, two, three!" Alejandro called out.

Angelina tossed the bouquet over her shoulder, aiming for Gabriella. Moments before the toss, Gabriella moved. The bouquet caught Kelly off guard, almost smacking her in the face. "Oh, my," she said as she grabbed the flowers. She sniffed them as she raised the bouquet to the crowd.

Next came the garter toss. Alejandro had a blast pulling the garter from around Angelina's leg. Alec had joined the crowd of bachelors on the dance floor. He wasn't paying a bit of attention when Alejandro flung the garter into the crowd. Somehow, the force of the garter shot across the room landing in his lapel pocket. Shocked, he looked down and retrieved the garter. "You didn't... I can't believe you aimed for me."

Alejandro yelled across the floor, "I didn't, but I guess we now know who will be married next in the family!"

Everyone laughed except Alec who continually told everyone that his career was foremost in his life. He was a bachelor through and through and didn't have his sights set on marriage now or ever.

Of course, there was a photo taken of the two winners. Angelina couldn't wait to give Alec a copy of it. She wanted him to remember the day he caught the garter and Kelly the bouquet.

They both attained their goals for the day, making memories they'd cherish for a lifetime.

Angelina still didn't know their destination when they left for their honeymoon. They had a late night flight, and that was all she knew. They both changed into travel clothes before leaving the reception.

Alejandro helped her into the limousine.

"Now, you can't keep our destination from me any longer. Where're we going?"

"Where do you want to go?"

She slapped at his forearm, "Come on now, quit teasing me and just tell me where we're going!"

He just smiled at her.

"Alejandro?" She wrapped her arms around his neck, rubbed her nose against his, and drew him in for a kiss. "I've waited all this time. Tell me where we're going."

"Ah," he said as she continued her seduction. "We're…"

"Tell me," she said as she pulled away. "I can't wait any longer. I've already waited long enough."

"Come here," he said and drew her into his arms. Kissing her, he pulled away. "We're going…"

"Yes."

"Somewhere warm."

She slapped him on the arm again. "Come on now."

They continued with this banter as the limousine headed towards the airport. She still had no clue as they walked towards the gate indicating a flight to Chicago. "We're going to Chicago? You mean I'm spending my wedding night in Chicago?"

"That's what it says…"

She was disappointed, thinking they were just going to Chicago.

Their seats were in first class. After they boarded, the flight attendant handed them a glass of champagne. He turned and raised his glass in a toast to her. "To my beautiful wife, I love you with all of my heart." He leaned over and gave her a brief kiss.

They sipped their drinks before the plane taxied to the runway. He reached for her hand as the plane's engines roared to life. He leaned over and said, "Are you ready to start our new life together?"

She smiled, nodded, and kissed his cheek. "Now more than ever."

When the plane reached its flying altitude, he jumped up from his seat and reached into the overhead bin and retrieved his duffle bag. He withdrew an envelope and returned his bag to the bin. "For you, my dear." He handed her the envelope with her name scrawled across it.

She looked at him quizzically. "What's this?"

"Open it and you'll see." She opened the envelope and withdrew its contents. Inside was an itinerary. The first line indicated their first destination of Chicago. Then she glanced at the subsequent arranged flights, their final destination… Bora Bora. She raised her hand to her mouth and gasped. "Bora Bora?"

As they journeyed to their honeymoon, he told her, "The one goal that I have is that we do whatever we want, whenever we want. I don't want to be tied to a schedule. I want everything to be spontaneous. I just want to enjoy each moment until the next one plays out. No planning whatsoever."

"Got it." she said as they waited for their plane to touch down.

When they arrived in Bora Bora, they were exhausted. They'd flown from Chicago to Los Angeles International airport, and then on to Tahiti where they picked up a short flight to Bora Bora. In all, they'd spent over nineteen hours in the air. They did their best to sleep on the planes, but both of them found it difficult. She waited for what seemed like an eternity to sleep in Alejandro's arms as man and wife, and she was going to have to wait a little longer.

When they arrived at their destination, they were whisked away to their private overwater bungalow where they were able to walk right out and enter the picturesque waters. The first thing they did was fall into bed and sleep. She'd waited for this night forever and she wasn't going to rush it.

It would be their first time making love and, like her wedding, she wanted to remember every moment.

When they woke, they were both starved. They ate and went about their day walking the nearby beaches and touring their little slice of heaven.

Alejandro arranged a special dinner. As far as he was concerned, this was their first night as husband and wife, and he was going to make it a memorable one. He arranged for a candlelit dinner for the deck of their bungalow. Soft music played in the background as they were served the island specialty, Poison Cru. It was a favored Polynesian dish of tuna marinated in coconut milk and lime. They danced to the soft music; then, Alejandro led her back to the table where a gift was waiting for her.

She smiled at him as soon as she saw it sitting beside her crème brûlée.

"Open it," he said.

She flipped open the lid and gasped when she saw what was inside. A Tahitian Black Pearl necklace and matching earrings lay in front of her. The pearls were unique to the islands. They were made by grafting locally cultivated Pinctada Margaritifera oysters. Although they were called black pearls, they formed a wide variety of colors, and the depth of color was determined by the amount of black pigment the oyster secreted.

Earlier in the day when they'd been shopping, Angelina had become fascinated by the whole process. They had been advised that, if they purchased the black pearl, they should choose a color that looked best on Angelina, taking into account her hair, skin color, and wardrobe colors she most often wore.

It had been a difficult decision for her and she'd decided to just move on and continue with her shopping. Alejandro had stayed back and chosen the lavender-tinted pearls. He had the clerk wrap up the set and deliver it to their hotel where he'd arranged for it to be given during their dessert.

Angelina didn't know what to say. Alejandro stood and reached for the pearls. He slipped the necklace around her neck. "Beautiful," is all he said as he reached for her hand. Placing her hand in his, she stood and followed him into their slice of paradise.

When they crossed into their bungalow, Alejandro smoothed her hair behind her ears. "I've waited too long for this night," he said as he kissed the side of her neck. Tugging on her hand, he led her into their bedroom. He pulled her again into his arms. "This is our night. I want you to remember every moment of it." Turning, she noticed the rose petals that were strewn across the floor leading to their bed, the candles flickering all about the room. He'd built a scene right out of a fairy tale for her.

She could still hear the soft music playing in the background. She noticed her lingerie had been laid out on the bed. He motioned for her to go change.

As she exchanged her sundress for her satin nightgown, she realized that he'd created this magical setting all for her. He wanted to make their first night together one that she'd remember for a lifetime.

The next morning she woke wrapped in Alejandro's arms. She glanced down at her string of pearls. She couldn't believe that he'd surprised her with the gift, along with the special touches to make the night an unforgettable one. She felt like she was truly living in a fairy tale.

Their honeymoon was an experience of a lifetime. Sunsets from their bungalow absolutely took their breath away. Nightly, as they sat on their deck overlooking the water, the orange and yellow hues mixed amongst the clouds on the horizon were the most amazing colors ever seen. After watching the sunset, they'd make their way to their bedroom where they'd spend the night wrapped in one another's arms.

During the day, they found themselves snorkeling right off their bungalow. They went on an all-day excursion, touring the lagoon and private islands that surrounded them. She loved walking on the pristine beaches, looking out at the water at the vivid shades of emerald, turquoise, azure, and royal blue. It was mesmerizing watching the change in the colors of the water. No one would believe the color of the water wasn't altered in their pictures. It was something she would never forget.

One of the highlights of their honeymoon was seeing a traditional Tahitian dance. They'd gone to one of the hotels for dinner and the show. They learned that the traditional Tahitian dance told a story of ancient legends and folklore of the Polynesian culture. The dances could be slow and sensual or fast paced and vigorous. They decided it was definitely something they were glad they'd done, as it was a beautiful insight into the Tahitian culture.

Before they knew it, their two weeks in paradise was coming to a close. They both got their wishes, and all too soon it was time to return home. They spent their last evening enjoying the view at sunset. He reached for her hand and held it close to his heart. "I've had a wonderful time."

"So have I. I couldn't have asked for more. I can't believe it's time to go home."

"I know. I'm not looking forward to my schedule the next few weeks. But instead of going home to an empty house, I'll be coming home to you." He kissed her knuckles as they finished watching the last rays of sun from their honeymoon disappear on the horizon.

# CHAPTER TWENTY-FIVE

Eight weeks had elapsed since their honeymoon, and Angelina had wrapped up another school year. She had moved the majority of her things to Alejandro's before the wedding and her parents had surprised her by moving the remainder of her clothes, along with their wedding gifts, to his house while they were on their honeymoon.

Both families surprised them with an impromptu celebration upon their return. They'd opened their gifts and described the true beauty of Bora Bora.

Angelina quickly adjusted to living with Alejandro. When she was in school, they pretty much got up at the same time. The hardest transition for her was sharing a bathroom first thing in the morning. They often found themselves bumping into one another. In time, they found the humor in it, but it took her a few days to see it.

Alejandro experienced a rough couple of weeks upon his return. His first day back greeted him with a six year old child who needed a kidney transplant. Matthew Johnson's parents discovered his kidney problems when he was just four years old, and now he was in dire need of a transplant.

Working with children challenged Alejandro, as pediatric cases drained him emotionally since he needed to be more sensitive to their needs. He tried to bring the medical jargon down to the child's level of understanding. He wanted each child to feel special in their own way, and dealing with a six year old was pretty challenging.

His own son would have been about the same age as Matthew if he'd lived. Alejandro often thought of Michael. He wondered what he would look like... What would his favorite subject be? Would he choose a career in medicine?

Alejandro was scheduled off for the long Fourth of July weekend and they were hosting a barbeque to celebrate. As they finished setting up the patio for the next day, and were enjoying their evening, they reminisced about the previous year, their engagement, and their spectacular wedding and honeymoon.

Alejandro changed the direction of the conversation and began to share Matthew's story. It was something he really needed to talk about. "We're hoping for a transplant, but you know how that goes."

"I know, sweetheart. I'll pray for him."

"His parents are such interesting people. They were eighteen when they married. His mother, Jane, worked her way through college and graduated with honors. His father, Duane, is extremely bright and double majored in Engineering and Business. Although they married young, they had supportive parents. Unfortunately, now they're facing Matthew's illness alone as both sets of grandparents are deceased. I'm so impressed with them. Often I look at Matthew and wonder about Michael... How tall would he be? What sports would he enjoy? You know, all the parent type stuff."

"Alejandro, we'll have that someday."    She reached for his hand and squeezed it.


The Fourth dawned with a severe thunderstorm. It awakened Alejandro suddenly in the night, and he couldn't fall back to sleep. He decided to get up and watch the early morning news. He made coffee and, just as he was ready to take a cup into Angelina, the news reported a horrific accident on the interstate. A drunken driver had crossed the median and drove straight into the path of a car carrying a young couple. The news reported that the couple was killed instantly and the drunken driver walked away unharmed.

"That's how it always goes. The innocent are killed," he spoke as he took Angelina her coffee.

"Did you say something?" Angelina asked.

Alejandro told her about the accident. "It's always the innocent that are killed so tragically."

They went on with their day as both families joined them for the barbeque. Alejandro grilled with Wyatt's assistance. Wyatt idolized Alejandro and followed him everywhere when he was around.

As they neared fireworks time, the phone rang—it was the hospital. Alejandro was off for the weekend, but they insisted on speaking with him. Angelina found him in the backyard sipping a cocktail, waiting for the fireworks to begin.

"Honey, the phone's for you. It's the hospital. They insist on speaking with you."

He looked at her quizzically and took the phone. "This is Dr. Alvarez."

"Alejandro, it's Robert…" Robert was covering for him while he was off for the weekend. "I have some bad news for you."

"What's wrong?"

"You know that little boy that you're waiting on a kidney for?"

"Matthew Johnson?"

"Yeah."

"Has his condition worsened?"

"No… His parents were killed this morning."

"Oh, no." Pausing momentarily, he said, "They were the couple killed on the interstate this morning, weren't they?"

"Yes."

"Does Matthew know?"

"Not yet. I thought you might want to be the one to tell him."

"I'll be right there."

Angelina overheard the conversation. "Matthew's parents were the couple that was killed this morning?"

He nodded.

"I'm going to the hospital with you."

"No, you've got your parents and family here."

"So do you. They'll understand."

Alejandro gathered everyone and broke the tragic news to his family. Now his only concern was Matthew and how he would deal with it.

They drove to the hospital in silence. She could tell the events were affecting him greatly. She reached across the seat for his hand.

"I don't know if I can do this," he said, squeezing her hand. "I just don't know… Michael's death keeps hitting me in the face. How am I going to tell Matthew about his parents?"

"Alejandro, that's why I'm here... I want to be here for you. Help all that I can." She looked at him while she spoke and watched his jaw clench. She said a prayer silently.

Alejandro pulled into his parking spot and quickly exited the car. He came around to the passenger side of the car, opened the door, and reached for her hand, helping her from the car as he flung his stethoscope around his neck.

Alejandro sought out Robert. He found him in the doctor's lounge reviewing a patient's file. He introduced Angelina to him. Angelina shook his hand, then turned all of her attention to her husband.

"What does Matthew know?" Alejandro asked.

"Only that his parents aren't here with him. We've been stalling all day, not knowing where they were. One of the nurses heard about the accident and put two and two together. Duane had convinced Jane to go home last night. He spent the night with Matthew and left early this morning to pick her up. They were headed back to the hospital when the accident happened."

Alejandro picked up Matthew's chart. "I'm going to go see him now."

Angelina followed him. Even though Alejandro was Matthew's his doctor, he wasn't acting as a doctor. He was there as his friend and Angelina was there to support her husband. She reached for his hand and clasped it tightly. As they neared Matthew's hospital room, she stopped walking. Alejandro's mind was elsewhere and her stopping caused him to misstep. He caught himself, saying, "What's wrong?"

"Have you thought through what you're going to say to him?"

"No."

"Shouldn't you?"

Looking down at the floor, he said, "I'm better talking extemporaneously. It'll be easier for me. If I think too much, I'll get too emotional. I have to be focused—I'm his doctor."

"I realize that, but—"

"Angelina, I know what I'm doing, okay?"

She nodded. "I think I'll stand out here while you tell him. I don't want to interfere."

"Interfere? Where did you get that? I need you, need you by my side. This is hard enough with Michael and…"

Angelina didn't say anymore. She followed him into Matthew's room to support him.

When they entered Matthew's room, she was taken aback by how small he looked lying in his hospital bed. She glanced sideways at her husband. She could see the fear in his eyes and the panicked look on his face.

Matthew was clueless as to what Alejandro was experiencing. He was just glad to see him. "Hey, Doc. What are you doing here? I thought you were off."

"I am, but something came up, and I needed to drop by the hospital to take care of it. My wife, Angelina, decided to come with me."

"Hi, I'm Matthew."

"It's nice to meet you, Matthew."

"Dr. Alvarez, do you know where my parents are? My Dad went to pick up Mom early this morning, and I haven't seen them all day long."

Angelina glanced between the doctor and his patient. Alejandro moved closer to Matthew. He sat on the edge of the bed while Angelina stood by his side. "Well buddy, that's why I am here."

"Something's wrong?"

"Yes, Matthew. I want you to know that I'm going to be completely honest with you."

"You always are."

Angelina placed her hand on Alejandro's shoulder, hoping to give her husband the strength he needed to share this horrendous news with the little boy.

"Matthew, your parents were on their way back to the hospital this morning when something terrible happened."

Matthew looked at him blankly.

"Your parents were involved in a car accident. I'm sorry to have to tell you this, but they were killed."

Angelina could tell that Matthew didn't understand what he'd just been told.

"You mean they'll be here later tonight."

Angelina knew her husband was having a hard time explaining himself, so she took over. "Matthew, I'm sorry but your parents won't be coming to see you again. They were badly hurt and died."

"No, that can't be." He seemed to finally register what they were telling him and he started crying.

Thankfully, Alejandro had grabbed a sedative before entering his room. He stood and removed it from his pocket. "Matthew, I'm not going anywhere, but I'm going to give you something to calm you down." As Matthew's tears and upset increased, Alejandro injected him with the calming drug. Shortly thereafter, he fell asleep with both Alejandro and Angelina by his side.

"He'll sleep for a while. Let's go for a few minutes. I have to check on a few things."

"How about I stay here?"

"Sweetheart, he's going to be out for some time. Please, I need you." He reached for her and pulled her into an embrace. They left Matthew's room arm-in-arm and headed for Alejandro's office. There he could think and decide what his next move would be.

# CHAPTER TWENTY-SIX

Alejandro didn't want Matthew to attend the funeral, but he insisted on attending. Several of Duane and Jane's friends attended the services, along with some of the doctors and nurses that they'd gotten to know because of Matthew's numerous hospital stays. Both of Duane and Jane's employers were supportive and had established trust funds in Matthew's name to collect money to help with hospital expenses and Matthew's education.

According to their attorney, there were no living relatives. They'd been in the process of setting up care for Matthew in the event that something happened to them, but never had the opportunity to finalize their plans because they were so focused on Matthew's health.

After they'd told Matthew about his parents, Angelina spent almost every waking moment of the day with him. She didn't want anything to happen to him, and he started to become very important to her.

From her first encounter with Matthew, Angelina had an overwhelming sense to protect him. Matthew, for all he'd been through, had a sense of humor, loved to play games, and was an avid reader. He loved the time he spent with Angelina and was disappointed when she'd miss a day of visiting him.

Angelina didn't want Matthew to feel like he'd been abandoned or forgotten. She made a point to let him know how important he was to her. Often, she'd stayed until late in the afternoon playing games with him. Many times she was kicked out by the nursing staff so that Matthew could rest. She looked forward to their visits and often would return to the hospital late at night to check on him. These were the evenings that Alejandro was busy either working late or out of town. Alejandro had no idea that she'd grown as close to Matthew as she had. Matthew was just as important to her as her students were— in fact, maybe even more important. She didn't want to see anything happen to him.

Alejandro had notified the appropriate authorities regarding Matthew's parents. The state would oversee him until he left the hospital, then he'd enter foster care since he had no living relatives.

Angelina didn't know what she'd do without Matthew in their lives. Alejandro shared that if Matthew's condition continued to worsen, he would need a transplant if he ever expected to leave the hospital. One evening, as they sat on the couch, she turned to him.

"I want to adopt Matthew."

Alejandro hadn't been paying too close of attention to her and he wasn't sure if he'd heard her correctly, "What'd you say?"

"He needs us. He knows he can count on us to be there for him."

Alejandro was stunned. "I don't know, Angelina, if this is the best thing for him."

"Why wouldn't it be? We want a family. He's alone without his parents to care for him. We'd be perfect for him. He trusts us…"

"Angelina, we haven't even been married six months. Don't you think we need some time together? Just the two of us?"

"Alejandro, what are you afraid of?"

"Nothing."

"You are. You're afraid of getting too close to him and then having something happen, aren't you?"

"I'm his doctor."

"That's easy—we'll just switch doctors."

"Angelina, please be rational. We can't just switch his doctor when he's comfortable with me."

"I understand that, but something needs to be done here. He can't just be farmed out to someone he doesn't know. He needs you—us to care for him when he has his transplant. We have to be the ones."

"Sweetheart, I don't know. I just don't know."

"Alejandro, what don't you know?"

"I care for him a lot. It's just…"

"Too close to Michael."

"Yes, that's it. I don't know if I could lose another child. And there's a chance…"

"Alejandro, you're a doctor. You know that life can be taken in an instant. Matthew's illness shouldn't prevent you from loving him as your own child. If we have him in our lives for only a short time, that's better than never having him a part of our family. I love him. I want to be able to call him my son for as long as I possibly can."

Alejandro didn't know what to say. He stood and started pacing the room. Angelina sat on the couch watching him. She witnessed a variety of emotions cross his face.

Finally, he turned to her. "Let's take that chance. You're right, we'll enjoy whatever time we have with him… And hopefully, he'll be able to be a part of our lives for a long time to come."

"Can we go tell him? Now, tonight, and see what he thinks about it?"

"Angelina, don't you think we need to investigate this a little further before getting his hopes up?"

"No. I think we need to see if he would even consider us as his parents before we move forward. He has to want us in his life before we do anything else."

"Okay, then. Let's go."

They arrived at the hospital shortly before eight. Matthew was in bed watching a cartoon.

"Hey there," Alejandro called as they walked up to his bed.

"What are you guys doing here?"

"We came to talk to you."

"What about?"

"Angelina and I were talking, and we have an important question for you."

"Okay, what is it?"

Angelina took Matthew's hand. "Matthew, you know how much Alejandro and I care about you."

Matthew nodded.

"Well, I was wondering how you would feel about us adopting you?"

Before either one of them could continue, he started shouting, "Yes, oh yes! I'd love that." Matthew had also come to care a great deal for Angelina and Alejandro. He missed his parents, but the fear that he'd first felt after hearing about their deaths lessened on a daily basis, especially since Angelina had been in his life. "I miss Mom and Dad a lot. But, if I had to choose a new set of parents, I choose you."

Angelina pulled him into her arms, hugging him tightly. He hung onto her, burying his head into her chest.

She turned towards Alejandro with a huge smile on her face. "We wanted to check with you before we proceed. I would imagine we'd have to become your foster parents first and then petition for adoption. We still have to meet with the authorities and this isn't cut in stone yet. We wanted to check with you first. And with the way you just reacted, we will move forward. We can't guarantee that it will work out, but we will do our best to take care of you and hopefully become your parents."

Alejandro added, "We'll never replace what you had with your parents."

"I know," Matthew said. "I'll never forget them. I don't care what you have to do. I just want a home to go to after I leave here." Matthew stopped for a second. "Will you still be my doctor?"

"I don't think so. It wouldn't be right to have me operating on you if I were to become your father. But whatever happens, know that I'll be by your side and we'll go through this together. As a family."

They sat with him until he fell asleep. Angelina stroked his cheek while Alejandro looked on. "Look at him. He's such an angel lying here." She looked up at Alejandro, "Thank you."

"For what?"

"For saying yes." She reached over and brushed a soft kiss on Matthew's cheek and then reached for her husband's hand. They left Matthew's room and headed home.

Angelina couldn't contain herself the next morning when she called Gabriella. "Alejandro and I are going to try and adopt Matthew."

"You're what?"

"You heard me. Gabriella, he's a wonderful little boy. I've come to love him, love him as if he were my own flesh and blood."

"And how does my brother feel about this?"

"Well, he was a little apprehensive at first."

"I can certainly understand that."

"Gabriella, he cares a lot about him, too. Even before this tragedy occurred, Alejandro used to come home and tell me about him. He'd go on and on about what a special little boy he was. The only thing that concerns me the most is that Alejandro is going to turn his care over to another doctor. I think that's what's really going to bother him."

"Why?"

"Because he wanted to see him through."

"But he'll still be seeing his care through, only this time it will be as a parent and not his doctor."

"I know. It's just… Never mind. When would you like to meet Matthew?"

"When are you going to tell everyone? I promise to keep my mouth shut until you do."

"I think we'll drop by my parents tonight and hopefully we can see yours as well."

"Just let me know so I don't ruin your news. I'd like to meet him as soon as you tell everyone."

"Gabriella, thank you for always being there for me. You're the best!"

"Anytime."

Angelina headed off to the hospital to see Alejandro and discuss their plans for the evening.

"Alejandro, what do you mean you can't meet with my parents this evening?"

"Honey, I have a meeting this evening. I'm sorry I forgot to tell you. I guess my mind's been elsewhere."

"Well, when are we going to tell our parents?"

"Can it wait until the weekend? I have such a busy week and I want to be focused on our discussion. If we wait until then, maybe we'll have some more details."

"I've already told Gabriella."

"Okay. And?"

"And what?"

"What did she say?"

"She's happy for us. She promised to stay mum until we tell everyone."

Angelina agreed to wait until the weekend to share their news. She called his mother and invited his parents for dinner.

"Anything wrong, dear?"

Angelina said no, that she and Alejandro just wanted to have the family for dinner. Then she contacted her mother. Jackie wasn't home, so she spoke with her father instead, who gladly accepted the invitation.

That evening in bed, as she laid in Alejandro's arms, she discussed her day. "I invited our parents to dinner Saturday evening."

"That's fine. What did you tell them?"

"Only that we hadn't seen them in a few weeks and wanted to have them over."

"You're sure about this?"

"As sure as I was the day that I accepted your marriage proposal. I love Matthew, and I know that he loves us, too. I want him to be a part of a family that loves him with all of their heart. I know we can do that. Who else would care for him? With his illness and—"

"Is that the only reason you want to adopt him? Is it because you feel sorry for him? That he'd remain in foster care?"

Turning towards Alejandro she said, "No, is that what you think? How could you say that? I love him. He's a special little boy and I want to be a part of his life."

"That's what I wanted to hear. I care about him, too. I don't want you taking pity on him, that's all."

"Pity? I thought you knew me better than that."

"I'm sorry. I'm pretty tired—I don't know what I'm saying. Forgive me?"

"Of course," but she moved out of his arms. She didn't understand why he was acting the way he was. She wasn't mad at him, she just didn't understand why he said what he said.

They went to sleep that night not under the best of terms. He was worried that she wasn't thinking the whole adoption thing through.

The next morning, when Angelina woke, she realized that she was alone in bed. She sat up and saw a note addressed to her sitting on the nightstand.

*Darling, I had to go into the hospital. I didn't want to wake you. We'll talk later.*

It was short and sweet, nothing more. Angelina reread the note and began to wonder if she should be upset. Alejandro never left her during the night without waking her and letting her know that he was called into the hospital. She decided to try and not let it bother her, but it did.

Angelina had just finished preparing the menu for their family dinner when Alejandro ambled in. He looked exhausted and it was only four o'clock in the afternoon.

"You look pretty tired."

"I am. I went in at two this morning."

"That early?"

"Yeah, I didn't want to wake you. You'd just fallen asleep, and I thought you should get your rest." He walked to the refrigerator and retrieved a bottle of water. He pulled a chair out from the table and fell into it. Rubbing his hand over his chin, he suppressed a yawn. "What are you working on?"

"My grocery list for tomorrow night's dinner. You do remember that we are having our parents for dinner, don't you?"

"Of course, I do. Why would you think that I'd forget something like that?"

"Well, after last night…"

"Angelina, let's not argue. I've had a pretty rough week. I'm sorry if I hurt you, but I'm still concerned about why you want to adopt Matthew. Yes, I know that we'll make fabulous parents. I know that we both love him. I just want to make sure that you want it for the right reasons."

"Alejandro, I want us to have a family. You know we have to adopt to have that family. We know

Matthew and his circumstances. I feel that we can provide him with everything that he needs right now. We understand where he has come from. We can sympathize with him over his parents' deaths. You knew his parents. I think they would want us to adopt him and provide for his future. I think we're the perfect fit for his situation, especially understanding his physical needs. I want to make sure that he has the medical attention that he requires. You're the best physician at what you do. You're the best person to become his father because you understand his condition. You could immediately determine if he were in a crisis. He needs us and we need him… Plain and simple. I don't know what else I can say to make you understand that."

Alejandro reached across the table for her hands. He drew them to his lips and kissed them. Holding onto them tightly, he said, "You're right. We're the best fit for him. I just hoped that we'd have had a little more time together before we had children. I understand how much children mean to you, I guess I'm just a little apprehensive. I love you, and I love Matthew. How about I get cleaned up and I'll take you out to dinner?"

She nodded and withdrew her hands from his. Alejandro headed off to the bedroom to change. She pondered their conversation. They'd be alright. He just had to get past Michael's loss. She'd help him, but so would Matthew.

The doorbell rang and Angelina answered it. Both sets of parents had arrived at the same time. She welcomed them and informed them that Alejandro was at the hospital but would be home shortly.

"Originally, he was scheduled off today, but he was concerned about one of his patients so he went in to check on her. He called about half an hour ago. He said he was getting ready to leave the hospital, so he should be home—"

"Good evening, everyone," Alejandro said as he walked through the front door. He quickly kissed her on the cheek and then turned towards their parents. He kissed both mothers and shook hands with his father and Ben. "Anyone care for a drink?"

"We just got here," his father said. "A glass of wine sounds good."

Alejandro poured the wine and Angelina set out the appetizers that she'd prepared.

"You okay?" she asked as they finished up in the kitchen. Alejandro looked upset.

"Yeah. I didn't want to tell you, but the patient I saw was Jessica. She was readmitted to the hospital a couple of days ago."

"Is she okay?"

"She had a rough night."

"And?"

"It's touch and go. She might need another kidney transplant."

"I should go see her."

"Let's wait and see how she progresses. I'll tell her you're concerned and that you said hi."

"Alejandro?"

"Let's leave it for now. We'll talk about her later. We have company right now and we have our own issues to deal with."

She preceded him out of the kitchen with a plastered smile on her face. His mother knew something was awry but kept it to herself. They were enjoying dinner when John asked how Matthew was doing.

"Well, Dad, that's one of the reasons why we asked you all to dinner."

Alejandro looked across the table at Angelina. Smiling at her, he turned back to his father. "Angelina and I have decided to adopt Matthew."

"Really?"

"Yes. We decided that since we're going to have to adopt to have our family, why not start with a child we know? Someone we care for and who cares for us in return."

Jackie jumped up to hug her son-in-law. Maria hugged Angelina.

"We're so happy for you," Alejandro's fathered interjected. "Have you started the proceedings?"

"We have an appointment to speak with Social Services. I hope we can set things in motion based upon our meeting. I know there's a lot that goes into this—looking at our finances, our backgrounds, but I don't think we'll have any problems. We've briefly talked with the social workers and they've started to put things into motion. Matthew's so excited. His only concern is that I won't be his physician any longer."

"You can still oversee his care."

"I know, Dad."

Everyone was excited with their news. "I'll call Joe and Alec and let them know our plans. Angelina already told Gabriella."

"She didn't say anything to me." Maria added.

"She was sworn to secrecy."

They enjoyed the remainder of the evening. On his way out, Alejandro's father mentioned that he'd like to meet with him, so they made plans to get together the following day.

After their parents left, they relaxed.

"Are we okay now?" she asked.

"Yeah, I think so."

They sat wrapped in each other's arms as they replayed the evening. Their lives were going to change shortly in more ways than one. They were going to have a family.

# CHAPTER TWENTY-SEVEN

While Angelina was out running errands, Alejandro went to his parents' house.

"Thanks for coming by."

"Dad, I was planning on calling you today. I need your advice."

"Son, are you sure about this adoption?"

"Yes and no. No, because I'm worried that Matthew's condition won't improve and that we'll lose him. I'm concerned about Angelina. I think she wants children so badly that she'll do anything to have a child. Since we have to adopt, Matthew's the perfect choice. We know him and understand his health… But it's just too soon. We haven't been married that long and—"

"I agree with you. But I also have concerns for you as well."

"Dad, I know I still have issues. At first I wasn't sure about this, but I am now. I just hope that nothing happens to Matthew because I'm not sure how Angelina will handle it."

They talked for a while about Tammy and Michael when Maria entered the room. "Alejandro, I didn't realize you were here."

"Hey, Mom."

Maria walked over and kissed him on the cheek. "Alejandro, I'm happy with your news, but I'm worried."

"I know Mom, so am I."

Alejandro spent a good hour going over the situation with his parents. "As I told Dad, I still have times when I struggle with Tammy and Michael's deaths, and I'm sure I will until the day I die. I know the only way we can have children is to adopt." He paused, "I hope I'm not being selfish. I just wanted a little more time with just Angelina before we have children. But then, I feel this is the right thing to do, a blessing in disguise. I knew Matthew's parents…"

"You're the only one that can answer the question for whether you should adopt Matthew. Your mother and I are here for you, but we can't tell you what to do. Only you and your wife can make that decision, and we'll be here to support you in whatever you choose." John hugged his son and patted him on the shoulder.

"We're both here for you if you need to discuss this further," said Maria.

Alejandro thanked his parents for their love and support. When he left their house, he still wasn't sure if he was doing the right thing in adopting Matthew. His heart kept telling him it was going to be okay, but logic kept rearing its ugly head making him unsure of their decision.

Alejandro returned to an empty home as Angelina had yet to return from her errands. He moved to the couch in the study where Angelina later found him. She entered the darkened room, turned on a lamp, and she saw him staring out at the backyard. He was in his own world and didn't recognize that she'd returned. She called his name, but he didn't respond. She placed a hand on his shoulder.

Alejandro turned to her, "Hey, honey. Get all of your errands run?"

"Yeah, where were you just now?"

"What do you mean?"

"When I came in, you didn't hear me."

"I was thinking."

"About what?"

"Lots of things... But it doesn't matter. Do you need any help?"

"No." She sat down beside him. Turning towards him, she placed her hand on his thigh. "What's bothering you?"

"Honey, I don't want to talk about it now. So how was your day?"

"Alejandro, don't shut me out."

"I'm not. I just need to think things through on my own."

"Alejandro?"

"Enough!" Alejandro burst. "Sometimes after an intense week, I like to sit alone and just let my mind wander, and this is the perfect time of day to do it. I'm fine. Don't worry." Alejandro had lost track of time. He'd been rehashing the conversation he'd had with his parents, and he was having doubts about the adoption. He wanted more time with just Angelina. And yes, he was thinking about Tammy and Michael and how their deaths impacted his life.

Angelina wasn't too sure what was going on with him. She told herself not to worry, but she did.

They went to dinner but ate mostly in silence. She was placing their leftovers in a box when his phone rang. It was his brother, Alec.

"What's up, Alec?"

"I hear congratulations are in order."

"Yep." He was pretty sure where the conversation was headed, so he asked his brother something trivial to change the subject. Alec was cognizant of what he was doing, though.

"I guess you can't talk right now."

"That's right."

"Call me later."

"Sounds great. How about we meet for lunch tomorrow?"

"One?"

"See you then."

Angelina had been watching Alejandro. "What did Alec want?"

"Not sure. I told him I'd meet him for lunch tomorrow. Now, I just want to go home and go to bed."

They drove home in silence. Alejandro headed off to bed while Angelina put the finishing touches on her lesson plans—she'd just returned to school at the beginning of the week. She was concerned about him. If he didn't open up soon, she would have to confront him. She loved him and didn't want the adoption to come between them.

Monday morning Alejandro got up, dressed, and headed off to the hospital with barely a word spoken to Angelina. She was lost and wasn't sure what was going on. She wandered into school just as the bell was sounding. She spent her whole day trying to get on track. She fumbled through her lessons, and actually lost her cool with her students' right before lunch. She didn't know what was wrong with her. Actually, she did, but didn't want to admit it. She and Alejandro were having problems. Thankfully, she had two free periods that afternoon where she could just sit and think.

Alec and Alejandro met for lunch at the deli across the street from the hospital. It was their normal stomping grounds when they met for lunch.

"What's up Alec?"

"I could say the same to you, but I know what's up. Is it true? Are you going to adopt Matthew?"

"Looks like it."

"And?"

"It's something Angelina is hell-bent on."

"What about you?"

"I know adoption is the only way we're going to be able to have a family, but I'm not sure Matthew is the answer."

"But you care for him, don't you?"

"Sure, I do."

"Then what's the problem?"

Alejandro looked at his brother. What *was* his problem? He loved Matthew. He knew he'd make a terrific son. So what was it?

"Alejandro?"

"You're right. What is the problem? Thanks, Alec."

"For what?"

"For making me see the forest from the trees. I've gotta go." Alejandro jumped up from the table and raced out of the deli.

Angelina was sitting in her classroom, staring out the window. She was oblivious to the door opening and closing. She felt a hand on her shoulder. Looking up, she saw him standing beside her.

"I'm sorry."

"Alejandro?"

"I was wrong. I'm sorry for not believing in us being a family. I love you, and I love him. We can make it work. I know we can."

Angelina stared at her husband, flabbergasted.

Alejandro squatted down beside her. He placed his hand on her cheek. "I love you, Angelina."

"I was scared… So scared that you didn't want a family with me. I thought you were regretting us."

"Why would you think that? You're the best thing that's happened to me. I'm sorry I withdrew. Withdrawing is how I deal with my problems. Now that I have you in my life, I have to share my feelings with you and not take them into myself. I know I still have problems with my past, Tammy and Michael's deaths… But I realize that I can't shut you out either. Sometimes the grief rears its ugly head and takes over, but with you in my life, the grief has lessened. Give me some time. With you by my side, I have no qualms that I'll be able to finally face their deaths head on." He drew her into his arms. "Please be with me. Stay by my side."

"Always."

Alejandro stood and Angelina stood with him, "I've got to go pick up my class."

Smiling, he told her he had to return to the hospital. "I rushed over here when I realized you were free. I had to talk to you before…"

"You chickened out." She smiled at him, teasing.

"No, that's not it. I wanted to... Oh, you." He kissed her and walked from the room. "See you tonight."

After he left, she felt like the weight of the world that she'd been carrying all day had been lifted. He was still dealing with Tammy and Michael's deaths. Even though he had vowed to love, honor, and cherish her, he still grieved. She needed to be cognizant of that.

Alejandro came home from work whistling.

"You're in a good mood. What's up?"

"Matthew's coming home."

"What? When?" Angelina said, her had going to her throat.

"Take a deep breath, will you? Matthew has improved slightly. We've decided to send him home. It's the best for him all around."

"Oh my gosh! We're not ready. We have to get—"

"Slow down! I've arranged to go to his house and pick up his stuff. That way he will have the things that are familiar to him."

"How? When?"

"Alec and Joe are coming by in a few minutes. My mom is coming by to help you. She'll be here—"

The doorbell rang and his entire family walked in.

Gabriella and Maria helped transform one of their spare bedrooms into a room fit for a boy. Alejandro, along with his brothers and father, brought Matthew's furniture and toys from his old room. He also located a picture of Matthew with his parents that he placed on Matthew's dresser. Matthew was surrounded by everything he knew and loved from his home—

everything except for his parents. By nine they'd finished converting the bedroom into a child's room.

"I can't believe he's coming home. Here... To our home."

"Believe it. By this time tomorrow, Matthew will be living with us."

In all of her haste, Angelina forgot to contact Mary about Matthew's homecoming. "What time will he be released? I forgot to call Mary and tell her I won't be at school tomorrow."

"Go to school. He'll be ready whenever you get here."

She walked into his arms, thanking him. She couldn't believe that tomorrow she'd be caring for Matthew.

Both of them had trouble sleeping. Alejandro got out of bed around two in the morning and sat outside amongst the stars. She woke shortly thereafter. She put her robe on and found him sitting in an Adirondack chair in the middle of the backyard. She grabbed two bottles of juice and joined him.

"Here," she said.

Looking up, he smiled at her and took her offering. He patted his leg and she sat down on his lap. She wrapped her arm around his neck. "I'm anxious, too."

"It's not that."

"Then what?"

"I couldn't sleep and didn't want to wake you. I was just remembering when we brought Michael home from the hospital. How excited we were. And you know what?"

"What?"

"I feel that same excitement. I'm excited about tomorrow and Matthew joining our family. I've missed having a little one around. You know we have to get him into school."

"Is he okay for that?"

"Sure is. He won't be able to go full-time at first. He's going to need to get his strength up after being in the hospital for so long."

"We have to enroll him."

"I'll call tomorrow. You'll be too busy at school. We'll see if he can start next week. By then we should have sorted out a schedule. Sound okay with you?"

"You're amazing. I'm the teacher and totally forgot about school. Thanks!"

"Not a big deal. We're both going to have a lot of adjustments to make."

"I realize that."

"But with you by my side, I know we're going to get through this as a stronger unit. I love you. Never ever dismiss that."

They sat under the stars, both dozing off just before four o'clock. The loud chirping of the birds startled Alejandro awake. It was near six o'clock and both of them were running late. He brushed a soft kiss on her lips, waking her. "Time to get up... You're going to be late."

Stretching, she removed herself from his lap. Hand-in-hand, they strolled into the house. It was going to be a glorious day.

Angelina left for school while Alejandro finished showering. He wasn't on service, so he decided to contact the school that Matthew would attend. He spoke with the principal and made an appointment to see him at ten.

Alejandro was a few minutes late as he received a call from the hospital concerning Jessica. It had taken him longer than expected to deal with her latest crisis. He promised the nurse he'd be in to see her shortly.

He arrived at the school and apologized profusely for being late. He'd called on his way informing the principal of his tardiness. "I received a call from the hospital just as I was walking out the door. Sorry about that."

"Not a problem. What exactly do you do?"

Alejandro explained that he was a surgeon and that Angelina was a teacher at a nearby school. Alejandro went through Matthew's personal history—his parents' recent deaths, his physical condition, and his hospital stay. He also discussed Matthew's need for a transplant and lastly that he and Angelina were going to eventually adopt him.

The principal called Matthew's teacher in to meet him. Alejandro introduced himself and re-explained Matthew's predicament. Everyone was on board with his needs. He would start school the following week. It would be part-time for the first week or so to see how his strength progressed. They would take it one day at a time, but Alejandro was assured that they'd work with him to make sure Matthew's transition back to school was a smooth one.

Alejandro arrived at the hospital and checked on Jessica. She was improving and hopefully would be released soon. She kept getting infections that he couldn't seem to get a handle on. He hoped that this was the last hospital stay for her. She was so sweet and he hated to see her go through the physical traumas that she'd endured over the last six months.

Alejandro then made sure his schedule was open for the next two weeks. Thankfully, he was scheduled off and he could take Matthew back and forth to school. Hopefully by the time he returned to service, Matthew would be strong enough to attend school full-time.

Alejandro was paged over the hospital intercom. He answered the call to discover that his father wanted to have lunch with him and Matthew prior to being released. Alejandro was excited that his father was taking such an interest in Matthew. Not only did his father join him and Matthew, but his mother surprised him as well.

"Matthew, we want you to call us whatever you want."

Matthew looked back and forth between Alejandro's parents and then said, "How about Grandma and Grandpa?"

In unison, they both agreed. They were thankful to have another grandson. They also missed Michael, but now they had a chance to make special memories with Matthew.

They hadn't even completed lunch when the door flew open and Angelina walked in.

"What're you doing here so early?" Alejandro asked as he placed a kiss on her cheek.

"Mary was so excited to hear about Matthew that she told me to leave after lunch. My aide, Jennifer, is going to substitute the rest of the week. It was Mary's idea, and she told me that if I needed to take more time, not to hesitate—just take it. I think I'll take

Monday off for sure, and we can take Matthew to school together. How does that sound?"

"Great!" Matthew said as he finished his lunch.

They left the hospital around four. They'd barely gotten Matthew settled at the house when the doorbell rang. Angelina's entire family filed into the house. Her mother had prepared dinner and had invited Alejandro's entire family. Alejandro feared that all of the activity would overwhelm Matthew, but he took it in stride. He met all of his future aunts and uncles, along with Angelina's parents.

He'd been so excited that he practically drifted off to sleep mid-sentence. Alejandro picked him up and carried him to his bedroom. A pain seared through his chest as this action brought back many of the same memories that he had with Michael. He suppressed them. Michael was gone. He could never be replaced but, in time, he'd be able to call Matthew his son.

Matthew settled in and adjusted to his new life. They both took him to school that first day. Angelina met his teacher and seemed to bond with her immediately. "I know he has to be behind. If you let me know where he needs additional help, I'll tutor him."

When they went to leave, Matthew hugged them. "Thank you."

"For what?" Alejandro asked.

"For wanting me... I love you both."

"We love you, too." Angelina had tears in her eyes as they returned to the principal's office. She met with the principal to make sure they were in agreement with Matthew's schedule and his special needs. Angelina was concerned but the principal told them that if Matthew seemed to tire, they would call them immediately. Hand-in-hand they left school.

"Alejandro…"

"He'll be fine. Stop worrying."

She smiled at him and squeezed his hand.

Matthew adjusted to school more quickly than either of them ever imagined. The night before Angelina was scheduled to return to work, she went to help Matthew prepare for bed. She stood in the doorway, watching him. He was looking at the picture of his parents that Alejandro had placed on his dresser. She wasn't sure what he was thinking when he looked up and caught her watching him.

"Angelina," he said and then walked towards her. When he reached her, he stopped, smiled up at her, and wrapped his arms around her waist.

"What's this all about," she asked as she knelt before him.

"Thank you," he said and then squeezed his arms more tightly about her waist.

"Why are you thanking me?"

"For taking me home. For wanting me."

"Of course I want you. I love you."

Matthew smiled up at her.

Just then, Alejandro walked in and joined them. Matthew hugged him as well.

"Everything okay here?" asked Alejandro. "How's school?"

Matthew lit up when he started to talk about his friends in school. "I love it! And I actually have friends."

"I'm glad. Anything else bothering you?"

Matthew thought for a second. He looked up at both Angelina and Alejandro and a huge smile crossed his face. They both realized then that everything was going to work out. Matthew seemed happy living with them and he was adjusting well to his new school.

Angelina returned to work mid-week while Alejandro stayed home and took Matthew to and from school. Angelina was impressed that Matthew wasn't behind in school. In all actuality, he was reading above grade level and his math skills were right on. Socially, he got along with all of the children and made some good friends. Physically, he was doing as well as could be expected. He still waited for his kidney transplant and underwent dialysis twice a week.

There were days that Angelina was ecstatic, and other days that threw her for a loop. Generally her down days coincided with Matthew's dialysis—she hated to see him suffer. Often, Alejandro was the one that took him for his treatment. Matthew thought it was neat that his "father" was able to do that.

Alejandro had become concerned as of late. He hadn't told Angelina, but she could see it in his eyes. Angelina was off one day and wanted to take Matthew to his dialysis. It had been agreed upon earlier in the week, but at the last minute, Alejandro argued with her that he needed to take him. She thought it strange that he insisted on doing so. Ultimately she'd won their dispute, but during his treatment she caught Alejandro reviewing Matthew's file. She confronted him in the hallway, but he stalled their conversation as he was paged to the OR.

Nervously, she waited for him that night. Alejandro was late and she'd already put Matthew to bed. He was fast asleep when Alejandro finally walked through the door.

Something was up. He looked like he'd been hit by a train. She watched him as he came into the room, hidden in the shadows. He brushed his hands across his eyes and dropped down onto the couch. He closed his eyes and threw his head back. She walked over and placed her hands on his shoulders, slowly massaging them.

"That feels so good. It's been another trying day. I'm beat. I think I'm going to take a shower and go to bed."

"Alejandro, can you wait a minute?"

"I really—"

"It's Matthew, isn't it?"

Sighing, he nodded his head. "His kidney function has declined again." Taking a deep breath he said, "He really needs that transplant as soon as possible. I spoke to Daniel and he said that we're going to have to add another dialysis treatment. I don't like that… We've just got to start praying harder to find a donor."

She was taken aback by his comments. "How long have you known this?"

He was silent.

"Be honest."

"A few weeks. I was afraid you'd hear something today when you took him to his dialysis. That's why I wanted to take him."

"Is that why I caught you looking at his chart?"

"Yes. I'm sorry I didn't tell you. It's just that I wanted to…"

"Protect me."

"Something like that. I know it was wrong."

"Yes, it was. He's going to be our son. I need to know everything about his condition. You need to be honest with me."

"I know. I was trying to protect you."

"I realize that. That's water under the bridge now that you've told me how critical the situation has become." She turned off the lights and followed him to their bedroom. He showered and joined her in bed. Reaching for her, he apologized again. He held her the entire night.

Waking at dawn, he wrote her a note and headed off to the hospital. It was Saturday and he wanted to get home as soon as possible so he could enjoy the day with his family. Jessica had been released from the hospital the week before and she'd returned home to her family. She'd dodged another bullet and thankfully wasn't rejecting her kidney.

Alejandro was fortunate that he had only two patients in the hospital—he was home by ten that morning. Angelina and Matthew had just finished breakfast when he walked back in the door. "Did you get my note?"

"Sure did, and it sounds like a plan to me."

"Huh? What are you talking about?" asked Matthew.

"How about a day at the zoo? It's perfect weather—not too cold. Do you feel up to it?"

"Uh huh."

"Then go get your jacket, and I'll go grab the camera."

Thankfully, the zoo wasn't too crowded when they arrived. As they walked through the gates, Angelina looked at her family and smiled. It was the first time they'd done something together and she was overjoyed. She finally had the family that she'd dreamed about since she was a little girl.

Alejandro threw his arm around her shoulders as they walked towards the sea lion exhibit while Matthew walked ahead of them. When they reached his side, he was leaning over the railing, pointing towards the sea lions. "Look at that," cried Matthew. He didn't get the response he was looking for so he called out to them again, "Mom, Dad look at that!"

The Mom and Dad titles caught both of them off guard. "What'd you say?"

Matthew looked at them. "I called you Mom and Dad."

"But Matthew—"

"You are my mom and dad now." He reached for their hands and they joined him along the railing.

Angelina had tears in her eyes. Alejandro caught her eye, winked and smiled at her. They were a family—a true family in every sense of the word.

# CHAPTER TWENTY-EIGHT

The holidays were a jubilant time as they celebrated their first Christmas together as a married couple. And to top it off, they had Matthew, too.

Angelina had a blast preparing for the holidays. She decorated every available space in the house with lighted garland, Christmas trees, and anything else that she could find that was festive.

She surprised Matthew with a Christmas tree for his bedroom. She took him shopping so he could choose whatever he wanted to decorate it with. He chose various birds to decorate his tree, along with brightly colored lights and garland.

She kept up her holiday tradition with Colleen as well, but Alejandro wasn't able to join them this time. Instead, Alejandro decided to start a family tradition all his own. He took Angelina, Matthew, Colleen, and Wyatt caroling. Since their house was located in a rural area, they caroled in both his and Angelina's family's neighborhoods. They had a blast and even recruited Ben and Jackie, along with his parents, to join the group.

Matthew still believed in Santa Claus, so Alejandro went all out. He found a form of a shoe that he could use to sprinkle with ash from the fireplace. It was perfect. He made it look like Santa had come down the fireplace—footprints led from the fireplace to the Christmas tree.

When Matthew woke Christmas morning, he went to the family room where he saw the shoe prints that led directly to the mound of Christmas presents. He ran to Angelina and Alejandro's room, bursting through the door screaming, "Santa's been here! Hurry up! Come on, let's open our gifts!"

Both Angelina and Alejandro were exhausted from the night before. They hadn't been able to get Matthew to go to sleep, and then they had to wrap all of the Santa gifts. It all added up to a Christmas Day nap for both of them.

They watched Matthew as he unwrapped his presents. The excitement he showed was overwhelming to Angelina.

Alejandro noticed a tear trickle down her face. He turned to her, brushed the tear away with his thumb, and said, "What's this all about?"

She smiled at him. "It's nothing. I'm happy— happy that we have Matthew in our lives."

They finished opening presents and then headed off to church, then over to her parent's house. They had decided to forgo what had turned into an annual early morning Christmas celebration at her parent's house because it was too late for Matthew.

After visiting with her family, they went to Alejandro's parents'. By the time they got home, everyone was exhausted.

Their first Christmas together as husband and wife was a memorable one, especially with Matthew in their lives.

Matthew's class was having a Valentine's Day party the following day. Angelina took him to the store to purchase last minute valentines for his class party. She had purchased valentines several weeks before, but when Matthew went to sign his name and add his sucker to the card, he decided he didn't like them at all—they were too girlie. She was tired of listening to Matthew's complaining, so she agreed to take him to the store so he could choose his own. He was so excited that he could barely contain himself in the car as they made their way to the store. It took him forever to make his decision since the selection of valentines had been picked over at that point. After some serious thought, he got a huge smile on his face and said, "Okay, Mom. I want these. They're perfect!"

"You're sure those are the ones you want?"

"Yep, I think these are just right!" he said as he perused the back of the box looking at the various cards.

"Ready to check out?"

"Uh, huh," he said as she pushed the cart towards the front of the store. The store was packed with shoppers. They slowly made their way to the checkout lane and stood in a long line—it seemed like everyone was there purchasing various sundries for Valentine's Day. The store seemed awfully warm to Angelina, but she attributed it to the larger than normal crowds. As Angelina reached into the cart to grab Matthew's valentines, she became lightheaded and quickly grabbed ahold of the cart, dropping the box onto the floor.

Matthew picked them up and noticed how pale she was. "Mom, are you okay?"

"I'm fine. It's just a little warm in here."

They made it through the checkout lane and headed out to the car. Matthew kept looking at her as they moved across the parking lot. "Mom, are you feeling better?"

"I am, Matthew. I just got really warm in there, that's all. The fresh air has really helped. Thank you for asking."

They hurried home so Matthew could address his valentines. Angelina started dinner, but had to sit down because she got dizzy. She realized she hadn't been feeling herself all day, but blamed it on all of the viruses going around school. Alejandro walked in as she sat there with her head in her hands.

He walked over to her, put his hand across her back, and leaned in to place a kiss on the top of her head. "Sweetheart, are you feeling okay?"

"Yeah, I'm just tired. I haven't quite felt like myself today. I guess I'm fighting what everyone else has. I had three kids out in my class today. I hear there's a virus or something going around."

"That's what I hear, too. We had a few nurses out this week, too. You need to take it easy. Maybe you should stay home tomorrow."

"I'll be fine. I just need a good night's sleep." Alejandro kissed her on the cheek, then went to check on Matthew. They huddled closely while Matthew completed his valentines.

"Dad, I think something's wrong with Mom."

"Why do you say that?"

Matthew proceeded to tell him about what happened while they were shopping. Alejandro thought about how he found Angelina when he came into the house. He decided he would watch her closely and, if she didn't seem better, he'd have her see the doctor.

Valentine's Day was unforgettable. Matthew made them special valentines. They were taken aback when they read them. He'd written how much he loved both of them, and he thanked them for becoming his parents. After reading her card, Angelina smiled and reached for him. She pulled him into her arms, telling him how lucky they were to have him be a part of their family. Alejandro brought home dinner, wanting to do something special to celebrate the day. He didn't want Angelina cooking since he was still concerned about her being ill and wanted her to take it easy.

Angelina placed the silverware on the table and reached for the plates when she again became lightheaded. She stumbled, almost dropping the dishes. She regained her balance and was able to set the plates down without incident. Alejandro noticed this out of the corner of his eye, but he didn't want to overreact. "Need some help there?"

"I'm fine—I just stumbled over my own feet."

They ate dinner, but Alejandro kept his eye on her the entire time. She mainly pushed her food around on her plate while they discussed Matthew's party.

Alejandro put Matthew to bed. After she cleaned up the kitchen, Angelina poked her head into Matthew's room, wishing him a goodnight and telling Alejandro that she was also heading off to bed. It was unusual for her to go to bed that early. Alejandro finished his story to Matthew and sought her out. She was in bed reading. He joined her and pulled her into his arms. "Sweetheart, are you feeling okay?"

"I'm fine. Just a little tired this evening. It's pretty chaotic whenever we have a party. Today was no exception."

"You know how I worry."

"I'm fine. Just go about your evening."

"If you insist," he said as kissed her and told her he'd join her shortly.

Before they knew it, spring break was upon them. They elected to stay in town and just be a family, doing whatever they felt like doing. Angelina was feeling much better. She guessed she'd had a virus since her symptoms disappeared as quickly as they'd appeared.

Alejandro had just arrived home for the day when his cell phone rang. It was the hospital.

Angelina watched him as he spoke, and his voice began to raise with excitement. She had no idea what was going on. He hung up the phone and grabbed her, calling for Matthew.

"What's wrong?"

"Nothing… Everything's right."

"What're you talking about?"

"Matthew, we got it."

"Got what?"

"A kidney!"

Angelina almost collapsed in his arms. She couldn't believe it. Their prayers had been answered. "We need to get to the hospital."

They arrived at the hospital and were greeted by members of the transplant team. Matthew was anxious, but greeted them with a smile. He knew that his life was going to change, but he was scared and couldn't wait for the surgery to be over. Angelina stood by and watched as they prepared him for surgery. Alejandro had phoned both of their families. His father was already at the hospital while Gabriella drove his mother. Alec and Joe would join them after their clinic closed and they finished rounding at the hospital for the day. Angelina's parents were out of town with Wyatt's hockey team and wouldn't be back until the following day. Colleen hurried to the hospital and was able to see Matthew before he went into surgery.

Alejandro went into the operating room while Matthew was being put under, but left before the actual surgery began. He needed to be with his wife.

Alejandro wished he was the surgeon—he'd be in control then. He'd performed this surgery countless times. He was comfortable with the procedure, but nervous because it was his son being operated on by someone other than himself.

Angelina sat beside him. She was extremely pale. He knew she was nervous, but that shouldn't account for her paleness. He made a note to keep his eye on her. Alejandro's parents and Colleen went to the cafeteria while Alejandro and Angelina waited for news on how the surgery was progressing. Angelina rested her head on his shoulder.

"Would you like something to drink?"

"No, thanks. I'm fine."

"Are you sure? You look like you don't feel too well."

"I'm just anxious and tired, that's all."

"You'd tell me if you didn't feel okay, right?"

She smiled at him and nodded. "What do you think?"

"I think no, but I have to believe you would."

They sat together for some time, just the two of them. Alejandro explained about the surgery and where he thought they were in the process.

The doors opened and a nurse came in to tell them they were closing. Daniel would be in shortly to tell them how the surgery went. Angelina decided to use the restroom before the doctor came in. She kissed Alejandro on the cheek. As she rose from the couch, Alejandro watched the expression on her face change. Angelina fell towards him, and he caught her before she hit the floor. She'd fainted dead away.

Alejandro laid her on the couch and called for a nurse. Just as the nurse entered the room, Angelina woke. "What happened?"

"You fainted."

"I what?"

"You heard me. See, I knew you weren't feeling well—I could tell by looking at you. We're going to get you checked out."

"Alejandro, I'm fine—just a little tired. Just help me to the bathroom and then I'll take a glass of juice. I feel better already. I guess I just need to eat something. I'm fine."

Alejandro knew better than to argue with her, but he knew something was wrong with her and had known it for some time. He'd watch her closely and, when he thought she'd overtaxed herself, he'd step in and help her out. This time he was going to make sure she saw her doctor.

Daniel came in and told them that the surgery had gone well. "He'll be out of it for a while, so why don't you go home and come back later?"

Angelina told Alejandro that she didn't want to leave the hospital. Instead, she thought they could just hang out in his office. Alejandro agreed and he led her to his office couch where she fell asleep almost instantly. While she was out, he paged Kevin, her doctor. Alejandro was tired of her making excuses. He had actually believed that she'd been fighting the virus that had been tearing through the community. She'd been fine for the last several weeks, but with the fainting he wasn't sure anymore. He wanted her checked out and wanted to know if something was wrong with her.

When Angelina woke, she saw a note laying on the table besides her. It read, "I've gone for coffee and something to eat. I'll be back shortly. Love, A."

She smiled and headed to his office restroom. She was still lightheaded and even somewhat nauseous. She chalked it up to the fact that she hadn't eaten since lunch the previous day. When she returned, Alejandro was seated behind his desk. He stood when he saw how pale she was. She even looked a little green around the gills.

"That's it."

"Huh?" she murmured.

"Angelina, quit lying to me."

"What're you talking about?"

"Something's wrong with you, isn't there?"

"Why do you say that?"

"You're awfully pale and you look like you're—"

She abruptly turned around and rushed back to the bathroom, slamming the door behind her. Alejandro rushed over and opened the door, finding her slumped over the toilet. He reached for a paper towel and wet it with cool water. He wiped her forehead as she sat slumped on the floor. "I think I have a bug."

"A bug? Angelina this has been going on for weeks. You're going to get checked out today. Your doctor's on his way here."

"I'm fine."

"Quit arguing with me. You're going to get checked out. If you're sick, you won't be able to see Matthew."

"Okay. I'll listen to you."

"Thanks. Now, if you're feeling better, let's get you up off the floor and back to the couch." Alejandro guided her back to the couch and sat beside her. Thankfully, he'd thought to get some soda crackers while he was getting their breakfast. He had a notion that she might need them.

Angelina's doctor came by promptly at nine. Alejandro led them into one of his examining rooms. Her doctor's office was offsite, but he'd agreed to see her as a favor to Alejandro. Alejandro left them alone. He'd already informed her doctor of the symptoms he'd witnessed. He'd hadn't trusted that Angelina would divulge what was going on, but she did—she told her doctor everything. She believed she had nothing to worry about since there were so many viruses going around school. She was sure she had one of them since she was so run down and just couldn't shake it.

Her doctor examined her and told her he wanted to run a couple of tests. He asked that she run over to his office to have her blood drawn and then he'd come back that evening with the results.

"Do you think there's something wrong?"

"I just want to check a couple of things. How about I see you at five? Your husband's office hours should be over by then."

"He's cancelled them for the remainder of the week since our son just had surgery." Angelina filled her doctor in on Matthew. She'd attributed all of the stress surrounding his illness to her symptoms.

"We'll see. I'll see you this evening."

"Sure."

Angelina filled Alejandro in on her conversation. He told her that he'd join her that evening when she got her results. Angelina ran over to her doctor's office to have her blood drawn. On the way back, she started to feel better.  She and Alejandro ate breakfast, and then they saw Matthew for the first time since coming out of surgery. He looked great. Her family arrived after returning home from Wyatt's hockey game. They were excited to hear the news. Neither of them told their parents of her fainting spell.

It was five o'clock when they headed back to Alejandro's office to meet with Kevin. Alejandro's secretary advised them her doctor was waiting. Alejandro reached for her hand as they walked down the hallway to his office. He had a feeling what the news was going to be. He couldn't be sure, but he'd had a dream about this day months ago—he'd known Matthew was going to have his transplant. He knew Angelina wasn't feeling well. He'd seen them walking down this same hallway... Walking towards his office to meet with her doctor. Alejandro hoped and prayed the outcome was the same as his dream.

Angelina's doctor greeted them with a huge smile on his face. "How's your son?"

"Great. Thanks for asking."

"Angelina, why don't you sit down?"

"Is the news that bad?"

"No, but I think you should sit down. What I have to say is going to come as a shock to both of you."

"Oh my," she said. "Let's get this over with then. Just tell me."

"Let me ask you. What're you doing in say, seven months?"

Angelina didn't understand his question. She just looked at him.

"Angelina, I'm surprised you didn't figure this out on your own."

A huge smile spread across Alejandro's face. He knew what Kevin was alluding to—his dream was just about to become true.

"Dear, you have no clue what I'm talking about, do you?"

"Not really."

Alejandro took over, "Honey, what I think Kevin is trying to say is…"

Kevin looked over at him, smiled, and nodded his head.

"Sweetheart, you're going to have a baby."

Angelina's eyes widened. "What? That can't be. You told me I couldn't have a child," she said as she covered her mouth with her trembling hands.

"Angelina, all I can say is that this is a miracle."

She was speechless, staring at Alejandro. A tear escaped her eye and slid down her cheek. Alejandro reached for her and pulled her into his arms.

"It's true, sweetheart. I knew it. I knew you were going to be pregnant."

"How?"

"I had a dream. I saw all of this. Saw Matthew's transplant. Knew you were going to faint. And I even saw Kevin here telling us about our miracle baby."

Kevin smiled at them both. "I'll leave you two alone. I need to see you next week in my office. In the meantime, here's a prescription for vitamins. You need to start taking them as soon as possible."

"I will," Angelina said, nodding vigorously.

Her doctor left them alone in Alejandro's office. She was totally shocked. She still couldn't believe the news. "Did I hear him correctly? Am I really pregnant?"

"Uh huh," he said as he placed a kiss on her forehead.

"How? I thought…"

"Let's not wonder how. Let's just be thankful that you are."

"I am, don't get me wrong. I'm just so shocked," she said as she wiped another tear from her face. Her periods had never been regular, and she hadn't thought twice about missing one.

"I am, too. I think we should wait a few weeks to tell our family."

"Definitely. I wholeheartedly agree." She threw herself back into his arms. "Thank you. Thank you so much."

"For what?"

"For sticking by my side... I love you so much," she said as she kissed him.

"Let's get that prescription filled and go see our son."

She nodded and hugged him again.

As they waited for her prescription, Alejandro sat staring at her. He realized that it was true. Pregnant women had a certain glow about them, and Angelina definitely was part of that crowd. She had a smile that couldn't be wiped from her face. And if his eyes weren't betraying him, she did indeed glow.

# CHAPTER TWENTY-NINE

Matthew recovered quickly from his surgery and was able to come home a week after surgery. After discovering that she was pregnant, Angelina couldn't believe how tired and nauseous she actually was. Morning sickness had a different definition in her book—she was nauseous morning, noon, and night. Now she understood what her friends had described while being pregnant. She'd also shed quite a few pounds since Matthew's transplant.

One evening, after an extremely difficult day with her morning sickness, Alejandro took a good look at his wife as she was putting Matthew to bed. After reading to him, Alejandro reached for her hand, leading her towards the patio. He guided her towards the chaise lounge and sat down, pulling her onto his lap. "Sweetheart, I can't help but notice how much weight you've lost."

"I can't eat. I'm nauseous all of the time."

"Have you talked to Kevin about this?"

"I see him next week. I'll talk to him then."

"You have to try and eat."

She put her hand up to stop him and said, "I know. Please don't lecture me. I try, but it just comes right back up. I'm sick all day long. I know some women experience this the entire nine months."

"Well, we can only hope that doesn't happen with you. You know, we're going to have to tell our parents soon."

"I know. Let's wait until after my appointment next week."

"That's fine."

"Will you be there for it?"

"It's on my calendar. I'll be there unless something comes up."

She wrapped her arms around his neck. "You know, I still can't believe we're going to have a baby. I have to pinch myself at least ten times a day. I'd truly given up the dream of our own child. What do you think happened?"

"I don't know what happened. It happens all the time when couples who think they can't conceive and then get pregnant out of the blue, most often when they've given up. Just call it our little miracle." He paused, not sure how she would take what he was about to say. "I just know I'm thrilled. I think you should quit work at the end of the school year. We don't need your salary. We have Matthew to worry about and, now our very own little one. I want you taking it easy. Enjoy this pregnancy. And most especially, I want you to enjoy motherhood." He kissed her and held her tightly in his arms. "I love you so much that it hurts sometimes."

"I know what you mean... I love teaching but I love you and our family even more. I won't sign my contract, and I won't tell Mary about the baby yet. I'll just tell her that I need to concentrate on Matthew. He's our priority right now and I need to be here for him." Smiling, she said, "I can't wait to tell our parents. My mother will be absolutely ecstatic. And yours..."

"My mother will be thrilled. She's missed having a grandchild since Michael died. Now she'll be able to spoil the baby, just as she did with Michael. Don't get me wrong, she considers Matthew her grandchild, too, but there's just something about my mother and a baby. Be prepared because that's her motto. She's there to spoil her grandchildren. My mom was heartbroken when Michael died, and now she'll have a new way of spending her time. I'm warning you because you'll get tired of seeing her, especially when there's a baby involved."

"Never. I love your parents. I'm fortunate to have such terrific in-laws. I've heard quite a few horror stories. And I, for one, am happy to report that I have the best that could ever exist."

"I'm glad to hear that. My parents feel the same way about you. I know they loved Tammy, but they love you as much or even more. There's a special connection between our families. It's kind of weird actually. But I'm just happy that you and Gabriella went to college together and became such close friends. Unfortunately, Colleen had to have her accident, but we probably would have never gotten together if it weren't for that. Fate allowed us to find one another. Fate has given me the opportunity to fall in love again. Fate has... It's provided us with this miracle that you're now carrying." Alejandro placed his hand on her stomach, thanking their lucky stars that fate played a role in making her life's dream a reality.

Alejandro's phone rang. He glanced at the caller ID. Rarely did his mother call him on his cell phone. He answered while Angelina got up to prepare for bed.

"Hi, Mom. How are you?"

"Good."

"How come you called on my cell?"

"I wasn't sure if you were at the hospital. I wanted to be sure that I reached you."

"Is something wrong?"

"Alejandro, what's wrong with Angelina?"

"Why do you think something's wrong?"

"Gabriella and I were discussing her. She's worried about her. She said she always looks pale and has lost a considerable amount of weight and—"

"Mom, she's been through a lot with Matthew. She lost a lot of sleep and still is not quite comfortable with his whole transplant. She's worried—"

"Alejandro, enough. Something's not right. You're both coming over here tomorrow and I won't take no for an answer."

"Mom, she's fine. We're fine."

"We'll see the three of you for dinner." With that, she ended the conversation.

Alejandro was staring at his phone when Angelina reentered the room. He told her about his conversation and their ensuing dinner plans for the following evening.

"What are we going to do? We can't tell them yet. It's too soon. Anything can happen."

"Let's just see what happens. Hopefully by tomorrow Mom will have calmed down and she'll have put it behind her."

"Knowing your parents, the answer to that statement is a big, fat NO."

The next day at school, Angelina worried the entire day. Thankfully Gabriella's class was on a field trip and she didn't have to face her.

They found a sitter for Matthew, as they didn't want him witnessing the potential fallout from their evening with his parents. Matthew was just as happy because he could watch one of his favorite movies instead of having to listen to a bunch of grown-ups.

"Tell Grandma and Grandpa I say hello."

"You have a good time with Julie." They kissed him goodbye and told him they'd see him in the morning.

Alejandro reached for her hand while he drove to his parents' home. Resting it on his thigh, he told her not to worry. He was sure his mother had settled down from their conversation the previous evening. Angelina informed him that she hadn't seen his sister that day since she'd been on a field trip. "I have to admit, however, that I did leave school right after the bell. I didn't want to face Gabriella any sooner than I had to."

"My sister can be a tad overbearing. I don't blame you for avoiding her. She's created this mess." He pulled into his parents' driveway. Angelina sat in the car while Alejandro exited and came around to open her door. He squeezed her hand and gave her a kiss on the cheek as she got out of the car. "Just try and smile and believe that it's all settled down."

Maria anxiously awaited their arrival. John had told her it was nothing and not to worry, but she insisted on confronting them. She was worried something was terribly wrong with her daughter-in-law, and she couldn't face it if she lost another.

The door opened as they approached. His mother was standing with a pained expression on her face. They both greeted her with a kiss on the cheek. Alejandro reached for Angelina's hand again as they headed off to the kitchen where his father and Gabriella were seated. Angelina immediately brought up Gabriella's field trip.

"One of the children decided to have a food fight in the middle of the park. He squirted his drink all over another student, and then one thing led to another. I've never been as mad at my class as I was today." Gabriella described the remainder of the trip while Maria finished preparing dinner. Angelina surmised it was her nerves that caused it, but she became nauseous just as dinner was served. She placed a small amount of food on her plate. Alejandro gave her a sideways look. Fearing he knew the answer to her fairly empty plate, he decided to carry the conversation. She picked at her food and never really took a bite. When everyone had just about finished, she reached for her plate along with Alejandro's. By doing this, she thought it would take the attention away from the fact that she didn't eat anything. Just as she placed their plates in the sink, she knew she was going to be sick. Excusing herself from the room, she ran down the hallway towards the bathroom, making it just in time. A few minutes passed before he excused himself as well.

"See, something is wrong," Maria commented as she stood to finish clearing the table. John looked at his wife and nodded his head in agreement. He'd noticed Angelina's weight loss but hadn't said anything. He thought it could've been stress-related, but after witnessing Angelina's condition, he questioned his first diagnosis.

Alejandro knocked on the bathroom door. "It's me," he said, entering. "You okay?"

She was washing out her mouth. He brushed her hair back from her face and then hugged her from behind. "I think we need to tell them."

Sighing dejectedly, she nodded in agreement.

"I know you wanted to wait until after your doctor's appointment, but I think it's best. I want to head off a confrontation with my mother. She's pretty astute, and my father has already figured out that something's up. I know him too well."

She dried her face and reached for his hand. "Let's do it."

They discovered that everyone had moved into the family room. His parents didn't take their eyes off of them. Alejandro squeezed her hand. She smiled at him and nodded. She wanted him to be the one to tell them of her pregnancy. They sat down on the couch. He placed his arm around her shoulder and reached for her hand. "Before you start in…"

"So there is something—"

"Maria, please let Alejandro speak," Angelina interrupted.

Maria nodded as they waited on Alejandro.

Alejandro smiled at Angelina. All eyes were focused on him. "I don't know how to say this, so I'm just going to—"

"Angelina, you're ill aren't you?" chimed in Gabriella.

"Gabriella, will you please let me speak?"

She nodded.

"As I was saying, we've had a miracle."

"A miracle?"

He nodded. "Yes, Mother. A miracle." He again looked at his wife. "Angelina is pregnant."

Everyone was stunned silent.

"Don't all congratulate us at once," he said.

"Oh my gosh," cried Gabriella. "How?"

He smiled at his sister. "We're not sure. Just that we are."

Maria rushed over to them. She pulled Angelina into her arms. "Angelina, I don't know what to say. I'm so happy for you both."

"We wanted to wait to tell you and my parents next week after my next doctor's appointment. You're the first to know."

"When did you find out?"

"When Matthew had his transplant. I hadn't been feeling well, but I thought it was a virus. After Matthew's surgery was completed, we went to Alejandro's office to rest. That was the first time I had morning sickness, although I'd been lightheaded off and on for several weeks. Alejandro called my doctor and he examined me in Alejandro's office. That evening we discovered I was pregnant. It was a glorious day for us. Matthew had successfully received his transplant, and we discovered I was going to have a baby. I'll never forget that day as long as I live."

"I'm so thankful for this miracle." Maria pulled Angelina into her arms. "I feared the worst. Angelina, you've been a wonderful addition to this family. I don't know what we would've done if there was something seriously wrong with you. When are you going to tell your family?"

"I think it's too late this evening. I guess we'll go by tomorrow and let them know."

"Please let me know, so I won't ruin the surprise. I can't wait to talk to your mother. We have so much planning ahead of us. There's the baby shower and—"

"Enough, Mom. Let's get through telling Angelina's family first before you start making all of your plans. I've already warned Angelina about how you like to spoil your grandchildren."

"I do not."

"Yes, you do. But let's not go there tonight."

His mother agreed. The conversation shifted to Matthew's recovery and their adoption. As the clock neared eleven, Angelina started yawning.

"I think I need to take the mother-to-be home."

Hugs and kisses were had all the way around. Angelina asked Gabriella not to spread the news of her pregnancy at school—she was planning on telling them but not right away. Angelina also told Gabriella that she wouldn't be returning the following school year. Gabriella didn't care if Angelina taught—she was thrilled that she was pregnant and that she was her sister-in-law.

Alejandro led her to the car. Once they were both settled in, she turned to him. "I'll call my mother first thing tomorrow morning and find out what's a good time for us to drop by. But first, we need to tell Matthew that he's going to be a big brother."

Alejandro started the car.

"I really wanted Matthew to be the first one to know about the baby. But just as long as he finds out before my family, I'll be happy with that."

They drove the remainder of the way in silence, as she fell asleep just as they pulled away from his parents' driveway.

# CHAPTER THIRTY

The next morning Angelina phoned her mother. She discovered that her family would all be home the following evening and not that day like she'd hoped. She paged Alejandro at the hospital and suggested that they take Matthew out to dinner to tell him the big news instead. She phoned Maria and told her that they wouldn't be able to tell her parents until the following day. Angelina assured her that her mother would be calling her immediately upon discovering the news.

That evening, Alejandro surprised Angelina with a bouquet of roses. "What're these for?"

"Just because I love you."

They also surprised Matthew with a trip to the local pizzeria. He liked playing video games while they waited for their pizza. Alejandro reached for her hand. He was sitting across the table from her. "This is it," he said.

"Yes, it sure is. I hope he's okay with becoming a brother."

"I think he'll be fine with it. When should we tell him?"

"Let's get our pizza first. Do you want to tell him?"

"Why don't you?"

The pizza arrived just as Matthew finished his game. They started eating and listened while Matthew discussed his day at school. When he reached for a second slice of pizza, Alejandro started. "Matthew, we have a surprise for you."

"What is it? Can I guess?"

"You can try. I'm not sure you'll be able to."

"Let me try. Give me a clue."

"Okay. Let's see... Angelina, what would be a good clue?"

"It's small."

Mathew jumped a little in his seat. "What else?"

"Let me give it a try," Alejandro said. "How about, we won't be able to see it for a while?"

"What else? Those aren't very good clues."

Angelina looked at her husband. "How about, it may like the color pink or blue?" She smiled at Matthew when she gave her clue.

"Are you having a baby?"

They both nodded.

"Cool. So I'm going to be a big brother? I'm going to have a little brother or sister?"

"Yes. How do you feel about that?"

"Wow. I can't wait! This is the best news except for when you adopted me."

He jumped out of his seat, ran over, and hugged Angelina. "When will it be here?"

"Oh, we have a few months yet."

They finished their dinner and went by Alejandro's parents' house after.

"Grandma, did you hear the news?"

"I sure did. What do you think?"

"I'm so excited. I can't wait. You know, I'll be the best big brother ever. I'm going to teach it the alphabet and how to count—"

"Honey, it'll be a while before he or she can do that. But I'm sure you'll be a great big brother."

While Matthew and Angelina talked with Maria, Alejandro sought out his father.

"Dad, I wanted to chat with you for a few minutes."

"What's up, son?"

"I wanted your thoughts on Angelina's pregnancy. What do you think happened? Don't get me wrong, I'm thankful. It's just…"

"Son, don't rack your brain trying to figure it out. Just be thankful."

"It's just—"

"Alejandro, don't question it. It's a miracle. You know medical science only goes so far. Sometimes we're wrong. It happens all the time when couples who think they can't have a baby pop-up pregnant. You're a fabulous doctor. If you're questioning your diagnosis, don't. Just move on."

"I just wish we'd known before. Then Angelina wouldn't have had to go through that heartbreak. That's all."

"I understand. But just live in the moment and enjoy her pregnancy."

Alejandro agreed. It just bothered him that he'd put her through that time. He took full responsibility for it.

The following day, they headed over to her parents'. When they pulled up in front of the house,

Angelina reminded Matthew not to say a word about the baby—it was a surprise. With it being Sunday, her entire family was present. Even Kelly had come in from Atlanta for the weekend.

Alejandro helped Matthew from the car while Angelina reached in the back for her bag. They walked around the back of the house and greeted everyone. Her mother was in the house preparing salads while her father had begun barbequing. Alejandro kissed Colleen and Kelly on the cheek. He hadn't seen them in a while since he'd missed quite a few of their dinners over the last few months. He shook her father's hand and asked if he could help. Matthew ran off to play with Wyatt. Angelina tried to help her mother, but Jackie insisted that she join the rest of the family on the patio. She was surprised that her mother hadn't said anything about her weight loss, but she was happy that she didn't have to deal with her about it. Alejandro's mother had quite honestly taken it all out of her.

"Time to eat," Ben called as he removed the burgers from the grill. Her mother and Colleen had brought the remainder of the dishes from the house while Angelina went inside to get Matthew and her brother. Dinner was a pleasant event for a change as it was the direct opposite of the one held with Alejandro's parents. She'd been stressed waiting for the next shoe to fall. Thankfully, she hadn't experienced any nausea in the last day or so—the last bout was at her in-laws. She could only hope that she was over it.

They finished dessert and, just as they were ready to clear the table, Alejandro stood. He reached for

Angelina's hand and she joined him. He put his hand around her shoulder and smiled at her.

"Alejandro and I have an announcement to make."

"You're not moving are you?" her mother asked.

"No, why would you think that?"

Her mother shrugged her shoulders.

"Matthew's okay, isn't he?"

"I'm great," Matthew chimed in.

Angelina smiled at her husband and he gripped her shoulders more tightly. "You'll never begin to guess…"

"Are either of you changing jobs?" asked Kelly.

"Nope. I think we should just tell them. What you do you think, honey?"

"Go ahead, Angelina. They'll never guess."

Taking a deep breath she started, "Our news… Let's see…"

"Out with it," cried Jackie.

"We're going to have a baby."

"You're adopting another child? Don't you think you should wait?"

"No, it's not that."

"I don't understand."

Chuckling, Alejandro thought that this was so much easier than dealing with his parents. Angelina took a deep breath, "We're pregnant."

"What?" Jackie stammered. "Are you joking? Did you find a surrogate?"

"No, Mom. We're expecting. I'm going to have a baby."

"I thought…"

"So did we. It's a miracle. Our little miracle."

Jackie jumped up in delight and ran to her daughter. Both Ben and James shook Alejandro's hand. Colleen and Kelly waited in line to hug their sister while Wyatt just stood there—he didn't know who to congratulate first. He was just excited for his sister, then he and Matthew went inside to watch a hockey game on TV.

"How long have you known?" asked Jackie.

Angelina detailed the events over the last several weeks. She told her family that they'd wanted to wait until the following week, but had to spill the beans due to Alejandro's mother.

"So, how have you been feeling?"

"Honestly, I've had morning sickness morning, noon, and night. I haven't been able to keep anything down."

"I noticed that you'd lost some weight but attributed it to Matthew's transplant. I knew how upset you were. How has Matthew taken the news?"

"He's thrilled. He can't wait to be a big brother."

"That's good to hear."

They enjoyed the remainder of the evening discussing the baby, Matthew, and life in general. When they decided to go home, Jackie told them that she'd be contacting Maria regarding their grandchild.

Alejandro laughed, "She's waiting to hear from you. My family is absolutely thrilled. Just do us one favor."

"And that is?"

"Don't go overboard like my mother. Please?"

Winking at her son-in-law, she said, "I'll try not to."

They left behind an overjoyed family. "Your parents were elated. I don't think I've ever seen your mother like that."

"I know. I certainly thought she'd be harassing me about my weight, but she never thought twice about it. She just assumed it was because of Matthew. And that's shocking because my mother was always on top of that."

Matthew fell asleep on the way home

"Alejandro, how's he doing?"

"Just fine. I'm actually thrilled with his progress."

"I can't believe how excited he is about the baby. He talks non-stop about being a big brother."

"I know, and I think it's driving Gabriella crazy. She took him for ice cream after school and couldn't wait to get him home. It's question after question. Actually, she thought it was cute how excited he is. Alejandro, he's really adjusted well between Duane and Jane's deaths, his transplant, and now the baby."

"He has. We're lucky, that's for sure."

When they arrived home, Angelina headed off to bed while Alejandro carried Matthew to his bedroom. He settled him under the covers. Rarely did Alejandro take the time to sit with Matthew while he slept. Tonight was a different story. He pulled a chair beside his bed and watched him sleep. His mind drifted back to a time when he used to watch Michael sleep. That had been the most enjoyable part of his day. He'd sit and watch his son sleep and dream of the future that laid ahead for him and his family. He'd dream of baseball games, boy scouts, all of the fun times that he would have with his son. He'd often dreamed of Michael's future siblings, but those days were over. Tammy and Michael were gone from his life.

Alejandro found himself brushing the hair aside from Michael's face. He was reliving their day.

They'd gone to the park. He and Tammy had a blast at the playground. While Michael climbed on the various apparatuses, he pushed Tammy on the swings. Afterward, they'd found themselves at Michael's favorite restaurant. Alejandro always enjoyed the time he spent with his family. They were his life.

The next thing Alejandro felt was a coldness sweep across him. His heart rate accelerated. And fear... A fear that he'd never experienced before consumed him. He screamed Michael's name and woke with a start. His heart felt like it was going to beat right out of his chest. For a moment, he thought Matthew was Michael. He was confused when he woke, Tammy wasn't there... Michael wasn't there... They were forever gone. Then he realized it was just a dream, one that he'd been having quite frequently.

He calmed himself as reality set in. Alejandro sat with Matthew for a few moments longer, then headed off to the den where he calmed himself with a drink. He'd been having these dreams a lot lately. They were so real and so unsettling. Before this round of dreams, he hadn't dreamt of his family in quite some time... Why now? What brought about these dreams, these feelings? He threw himself down on the couch. Raising a hand to his forehead, he took a deep gulp of bourbon. Closing his eyes, he rehashed his day and tried to determine what was causing them.

Angelina found him sitting in the den in the middle of the night. When she'd awakened and he hadn't been beside her, she'd become worried. The last she'd seen him, he was putting Matthew to bed. When she found him, he was clutching his drink in one hand while the other was flung across his eyes. She sat beside him and reached for his glass.

He hadn't heard her enter the room. Softly, he said, "What're you doing up? I thought you went to bed."

"I did. Alejandro, aren't you coming to bed? It's almost four in the morning."

"It is?"

Shaking her head, she moved closer to him and placed her hand on his chest. "Honey, is something wrong?"

"No. Why would you ask?"

"Just a feeling, that's all."

He reached for her and pulled her into his arms. They both drifted off to sleep there, and it's where Matthew found them the next morning, nestled in one another's arms.

He wasn't sure what to do. He stood there looking at them and then tapped Alejandro on the knee. Alejandro jumped up, practically knocking Angelina to the floor.

"Matthew, is something wrong?"

"No. But it's morning. I have to get to school."

It took a few seconds before they both became fully alert. Alejandro looked at the clock and it was almost seven. He needed to get to the hospital. Angelina rushed to the shower and dressed while Alejandro quickly prepared breakfast. When Angelina reappeared almost forty-five minutes later, Alejandro had also showered and dressed. He ruffled Matthew's hair and kissed Angelina goodbye. "I've gotta go. I'll see you both this evening."

Alejandro rushed out the door. She wasn't sure what was up with him but she'd find out.

# CHAPTER THIRTY-ONE

Alejandro was feeling run down. He'd been pushing through the week since they'd told Angelina's parents of the pregnancy. He'd just seen his last patient of the day and decided to stretch out on his office couch. It was early. He thought he'd get some rest before going home for the weekend since he was off and they had no plans. Alejandro covered his eyes with his forearm and drifted off to sleep. His dreams were again filled with memories.

Angelina had expected him for an early dinner. They'd planned all week to visit his family. She knew his last patient left before noon and that he'd given his staff the remainder of the day off. It was nearly four o'clock and she hadn't spoken with him. She was getting worried because he always stayed in touch with her. She'd tried his office and cell phone, and even had him paged at the hospital. No answer.

Angelina called his mother and asked if she could drop Matthew off at their house. She let Maria know she was worried that she hadn't heard from Alejandro. Maria told her not to worry, that she was sure he was just fine.

"I know, it's just that he hasn't been acting like himself. I'm concerned. I'm going to run by his office just to make sure he's okay."

"I'll be waiting for you. Angelina?"

"Yes."

"I'm sure he's fine."

"I hope so. I just have this bad feeling, that's all."

Angelina dropped Matthew off at his grandparents and headed to the hospital. The closer she got to the hospital, the more anxious she became. She pulled into the garage and sought Alejandro's parking place. She breathed a sigh of relief when she saw his car parked in his assigned spot.

She quickly found a parking spot and hurried to the clinic entrance. She pressed for the elevator, but it was too slow so she ran for the stairs. She entered the stairway and headed up the stairs towards his office. She was out of breath as she entered the hallway and had to stop to catch her breath. No one was in the hallway as she neared his office. The main door was locked, so she headed for his private door. Her hand shook as she tried the door—it was unlocked. Slowly she turned the knob and pushed open the door. Alejandro laid on the couch.

She closed the door and called to him. He didn't respond. She ran to his side and noticed he was covered in perspiration. She reached for his forehead. He was burning up. She tried to wake him. He was mumbling. "Alejandro?"

She stroked his cheek as he continued to mumble. "Honey, wake up. I'm here."

"Tammy. Is that you?"

*Tammy,* she thought. *What's going on with him?*

"Michael? It's time to go…"

He was dreaming. He had to be.

"Michael, go get your mother and we'll head on out…" He continued to mumble.

She shook his shoulder and he opened his eyes.

"Tammy?"

"No, Alejandro. It's me, Angelina."

He blinked several times until she came into focus. He brushed his hand across his forehead. Blinking several more times, he finally said, "Angelina? Where are we?"

She stroked his forehead and told him that he was in his office. "I've been calling you for hours. You were supposed to be home some time ago. It's almost seven. I got worried, so I dropped Matthew off with your mother. Alejandro, you have a fever. Can you sit up?"

Alejandro dragged himself to a sitting position. "Go into the examining room down the hall. There's a thermometer in there. Can you also bring me a glass of water on your way back?"

Angelina nodded and hurried to gather the items. When she reentered the room, Alejandro had slumped back down onto the couch. She reached for him and helped him sit up. She took his temperature. "Your temperature's 103."

"I knew it was pretty high." He gulped down the water and brushed aside her hand. He tried to stand, but quickly sat back down. "Give me a minute to get my bearings and we can go home. I want to grab an aspirin before we head out. Can you call my mom and see if Matthew can stay with her overnight? I don't want him exposed to whatever I have."

"Sure." Angelina left the room so she could get another glass of water. She called Maria and told her she'd found Alejandro and that he was sick. Maria agreed to keep Matthew all weekend—she didn't want him getting sick. Angelina asked if John was home.

"I expect him shortly. Why?"

Angelina asked that he meet them at their home. She wanted him to examine Alejandro.

"Do you want him to meet you at the hospital?"

"No, I think I can get him home. He's taking some medication and then we'll leave. We should be home in about fifteen to twenty minutes."

"I'll send John over as soon as he gets home."

Angelina gathered everything that Alejandro instructed her to obtain from his office. She helped him get his jacket on and helped him from the couch. Placing her arm about his waist, she got him to her car. On the way to the car, he told her that he had a pounding headache and just wanted to lie down on the backseat. As she neared their driveway, she saw John waiting for them. He hurried to the car and helped Alejandro inside. "Son, what's wrong?"

"I think I have the flu. I have this pounding headache, high fever…"

"Let's get you inside." John helped him inside while Angelina gathered the supplies. Alejandro made his way to the den and fell onto the couch.

"I've been so tired this last week. I thought I was just putting in too many hours, but I guess I was getting sick."

"Looks that way. Let's check your temperature." John took his temperature and said, "It's still high, but looks like it's come down some since Angelina called your mother." John examined his son and helped him to bed. "You need to rest and drink fluids.

I'll check on you tomorrow. Angelina, Maria asked that I bring Matthew a change of clothes since he'll be with us this weekend. Your mother is excited to have her grandson all to herself for a few days, although she's sorry to see that you're not feeling well."

Angelina ran off to put an overnight bag together for Matthew.

"Dad, thanks for everything."

"No problem, son. You've been working too hard lately. You need to take it easy this weekend."

Alejandro stared off into the distance.

"Did you hear me?"

"Huh? Oh yeah, Dad. I heard you."

"What's bothering you? You seem miles away."

"Nothing. Nothing at all... Thanks for helping Angelina with me. I really appreciate it."

John squeezed his son's shoulder and told him to rest. "I'll see you tomorrow."

Alejandro thanked his dad and then closed his eyes. Angelina accompanied her father-in-law from their bedroom. "Is he going to be okay?"

"Should be. We need to watch his fever and make sure he gets plenty of liquids. Angelina, you need to take care of yourself, too."

"I will." She closed the front door behind John. Turning, she leaned her back against the closed door. She remembered the way Alejandro had been acting when she'd entered his office. Lying there, he was murmuring Tammy and Michael's names. Something other than his illness was bothering him and had been for some time.

Angelina checked on Alejandro and he was sleeping soundly. She decided to phone Matthew to tell him about Alejandro and that he'd be spending the weekend with his grandparents.

As she prepared to get off the phone, she told him how much they loved him.

"Mom?"

"Yes, Matthew?"

"Take care of him." Matthew didn't want something to happen to Alejandro. He was worried and just needed reassurance that he was going to be okay.

"I will. He's just got the flu and will be better in a few days. I'll call you tomorrow. Listen to your grandparents."

"I will, don't worry. And Mom?"

"Yes?"

"I love you."

"I love you, too," Angelina ended the call and smiled. They'd done the right thing in adopting Matthew. He was a good boy and she was glad that they could call him their son.

Angelina turned off the remainder of the lights in the house and headed to their bedroom. Alejandro laid in the same position. She decided to take a bath and relax. She'd just gotten into the tub when she heard Alejandro call out. She jumped up from the tub, wrapping herself in a towel. Hurrying from the bathroom she found Alejandro moving his head back and forth in his sleep. As she neared him, he shouted Tammy's name. He sat up in bed with fear in his eyes. She stroked his cheek.

"Alejandro, it's me. Angelina."

Swallowing, he closed his eyes. Turning his head towards her, he reopened them. "Honey, I know it's you." He reached for her hands. Holding them tightly, he added, "Thank you for finding me." He recounted his afternoon, "I saw my last patient and let my staff go early for the weekend. I got so tired, so I thought I'd lie down and take a quick nap. I don't know what happened. I must have been sleeping for at least six hours before you showed up."

"I got worried when I couldn't reach you. I called your mom and dropped off Matthew before I came looking for you. You don't know how relieved I was when I saw your car in the hospital garage. But when I opened your office door and saw you on that couch, my heart dropped. You're never sick. I felt myself begin to panic. When you finally recognized me, I felt better."

"Recognized you? What do you mean?"

"It doesn't matter right now. You just need to concentrate on getting better. I'm going to get dressed and come to bed. You rest and I'll be right back."

Angelina put on her nightgown and slid into bed beside her husband—he'd already fallen back to sleep. She laid there staring at him. She stroked her hand across his forehead, pushing his hair aside. He was still quite warm. She woke him to give him his next round of aspirin before falling asleep herself.

At around three in the morning, he woke her, calling out Michael's name. He was reliving the night that he lost his family. As far as Angelina knew, he hadn't experienced those dreams in a very long time—something was eating at him. She held him as he settled back into a normal sleep. She'd known he'd been bothered by something recently, and now she had her answer.

The sun woke Angelina and she looked at the clock. It was just after six. Reaching over, she felt

Alejandro. He still had a fever but felt much cooler. She rose and dressed. She hoped that he'd sleep most of the day. She headed off to the kitchen where she made herself a cup of tea. She sat at the table recounting the previous day's events. She decided she'd talk to Maria about his nightmares. Maybe she'd have some insight before she talked to Alejandro.

While Alejandro slept, Angelina called and spoke with Matthew before speaking with Maria about Alejandro.

"Angelina, what's troubling you? I can hear it in your voice."

"It's Alejandro."

"I thought you said he seemed better."

"His fever is down…"

"And?"

Angelina didn't respond.

"What's troubling you, dear?"

"Maria, I'm not sure. It's just a gut feeling…"

"What?"

"Alejandro has been dreaming of Tammy and Michael."

"What makes you believe that?"

"I've heard him call out their names. Why? Why do you think he is dreaming of them?"

"Have you talked to him about it?"

"No, not yet. It's just…"

"What? Angelina, you have to ask him. I can't say for sure, but I would gather it has something to do with your pregnancy? When did these dreams begin?"

"I'm not sure. I've only witnessed it a couple of times, but my instincts tell me they've been happening for a while. I know he's been having trouble sleeping at night. I believe that's why he's gotten so run down. He doesn't take care for himself. He worries too much about me, Matthew, his patients. I'm always telling him to slow down, but you know him. He just doesn't listen."

"He's a lot like his father—driven by his family and patients. Dear, when he's feeling better you must talk to him. He'll tell you what's bothering him. I know he will…"

Angelina checked on Alejandro and his fever had broken. He was sleeping soundly. It was mid-afternoon, and she'd grown pretty tired herself. She slipped into bed beside him and fell asleep.

When she awoke near five, Alejandro was lying on his side, looking at her. "Honey, are you feeling alright?"

"I'm fine. I was sleepy so I decided to take a nap. What about you?"

"Better, much better. My fever broke a while ago. I'm still pretty exhausted and my headache is better, but…"

"Do you want another aspirin?"

"Not yet. I just want to lie here and look at you."

"I'm fine. How about something to eat?"

"I don't want you waiting on me."

"Alejandro, you have to eat. I'll go fix us a cup of soup. I'll be right back."

Alejandro laid on his back, waiting for her to return. He rehashed what had occurred over the last few weeks, days, and hours. He'd been thinking a lot about Tammy and Michael. He assumed it had to do with Angelina's pregnancy. All of the memories… He hadn't been sleeping. Really, hadn't been able to concentrate on anything of late. He hoped that Angelina hadn't picked up on this. He had to rid himself of his past. He thought he'd done that when he'd married Angelina. He knew they'd always be with him, but he had to stop being consumed by their memories. He had to let go for once and for all.

As Angelina heated their soup, she contemplated how she was going to bring up Tammy and Michael. She didn't want to upset him, but she wanted—no, needed to get to the bottom this.

She carried their soup to the bedroom. Alejandro looked much better. He had color in his face and seemed more relaxed. She sat beside him while they ate. He finished his soup and put his cup on the nightstand. As he leaned back onto the headboard, she took a deep breath and said, "Alejandro, what's troubling you?"

Stammering, he asked her what she meant.

She repeated her question. "I know something's wrong. You haven't been yourself for weeks now. When I found you in your office, you were calling for Tammy and Michael. Then, after I brought you home, you had a nightmare. You were dreaming of the night they were killed. Why now? What's bringing those memories back?"

He reached for her hand. They sat in silence for some time. He didn't know what to say. Where to begin? He said, "I love you."

"I know that."

"Then what's the problem?"

"Alejandro. You're having nightmares. Nightmares about your former wife and son... How long has this been going on? I want to know. I want to help you."

He looked away from her, still clutching her hand. They continued to sit there. He squeezed her hand and began to speak. "I started with my dreams the night we told your parents about the baby. I don't know why. They just came back out of the blue. I've tried to lock them away again. I love you. I don't want my memories to hurt us. I just…"

"Alejandro, it's okay. I understand."

"But how can you?"

"They were everything to you."

"Yes, they were. But that's the past and this… this is the present."

"And you're trying to protect me?"

"Always."

"But now there's not just you and me. There's you, me, Matthew, and our unborn child." She squeezed his hand and brushed her hand across his cheek. "Alejandro, I think you're trying so hard to protect me that their deaths are haunting you. You couldn't protect them and you're worried that you can't protect me or the baby."

"That's not true."

"Really? You said you started with the dreams the evening we told my family about the baby. Why else would you begin to have these nightmares? You're afraid. Afraid that you won't be there to take care of us, afraid that something will happen that you can't control. Your dreams… Are they reaching out for you?"

He nodded.

"See what I mean? You're trying to right the wrong that happened. You're trying to make sure that nothing will happen to them. That's the only way that

I can fathom why you're having these dreams. I sense that it is a need to protect."

"Maybe you're right. I blame myself for believing that you couldn't have children. I guess that I have this desire to protect you from all bad. I believe that I couldn't protect them, so I guess I believe that I can't protect you. I need to get over that fear and need to protect. My father told me it wasn't my fault."

"Your fault?"

"Your misdiagnosis."

"Who said there was a misdiagnosis? I never—"

"I know. It's just that I believe I did you a disservice…"

"Alejandro. Get that out of your mind. This is a miracle. Our miracle child. You did not misdiagnose my condition. Everyone at the time, including the specialists I saw, thought I was infertile. I'm lucky. We're lucky. We have to believe that. Please stop blaming yourself. Please do that for me, for the baby. If you can't let this go, it will hang over our heads the remainder of our lives. Please let it go. Do it for me."

He reached over and pulled her into his arms. "I love you so much. I'll do my best to let it go. I thought I'd let it go a long time ago. I might need your help."

"I'm here. I'll always be here for you. You are my love, my life. I'd do anything for you. I can't see you suffering any more. Let Tammy go. Let Michael go. They would want you to be happy. You'll always have the memories, but now it's time to make new ones."

"I know. And I will."

# EPILOGUE

Angelina sat in the living room, admiring the holiday decorations. It was Christmas Eve and she had so much to be thankful for. They'd experienced a lifetime of memories in the last year, and the best miracle of all she held in her arms... Their daughter. They named her Angelina-Maria but were going to call her Angel. She was a special gift sent to them, born surprisingly on Thanksgiving Day (albeit two weeks late).

For the last several years, Thanksgiving had been filled with sadness. Two years ago, Alejandro had delivered the horrific news of her infertility. And now, the sadness had been reversed with utter jubilation. The most precious gift of all was born to them on this day.

When her water had broken, Alejandro fell to pieces—one wouldn't know that he was a successful surgeon. He'd had difficulties getting himself together, let alone helping Angelina to the car. On the way to the hospital, she'd had to remind him to slow down. At one point, he'd almost run a red light. "You'd think you never experienced this moment in your life before," she'd said as they pulled into the hospital garage.

"I know. I can't seem to get my act together."

"It's okay, Alejandro. Everything's going to be just fine." She'd reached for his hand, squeezed it, and he'd smiled at her, then exited the car and retrieved a nearby wheelchair. Helping her into the chair, they'd headed into the hospital. The nurses couldn't believe how nervous he was. After what seemed like a prolonged labor, Angelina had delivered their precious bundle of joy in the early morning of Thanksgiving.

"Do you know what today is?" she'd asked. He'd just looked at her, not quite understanding her question.

"It's Thanksgiving."

"It is, isn't it?"

"Yes, and now we have something to be thankful for." She'd reached for his hand and added. "Let's put to bed the past and always remember this day and all that we have."

He'd smiled at her and leaned over to kiss her. "Yes, I'll try and forget that day. Looking back, I should have waited to tell you."

"I'm glad you didn't. Yes, we had sadness associated with that day, but look at what we have now. Our miracle sent to us from above."

Alejandro walked into the room as Angelina admired her daughter. He approached her and placed his hand on her shoulder. "She's absolutely beautiful," he said as he stroked Angel's forehead. "We have so much to be thankful for this holiday season," he said as he sat beside Angelina on the couch. "She's precious, absolutely precious.

Angelina, I love you more today than the day we married. You're my life, my love…"

She looked up at him.

"This is my world. You, Matthew, and our precious Angel. I can't thank you enough for making my dreams come true."

He started to speak, but she stopped him. "Alejandro, I know how much you love us, and I know how much you loved Tammy and Michael. Let's enjoy today and dream of tomorrow. We can't go back, but only forward. What's in the past is that—the past. We have an endless future ahead us. Let's enjoy all that it has to offer."

Alejandro was in a good place in his life. Ever since they'd had their last conversation about Tammy and Michael, he'd overcome his nightmares. He'd placed them in a safe spot in his memory. They'd always be a part of his past, but now he had a wonderful future ahead of him filled with lots of love. *Miracles really do happen*, he thought. *I've been blessed with a wonderful family and will be thankful for them for all eternity.*

# ABOUT THE AUTHOR

Anne Stone has been a fan of romance since reading Katherine by Anya Seton her senior year of high school. In college, she penned her first novel which ended up at the bottom of a desk drawer after being rejected by a publishing house. She's constantly dabbled in drafting stories but her career always seemed to get in the way. Anne decided to take the plunge and self-publish. Self-publishing allows her to write the kind of book that she enjoys reading and doesn't put a limit on her creativity. Originally from St. Louis, Anne currently resides in Wisconsin with her Cavalier King Charles Spaniel.

You may contact Anne Stone by visiting her website: www.AnneStoneAuthor.com
Facebook: Anne Stone Author
Twitter: @AuthorAnneStone

If you enjoyed reading Life's Second Chances, please consider leaving a review. The best compliment an author can receive is from readers leaving a review.

.